"YOU CAN'T DENY THAT YOU WANTED ME TO KISS YOU LAST NIGHT, JULIA. YOU WANTED IT AS MUCH AS I DID. I COULD TELL."

Her eyes widened incredulously. "But how . . . how did you know?"

He traced the outline of her mouth with a callused finger, studying her with a gaze so intense that her breath caught in her throat.

"Your eyes were sending messages to me, sweet Julia. You were looking at me like you *wanted* me to kiss you . . . the same way you're looking at me now."

"I didn't . . . didn't realize I was so . . . transparent," she choked out.

"Wanting to be kissed isn't a sin, you know."

"But the way you kissed me wasn't exactly chaste, Tyler."

"God wouldn't have invented kissing if He didn't intend for us to enjoy it."

Amusement sparkled from his eyes and Julia's heart thundered in her chest as he edged closer and bent his head . . .

Loving Tyler

Susan Sawyer

AVON BOOKS ◆ NEW YORK

LOVING TYLER is an original publication of Avon Books. This work
has never before appeared in book form. This work is a novel. Any
similarity to actual persons or events is purely coincidental.

AVON BOOKS
A division of
The Hearst Corporation
1350 Avenue of the Americas
New York, New York 10019

Copyright © 1995 by Susan Sawyer
Published by arrangement with the author
Library of Congress Catalog Card Number: 94-94477
ISBN: 0-380-77890-4

First Avon Books Printing: January 1995

AVON TRADEMARK REG. U.S. PAT. OFF. AND IN OTHER COUNTRIES, MARCA
REGISTRADA, HECHO EN U.S.A.

Printed in the U.S.A.

RA   10 9 8 7 6 5 4 3 2 1

With all my love
to my husband, Ron,
my real-life, twentieth-century hero—
who happens to be the perfect combination
of Renaissance man,
dragon slayer, and dream maker.

Loving Tyler

Chapter 1

"**B**lasted Yankees! They're the ones responsible for the leak in our roof," Odelphia Hopewell muttered, glaring through her thick spectacles at the puddle of water on the floor. Silver curls bobbed around her wrinkled face as she shook her head in dismay. "In all of my sixty-one years, I've never lived in such atrocious conditions!"

"Mama and Papa would roll over in their graves if they could see the sorry state of their house now." Dorinda Hopewell, a shorter, plumper version of her older sister, fingered the faded brocade drapes and blinked back the moisture from her eyes. "Everyone used to say the Hopewells owned the loveliest house in all of Rome, Georgia."

Standing at the doorway of the bedroom, Julia Carey quietly observed the exchange between her maiden aunts. One reddened hand clenched a tattered rag; the other gripped the handle of a tin bucket. Hoping she could ease some of the women's misery, Julia drew in a deep, steadying breath and swept across the room.

"The War has been over for three years, Aunt Odelphia, and I'm afraid blaming the Yankees for a spring shower and a leaky roof won't get us anywhere," she pointed out diplomatically, kneeling to wipe the water from the oak floor. "And I'm certain Grandmother and Grandfather Hopewell

1

would understand that keeping up a house this large requires a great deal of money."

"Money we don't have, thanks to the Yanks," Odelphia grumbled.

"And without a man around the house to do the labor, the repairs will cost a fortune," Dorinda added sorrowfully.

A batch of thunder rumbled from the Georgia skies just as Julia set the bucket on the floor to catch the drips from the ceiling. Overhead, rain pelted against the tin roof with a relentless clatter. Across the room, another section of the ceiling cracked and crumbled, sending bits of plaster and new streams of water gushing to the floor.

"Come on, Dorie." Odelphia sighed, heading for the stairs. "We're going to need the mop."

"And some more buckets." Dorinda's short legs scurried to catch up with Odelphia's long, brisk strides.

As the ladies disappeared into the hall, a heavy weight filled Julia's chest. Tilting back her head, she studied the damage to the ceiling. The leaks were getting worse by the minute, and she was helpless to do anything about it. Her meager wages from teaching school barely covered the costs of food and clothing, and the expenses of replacing the roof were simply out of reach.

But taking care of the house was her responsibility, Julia reminded herself with a stern shake of her head. *It's all up to you now, Julia. You promised Papa, didn't you?*

Remembering her father's last words, Julia straightened her narrow shoulders. On his deathbed, Jeremiah Carey had made only one request of his daughter: to take care of the family after he was gone. Julia had assured the dying man that she would always provide a home for their family.

And she fully intended to keep her promise to her beloved father, no matter what the cost.

In the two months since the Reverend Carey's death, Julia had devoted herself to running the household and providing for her family, along with teaching every day at the schoolhouse. Most of the time she enjoyed taking care of her younger sister, Kate, and tending to the needs of her aunts. But sometimes, like today, Julia wished she could count on Lucas for help with maintaining the stately old family home.

But Lucas was no help at all. Julia's half brother, fifteen years her senior, had drifted from place to place, from job to job, from dream to dream, since the end of the War. Julia suspected the brutality of the battlefield had spawned her brother's restless spirit. Since wearing the gray uniform of the Confederate army, Lucas had never returned home for more than a day or two at a time. Months often passed without any word from him at all.

Though coping with the loss of her father and her brother's absence had not been easy for Julia, she supposed all the differences in life had been even harder for her mother's sisters. Before the War, Odelphia and Dorinda had lived in pampered luxury. Their days had been centered around parties and socials and teas. Now their old way of life had vanished like a cool breeze fading into the relentless heat of a summer afternoon. Since the conflict erupted between the North and South, the elderly sisters had dealt with more changes than they'd encountered during their entire lives.

And Julia shared the heartache of their losses. Together the women had grieved for the loss of Capitola, Julia's mother, when she'd died giving birth to little Kate six years ago. They'd consoled each other when Lucas marched off to war. They'd

comforted each other after severing ties with their
beloved Chocolate, their only slave, relinquishing
her into the world of freedom. And they'd worked
side by side, defending their home, when Union
troops had descended upon Rome.

After hiding their best furniture in the cellar and
attic, they'd buried the family silver behind the
barn and prayed for a reprieve from the approaching troops. Miraculously, their prayers had been
answered. Though Sherman had burned the industrial and business sections of Rome, the town's resi-
dences were left unscathed.

Now, in the spring of 1868, the South was making
strides in rebuilding the war-ravaged land. Railroad
tracks, ripped to shreds by Union forces, were being
restored. Schools were being set up to educate the
children of the South, both black and white. And
businesses were springing back to life again.

But worthless Confederate greenbacks couldn't
put food on the table or clothing on their backs.
And Julia didn't have the heart to remind her aunts
that the house needed much more than a new roof.
With each passing day, it was becoming more and
more difficult to ignore the peeling wallpaper, the
rotting porch steps, the worn rugs, or dozens of
other items needing replacement. If only she could
find some way . . .

A plan simmering in the back of her mind for
weeks bubbled to the surface of her thoughts just
as her aunts came back into the room. Straightening,
Julia brushed back a few wispy tendrils of chestnut
hair from her forehead. Then she smoothed down
the folds of her blue muslin dress and stepped forward. Did she dare approach Aunt Odelphia and
Aunt Dorinda with the idea?

It didn't seem fair to ask them to make another
radical adjustment in their lives. Yet, Julia knew

something had to be done or they would lose what little they possessed. The house was their only asset, and they would have to use it to its best advantage.

"I believe I know of a way for us to make repairs to the house," she announced brightly.

"I know of a way, too." Odelphia set the mop over the new puddle in the floor. "A wealthy husband for you could be the answer to all of our problems."

Dorinda's eyes widened. "Did that nice Horace Bates ask you to marry him yet, Julia?"

"You could do much worse than Horace, you know." Odelphia mopped up the water with brisk, efficient strokes. "Why, I'd wager he's made a fortune since the end of the War with that general store of his."

"Actually, Horace and I haven't discussed marriage," Julia clarified, quickly snuffing out the sparks of matchmaking delight in her aunts' eyes. "And I don't expect the subject will ever come up between us."

Because she would refuse to discuss marriage with an eternal pessimist like Horace Bates, she added silently. Though Julia had nothing against marriage, she couldn't imagine herself assuming the role of devoted wife to any man. Though she longed for a husband to love and a family of her own, her hopes and dreams for marriage had been crushed on the day that a Union bullet had pierced Brent's heart.

Brent. Julia's heart ached at the memory of her fiancé. His ready smile and sparkling blue eyes had filled her life with love and laughter before the War. But the Battle of Chickamauga had shattered their plans for a future together. And Julia was certain she could never love another man the way she had loved Brent Harrington.

Now, at twenty-three, Julia felt she was past her prime for indulging in the frivolities of courtship. She didn't care for batting her lashes or bantering with eligible bachelors. She simply had neither the desire nor the time for such foolish nonsense. Besides herself, she had three other mouths to feed and no time to be bothered with the foolish pleasures of a man. All of her energies were focused on taking care of her family. And what man in his right mind would want to assume the responsibilities of a ready-made family?

Besides, Julia was convinced she was much too plain to snare the affections of a man whose character was suitable enough for marriage. Every morning her reflection in the mirror reminded her that her green eyes were too deep-set to be considered her most attractive feature, her smile too wide to be called dainty. Her chestnut hair was too thick and unruly for curling into fashionable ringlets, so she usually pulled it back from her face and coiled it into a loose bun at the nape of her neck. In her opinion, she possessed only two redeeming features: None of her teeth were missing, and her eyebrows and lashes were dark enough to be seen without the benefit of spectacles.

"So tell us about your idea, Julia." Odelphia finished mopping the floor and wiped off her hands. "Dorie and I aren't a pair of sniveling, spineless ninnies, you know. We're pretty tough geezers, if I say so myself, and I doubt you can shock us to death with anything you have to say."

In spite of Julia's worries, she couldn't keep her lips from twitching with the hint of a smile. Maybe she'd underestimated her aunts. Though Odelphia had slowed her brisk pace in recent years and Dorinda thrived on her memories of their old way of life, they were survivors, and hearty ones, who'd

withstood the strife of the Civil War. And maybe
they could adapt gracefully to another change in
their lives.

Julia folded her hands together and began. "Since
the trains are operating on a regular schedule again,
I've noticed lots of new faces in town lately. The
businesses which have reopened since the end of the
War—and the new ones springing up—are drawing
lots of customers and salesmen to the area."

Dorinda nodded in agreement as she placed a
bucket on the floor beneath the new leak. "Several
new families have moved to Rome, too, like the
young couple with three children who joined the
church last Sunday."

"And all of them need a place to stay when
they arrive in town," Julia said. "With the growing
number of passengers getting off the train every
day, Mrs. Chandler's boardinghouse has been full
for months. There isn't any other place in town
to accommodate overnight visitors. But we have
plenty of rooms to spare here."

"You mean . . . you mean you want to open our
home to . . . to strangers?" Dorinda clutched her
throat and shuddered.

"Of course that's what she means," Odelphia
retorted. "And I, for one, think it's an ingenious
idea."

"You do?" Dorinda looked at her tall, reed-thin
sister and blinked in disbelief.

Odelphia straightened her spine. "Of course. Now
let's listen to what she has to say."

At that moment a new torrent of rain pelted
the roof and rattled the windowpanes. The water
cascaded from the ceiling, dripping into the tin
buckets with a pinging sound.

Sighing, Julia retrieved a small, threadbare rug
from the floor before another leak could break

through the ceiling. "We obviously have to do something to keep our house livable and operative for our family. Taking in boarders is a respectable way to support ourselves. Naturally we would be discretionary in our clientele—like families waiting to move into permanent homes or gentlemen of good breeding who need a place to stay while they're visiting Rome on business. We could offer room and board by the day or the week, and use the money to repair the house."

"Oh, my." Dorinda paled. She lowered her plump frame to the edge of the iron and brass bed, clinging to the bedpost for support. "Mama and Papa would have been appalled to accept money from total strangers like that. Why, Papa would say that taking in boarders is . . . is . . . beneath us."

"But Papa wasn't left penniless by the War, Dorie." Odelphia patted her sister's round shoulder affectionately. "And he'd want us to keep this house, no matter what the cost. We have plenty of empty rooms that could bring in some extra income. Why, all of these bedrooms up here on the third floor could be rented out. Even this room, once we get the roof fixed."

Dorinda wrinkled her nose. "But we'd have to clean up after all those strangers . . . like . . . like . . . like hired women!"

"Adding a few more plates to the table and washing a few more linens shouldn't be too much of a burden on any of us." Julia rolled up the small rug and placed it under the bed. "We have to prepare meals and launder our own things, anyway."

"Unfortunately." Dorinda fingered the lace jabot beneath her sagging chin and gave a wistful sigh. "You know, life was a lot easier when Chocolate took care of all those things for us."

"But Chocolate has her freedom now, and it's up

to us to take care of ourselves." Odelphia pushed up her glasses to the bridge of her nose and lifted her chin. "There isn't any reason why we can't fill this old place with laughter and conversation again by taking in boarders. Don't you remember when Mama and Papa used to invite strangers to our house for Sunday dinner after church? By the time dinner was over, nobody was a stranger any longer."

"We could offer the same hospitality to boarders every day," Julia pointed out. "Of course, it will take some time to fix up all the bedrooms again. But we could start with one or two boarders, then add more as we're able to furnish the rest of the rooms."

Odelphia narrowed her eyes, as if combing her memory. "You know, there's an iron bed in the cellar. And we still have those two bedroom suites we hid in the attic when the Yankees came through town."

"I suppose we were luckier than most folks in Georgia," Dorinda admitted. "We didn't lose our house, after all."

"I think we're among the most fortunate families in the South," Julia added quietly, gazing around the room.

In its glory, the Hopewell house had been the showplace of Rome. Fourteen-foot ceilings and elaborate woodwork graced the eight bedrooms on the second and third floors and the magnificent parlor, study, and dining room on the main level. Now the polish had faded, ravished by war and time and neglect, but the house's stately character remained intact.

To Julia, something of the Greek ideal was built into the white Doric columns that adorned the front of the house, an ideal that sought values in living beyond monetary standards. The Hopewell house meant permanency and stability, a sense of family and love and caring. It was the only permanent home she'd ever known, and she would fight with her bare hands to defend it.

Julia ran her fingers over the fireplace mantel, admiring the carved woodwork and the beveled mirror hanging above it. "I hope both of you realize how much I adore this house and how much it means to me that all of us are living together," she said. "Now that Papa's gone, you and Kate— and Lucas, wherever he may be—are all the family I have."

"Why, you know where Lucas is, dear." As Dorinda pulled up from the edge of the bed, the mattress creaked and groaned beneath her weight. "He's somewhere in Tennessee, working on the railroads that the Yanks destroyed."

"One of these days, your brother will come to his senses." Odelphia joined her niece in front of the fireplace. "He's just sowing wild oats right now. He'll come back home and settle down with Elizabeth soon. Though I don't know how much longer that pretty little thing will wait for him."

Julia tried to smile. "Maybe Lucas is more like Papa than I thought, always on the road and never with us. Until we came to live here, I never really felt as though we had a home of our own. Of course, Mama never seemed to mind pulling up roots every few months, but I think she would have followed Papa to the ends of the earth."

"I thought it was rather romantic, the way she picked up and moved every time the bishop changed Jeremiah's circuit route." Dorinda sighed. "I always admired the love between our baby sister and Jeremiah Carey."

Julia's eyes swelled with moisture at the memories of her beloved parents. "Papa never was one to worry about the basics of life. He was more concerned about saving lost souls than feeding his family. But both Mama and Papa left us with lots of wonderful memories. I want Kate to grow up surrounded by the same love in our home, even if our parents no longer share it with us. And I want Lucas to realize that he always has a family waiting for him, a place to come home to, if he ever decides to settle down."

"In the meantime, we'll be getting the house fixed up from the money we take in from boarders." Behind the thick spectacles, Odelphia's eyes sparkled with excitement. "And we can start by spreading the word to the auxiliary ladies at church. They may know of someone who needs a place to stay. We can put up a notice at the train station, too."

"Sounds like a lot of trouble and work to me." Dorinda frowned as she held out her chubby, white hands and examined them. "Washing all those dirty linens and dishes will ruin my hands, I fear."

"Would you rather be mopping up water every time it rains?" Odelphia shuddered at the thought. "If we can pay for repairing the house by taking in boarders, we won't have to worry about the roof caving in. We might even meet some interesting people."

Dorinda still wasn't convinced. "But the bother! Cooking all those meals and—"

"All those rich, tasty desserts. Just think, Dorie!" Odelphia smiled. "We'll have to keep plenty of desserts on hand for our guests."

"We'll need to stock a good supply of treats, like cakes and candies and pastries," Julia agreed.

"Pies, too," Odelphia insisted. "Why, I'd wager we'll need Dorie to make a couple of fresh pies every day."

"You'd want me to make pies . . . every day?" Dorinda, who never volunteered for anything other than preparing sweets for the family, suddenly perked up. Indulging in rich pastries was her weakness, and the promise of keeping a hefty supply of decadent desserts in the house was too appealing for her to resist. It took only a moment for Dorinda to agree to the plan. "Well, I suppose it won't hurt to take in a few boarders. And it might be nice to have some guests around the dinner table again."

Beaming, Odelphia turned to her niece. "It's settled, then. When do you want to open the doors, Julia?"

"In a week or two. As soon as we can fix up one or two rooms, Hopewell House will be in business."

"Hopewell House!" Dorinda giggled like a schoolgirl. "You know, that has a nice ring to it . . ."

As the ladies continued to discuss the new venture, Julia suddenly noticed that the incessant battering of rain on the tin roof had stopped. Morning sunshine streamed through the windows, filling the room with light.

She stepped over to the window, her heart swelling with hope. Maybe the storm was truly over now, she thought. And maybe she could keep her promise to Papa, after all.

"Damn it all to hell," Tyler McRae muttered as the train rattled through the North Georgia mountains. Fuming, he ran a finger along the damp rim of his collar.

It was hot and stifling in the crowded passenger car, but opening a window was out of the question. The storm of the century was raging outside, and pellets of rain were beating against the glass, sounding like little shots of gunfire in his ear.

Tyler gazed through the rain-drenched window. Streaks of lightning shot through the dark Georgia skies. He assumed the heavens were full of thunder, too, though he couldn't distinguish nature's booms from the roars of the snorting train.

Normally Tyler enjoyed the rhythmic motions of riding the rails, welcomed the sight of the scenic Georgia countryside after the train pulled out of Union Station in Chattanooga. In recent months he'd been a frequent passenger on the route between Chattanooga and Atlanta, and always looked forward to the journey.

He liked Atlanta. The city would be the center of the South someday, he thought. Already it was rising from the ruins of Sherman's march to the sea. And he intended to play a part in the city's ascent to greatness by building a new hotel on Peachtree Street. He'd purchased the land for a song, a prime parcel of ten acres in the center of town. Plans were under way to pattern the Atlanta hotel after The McRae, Chattanooga's most opulent hotel.

But today Tyler McRae wasn't going to Atlanta. All of his ambitious plans for launching a second hotel had been temporarily suspended because he was heading for Rome, Georgia.

And he would rather be going to hell.

Maybe I'm already there. He shifted restlessly in the hard seat, feeling beads of sweat trickling down his back.

Or maybe Jeremiah Carey was the one responsible for bringing hell to earth, spurred by one of his hellfire and brimstone sermons.

Tyler's temperature rose another notch at the thought of Jeremiah Carey. The man was nothing but a horse thief hiding behind a pulpit.

Carey had breezed into The McRae two months ago, asking for a job in the livery. Tyler's livery manager was impressed with the energetic man, who was full of promises and assurances about his skill with horses and buggies. He had hired him on the spot.

As Carey had worked in The McRae's livery, he'd settled into one of the hotel's more modest rooms and taken his meals in the dining room each day. He'd promised to pay for his food and lodging at the end of the month, insisting the arrangement was only temporary until he could find a place of his own.

At first the livery manager had been pleased with Carey's performance. A tall man with an easygoing smile and sandy brown hair sprinkled with streaks of gray, Carey seemed to have a way with people and a knack for handling horses. Business picked up considerably during the first few days of his employment. Several traveling businessmen rented buggies with teams of horses for overnight trips, while numerous visitors to the city, arriving by train, had hired horses from the livery for use during their stays in the area.

Then, one morning, Carey failed to show up for work. Within a few hours, the livery manager realized that Carey had disappeared, leaving behind nothing but an empty hotel room and an unpaid tab at The McRae.

Odder still, none of the customers had returned with the horses and buggies they'd rented from the livery.

It soon became apparent that a master theft had occurred at The McRae's livery. The missing stock alone was worth thousands of dollars, to say nothing of the cost of the lost equipment. Along with Jeremiah Carey, twelve horses, four new buggies,

and every bit and bridle in the place had vanished.
Tyler suspected Carey had sold the livery's stock
and equipment, piece by piece, instead of renting
it out. Or he'd set up the robbery with a group of
conspirators, acting as though he were hiring out
the horses and buggies, yet knowing the merchandise would never be returned to the livery.

Tyler informed the authorities of the theft, but to
no avail. Law and order were hard to come by in
the aftermath of the War. It was only yesterday,
when he'd stumbled across a faded handbill, that
Tyler decided to take the law into his own hands.

The handbill, tattered and torn, invited lost souls
to attend a March revival meeting on the banks of
the Tennessee River. Conducting the service was
the Reverend Jeremiah Carey of Rome, Georgia.

Finding out Carey's true identity infuriated Tyler.
A man of God, a man who preached righteous
living, was nothing more than a common horse
thief.

What did you expect? A bitter ache filled Tyler's
chest. All his life, people had betrayed him. First
his own parents, and then Sarah . . .

New beads of perspiration popped out along
his forehead. He yanked a handkerchief from his
pocket, pulling out a wad of bills at the same time.
"Damn it all to hell," he muttered.

Seated across from Tyler were an elegantly
dressed woman and a slender man wearing a
threadbare suit. The woman's eyebrows rose a
notch at the sight of the money spilling out of Tyler's
pocket. The man's Adam's apple bobbed nervously.

Distracted by his thoughts, he stuffed the money
back into his pocket. Tyler had never been a church-
going man, but discovering a minister was no better
than a common horse thief destroyed what was left
of his fragile faith in the goodness of humanity. And

it confirmed his belief that very few men could be trusted.

Now that Tyler knew where to find Jeremiah Carey, he intended to track down the imposter in the little town of Rome and demand payment for his loss or the return of his goods. Armed with his livery manager's description of Carey, Tyler was confident he would have no problem finding the man. Then he would turn the scoundrel over to the authorities. Justice was all he wanted; nothing more.

Of course, this wasn't the first time he'd gone after a scoundrel like Carey. Tyler McRae never permitted anyone to get away with making a fool of him. He'd jumped on more than one train to avenge his losses, leaving hotel manager Forrest Utley in charge of The McRae during his absences.

Thank God for Forrest. Tyler smiled to himself. At least there was one honest person in this world. During the War, tall, lanky Forrest had saved Tyler from certain death by stepping into the line of fire and shielding him from the blast of a Yankee bullet. The limp in Forrest's left leg constantly reminded Tyler that he could trust the man with anything—even his own life. Confident he was leaving The McRae in competent hands under his friend's management, Tyler felt free to travel whenever or wherever the need arose.

But it wasn't money he was after. God knows he didn't need it. He had more than enough to last a lifetime or two. It was the principle. Tyler McRae was tired of people not living up to their promises. He'd been swindled one too many times.

Forgiveness was another matter, of course. He would never forgive Jeremiah Carey for making a fool of him, for robbing him blind. Just as he would never forgive his father for breaking his promises to him. Or Sarah.

I will find Jeremiah Carey, Tyler promised himself. And he will pay for his sins, just like any ordinary man.

At that moment the train entered a tunnel winding through the North Georgia mountains. Darkness as black as midnight engulfed the passenger car. The clatter of the churning wheels intensified, echoing through the cavernous passage with a deafening roar.

Out of the darkness, something hard crashed into Tyler's jaw. He curled his hands into fists to defend himself just as a hand plunged into his pocket. The thunder of the train muffled the sound of gunfire, but Tyler knew what had happened the instant a hot flash of pain exploded through his upper arm.

Then a new type of darkness engulfed Tyler McRae. He slumped down into the seat as the train continued on its way, rattling down the North Georgia tracks.

"Don't you just love the smell in the air after a good spring rain?" Odelphia inhaled deeply as she strolled through the streets of Rome with her sister. Throughout the afternoon, the gray skies had changed into a vivid blue; the stormy clouds had been replaced with white fluffy ones.

"It does smell good," Dorinda agreed, admiring the pink azaleas and white dogwoods blossoming along their path. "It's like everything has been washed clean—the trees, the buildings, even the grass."

"Except for the streets," Odelphia noted, frowning at the muddy trail in front of them. She tugged at her sister's arm. "Let's get on the other side of the street, Dorie. It's not as muddy over there."

They'd taken only two steps forward when the shrieks of a train whistle pierced the air. Odelphia stopped in the middle of the street, shielded her eyes from the sun with her hand, and gazed into the distance. Puffy clouds of black smoke drifted through the Georgia skies.

"Train's a-comin', Dorie! Let's get on over to the depot and see who's coming to town."

The train was chugging to a stop by the time the Hopewell sisters reached the depot and joined the crowd of people gathered on the platform. Though some individuals were on hand to greet arriving passengers, others were waiting to board the train for the next leg of its journey into Atlanta. And a few, like the Hopewell sisters, were merely curious observers who enjoyed the excitement of the train's arrival.

Greeting the train from Chattanooga was a daily ritual for the ladies, who enjoyed watching the flurry of activity and the host of arriving and departing passengers. But today they sensed that something was dreadfully wrong when the porter practically leaped from the train onto the wooden platform.

"Is a doctor here?" he shouted, obviously distraught. "We need a doctor!"

A man with gray sideburns and a neatly trimmed goatee stepped out from the crowd. In his hand was a black leather bag. "I'm a physician," he announced. "What's the problem?"

Odelphia nudged Dorinda with her elbow. "Doc Kramer! What's he doing here?"

Instead of answering, Dorinda gaped. "Oh, Odie! Look at that poor man!"

She pointed to the train, where two railroad employees were carrying a passenger down the steps. The man's body was limp and lifeless, his face pale, his eyes closed. A dark red stain appeared on the sleeve of his suit.

"My goodness." Odelphia gasped. "He's been shot!"

Melee broke out. A woman screamed. A baby squalled. Someone shouted for the sheriff. Several men broke into a run. Arriving passengers grabbed their bags and ripped through the crowd with the speed of a tornado.

"Please return to your seats," the porter urged. "The sheriff will want everyone to stay for questioning."

Still, passengers scurried away from the train, ignoring the porter's plea. In the midst of the uproar, Odelphia and Dorinda worked their way through the crowd and followed Doc Kramer inside the depot building. The ladies stepped into the frame structure just as the railroad workers placed the wounded man on a wooden bench.

For a few moments the sisters stood in silence, watching curiously as Doc Kramer cut off the sleeve of the man's suit and examined the wound. Then Odelphia stepped up and peered over the doctor's shoulder. "How bad is it, Doc?"

"He'll live," Doc Kramer answered. "But he'll need to get plenty of rest after I remove the bullet."

"Can we do anything to help?" Dorinda asked, stepping up to join them.

The doctor looked up from his patient. "As a matter of fact, there is something you ladies can do. This gentleman isn't going anywhere for a while, and he'll need a place to recuperate. Could you check with Mrs. Chandler and see if she has any rooms available at her boardinghouse?"

"We'd be happy to, Doc, but it isn't really necessary," Dorinda returned. "We just saw Mrs. Chandler on our way to the depot. She was hammering a 'No Vacancy' sign on the door."

Doc Kramer frowned. "Well, now, that presents a problem. We certainly can't put this man back on the train to Chattanooga in his condition."

"I know where he can stay," Odelphia volunteered. "A new boardinghouse just opened up in town this morning."

"You don't say." Kramer's eyebrows rose in surprise. "Odd, but I don't recall hearing anything about a new boardinghouse."

"That's because we just decided this very morning that we're opening the Hopewell House." Odelphia smiled. "So we'll be glad for this poor young man to come with us after you clean him up."

The doctor's face lit up in a smile. "Wonderful! We'll make sure he gets there shortly."

"Fine. We'll go on home and get ready for him." With a curt nod, Odelphia turned and headed for the door.

Gasping in horror, Dorinda trailed after her sister. "Have you lost your mind, Odie? We're supposed to be running a boardinghouse—not a hospital! We don't know anything about taking care of a strange man who's just been shot! We're not doctors!"

"Of course we're not," Odelphia agreed. "But you heard Doc Kramer! This man isn't on his deathbed. He just needs a place to stay."

"But Julia won't like it, Odie. We're not ready to take customers just yet. We haven't fixed up the extra bedrooms and—"

"For goodness sake, Dorinda, taking in boarders was Julia's idea! She'll be happy when she finds out we've brought home our very first customer."

"But Julia doesn't like surprises," Dorinda mumbled. Slowing her pace, she shook her head in dismay as she continued down the street. "I'm afraid Julia won't like this at all."

Chapter 2

Returning home after a pleasant visit with Elizabeth, Julia sauntered through the garden plot located behind the house. She smiled as she surveyed the tiny green shoots sprouting up through the moist Georgia soil. A sense of peace flowed through her, a peacefulness she hadn't known in weeks. Not only was her garden blossoming with the first signs of life, but prospects for the future looked brighter than they had in months.

Keeping enough food on the table throughout the summer had been Julia's primary motivation for planting a spring garden. Now that boarders would be sharing meals with them, Julia was glad she had taken the time to plant a large crop of vegetables, including corn, tomatoes, carrots, and beans. And sweet, luscious strawberries—perfect for making preserves and jams and pies—would be ripening within a few days.

Though it would be several weeks before they would be ready to accept their first customer, Julia was already looking forward to opening the third floor of their home to overnight guests. She intended to open the four upper rooms, one by one, buying a few good used pieces of furniture along the way to add to the existing furnishings. By her estimation, the bedrooms on the top story of the house should bring in enough money to pay for a new roof by the end of the summer. Other repairs would follow with a steady stream of boarders.

Shielding her eyes from the afternoon sun with her hand, she gazed at the white clapboard house, shaded by sprawling magnolia trees. The Greek columns lined the front porch, and black shutters graced the long, narrow windows. But two shutters were missing, the entire place needed a fresh coat of white paint, and the columns were—

"Julia, Julia!"

Startled by the frantic cry, Julia turned. Her heart leaped into her throat when she saw her sister running across the lawn, blond braids flying wildly behind her. "What's wrong, Kate?" she called, picking up her skirts and dashing from the garden.

"Come quick, Julia!" Kate pleaded. "There's a naked man upstairs—in your bed!"

Julia's eyes widened in horror. "What?"

Kate pulled at her arm, tugging her toward the house. "He was a passenger on the train from Chattanooga—and he's been shot!"

"He was shot . . . in our house?"

"No, no! He was shot while he was riding on the train. Doc Kramer has already removed the bullet, but he wants to talk to you about taking care of him."

"Me? Taking care of . . . ?"

But there was no more time for questions. Kate was already halfway across the yard. Julia picked up her skirts and ran after her, following the young girl into the house, up the stairs, and down the hallway.

The door to her room was open. Julia stumbled to a halt as she surveyed the scene in front of her. Not only was there a man in her bed, but surrounding him were Odelphia, Dorinda, Doc Kramer, and Sheriff Mitchell.

Confusion swarmed through her as she stepped into the room. Dear heavens, what was going on?

Kate cautiously edged her way to the side of the bed. "Is that man . . ." Pausing, she gulped. "Is he going to live? He's not going to die here in front of us, is he?"

As she saw the fright in Kate's eyes, heard the tremor in her voice, Julia's heart rolled over. The child had already witnessed too many heartaches for her tender age. Julia was certain Kate's memories of their father's recent death were all too vivid at the moment, and she didn't want her to be exposed to another death.

"The gentleman is going to be fine, Kate," Doc Kramer assured the worried girl. "He's lost a lot of blood, but the bullet came out clean. All he needs is a few days of rest."

Kate breathed a sigh of relief. "That's good to hear. I'd hate for him to die."

Julia wrapped an arm around her sister's shoulders. "Doc Kramer said he's going to be fine," she reminded the young girl. "There's no need to worry, Kate."

"I'm glad. I wouldn't want anyone else to die around here." With forced effort, she flashed a brave smile.

Relieved that Kate seemed to be accepting the doctor's prediction, Julia turned to Sheriff Mitchell, a paunchy man with a thick Georgia drawl. "Would someone mind telling me what's going on here?"

"Of course, Miss Julia." Sheriff Mitchell removed his broad-brimmed hat and held it in front of his round belly. "It seems there was a shooting on the train from Chattanooga—and this gentleman was the victim. Unfortunately, most of the passengers who might have been witnesses took off in all directions when the train stopped at the depot. Scared out of their wits, I suppose. I only managed to question a few of them."

"Which means whoever was responsible for shooting this man was probably a passenger— and simply got lost in the crowd," Julia surmised.

"I'm afraid so," the sheriff admitted. "From what we can piece together, robbery was the motive. One fella said the shooting must have occurred when the train passed through a tunnel on the route. No one noticed this man had been shot until everyone got up to leave."

"He was lucky that Doc Kramer was at the train depot to remove the bullet on the spot," Odelphia chimed in.

"Seeing how this poor fella needed a place to stay, and Mrs. Chandler's boardinghouse is full up, your aunts volunteered to let him stay here," Doc Kramer added.

"Our very first customer!" Odelphia beamed with pride.

"I see," Julia murmured, though she didn't really understand why her aunts would think that a man who had been shot and robbed would be a good candidate for their first paying customer.

Doc Kramer pulled a bottle out of his bag and handed it to Julia. "He's unconscious at the moment, and running a bit of a fever. He'll probably have a rough night until the fever breaks. I'll be leaving this bottle of morphine with you to give him when he wakes."

"You're leaving me in charge of your patient . . . overnight?" Julia asked.

"It won't be as difficult as it sounds. He'll probably sleep most of the time." Doc Kramer picked up his bag to leave. "Send for me if he has any problems during the night. Otherwise, I'll be back in the morning to change his dressings."

Sheriff Mitchell followed the physician to the door. "I'll be back in the morning to see him, too. Maybe by then I'll be able to question him. Or I might have some leads on the case."

"We'll be expecting you then," Julia agreed. She turned to Kate. "How about seeing our guests to the door?"

"Sure, Julia."

After Kate and the men left the room, Julia turned to her aunts and frowned. "Well, ladies," she said. "You're certainly full of surprises."

"You don't seem too happy about getting our first boarder so quickly," Dorinda commented with a nervous laugh.

"I'm just concerned that our new boarder may be a threat to us," Julia admitted with genuine sincerity. "There could be a reason for someone shooting him, you know. Did you ever stop to think this man could be in trouble?"

"Psshaw," Odelphia said. "He's as harmless as a flea."

"Fleas aren't harmless, Aunt Odie. They're nothing but trouble. We don't know anything about this man and—"

"We know he was wearing a fine-looking suit until Doc Kramer had to cut the sleeve from his jacket." Odelphia lifted her chin with an air of defensiveness.

"We know he was shot while he was a passenger on the train from Chattanooga," Dorinda added.

"And we know he was carrying a nice-looking traveling bag with him." Odelphia pointed to a bag made of fine leather on the floor of the room.

"But do you know his name? Where he's from?

Or why he was shot? The man could be a criminal on the run, for heaven's sake!"

"I told you she wouldn't like this, Odie," Dorinda warned.

Ignoring her sister, Odelphia frowned. "I thought you'd be proud of us, Julia. What's wrong with being a Good Samaritan? Isn't it our Christian duty to take care of those in need?"

Julia sighed, determined not to feel bad about reprimanding her aunts when she was only trying to look out for their welfare. "It doesn't hurt for any of us to be cautious about the activities of our overnight guests. But if the sheriff believes he was merely an innocent robbery victim, I suppose it doesn't hurt anything for him to stay until he can get back on his feet. He certainly can't do any harm to anyone if he's unconscious."

Dorinda breathed a sigh of relief. "An innocent victim, I'm sure."

"He's innocent till proven guilty, and we'll treat him as we would any guest," Odelphia announced. "And now that he's settled, we need to have some chicken broth and biscuits ready for him when he wakes up."

As the two ladies headed for the kitchen, Julia slumped into a rocking chair beside the bed and sighed. Opening their home to boarders had been her idea, and she knew Odelphia and Dorinda had only been trying to help when they'd volunteered to take in the injured passenger. But she hadn't expected their first boarder to be arriving today. Why, they didn't even have a room ready for him! He was sleeping in *her* bed, for goodness sake.

Contending with the man's unexpected arrival, Julia had barely had a moment to catch a glimpse of him. Now she glanced over at him, studying him for the first time. What she saw nearly knocked the breath from her lungs.

His hair was as dark as a raven's feathers against the white pillow casing, sweeping back from his forehead in thick waves that stopped just above his shoulders. Dark lashes framed closed eyes, lashes that were as sinfully thick and luxurious as the mustache that curled over the top of firm, thin lips. His high cheekbones, thick brows, and straight, aristocratic nose were just as appealing as his olive complexion and firm chin.

Somehow, it seemed sinful for God to make such a beautiful creature. There was something about him—the stubborn thrust of his chin, the alluring curve of his jaw, or the combination of all his appealing features, she didn't know which—that mesmerized her.

To make matters worse, the other parts of the man that weren't covered by the pristine white sheets were just as fascinating to Julia. His shoulders were wide, his neck thick. Wisps of dark hair grew in curly mounds over his broad chest. The upper part of his left arm was bandaged in a white cloth. Even in his unconscious state, there was an aura of vitality throbbing from every visible inch of him. There was no doubt he was alive, nor that he was fighting to live.

Her imagination took flight. Who would want to shoot this man? Certainly he must have a wife at home who was worried about him. Or was he a drifter, like Lucas? Was he full of anger and hate that wouldn't allow him to settle down? Or full of bitterness that drove him to the ends of the earth? Her brother's emotions had never allowed him to find any peace since the War ended.

Julia pursed her lips together and sighed, suddenly aware that the blissful sense of peace she'd found in the garden had vanished.

It was going to be a very long night.

It had happened, just as he'd feared. He'd gone to hell. The agonizing pain in his upper arm was all the proof he needed.

It was all coming back to him now. The darkness. The explosive sound of gunfire. The pain erupting in his arm. Then darkness of a different kind.

He struggled to open his eyes. The room came into focus, bringing into view a walnut dresser with a marble top. Then a chipped porcelain bowl on a washstand. A pair of long, narrow windows. Worn drapes that lacked their original luster, but looked clean. Once stylish wallpaper, now faded and peeling.

He shifted uncomfortably. There was more. Touches of femininity everywhere. The soft glow of a lantern. Dainty lace edging on the pillow casing. Delicate, fine stitches on a homemade quilt. And the scent of lilacs . . .

He craned his neck and glanced to his right. A woman was sitting in a rocking chair, peacefully dozing. He edged forward, scrutinizing her with interest.

She was nothing like the loose women he'd known, the women who paraded along back streets or sold their wares behind closed doors. Her dress was too plain and worn, made of muslin instead of silk, loose-fitting instead of tight, simple instead of gaudy.

In fact, nothing about her was pretentious. Not a speck of paint or powder marred the creaminess of her complexion, the natural arch of her thick brows, or the fullness of her red lips. Her hair was styled simply, pulled into a loose coil at the nape of

her neck, and a few wispy tendrils dangled around
her forehead and temples.

Sitting there beside him, dozing in the rocking
chair, enveloped by the golden glow of the lantern,
she looked like a goddess . . . an angel of mercy,
keeping watch over him by night . . .

Nonsense.

No one had ever watched over him before. No one
had ever cared enough about Tyler McRae to give a
hoot about him. Besides, angels didn't exist, except
in dreams. There was too much evil in the world
for anyone to accept the crazy notion of angels.

Maybe he hadn't gone to hell, after all.

Maybe he'd just gone crazy.

A hot flash of pain shot through his arm, and
darkness engulfed him once again.

Sometime later, he heard the swish of a woman's
skirts. Lifting his head from the pillow, he saw the
woman again. Only this time, she wasn't peacefully dozing in a rocking chair. She was standing in
the corner of the room, bent from the waist, rifling
through a bag on the floor. *His* traveling bag.

A wave of furor washed through him. She wasn't
the innocent angel she'd appeared to be, after all.
She was stealing him blind. And she wouldn't get
away with it. Groaning, he closed his eyes and
waited to make his move.

Hearing his moans, Julia quietly rose, leaned over
the bed, and placed a cool hand over his feverish
forehead. He opened his eyes and gazed up at her.

As she looked down at him, Julia's lungs stopped
working. Vivid blue eyes burned into hers with
an alarming intensity, glistening with a power so
primitive and raw that a flame rose to her cheeks.

"Watch what you're doin', darlin'," he warned.
His voice was like black velvet, rich and lush and
tempting. "I may be delirious, but I'm nobody's
fool."

"You're running a fever," she said as evenly as she could, though her heart was racing uncontrollably. The hot touch of his skin suddenly scorched her fingers. She removed her hand from his forehead.

He stretched out his arm, clamped a hand around her wrist, and yanked her toward him. "I'm not crazy, lady. I know what you're trying to do."

"I don't think you understand," she countered, her voice shaky and uneven. "I'm merely trying to make sure you feel as pleasant and comfortable as possible under the circumstances."

As if to prove her point, she worked her wrist out of his clamplike grip and reached behind the wavy locks of raven hair spread across the white linens. After she fluffed up the pillow, a lazy grin sprouted at the corners of his lips.

"That's not how you please a man, darlin'." In one swift movement, his hand whipped around to the back of her head. Strong fingers plunged through her hair, then fastened around her neck and pulled her down. As she lost her balance, her feet slid across the wooden floor. Within the space of a heartbeat, her breasts were crushed against the man's bare chest. And her lips were only a breath away from his.

His eyes locked on her mouth. "This is how you please a man," he warned with a groan of unbridled desire.

With the full length of her trembling body sprawled over his, terror slammed through her. Julia knew exactly what he intended to do. Her instincts warned her to run for dear life or scream for help—anything to remove herself from the clutches of this ruthless, dangerous man. But she couldn't breathe, couldn't speak, couldn't move.

Just as she feared, he ground his lips against hers.

The raw, primitive surge of his mouth branded her with a kiss that was hot and hungry, scorching with passion and burning with untamed promises.

Though Julia expected the touch of his lips to be demanding and gruff, she never expected to be mesmerized by its power. She had the strange feeling that she'd never be able to erase the memory of his mouth clamping over hers. Her head started to swim, and her weight sagged against the length of his masculine frame. He was kissing her senseless, and she was powerless to stop it.

Her breath finally returned, coming in short, terrified gasps. Panic tore through her. Summoning up the last bit of her strength, she flattened her palms against his chest. Hot flesh scorched her fingers; she could feel the frantic thumping of his heart through the curly mounds of dark hair covering his chest. With a cry muffled beneath the pressure of his lips, she pushed with all her might. To her horror, his hand tightened around her neck, locking her in place. Though a bullet had ravaged his body with fever, it had not subdued the power soaring through his limbs. The man was a pillar of endurance.

"Oh, Jesus, you're sweet," the man murmured into her mouth as he kissed her. "As sweet as I've ever tasted . . ."

Out of desperation, Julia attempted to escape one last time. Using both hands, she pinched the curly dark hairs on his chest between her thumbs and forefingers.

Then she plucked the hairs out of his chest by the roots.

Yelping like a wounded puppy, the man shoved her off the bed. His hand flew to his chest, massaging the tender skin. "Goddamn it. What in the hell did you do that for?" he demanded. His eyes were wide, full of shock and pain, as he stared at her. His wounded expression reminded Julia of a little boy who had just been wrongfully accused of stealing cookies from the bakery.

"I could ask you the same question." She rubbed her bruised lips, trying to wipe away the memory of his touch. But even as her fingers glided across her mouth, she knew it would be impossible to ever forget that searing kiss. She'd never experienced anything like it in her life, and she knew she'd never know anything like it again. Until now, she'd only been kissed by Brent. And his kisses had been sweet and tender, nothing like this man's hot, scorching touch.

"I already told you what I was doing. I was just showing you how to please a man." His fingers moved over his chest with slow, seductive strokes as his eyes raked over her petite frame with blatant approval. The hint of a smile played on his lips. "But it looks like you need a few more lessons, darlin'."

"Don't stake your life on it." Infuriated by his arrogance, enraged by his audacity, she spun around and turned her back to him. She stalked to the washstand and tried to compose herself as she dampened a rag in the basin and returned to his side. "Judging by your despicable behavior and foul mouth, I should let you lie here and burn up with fever." In spite of her admonishments, she placed the cool fabric on his forehead.

"But you're not," he observed wryly.

The curve of her back went rigid. "I promised Doc Kramer I would watch you tonight."

"And you always keep your promises?"

"Always." She folded her arms across her chest. "You're a lucky man, you know. The bullet only missed your chest by a few inches."

"Lucky?" Tyler sneered. "Yeah, I'm damn lucky to get hit in the arm."

"I know you're in pain, but please curb your tongue. We do not allow such foul language in this household."

"Is that so?"

She pursed her lips together. "Only gentlemen are permitted lodging here."

"And I'm not a gentleman?" He pulled up the sheet and peered at the lower half of his naked body. Then he looked up at Julia and grinned like the devil. "It seems to me that I'm perfectly qualified to be called a gentleman. Care to check for yourself?"

Rage filled her veins. He was mocking her, trying to humiliate her, and Julia hated him for it. Though she had no doubt that this man was all male, she had no desire to see the evidence of his masculinity. Yet she couldn't give him the upper hand in the situation, either. "As soon as you're able to find other accommodations, I think it would be best if you leave Hopewell House," she announced with a quiet firmness. "My sister is only six years old, and my aunts have a few hairs that haven't turned silver. I'd hate for your language to offend or corrupt anyone in this household."

"And just who the hell are you? Some kind of nun?"

She bristled. "I'm just a woman who doesn't want her family to be exposed to your foul mouth." She spooned out some kind of liquid from a brown bottle. "I'm sure your family will be worried about you. If you'd like me to send a wire to anyone at your home, I would be—"

"That won't be necessary," he snapped, more harshly than he intended. His only resemblance to a home was The McRae, and Forrest Utley was the closest thing to a family that he had. He fully intended to check on business with Forrest in a day or two. But he'd be damned if he'd ask this woman to send a wire for him.

"Are you sure? It wouldn't be any trouble. If you—"

"I'm sure, lady. I don't have any family."

"No one?" The natural arch of her brows rose higher.

"No, no one." His voice was flat, lifeless. As lifeless as his soul.

She winced. Was she feeling sorry for him? Or had his harsh reply wounded her? Damn it all to hell. He felt so lousy that he couldn't tell what she was feeling. But why was this little sliver of a woman getting under his skin?

She held the spoon to his lips. "Doc Kramer said you should take this."

The sweet lilt in her voice was like a soothing caress, wrapping around him. He tried to ignore the comforting sensation, tried to disregard her words. When he didn't move, she added, "It's morphine. It'll take away the pain."

What the hell? He didn't want to be here anyway. Maybe a good shot of morphine would make him forget this cozy room with its lantern glow, its homemade quilts, its lilac scent. He swallowed the liquid in one gulp, then wiped his mouth with the back of his hand.

"So where in the hell am I?" he demanded.

"You're in Rome, Georgia, at Hopewell House. My aunts and I have just opened our home to boarders. You're our first customer. I'm Julia. And you're . . . ?"

"Tyler. Tyler McRae. And don't try to get sweet with me, lady. Where are my clothes?"

He threw back the covers. Julia hastily stepped back and whirled around. A blush crept from her neck to the roots of her hair. "You are in no condition to leave, Mr. McRae. Doc Kramer said—"

"I don't give a damn what any doctor said," Tyler snapped. He swung his legs over the side of the mattress and stood upright. Then he jerked the quilt off the mattress and wrapped it around his torso. The room swam in front of him. Nausea jolted his stomach.

Moaning, he slowly lowered himself to the edge of the bed. He clutched the bandage on his upper arm and squeezed his eyes shut. "Damn it all to hell," he muttered, resting his head on the pillow.

A few seconds later, he cleared his throat in an awkward attempt to break the silence between them. "I suppose I should thank you," he admitted, but the reluctance in his voice spoke volumes.

"For what? Plucking out the hairs on your chest?"

Taken aback by her humor, he smiled. But the slight curve in his lips vanished when a disturbing thought entered his mind. Was she trying to soften him up and get him to apologize? If so, she was in for a long wait. They would both be dead and gone before he'd voice one apologetic word. "You know damn well what for, lady. For taking me in."

He could have sworn compassion was glowing from those indecently beautiful green eyes of hers. "I didn't do it for you," she said. "In fact, I haven't done anything by choice. My aunts were the ones who insisted on bringing you here. They were at the train depot when Doc Kramer removed the bullet from your arm. They were the Good Samaritans. Not me."

For some reason, he felt disappointed. He would have liked to believe she was his own private angel sent from above, an angel who'd winged her way to his side by her own free choice. But an angel didn't plunge through a man's traveling bag like a pickpocket off the street, he suddenly remembered.

He regarded her, wary. "So they picked up a man at the train depot and brought him home—like they'd pick up a mangy, stray dog?"

"If you knew my aunts, you'd understand. They're very interesting women."

"Or maybe desperate ones." His eyes narrowed with suspicion. "Maybe you're desperate, too. Desperate enough to rummage through a traveling bag that belongs to an unconscious man."

Julia bristled. Her lips formed a tight line, and Tyler knew he had hurt her again. A twinge of regret sliced through him, but he tried to ignore it. Why should it matter?

"I was looking for some kind of identification—a name, an address, a piece of paper that would tell me something about you. I've never taken a thing from anyone in my life. And I don't intend to take advantage of anyone now—especially not someone in your condition."

His face burned with shame when he realized she was telling the truth. He shifted uncomfortably, feeling some strange emotions that he couldn't define. Long ago he'd lost his soul, buried it along with a wagonful of shame and grief and heartache. And he didn't need some woman trying to resurrect something that he no longer wanted or needed.

His eyes burned a trail down the length of her. Sweet Jesus, she was tiny, probably only a couple of inches over five feet. Her body curved in all the right places with enticing dips and swells, from the fullness of her breasts to her gently rounded hips. Her waist was so small that Tyler figured he could put his hands around it.

She turned and raised one hand to knead the nape of her neck. Then she loosened her narrow shoulders and rotated her head in an imaginary circle. Watch-

ing her, Tyler became acutely aware of how exhausted she appeared, how fragile, how vulnerable.

For cripes' sake, it was a miracle he hadn't killed
her, yanking her down on top of him, kissing the
life out of her, treating her like some harlot out of
the slums.

Turning back around, she leaned over the bed and
pulled the quilt up to his chin. He glanced up
at her uncertainly. In spite of everything he'd
said and done, her touch was tender, her expression full of concern.

His eyelids suddenly felt like a ton of bricks. The
pain in his arm intensified. He closed his eyes and
sighed. "Feel . . . like hell," he muttered.

Watching him struggle against the pain, Julia
sensed this was a man who did not easily suc-
cumb to defeat. Since the War, most men were
merely struggling to survive, haunted by memories
of bloody deaths and brutal battlefields. The conflict between the North and the South had sapped
their strength to live; many acted as though they
were nothing more than walking corpses who had
not been given the grace to die. But this man was
different. Even in his weakened state, he was full
of fight and defiance.

This man is a survivor, she thought. As her gaze
swept over him, she wondered what had happened
to his family and what kind of heartaches he'd
endured. She suspected he was wary of trusting
anyone. Why else would he accuse her of trying to
steal from him?

"I'm sure you'll feel better tomorrow," Julia returned, unable to resist placing a hand over his
forehead to check on his temperature one last time.
He was still burning with fever, but she was certain
he would not awaken before dawn. The morphine
was already taking effect, and he should be able to
sleep until morning.

Suddenly realizing she was exhausted, Julia quietly slipped out of the room. Yet even in her frazzled state, she felt certain that sleep would not come easily for her. Not even the blissful state of sleep would be able to erase the knowledge that her new boarder was a very dangerous man. Nothing would ever make her forget the memory of his seething kiss, a memory that still scorched her lips like a fire raging from the depths of hell.

Chapter 3

The sweet aroma of freshly baked bread wafted through the kitchen shortly before dawn. Julia set the loaves on the table to cool, then inserted two trays of neatly cut rounds of biscuit dough into the oven.

Breakfast was the only meal of the day that Julia prepared, other than fixing lunches for Kate and herself every morning for their noon meal at the schoolhouse. Aunt Odelphia and Aunt Dorinda were responsible for cooking supper each evening. Except for the summer months, Julia's teaching job kept her busy throughout the afternoon, and the cooking arrangement worked out nicely for everyone.

Julia usually enjoyed the quiet moments of privacy in the kitchen before the eruption of the hustles and bustles of the day. Ordinarily she relished the sight of the sunrise through the kitchen window, the sounds of a rooster's crow, the smells of baking bread.

But the day was not starting out to be a normal one. After her disturbing encounter with the new boarder, she'd traipsed up to the third floor, staggered into the one unoccupied room that contained a mattress and pillow—the one with the leak in the ceiling—and tumbled into bed without bothering to change her clothes. She had been too weary to bother removing her blue muslin dress. Besides, all of her gowns were hanging in her wardrobe. And she didn't dare return to her room to retrieve a fresh gown as long as Tyler McRae was sleeping in her bed.

So she'd tried to sleep on a bare mattress without any linens and prayed that rain wouldn't fall from the skies and trickle through the leaky roof. But sleep was elusive. Her wanton behavior sent waves of shame washing through her. The memory of Tyler McRae's kiss burned through her like a scorching heat, and she struggled to forget the disturbing sensations soaring through her from the touch of his lips on hers, from the feel of her breasts crushed against his bare chest.

"Shame on you," she scolded herself, pulling the tray of golden, flaky biscuits from the oven. Why had she allowed her emotions to soar out of control last night? It was disturbing to think a man like Tyler McRae could elicit such unfamiliar feelings in her.

Behind her, footsteps shuffled across the wooden floor. Turning, she nearly jumped out of her skin. Tyler was standing in the doorway, or rather, propped up against it, watching her intently.

His hair was wild and tangled, his skin tanned and smooth. A shadow of beard appeared along the line of his jaw. For the life of her, Julia couldn't prevent her eyes from traveling like a wandering gypsy down his tall, muscular form. To her horror, she discovered he was wearing only three things: a quilt bunched around his waist, a bandage over the upper part of his left arm, and a rakish grin across his lips.

Stunned, she lifted her eyes to his face. "You cannot walk around the house like that, Mr. McRae!"

His blue eyes twinkled mischievously. "Gentlemen don't do such things?"

"I've already told you—there are other people in this house besides you!"

"But I thought I was your first—and only—boarder."

"And the last, if the rest are like you." She frowned. "You shouldn't be out of bed, you know. Doc Kramer won't appreciate it if I don't—if you don't—if—"

Flustered, she stumbled to a halt. He picked up where she left off. "So you'll be in trouble with the doc if you don't make me behave?"

She seriously doubted if anyone could make this man behave. And that infuriated her. Julia liked to be in control of her life, her house, her family. By refusing to cooperate with her, this man wasn't fitting into the nice, neat mold that she'd carved out for herself and those around her. He was a rebel who couldn't be tamed, disrupting every inch of her household, every part of her safely guarded life.

"If you're hungry, I suggest you return upstairs and I'll bring breakfast to you," she announced stiffly. "I hope you like chicken broth."

He wrinkled his nose. "I'd rather have some fresh bread . . . with some jam or preserves."

"Since you made it down the stairs by yourself, I don't suppose bread and preserves would hurt if broth doesn't appeal to you," she conceded.

Tyler swayed, grasping the doorframe for support. "Damn," he muttered. "I'm not sure I can make it back up the stairs by myself."

"Oh, for heaven's sake!" Julia turned with a swish of her skirts. With a boldness born of necessity, she draped his arm over her shoulder. "Don't put all your weight on me," she warned, "or both of us may tumble down the steps."

He had the audacity to caress her shoulder with the palm of his hand. Then he had the nerve to look down at her with his inexcusably beautiful blue eyes. And to make matters worse, he was brazen enough to flash a disarming smile. "I'll be careful," he promised solemnly, though Julia knew he meant not a word.

She wrapped her arm around his back to balance herself, but the touch of his bare flesh against her fingers sent her heart slamming into her ribs. The closeness of him not only heated her skin, it numbed her brain as well. As they trudged through the breezeway that connected the kitchen to the main house, Julia hated herself for reacting so violently to this barbaric man.

They'd taken only one step up the staircase when Tyler stopped cold. "I can't hold on to the banister and the quilt and you at the same time. Think I should just drop the quilt, forget the railing, and concentrate on holding on to you?"

Julia gritted her teeth. Dear heavens, would he never stop tormenting her? "Maybe we should consider fixing up a room for you in the barn where there aren't any steps to contend with," she ground out.

He dismissed her suggestion with a shrug. "I rather prefer the comfort of the bed you've given me."

She felt a flush rise to her cheeks, but dared not comment. He wrapped his right arm around her shoulders and leaned heavily against her while clinging to the quilt draped around his waist with his left hand. Each step became a strange mixture of torture and delight for Julia as they trudged up the stairs together at a snail's pace.

When they finally reached the bedroom, Julia had the horrible feeling that Tyler was going to faint. His face was pale, beads of sweat were popping out along his brow, and he was staggering like a drunken sailor.

She guided him over to the bed and pulled the quilt up around him. Obviously his fever had broken, but he needed food to regain his strength. "I'll be right back with your breakfast," she announced, hastily leaving the room.

In the kitchen, she prepared a kettle of hot tea and sliced one of the bread loaves. After generously buttering each piece, she topped the slices with several tablespoons of strawberry preserves. Then she set the plate of food and mug of tea on a wooden serving tray. Just as she started up the steps, a knock sounded at the door.

Balancing the tray on her hip with one hand, she opened the front door. The rising sun cast a golden glow over the porch where Sheriff Mitchell was standing.

After one swift glance at Julia, a puzzled frown crossed the sheriff's face. "Good heavens, Miss Julia! You look like you haven't had a wink of sleep all night! Did your boarder give you some problems?"

More than you'll ever know, Julia wanted to say. She smoothed back a few wayward tendrils from her forehead, cringing at the thought of how she must look to the sheriff. "He was very restless," she conceded. "I'm on my way upstairs with his breakfast."

"Sorry to disturb you at the crack of dawn, but I wanted to get an early start today." Sheriff Mitchell eyed the bread and preserves on the tray and licked his lips. "I thought it would be best if I dropped by here before heading into town."

"No problem, Sheriff. I'm always up before the sun." Julia bit back a smile, noticing the sheriff's fascination with the food on the tray. "Would you care for something to eat, too?"

The sheriff grinned. "Can't turn down a taste of your bread, Miss Julia."

After returning to the kitchen to retrieve some more bread and another mug of hot tea, Julia accompanied the sheriff to the second floor. Tyler was sitting up in bed when they entered the room. Remembering that he had not been conscious during the sheriff's last visit, Julia promptly introduced the gentlemen as she served them both.

Tyler regarded the gold star on the sheriff's vest with a contemptuous glare. "So what do you want?" he demanded.

Slow-moving and easygoing with a drawl as thick as maple syrup, Sheriff Mitchell appeared not to be concerned with Tyler's gruff demeanor. He washed down a slice of bread with a gulp of hot tea before answering. "I'm just trying to piece together the events on the train, son. Care to tell me what happened?"

"What good would it do? You'll never be able to catch the bastard who shot me." Tyler crammed some bread into his mouth, as if he were finished with the conversation.

"I might be able to solve this case if you'll cooperate with me," Sheriff Mitchell contended. "Course, some folks don't talk when they got somethin' to hide, or when they give a man cause to shoot 'em."

"You son of a bitch." Every muscle in Tyler's body stiffened at the insinuation. Julia had the horrible feeling he was going to leap up and knock the sheriff's head off. She was almost relieved when he simply bolted upright in the bed and shoved an outstretched finger in the sheriff's face.

"Listen, mister, I've done a helluva lot of stupid things in my life, but dodging the law isn't one of them. Good God, I nearly had my arm blown off, and you're blaming me for causing it! Is that your idea of justice? And even if I were a troublemaker, it doesn't give anyone the right to shoot me in the dark."

His strength sapped from the outburst, he sank back into the pillow. The fury had vanished from his expression, replaced with a wounded look that reminded Julia of a little boy who was being punished for a prank he didn't instigate.

The sheriff's voice broke into her thoughts. "I'm not working against you, son. I'm working for you. I'm just looking for a motive and a suspect. But I can't find the person who shot you unless you tell me what happened."

Tyler heaved a weary sigh and raked a hand through his tousled hair. "It was hot as Hades on the train, as crowded as a cattle car. Then we passed through a tunnel. Couldn't see a damn thing. Couldn't hear much, either, other than the train's thunderous roars. Something smashed into my jaw, and my arm felt like it was exploding. Next thing I knew, this lady here was rummaging through my traveling bag."

Furious, Julia felt her pulse rate quicken. How dare he distort the truth! She hastily defended herself. "You know I was merely trying to find some identification," she corrected.

"Remember anything else—like someone watching you?" Sheriff Mitchell prompted.

His eyes narrowed intently, as if he were combing his memory. "Once, I pulled a handkerchief from my pocket, and my money slipped out. A wad of it."

"How much?" the sheriff asked.

"About fifteen hundred."

Julia's eyes widened. Tyler McRae must be a very rich man to carry that much cash with him.

Or a very foolish one, if he'd lost every penny to his name.

"Didn't notice anyone ogling me," he continued. "Unless you count the lady sitting across from me. But I didn't pay her much notice. She wasn't my type. And it looked like she was traveling with the skinny little guy sitting next to her."

Julia wondered exactly what kind of woman was his type, then despised herself for her wayward thoughts. She didn't have any interest in this crude, foulmouthed barbarian who possessed the most beautiful blue eyes she'd ever seen.

"All I know for certain is that my money has disappeared, I nearly got my arm blown off, and I can't even find my damn clothes," Tyler finished with a disgusted sigh.

"Doc Kramer had to dispose of your suit," Julia informed him. "He had to cut off the sleeve of your jacket. It was ruined from all the bloodstains . . ." She shuddered at the thought.

Sheriff Mitchell scratched his head as he ambled across the room. "Looks like we got a case of robbery on our hands," he surmised. "But without any witnesses, it's difficult to make a case."

"What a surprise," Tyler muttered.

"Since you'll obviously be here a few more days, I'll drop in and let you know if I come across anything."

"You do that." Tyler scowled. "I won't be holding my breath, you know. I'll just take care of my business and get the hell out of this godforsaken town."

After escorting Sheriff Mitchell to the door, Julia returned to Tyler's side. He was still wearing a scowl on his face, and a stab of irritation shot through Julia. Why was he always so uncooperative with everyone? The man couldn't even be cordial to a sheriff who was trying to help him!

"What are you staring at?" he grated.

"The rudest, most ungrateful man I've ever met," she responded quietly. "Sheriff Mitchell was only trying to help, you know. There was no call for your uncivilized, ill-mannered, impudent behavior."

His grin was lazy, arrogant, disarming. "You and Sheriff Mitchell may not have appreciated my winning ways today, but I don't recall that you objected too much last night. Until those itchy little fingers of yours decided to pluck the hairs from my chest, I was giving you the thrill of your life. And you were enjoying it. I could tell by the way you opened your mouth to me, the way your breath came in short little gasps, the way your hot little body was wiggling over mi—"

His voice halted as she hurled back her arm and smacked him across the face. "Who do you think you are, Tyler McRae?"

Then she whirled around and yanked open the door to the wardrobe. She hated him. Never before in her life had she hated anyone. But this man evoked emotions she never knew she had.

Hot tears burned her eyelids as she pulled out a clean dress and some nightgowns from the wardrobe with trembling fingers. Her hand smarted from slapping him, and she could feel his stunned gaze boring through her.

"I'll be leaving shortly," she announced without bothering to turn around. "My aunts will be tending to your needs while I am gone for the day. Should I ask Sheriff Mitchell to protect them from you?"

"That depends. How old are they?"

She was grateful he could not see her face. The nerve of him! "Sixty-one and fifty-eight," she ground out.

"Naw, you don't have any reason to worry. Until you get home, that is." He paused. "If you're looking for some clothes for me, you're wasting your time. Those aren't exactly my style. Besides, I have clothes in my traveling bag. But if you'd care to get my bag, I'll—"

"You can get your own clothes from your traveling bag." She whirled around to face him. "And I believe you can get dressed all by yourself, too. I have better things to do than fool with the likes of you."

She wanted to say more. She wanted to tell him where to go and how to get there. And she wanted to wring his neck until something like regret crossed his face, staining his high cheekbones with a deep crimson.

"This is your room." The grating edge to his voice disappeared, replaced with a tone of sudden understanding. "You gave me your bed, didn't you?"

She didn't answer, didn't have to. He already knew the truth of the matter. Cursing himself as she stormed out of sight, Tyler slumped back into the softness of the bed.

Rome, Georgia, wasn't exactly the place of his dreams, after all. A horse-snatching preacher led him here, then a potbellied sheriff accuses him of causing his own shooting. He'd never met a sheriff with an ounce of competency, and he figured this one wasn't any different. It had been useless to tell him about the shooting.

But he hadn't expected Julia's reaction to his rudeness. What he saw in her eyes stirred up emotions he'd forgotten he'd ever had. Beneath those thick,

with the confidence of a pagan warrior. All it took
was a carefully chosen word, a menacing scowl,
or a fist in the jaw. But how could you control a
six-year-old who looked like a cherub?

He didn't feel like contending with a child, especially if she were like most of the unruly children
who stayed at The McRae with their parents. They
poked their fingers into everything and asked questions that were impossible to answer. They cried
without warning. And they threw temper tantrums
without cause.

He opened his eyes and glared at her, hoping
she'd take one look at him and run. But she simply
continued to peer at him with wide-eyed innocence
and announced, "You look like you're mad."

"I'm not mad," he denied with a shrug. "I'm
Tyler. Who'd want their name to be Mad?"

She giggled. "You're silly."

It had been a while since Tyler had made an
effort to be nice to anyone. But that girlish giggle,
full of innocence and joy, pierced into the depths
of his heart, dredging up a part of him that hadn't
surfaced in a long time. "No, I'm not silly, either.
I'm Tyler. Are you Silly?"

Her laughter was as free as the wind, uninhibited,
as only a child's can be. "No, silly. I'm Kate."

"That's a nice name. Better than Silly or Mad,
don't you think?"

"I like it. My real name is Kathryn, but all my
friends call me Kate. You can call me Kate, too."

"Does that make us friends?"

"I guess so." She wrinkled her nose. "Don't you
want me to be your friend? You look like you
need one."

Taken aback by her candid observations, he
scowled. "Men don't need friends. We're big and
strong and tough. We can take care of ourselves."

He wasn't as convincing as he thought. Her bow-shaped mouth twisted into a frown. "Julia says everyone needs friends." Her wide eyes traveled over the bandage on his arm. "Does that hurt?"

He nodded. "'Fraid so."

"Then don't you need a friend to help make it better?"

"I don't think so." Tyler grimaced, shifting his weight. Heaven help him, he was already losing an argument with a little girl. "You'd better go, Kate. Your sister might get mad if she knew you were up here, talking to me."

"She's already mad. She's running late this morning, and Julia's never late." She tilted her head, studying him intently. "Did you do something to make Julia mad?"

"Probably. She doesn't like me very much, I'm afraid."

"Why not?"

"We're just different, I suppose."

She sighed. "Maybe she won't be so grumpy when we get to school."

"You and Julia go to school?" Terror sliced through him. Good God, had he mauled a schoolgirl?

"She's my teacher," she explained simply. "She teaches me and all the other kids at school, too."

He breathed a sigh of relief. "Must be nice, having a sister. Especially if she's your teacher."

"You don't have a sister?"

"No." *Not anymore.*

"That's too bad. Sisters are nice. But most of the time, Julia acts more like my mother. Ever since Mama died, Julia is always doing stuff like telling me to sit up straight and checking to see if I washed behind my ears. She even makes me eat green beans! And I hate green beans." She leaned forward, lowering her voice to a whisper. "But I don't really eat them, you know. Julia just thinks I do. I put them in my mouth and pretend to chew them up. But I spit them into my napkin when she's not looking."

Suddenly, Julia's voice sounded from the first floor. "Hurry, Kate! We don't want to be late to school!"

"Coming, Julia!" Kate whirled around and bounded across the room. At the door, she paused, then scurried back to Tyler's side. "You won't tell Julia about the green beans, will you? 'Cause I could get in big trouble."

"Don't worry." For the life of him, he couldn't prevent his lips from curling upward. Who could resist the charm of this winsome imp? "Your secret is safe with me."

Stretching up on her toes, she leaned over and planted a wet kiss on his cheek. The effect of that simple gesture was more disarming to Tyler than the bullet that had ripped through his flesh. He was so stunned that he was still staring at her, wide-eyed, when she smiled.

"You know something? I think I'm going to like having you for a friend." Then she spun around, darted across the room, and skipped into the hall.

Thirty minutes later, Julia stood at the entrance of the one-room schoolhouse and rang the bell, signaling the start of classes for the day.

The school's seventeen students, ranging in age from six to fourteen, were congregated in the spacious yard that surrounded the white frame building. Some of the younger girls were examining the contents of their friends' lunch pails. A few feet away, another group of children played a game of hopscotch while a trio of ten-year-old boys chased after a grasshopper. Older students were huddled in groups of twos and threes, sitting on overturned logs or standing under the shade of a sprawling magnolia tree.

School should have started ten minutes ago, though none of the children seemed to notice—or care, for that matter. They were too busy enjoying each other's company and taking advantage of the cool morning breezes, the May sunshine . . . and their teacher's tardiness.

Julia cringed with shame for her belated arrival. Promptness was one of the many virtues she tried to instill in her students. She believed in setting an example for her pupils, and genuinely tried to live by the standards she taught in class each day.

Only yesterday she had lectured on the importance of timely arrivals. "People value promptness in others," she'd told the students. "Always being on time means you're dependable, responsible, and organized. And promptness shows that you're considerate of other people's time, as well."

And she sincerely believed every word. Julia Carey had never been late to anything in her life. Until this morning. Until Tyler McRae had barged into her life.

His parting words still burned in her ears. And it was the slight edge of truth in his accusations that sent a hot flush of shame to her cheeks.

Had she actually enjoyed being crushed in his arms? Closing her eyes, she grimaced at the vivid memory, not daring to admit it was true. For a fleeting instant, when she'd been sprawled out on top of him, when his lips had branded hers with that searing, unforgettable kiss, hot waves of passion had shot through her.

To make matters worse, he'd detected that heated rush of longing. And Julia Carey was more ashamed of herself than she'd ever been in her life. How could she, a minister's daughter, a woman of virtuous beliefs, have felt such stirrings of desire? She'd never lost control of her conduct with Brent. But she'd behaved like a wanton woman with the guest in her house, and she was certain her guilt would plague her for the rest of her life. She never wanted to see Tyler McRae again.

Even if she could have spared a few moments before leaving for school, she did not dare go back into that room. She could not, would not, face Tyler McRae again until she was forced to do so. Though she fully intended to make certain that he received proper care until he recovered, as she'd promised Doc Kramer, she would not permit herself to be alone with him again. He was far too dangerous to risk the chance.

"Look what I found, Miss Julia!"

Eight-year-old Daniel Young bounded up the steps and held out his hand, jarring Julia from her thoughts. A frog dangled from the boy's fingers.

"How interesting, Daniel." Julia forced a grim smile. "That's the third frog you've found this week, isn't it?"

"Yes, ma'am." He beamed with pride.

"And I'm sure you remember the rules, don't you?"

His smile vanished. "Yes, ma'am. No frogs allowed in class."

While Daniel retraced his steps and returned the frog to the school yard, Julia rang the bell one last time. "Time to get to your desks, class," she announced.

As the youngsters filed up the steps and into the classroom, Julia offered warm, personal greetings to each of them. But it was young Sam Springer who captured most of her concern and attention that bright spring morning. Julia knew something was troubling the young boy the instant he trudged into the schoolhouse. For several weeks she'd been attuned to the dullness of his eyes and the absence of his usual curiosity. Normally the freckle-faced, red-haired imp dashed into class like a streak of lightning. But this morning he seemed more distracted than ever.

Unable to concentrate on the arithmetic lesson, Sam failed to solve several simple problems. He fell asleep when he was supposed to be reading. He never raised his hand to answer any questions during geography, his favorite subject. And when the rest of his friends were admiring Daniel's frog-catching abilities during lunch, Sam sat by himself under an oak tree at the edge of the school grounds, looking for all the world as though he'd lost his last friend.

Observing Sam's despondency as the other children laughed and played, Julia felt her chest tighten. She quietly crossed the school yard to join him. Approaching him beneath the oak tree, she noticed Sam's lunch pail was missing.

"Forget your lunch this morning?" she asked.

Shrugging, he looked up at her. His eyes were dull, his expression lifeless. "Didn't forget. Just didn't want any."

Sitting down beside him, she reached into her own lunch pail and pulled out two biscuits, several slices of cheese, and an apple. All morning she'd looked forward to eating the noon meal. In her haste to get ready for school, she'd not taken the time to eat breakfast. But now, satisfying her appetite did not seem as important as offering some comfort to Sam.

"You know, I'm not very hungry today," she lied smoothly. "Would you like to share my lunch with me?"

His thatch of red hair flamed beneath the rays of the spring sunshine. He gave his head a vigorous shake. "I'm not hungry, either," he insisted. But in spite of the adamant denial, his hungry eyes betrayed him. He never once removed his gaze from the flaky biscuit in Julia's hand.

"Well, that's too bad." Julia sighed dramatically. "Guess I'll just have to leave my lunch for the birds."

For a fleeting instant Sam looked like he was on the verge of snatching the food from Julia's grasp. But something held him back, restraining him from doing so. Stiffening, he pursed his lips together and turned away from her.

The boy was so unlike his normal, energetic self that an ache swelled in Julia's chest. "Sam, sometimes it helps to talk to someone you trust if something is bothering you. Is there anything you'd like to talk about? Something at home?"

He jerked back around, his eyes wide, his face pale. Against the whiteness of his skin, hundreds of freckles seemed to stand at attention. "Ain't nothin' wrong at my house," he denied hotly. "Who says there is?"

"No one," Julia quickly assured him. "It was just a guess. You haven't been very attentive in class, like you're thinking about something else. And I just wondered if anything was wrong."

"I already told you. Nothin' ain't wrong. And I ain't hungry, either."

He scowled at her, and Julia saw a thousand emotions written there. The most prominent were denial and anger, fear and shame. She'd seen that expression before, that very morning, on the face of another male . . .

Sam leaped up and trudged off, his shoulders slumped, his steps heavy. Sighing, Julia took one of the biscuits for herself, then left the rest of her lunch on the ground beside the tree. Maybe Sam's hunger would overcome his pride before the start of the afternoon school session, she prayed.

As she sauntered back to the building, two girls skipped across the lawn and fell into step beside her. Julia didn't see Sam again until she rang the bell to start the afternoon session of classes. While the rest of the children bounded into the schoolhouse, Sam darted behind the trunk of the oak tree.

Standing beside the door and ushering the children up the steps, Julia didn't press Sam to return to class with the group.

By the time Sam came into the classroom, the rest of the children were already seated at their desks. As he slipped into his chair, he wiped his mouth with the back of his hand. Julia was delighted to see some biscuit crumbs on his shirt.

But she knew something far greater than hunger pains was responsible for Sam's withdrawal. By the end of the day, she decided that paying a call on Sam's mother was in order. Though she'd never met Sophie Springer, rumors abounded about the loose morals of the woman who lived with her son in a run-down shack on the outskirts of town. Julia had never heard any mention of Sam's father, so she assumed he was either dead or living apart from the family. Still, something was wrong with Sam, and Julia intended to find out the reason behind the young boy's change in temperament.

She was still mulling over her worries about Sam as she closed up the schoolhouse and headed home later that afternoon. After permitting Kate to go home with her best friend, Maggie O'Neill, for a few hours of play before dinner, Julia padded up

the worn pathway leading to the front entrance of
Hopewell House.

Aunt Odelphia and Aunt Dorinda were sitting
in a pair of wicker rockers on the front porch. The
ladies were dressed for their daily walk, wearing
wide-brimmed hats and pastel walking dresses.
Two parasols were propped up by the door.

"We were waiting for you, Julia," Dorinda announced brightly.

"We didn't want to leave that nice Mr. McRae in
the house all by himself while we took our afternoon stroll," Odelphia added.

That nice Mr. McRae? Julia frowned in confusion.
Surely Aunt Odelphia was teasing!

"He was sleeping like a babe a few moments ago,
but I'm sure you'll want to check on him while
we're gone." Rising, Dorinda smoothed down the
folds of her brown skirt.

"He won't be any trouble, I'm certain." Odelphia
crossed the porch and picked up the parasols. "Doc
Kramer dropped by this morning and said our
patient was healing nicely."

"A gentleman as charming as Mr. McRae could
never be considered a bother." Sighing, Dorinda
adjusted the floppy hat perched on the top of her
silver curls. "You know, I believe he's the most
charming gentleman I've ever met in my entire
life."

Julia stopped cold. Were they discussing the same
man who'd yanked her down on top of him and
kissed the daylights out of her? "Are you certain
we don't have more than one boarder?"

"Goodness no, Julia!" Dorinda opened her para-
sol and stepped down from the porch. "One boarder is all we can handle at the moment."

Joining her sister, Odelphia waved good-bye to
Julia. "See you in about an hour, dear."

Confused and troubled, Julia remained motionless on the porch long after the two ladies disappeared down the street. Aunt Odelphia and Aunt Dorinda acted as though the man upstairs was a saint. Why did they think Tyler McRae was a perfect gentleman? Nothing could be further from the truth. If that impudent man was behaving like a civilized human being, Doc Kramer must have doubled his dosage of morphine that morning.

Just as she stepped into the house, another realization hit her with full force. No one else was home. Aunt Odelphia and Dorinda were taking their afternoon stroll, and Kate was visiting Maggie. Which meant she was in sole charge of Tyler McRae.

Confronted with the disturbing thought of facing him once again, Julia struggled to keep from running out the door. She didn't want him here, didn't want him sleeping in her bed. And she didn't want to be concerned about his welfare.

But her conscience would not allow her to totally ignore him. After all, hadn't she promised to make sure he was comfortable during his recovery? She wouldn't want to live with the guilt if he took a turn for the worse because she'd ignored his suffering.

With reluctance, she tiptoed up the stairs. When she peered into the bedroom, she saw the steady rise and fall of his chest, the relaxed form of his body sprawled out beneath the quilt, the closed lids of his eyes. She breathed a sigh of relief. "As long as he's asleep, he's harmless," she mumbled to herself.

Just as she turned to leave, the rustle of bed coverings and a low, guttural moan stopped her cold. Dear heavens, was he hurting? Had his fever returned . . . or worse? She swept across the room, rushing to his side.

She leaned over the bed, studying him. His eyes were still closed, but the lines of his jaw were clenched tightly, as if he were in pain. She placed a hand on his forehead, relieved to discover he was not burning with fever. Brushing back a few errant strands of hair around his temple, her fingers lingered in the dark, silky waves. His hair was thick and soft, so rich and tempting . . .

His dark lashes fluttered open. A hint of mischief sparkled from his eyes as he gazed up at her. "Now that I'm awake . . . am I no longer harmless?"

Stunned, she jerked back her hand. "You were supposed to be asleep!"

"I was just resting, like your aunts ordered me to." His lips curled into a rakish grin. "But it's nice to know you'd come running to my aid if I'd really needed you."

She glared at him. "If you're truly in pain, I'll be glad to send for Doc Kramer. If you're chilled, I'll bring you another quilt. If you're hungry, I'll fix you some food. But I don't care for playing your silly little games, Mr. McRae."

"Ah, I see." His voice was low and taunting. "Too dangerous for you?"

She pursed her lips together, not wanting to admit he was right. Deep inside, she sensed that Tyler McRae and his little games were far more dangerous than anything she'd ever encountered. "Recovering from your injuries should be your primary concern at the moment, Mr. McRae. Not bantering with me."

"Fine," he snapped. "I'll concentrate on getting the hell out of here instead of focusing my attention on you." Struggling to sit upright, he pressed his weight against his uninjured arm. The sheet fell to his waist, revealing the broad expanse of his bare chest. As he hoisted himself into a sitting position, beads of perspiration popped out along his forehead. "You wouldn't deny a drink of water to a man who is trying to recover from a fever and a gunshot wound, would you?"

"Not if he were truly thirsty," she conceded, propping up the pillows behind his head and trying to avert her eyes from the dark, curly mounds of hair covering his chest.

He moistened his lips with his tongue. "I could use a little something to drink. Honest."

This time he wasn't joking, Julia sensed. She quickly picked up a water pitcher from the table beside the bed and poured the liquid into a glass. Then she cupped one hand around the back of his head and lifted the glass to his lips. His fingers clamped around hers, steadying the glass as he tilted back his head and guzzled down the water in one long gulp.

When he'd finished, his grip tightened around Julia's hand. "Just saying 'thank you' seems a bit inadequate. I'd rather express my gratitude to you in other, more appropriate ways . . ."

As his gaze locked on her mouth, Julia forgot how to breathe. Her own gaze strayed to the sensuous line of his lips and lingered there, unable to tear away. For a fleeting instant she found herself remembering the way those hungry lips had devoured hers, wondering if another kiss could produce the same mind-boggling sense of excitement and passion . . .

The touch of his hand shifted across her fingers, sending a jolt through Julia. Silently reminding herself that she should not be entertaining such inappropriate thoughts, she hastily pulled away from his grasp and struggled to regain her composure. "You must have made quite an impression on my aunts today," she remarked as casually as she could, returning the empty glass to the table. "For some odd reason, they think you're a very charming man."

"Maybe it's because I didn't accuse them of trying to steal my traveling bag." He hedged as a tinge of crimson stained his cheeks. "Or because they didn't get kicked out of their own rooms—their own beds, even—just to accommodate me."

The remorseful timbre of his voice caught Julia off guard. Dear heavens, was he apologizing for the way he'd treated her? She leaned against the edge of the bed, scrutinizing him, wondering if he were truly as regretful as he sounded. "You didn't exactly kick me out of my own bed," she reminded him. "You weren't even conscious when you arrived here."

He rested his head against the pillows, wincing as he fingered the bandage across his arm. "Still, finding out that your aunts had given your room to a stranger—one who later attacked you, I might add—couldn't have been the most pleasant experience of your life."

"It was surprising, I'll admit. I'm not accustomed to walking into my room and finding a wounded man in my bed. Or any man, for that matter," she added quickly, dropping her gaze in embarrassment.

"There's always a first time for everything, darlin'." Suddenly sounding groggy and fatigued, he slumped down into the pillows and closed his eyes.

After tucking the sheet up under his chin, Julia hastily slipped out of the room. Being alone with him again had been just as disturbing as she had anticipated. Something about Tyler McRae caused every nerve ending in her body to tingle when she was near him.

Thankfully, she had more than enough chores to keep her hands and mind occupied for the rest of the afternoon. Airing out the third floor was her first priority. Until Tyler McRae was out of her bed, she intended to make her living quarters as comfortable as possible.

During the winter, Julia closed off the unoccupied rooms in the house. Now, with the advent of warm spring days, the top story had become hot and musty. After opening all of the windows, Julia put fresh linens on the bed and dusted the sparse furniture. Satisfied she could sleep comfortably after the fresh spring breezes filtered through the windows, she retreated down the stairs and went outside.

A barn, a smokehouse, a springhouse, and a well were located in the yard behind the main house. Like most of Rome's residents, Julia and her family owned a small herd of livestock to provide for their needs. There were enough chickens for eggs and poultry, two cows for milking, and several hogs for slaughtering. They also owned a pair of horses, Tulip and Petunia, which pulled the family's buggy.

After feeding the chickens, Julia was delighted to discover that most of the strawberries had ripened. She spent over an hour picking berries, filling a large basket with the fresh, ripe fruit. Then she stood back and studied her surroundings with a critical eye. For the first time she noticed that a few of the wooden slats around the hog pen were cracked. So much needed to be done, she thought, a heavy weight filling her chest. As soon as she saved up enough money to repair the roof, she would have to start setting aside money to fix the hog pen.

Aunt Odelphia and Aunt Dorinda had returned from their walk by the time she retreated into the house. Wearing aprons over their dresses, the ladies scurried across the breezeway and into the kitchen to prepare the family's dinner. While Odelphia boiled a pot of water for stewing chicken and Dorinda measured out flour for dumplings, the two women chattered about the charms of "that nice Mr. McRae." Not caring to listen, Julia wandered into the parlor and occupied herself by dusting the furniture until she heard the sound of Kate's footsteps pattering across the front porch.

Kate returned from Maggie's house just in time to help Julia set the table for dinner. But as Julia handed four sets of utensils to Kate, little lines of confusion creased the young girl's forehead. "We only have enough forks for us, Julia. Aren't we going to ask the man upstairs to eat dinner with us?"

"I don't think Mr. McRae feels like sitting up at the table and eating with us tonight. One of us will take up a bowl of chicken and dumplings to his room a little later," she said, praying she would not be the one drafted for the task.

"Oh." Kate's green eyes clouded with disappointment. "Will he eat with us at the table tomorrow night?"

"I'm not sure," Julia admitted, setting out the plates on the table. "He needs lots of rest."

Kate trailed behind Julia and placed the utensils beside each plate. "Then what about my birthday? It's only three days away. Could Mr. Tyler come to my birthday dinner?"

"Well, I . . . I . . ." Surprised by the request and Kate's fascination with the boarder, Julia fumbled for an answer. Surely Tyler McRae would be gone in another three days! "I'm not certain, Kate," she answered honestly. "If he's healing as nicely as Doc Kramer says, he may not be staying here by then."

"But he might stay an extra day if you ask him to come to my birthday dinner."

Not wanting to encourage any further contact between Kate and the new boarder, Julia kneeled down and pulled the young girl into her arms. "We don't know anything about Mr. McRae, sweetheart. He may have to leave by then. Besides, why are you so concerned about Mr. McRae being here for your birthday? He's a stranger to us, after all."

"Mr. Tyler isn't a stranger, Julia! I talked to him this morning before we left for school."

Julia's breath caught in her throat. "You talked to . . . Mr. Tyler?"

Kate nodded sheepishly. "I just wanted to see if he was better. But he looked lonely up there in that room all by himself. He told me he doesn't want any friends, but I think he needs one." She wrapped her arms around Julia's neck. "Oh, Julia, I want Mr. Tyler to come to my birthday dinner more than anything else in the whole wide world! Will you invite him, Julia? Please, just for me?"

When she saw the excitement in Kate's eyes, heard the pleading sounds in her voice, Julia's heart sank. In less than twenty-four hours, their new boarder had managed to edge his way into the hearts of two elderly women and a six-year-old child. And if he could weave a web of deceptive charm over her family, what else was he capable of doing? She didn't want to find out.

Yet Julia could not bear to disappoint Kate on her birthday. How could she deny this simple request?

She playfully tugged on the thick braid that dangled down Kate's back. "If it means so much to you, Kate, I'll invite him."

"Promise?"

Julia grinned. Kate was well aware that Julia's promises were never broken. "Promise."

With a yelp of excitement, Kate tore out of Julia's arms and whirled around. Julia watched in silence, praying she would not regret her hasty vow.

Chapter 5

After dinner, Julia set the basket of freshly picked strawberries on the kitchen table. Then she pulled up a chair and culled through the plump, ripe berries, removing the green caps and stems.

By far, the crop was the best since the War. Even after she set aside the major portion of the harvest for jams and preserves, the large yield would allow them to enjoy plenty of Aunt Dorinda's strawberry pies and shortcakes within the next few weeks.

Admiring the perfect color and shape of one of the berries, Julia couldn't resist the temptation of sampling its sweet, juicy taste. But no sooner had she popped the berry into her mouth, Kate came up behind her and peered over her shoulder.

"Oh, strawberries!" Kate licked her lips. "Can I eat some, too?"

Julia nodded. "Wash your hands and you can help me."

As Kate scrambled to the washbasin, Odelphia spooned out a generous portion of chicken and dumplings from a large pot on the stove. "Seeing that you and Kate are busy, I suppose Dorie and I should take Mr. McRae's dinner to him."

"I'm sure he's hungry," Julia remarked, relief swamping her. Wanting to avoid any more confrontations with their boarder, she had hoped her aunts would volunteer to deliver his evening meal. Grateful for the reprieve, she scooped up a cup of strawberries. "He might enjoy some fresh strawberries, too," she offered, placing the cup on the serving tray.

As soon as the ladies left the kitchen, Julia returned to her work. With Kate's assistance, the task of plucking the stems and caps from the berries went quickly. Julia had just gleaned the last berry from the basket when her aunts returned to the room.

"Mr. McRae ate every bite of our chicken and dumplings." Odelphia smiled as she glanced at the empty bowl on the tray. "Said it was the best he'd ever tasted!"

"And he loved the berries, too." Dorinda snatched a handful of strawberries for herself from the bowl on the table. "Why, he insisted he couldn't think of a single place in the world that served better food than we do!"

"When word gets round about the meals at Hopewell House, he said, customers will be knocking down our doors," Odelphia added.

"You must have made quite an impression on our first boarder." Julia grinned. "It almost sounds as though he's smitten with the two of you."

Dorinda's eyelashes fluttered. "Don't be silly, dear," she protested, though Julia could tell she wished it were true.

"Mr. McRae is simply grateful to us for taking care of him," Odelphia explained. "Good Samaritans, he called us."

"Maybe he's finally coming to his senses." Rising, Julia wiped her hands on her apron. "He wasn't nearly as polite to me last night or this morning. In fact, he was insufferably rude."

"Maybe he just wasn't feeling well then, dear," Odelphia rationalized.

"He wasn't nice to me at first, either," Kate piped in. "When I first saw him this morning, he looked like he was mad. But he said he wasn't mad. He said he was Tyler! I thought that was funny, and we laughed."

Kate giggled at the memory, but the subject of Tyler McRae was no laughing matter to Julia. In fact, nothing seemed funny to her at the moment. Weariness plagued every muscle in her body. The tips of her fingers were stained with strawberry juice, her back ached from working in the garden, and she felt as though she hadn't slept in weeks. Tired of hearing about the wonders of Tyler McRae, she politely excused herself for the night.

The first light of dawn was peeping through the bedroom curtains when she awoke the next morning. Julia groaned, knowing she'd overslept. She was praying she wouldn't be late for school for a second day in a row just as Kate's voice sliced through the air.

"Julia, come quick! Mr. Tyler is bleeding!"

Terror shot through Julia. Dear Lord, what was wrong? She jumped out of bed, grabbed her robe, and bolted out of the room, taking the stairs two at a time. But as soon as she stepped into her former bedroom, she stopped cold.

He was standing at the washstand, wearing a pair of wrinkled pants. Stretched out to his full height—at least an inch or two over six feet, she estimated—the man was a vision to behold. Even with a gunshot wound, masculinity and power and strength radiated from every pore.

Morning sunlight streamed through the window-panes, casting a golden glow over him. Except for a towel draped around his neck and the bandage wrapped across his upper arm, his torso was bare.

Bands of muscles filled his broad shoulders, and mounds of dark hair covered his chest. The curly, dark nests of hair trailed down over a taut stomach and disappeared beneath the waist of his pants.

Julia's heart pounded uncontrollably. *You're just winded from racing down the stairs,* she tried to tell herself, even though she knew it wasn't true. The magnificence of the bare-chested man in front of her was the reason for the frantic beat of her heart. Mesmerized by the sight of him, she didn't notice Kate's presence beside her until she felt a tug on her gown.

She looked down at her sister, who was already dressed for school, wearing a calico dress topped with a white pinafore. "See, Julia! Mr. Tyler is bleeding! It's a good thing I came to say good-bye to him before we left for school, isn't it?"

Julia's gaze returned to Tyler. He was holding a razor in his hand. Mounds of soapy lather covered his chin, jaw, and cheeks. Drops of crimson drizzled from his chin and dotted the white towel that was carelessly slung over his shoulder.

"Yes, it's fortunate that you called me, Kate. Mr. McRae obviously needs some help." Julia bit back a smile, trying not to make light of the little girl's concern. In her six-year-old eyes, the man probably looked like he was bleeding to death.

"You'll be okay now that Julia is here, Mr. Tyler," Kate offered in her most grown-up voice. "She'll take good care of you."

"I have no doubt," Tyler mumbled ungraciously, wiping the blood from his chin with the towel.

Taking Kate by the shoulders, Julia spun her around to face the door. "Run along downstairs, Kate. I overslept this morning, and Aunt Odelphia and Aunt Dorinda are probably waiting to eat with you. We don't want to be late for school again today."

Kate looked up at her sister. "Remember your promise?" she whispered.

Julia nodded, giving the girl a reassuring hug before nudging her toward the door. At the moment, extending a dinner invitation to Tyler McRae was the last thing she wanted to do. But she couldn't bear for Kate to be disappointed on her birthday.

Taking a deep, steadying breath, Julia turned back to Tyler. Bent from the waist, he was peering into a mirror, twisting and contorting his face, examining the nicks on his chin. With his movement restricted by the bandaged wound on his arm, the relatively simple process of shaving had apparently turned into a nightmarish task.

"I'm sorry if Kate disturbed you," she said with genuine sincerity.

Without looking up, he grunted. "Do you always allow her to run through the house like an untamed bronco?"

A hot flash of anger shot through Julia. She pursed her lips together, making an effort to maintain her composure while defending the innocent actions of her sister. "She's only a little girl. One who is very concerned about you, I might add. And it looks as though she had good reason for calling me in here. I suspect that slashing your face with a razor is not the most enjoyable way to begin the day."

Muttering an oath, Tyler clenched his fists. Then he looked up at Julia and froze. His turbulent, expressive eyes darkened with passion. Looking down at herself, Julia knew the reason why.

A sickening feeling swept through her. Dear heavens, she'd slung her robe over her shoulders when she'd leaped out of bed. In her haste, she hadn't slipped the garment over her white cotton gown. The thin fabric concealed nothing from Tyler McRae's probing eyes. She could feel the heat of his gaze scorching through the gown and licking her skin like a searing flame, leaving her weak and confused and reeling with unwelcome emotions. She burned from the intensity of his scrutiny and from the shame of her inappropriate dress.

Tyler thought it would be interesting to watch her squirm beneath his seething glare. Very interesting, considering her gown was thin and transparent, revealing more than it concealed. And more than he'd bargained for.

His breath caught in his throat as he drank in the sight of her. Holy Mother of Jesus, she looked like a sleepy-eyed angel who'd just been plucked from a cloud. Thick strands of tousled hair streamed down over her shoulders like a tumbling waterfall, the rich chestnut color shimmering with hues of red and gold. Beneath the flimsy fabric of the gown, her breasts jutted out like melons, full and ripe and yearning to be touched. The sheer material exposed the dark circles around the tips of her breasts, the nipples protruding like little hard buds, the outline of her tiny waist. And a dark triangle of hair at the top of slender thighs.

Pure lust pounded through his veins as she slipped the robe over her gown, lust so powerful and consuming that it nearly obliterated the soft purr of her voice.

"My father was confined to bed for several weeks before his death," she was telling him. She shoved her arms into the sleeves of her robe and draped the garment around her tightly. "I shaved his beard many times during his illness. And I never nicked or cut his face with the blade of a razor."

"But you didn't have any reason to want your father dead," he grated.

She boldly met his gaze. "I have no desire for any harm to come to you, either."

Why was she being so damn nice? Tyler knew he would be cutting his own neck if he tried to shave himself again. Holding the blade steady was next to impossible. When he held up the razor to his face, a burning pain shot through his arm. And to make matters worse, the stubble of beard along his jaw was itching like crazy. Like it or not, he needed her help. He'd burn in hell before he'd ask for it. But if she was volunteering . . .

"Then I'm all yours, darlin'." He practically threw the blade at her. Without a word, she stepped forward, accepted his offering with a gracious nod, and lifted the razor to his face.

Tyler never expected her boldness, her confidence. Nor did he expect the strange sensations swarming through him the instant her fingers caressed the line of his jaw and ever so gently tilted his head to one side.

Her touch was tender, tentative, tantalizing. But Tyler felt as though someone had rammed a fist into his gut. Her warm breath on his chest ignited shafts of longing that bolted straight to his loins. Passion, raw and flaming, burned a fiery trail of desire through him.

She stretched up on her toes to shave him, straining her arms. "I can't see what I'm doing when I have to reach up over my head," she admitted. "Would you mind sitting down?"

Would he mind? Good God, he *needed* to sit down.

He plopped down in a straight-back chair. She stepped between the wide vee of his legs. Keeping one hand on his jaw to steady his face, she glided the razor over his cheek.

Each stroke was gentle, precise, efficient. Tyler

had no complaints about her skillfulness with the blade. It was everything else about her that was driving him insane. Like her lilac scent. The soothing stroke of her fingers. The warmth of her breath in his hair. The supple grace of her limbs. The way her legs brushed against the inside of his thighs. And her breasts, full and ripe and tempting, directly in his line of vision.

He squeezed his eyes shut, trying to suffocate the urge to lean forward and bury his head in those luscious, soft mounds.

She wiped off some dabs of lather from his cheek with the edge of the towel. "Would you like for me to trim your mustache, too?"

His eyes shot open. "No." Tyler McRae wasn't a fool. He wasn't stupid enough to subject himself to any more torture.

"It's not any trouble." She slipped the towel from his neck and wiped her hands on it. "I have some scissors right here in the drawer and—"

"What's this?"

Tyler grasped her hands. Though they were delicate, feminine, a sharp contrast against his own, the tips of her fingers were tinged with pink stains.

She shrugged, edging her hands out of his. Did his touch bother her? "Oh, it's nothing. Just stain from the strawberries."

"The strawberries from dinner last night?"

She nodded. "They're from my garden. It's a bumper crop, too. I have enough berries to make preserves to last through the winter. If all the plantings yield as much as the strawberries, we'll have enough corn and tomatoes and beans to last all—"

"Wait a minute." Tyler raked a hand through his hair and frowned. "You grow your own food. You put up preserves. You make the best damn bread I've ever tasted. You handle a razor bet-

ter than most men could ever hope to. You teach
school every day and take care of everyone in this
house. And now you're opening up your home to
boarders?"

Roses blossomed on her cheeks. "It's my life, Mr.
McRae, and I make no apologies for it."

"Good God, woman, I'm not fishing for an apology! I'm just wondering why in the hell you'd want
to do all that. Why in tarnation don't you just find
yourself a rich man, get married, and quit working
yourself into an early grave?"

Her eyes flashed like fiery emeralds. "This may
come as a surprise to you, Mr. McRae, but my life
is not as dreary as it may sound to you. And I'm
not interested in finding a man to save me from
all my responsibilities. I don't need one. I've never
met a man who was capable of taking care of himself, much less a house full of women. Besides, I
like my life. I like gardening. I like teaching school,
baking bread, caring for my sister. In fact, I love
everything about my life, especially taking care of
my family."

Skepticism and doubt were written in every line
of his face. Crossing his arms over his chest, he
grunted. "Just sounds like a lot of trouble to me.
A lot of headaches and responsibility."

"It depends on what you want out of life, I suppose. I don't consider my family to be a burden
at all."

He hedged, just long enough for Julia to detect
a flash of longing in his expression. Then a snarl
quickly covered up his thoughts. "Families aren't
for everyone," he insisted. "Especially not for people like me."

"Everyone needs a sense of family." *Even you,
Tyler McRae.* There was such a contrast between
this man and her father, she thought. Tyler McRae

was rigid, rough. Nothing at all like kind, gentle Papa. Shaving her father's beard had been much easier than holding a razor to Tyler's face. But then, her father had not caused her hands to tremble or the blood to race through her veins.

Surprisingly, she'd felt no fear when she'd accepted the challenge of shaving him. If he'd willingly given her possession of a razor, practically daring her to use it on him, she doubted she had any reason to worry about being attacked.

But she was grateful that he'd closed his eyes when she'd glided the razor over the firm line of his jaw. She didn't want him to see the sheen of perspiration along her brow, the slight tremble in her hands, her fascination with the grooves and planes of his arresting face.

Undoubtedly God had never made a more handsome creature.

Nor a lonelier one. Julia was convinced he needed a sense of family in his life, a sense of love and caring.

He snapped up from the chair and stalked to the window. Julia headed to the door, assuming the conversation was over. But she'd taken only two steps when she realized that she'd almost forgotten her promise to Kate.

"Kate's birthday is Saturday," she said. "She has specifically requested the honor of your presence at her birthday dinner. Hopefully by then you'll feel like joining us downstairs at the table for dinner."

His head snapped around. "Kate wants me . . . at her birthday?"

"Yes, Kate wants you there." She gave a tiny smile, amused by his surprise. Couldn't he see that Kate obviously adored him?

"Damn it to hell!" Tyler grated. But even he knew when his back was against the wall. Resigned, he shrugged. "Might as well go, I suppose. If not, you'll starve me to death, I'm certain."

Julia's little grin spread across her lips and blossomed into a full-blown smile, a smile so dazzling that Tyler could have sworn the earth moved beneath him. At that instant he wanted nothing more than to crush her in his arms, bury himself in the happiness radiating from her.

But he didn't have the chance.

Spinning on her heels, she turned to leave. "Six o'clock, Saturday," she called over her shoulder.

And then she was gone.

Chapter 6

On Saturday morning, Doc Kramer inspected the wound on Tyler's arm and nodded with approval. "Looks like you're healin' nicely, son. No fever, no infection." He stepped back from the bed and pulled a roll of bandages from a black leather bag. "And your color looks good, too."

"A little fresh air and sunshine has helped, I suppose. I've been walking into town the last few days to keep from going stir-crazy," Tyler said, wincing as the older man draped the snow white cotton around his upper arm. "How long have I been holed up in this place, anyway? A couple of years?"

Doc Kramer chuckled. "About a week. The ladies here tell me you've been sleeping a lot, so it's no wonder you've lost track of time."

"Other than stepping outside to stretch my legs, all I've done is sleep—and eat like a pig." Tyler patted his taut stomach. "These Hopewell ladies serve the best damn food I've ever tasted in my life. I've probably put on ten pounds since I've been here."

"Don't complain, son. You're a lucky man. Only healthy men can boast about a hearty appetite." The doctor tightened the white cloth around Tyler's arm, then snipped off the remaining fabric with some scissors and tied the ends of the bandage into a sturdy knot. "Your arm may feel tight and stiff for a while, but the worst is behind you."

Tyler ran his fingers over the fresh dressing. "Maybe so, but I'm itching like hell."

"That's because your wound is healing. You're almost as good as new. By tomorrow you should be able to get on with your business." The doctor closed his black medical bag. "What brought you to Rome, anyway?"

"Business." *Business with a son of a bitch masquerading as a preacher.*

When he offered nothing more, Doc Kramer picked up his bag. "Well, I hope the rest of your visit here goes more smoothly than your arrival into town. Has Sheriff Mitchell made any progress on finding the scoundrel who shot you?"

"I've dropped by the jailhouse a couple of times and talked to him, but he doesn't have a damn thing to report. Seems he can't find a single witness." Tyler shrugged. "Actually, I didn't expect him to. It was too dark and noisy on the train for anyone to see or hear anything." *To say nothing of the sheriff's incompetency*, he added silently.

The physician frowned. "That's too bad. Any man who robs someone blind should have to pay for his crimes."

"Can't argue with you on that point, Doc. That's always been my own personal theory for dealing with bastards like the one who blasted a hole in my arm." His fingers knotted around the edge of the fresh dressing. "I'd go after that son of a bitch myself and crush his skull into little pieces if I knew where to start looking for him."

Doc Kramer stroked his gray goatee and gazed thoughtfully at Tyler. "Considering the circumstances, I think you'd be better off concentrating on other endeavors, son. And be grateful you only lost your money on the train—and not your life."

Feeling a rush of anger, Tyler glared at the gray-haired physician as he turned and exited the room. Then he hurled back the quilt, set his bare feet on the floor, and stalked to the window. The morning was overcast and dismal, just like his mood. Dark clouds hovered in the gray skies; thunder rumbled in the distance.

He gazed aimlessly through the glass panes. Dammit, he didn't ask for the doc's opinion, didn't want any interference from him.

But as much as he hated to admit it, the old man was right.

Tyler despised the thought of letting anyone get away with blasting a hole through his arm and robbing him blind. Ignoring the matter went against every instinct he possessed. But after almost a week of examining the situation from every possible angle, Tyler had reached the same conclusion as Doc Kramer. Without any leads or witnesses, tracking down the culprit who'd shot and robbed him was almost hopeless. For once in his life, he'd leave the matter in the hands of the law. And he would concentrate on other problems, ones that could be solved.

Like the reason he came to Rome in the first place. *Jeremiah Carey.*

The sounds of approaching footsteps shattered Tyler's thoughts. He swung away from the window, listening intently. He'd become so attuned to the daily routines in the Hopewell household that he could distinguish the permanent residents by the sounds of their footsteps in the hall.

Kate's little shoes usually skipped over the wooden floors, pattering in a staccato rhythm. A slow, weighty pace meant that Dorinda was pushing her heavyset frame through the halls, while brisk clatters signaled Odelphia's arrival.

And then there was Julia.

Her steps were light and airy. Sometimes he could even hear the rustle of her skirts from the hall, smell the scent of lilacs drifting around her. But she hadn't entered his room since she'd shaved his beard and issued the invitation to Kate's birthday dinner. Each time she'd passed the door, she'd scurried by the room as if the devil himself were nipping at her heels.

Nonetheless, his needs had not been neglected in recent days. Each morning and evening, little Kate had stopped by, charming him with her laughter and smiles. And the silver-haired Hopewell sisters had pampered him like a baby, tending to his every whim, doting over him as if he were royalty. They'd fed him like a king, fluffed his pillows, emptied his chamber pot. Even the opulent McRae hotel did not offer such personalized attention and service to its guests.

Still, each time someone opened the door to his room, he'd found himself hoping to see Julia standing there. And as soon as she arrived home from school each afternoon, he'd either wandered through the house or gone outside to catch a breath of fresh air, hoping to run into her.

But he'd never been able to snatch a moment alone with her. If she wasn't preoccupied with some household chore, she was rushing from one task to the next. Asking her to accompany him on a walk into town yesterday afternoon hadn't worked, either. She'd politely refused his invitation, insisting she could not spare the time away from her family and household chores.

Which was probably for the best, Tyler supposed. He'd been able to send a wire to The McRae during his trip into the business district. At least Forrest would know he hadn't dropped off the face of the earth since leaving Chattanooga, he consoled himself.

Now, as the patter of footsteps came closer, Tyler noticed his heart was racing. A stab of irritation shot through him. Sweet Jesus, what was wrong with him? Why should he care if she ever set foot in his room again? He didn't want to see the compassion shining from those thickly lashed green eyes, the innocence radiating from those bow-shaped lips, the beauty glowing from those apricot-tinted cheeks. Nor did he care to hear her voice, as soft as spring rain, extolling the joys of family life. Nothing about families appealed to him. He knew all too well about the dangers of getting snared in that deceptive web of security.

Yet he couldn't prevent himself from straining to hear the conversation outside the door as Julia and Kate swept through the hall.

"We'll be prepared for the rain this time," Julia was predicting. "If we set out all these buckets before it starts raining, maybe we won't have to spend all afternoon mopping up water from the leaks."

Kate sighed. "But it's my birthday! On today of all days, why does it have to be raining?"

Julia laughed. "Rain doesn't have to spoil your birthday, Kate! Spring showers don't last long. I'm sure it won't be raining this afternoon. In the meantime, God is making sure our garden is getting plenty of water so our plants will grow and we'll have lots of good things to eat all summer and . . ."

The voices faded. As the sisters ascended the stairs to the third floor, Tyler plunged through his traveling bag and retrieved a pair of trousers and a clean shirt. The clothing was too wrinkled to be presentable. But if the old biddies could press them before dinner . . .

"Bloody hell." He hurled the clothes across the room.

Peering into the beveled mirror above the dresser, he groaned. Was this the same man who'd left Chattanooga, intent on stalking down the son of a bitch who'd cleaned out his livery? He thought not. The stranger in his reflection was more concerned about getting his damn pants pressed to go to a six-year-old's birthday party.

Clenching his jaw in determination, Tyler picked up the razor strop from the dresser. He'd agreed to eat dinner with the family, nothing more. He hadn't agreed to open himself up to this kind of torture. He didn't need it. He'd just stuff food into his mouth, enjoy every bite, and manage to endure the evening. And he would be so aloof, so disgruntled, that Kate and Julia would never dream of inviting him to join them at the dinner table again.

Then he would forget all about Hopewell House. In the morning he would leave this place, forget he'd ever been here. And he would resume his search for the Reverend Jeremiah Carey.

The showers began just as Julia and Kate positioned the tin buckets on the floor. But it was a soft spring rain, unlike the violent thunderstorm earlier in the week, and Julia prayed the leaks would be few and far between.

By midmorning, however, the light showers had become a heavy downpour. Armed with three more tin buckets, Julia trekked up to the third floor, hoping she could ward off any further water damage by setting out additional containers for catching stray leaks. Climbing the stairs, Julia grasped the handles of the tin pails with one hand while holding up her skirts with the other.

The buckets clattered and clanged together as she worked her way up the first flight of steps. Just as she swept past her former bedroom, Tyler opened the door and stepped into the hall. "Hellfire, woman! Are you trying to wake the dead?"

She stumbled to a halt, startled by the tingling sensations spreading through her as she gazed up at him. Bare-chested and barefooted, he was so devastatingly handsome that she almost forgot how to breathe.

"I was just on my way to the third floor," she choked out. "We always have to set out buckets on the top floor of the house when it rains, and I . . ." She paused, losing her train of thought somewhere between the amusement sparkling from his eyes and the intriguing width of his bare chest. She'd never realized a man's shoulders and chest could possess so many muscles . . .

"Let me give you a hand," he insisted, reaching for the buckets.

"It's not really necessary. I can manage by myself."

"Of course you can." He grinned. "And you'll break my eardrums in the process."

Removing the buckets from her unsteady grasp, he motioned for her to lead the way up the stairs. Disconcerted by the power of his smile and its unsettling effect on her, Julia picked up her skirts and swept past him without a word.

When they reached the third floor, she tilted back her head and groaned. Water was dripping from two new leaks in the ceiling, culminating in large puddles on the floor. "I was afraid of this," she mumbled, grabbing a mop from the corner of the room.

Tyler frowned as she began mopping up the water. "You could avoid all this backbreaking labor, you know, with a fairly simple solution. A new roof would—"

"Cost a great deal of money, Mr. McRae." She was being curt and short with him, she knew, but she couldn't help herself. Did he think she was stalling to buy a new roof because she actually enjoyed mopping the floor?

She shoved the mop over the puddles with quick, efficient strokes, trying to swab up the water before it could seep across the rest of the oak floor. Tyler trailed behind her, positioning the buckets around the room to catch the drips from the ceiling. "I'm afraid if you don't make plans for a new roof in the near future, this wonderful old house might be damaged beyond repair," he remarked as she set the mop over the last puddle.

"I'm well aware of that fact, Mr. McRae. Every time it rains, a new leak breaks through. Hopefully I'll be able to remedy the problem in another month or . . ."

Her voice trailed off as he reached out and took the mop away from her. Julia glanced up and froze. He was standing so close to her that she could almost count every lash framing his inexcusably beautiful blue eyes.

"Don't you think it's time we dropped the formalities? Mr. McRae sounds a bit stuffy to me. I'd much prefer that you call me Tyler." His lips curled upward into a grin that was devilishly handsome. "After all, we're not exactly strangers to each other. As I recall—"

"We're not exactly friends, either," she interrupted, praying he wouldn't make any snide remarks about the intimacy of their first encounter.

She had no desire to remember that searing kiss of his. No desire at all.

"I suppose you're right," he conceded. "After all, friends don't avoid each other the way you've been avoiding me the last few days."

"Ignoring you has never been my intention." She dropped her gaze, fidgeting with the cuff of her sleeve. "It's just that I've been extremely busy this week with my responsibilities at home and at school."

"Have you honestly been too busy to tend to your first boarder?" He placed an outstretched finger beneath her chin, tipping her head back and forcing her to meet his questioning gaze. "Or are you afraid of being alone with him again?"

Taken aback by his perceptiveness, Julia swallowed convulsively. Yes, she was fearful of what might happen between them. Though she would never admit it, she was terrified he might kiss her again. And even more frightened by the possibility that she might not be able to resist the touch of those hungry lips on hers, searing through her with more passion and fire than she'd ever dreamed possible.

Her mouth went dry at the thought. No matter how hard she'd tried to forget that scalding kiss, it still burned like a fiery flame in her memory. Now, as she gazed up at the sensuous line of his lips, a disturbing question skittered through her mind. Were Tyler McRae's kisses always so fervent and passionate?

Surely not. Surely there could never be another kiss like the first one.

Of course, there was only one way to find out. She moistened her parched lips with her tongue, suddenly tempted to yield to her unthinkable thoughts. If he kissed her again, surely she would discover that it was impossible for all of his kisses to be so soul-jarring and unforgettable . . .

At that instant, thunder rumbled through the Georgia skies, rattling the windowpanes and booming through the house like the blasts of a cannon. Julia nearly jumped out of her skin as a large piece of plaster snapped away from the ceiling and plummeted to the floor.

"Oh, for heaven's sake!" With a frustrated sigh, she scurried to wipe up the mess.

Tyler picked up the broken bits of plaster while Julia scrubbed the residue off the floor. When they'd finished, Julia quietly thanked him for his help. He retreated into the privacy of his room while she returned to the main floor to check on Kate.

Restless from being confined to the house and too excited about her birthday to sit still for more than a few minutes at a time, Kate tagged behind Julia for the remainder of the morning. When the skies cleared and the rain subsided in midafternoon, the sisters retrieved the tin buckets from the third floor and headed back downstairs together.

As they scurried past Julia's former bedroom, Kate paused beside the closed door. "Why don't you ever stop and talk to Mr. Tyler, Julia?"

Julia stopped, forcing a pleasant smile. "Because Mr. Tyler is much better now, according to Doc Kramer's report this morning, and he doesn't need me to take care of him any more." Turning, she continued down the stairs.

"But why don't you just stop and talk to him for a few minutes?" Kate persisted, trailing on her heels.

"Because I . . . because he . . . because we . . ." Reaching the foyer, Julia stumbled to a halt. She leaned against the railing at the foot of the stairs and sighed. How could she explain something to a child that she didn't understand herself?

"I know why." Kate twirled her braided hair around her fingers and smiled. "You don't have time to talk to him. You're going to be too busy getting ready for my birthday dinner this afternoon!"

Julia grinned and pinched the end of Kate's nose. "You're too smart for your own good, young lady."

"I know," Kate returned with an innocent shrug. "But I think Mr. Tyler has been lonely, all by himself in that room this week. And I want to be sure he hasn't forgotten about coming to my birthday dinner tonight. So could I knock on his door and remind him about eating with us?"

Julia started to refuse, then changed her mind. What harm could it do? After all, he'd agreed to join them for dinner. "Tell him we'll be expecting him at six."

As Kate scrambled up the stairs, Julia set off for the kitchen. After placing the tin buckets in one corner of the room, she donned an apron, set a large mixing bowl on the table, and pulled out the ingredients for making her sister's birthday cake. But the mere thought of sitting across the dinner table from Tyler McRae sent a hot flush to her cheeks and a tremble to her hands.

Frustrated, she added sugar, eggs, and cream to the flour and tried to forget about her disturbing encounter with Tyler McRae. But shame plagued her, shame for feeling emotions that a woman of honor and integrity should not feel. No man had ever affected her like Tyler McRae. Not even Brent, the love of her life, had aroused such tumultuous feelings in her.

But why was a foulmouthed, crude scoundrel turning her life upside down? Every time she was near him, she seemed incapable of controlling her emotions.

She mixed the ingredients together, whipping the mixture into a creamy batter with a wooden spoon. No matter how hard she tried to avoid him, she was acutely aware of his presence. Even though she'd kept her distance from him in recent days, he was never far from her thoughts. Trying to adhere to her Christian principles, she'd diligently prayed for his speedy recovery each morning and evening. She only hoped God would overlook the selfishness of her plea. The sooner Tyler McRae recovered, the sooner he would be on his way. Then she could get her life—and her emotions—under control.

Now all she had to do was endure one more evening with him. She shuddered, dreading the thought of coming face-to-face with him again, as she poured the cake batter into two baking pans. She was filling the second pan when Kate skipped into the room.

"How much longer until dinner?" Kate stretched up on her toes, leaned over the table, and poked a finger into the mixing bowl to sample the batter.

"Too long for you to be asking, birthday girl." Julia scraped out the remaining batter from the bowl. Then she smiled down at the young girl and handed the wooden spoon to her. "Other than making your cake, I haven't even started cooking dinner yet."

Kate ran the spoon along the side of the bowl, scooping up the leftover batter. "We'll need lots to eat. Mr. Tyler said he'll be hungry."

"We'll have plenty of food, Kate. More than enough for all of our guests," Julia assured her, placing the baking pans into the oven.

"All of our guests? Who else is coming to dinner?"

"Elizabeth, for one." Engaged to their half brother, Lucas, Elizabeth Fielding was a frequent dinner guest. "She didn't want to miss being here for your birthday, and I thought you'd like for her to join us."

"Oh, goody! I love Elizabeth!" Kate dropped the spoon and clapped her hands. "And who else did you invite?"

"Just one other person." Julia paused, suspecting her sister would not be pleased with the news. "I invited Sam."

"Sam from school?" As Julia nodded, Kate froze. "How come you asked him?"

"Because I think Sam needs a hot meal and some friendship," Julia admitted honestly.

Kate shoved aside the empty mixing bowl. Her lower lip protruded. "But I don't want him here on my birthday, Julia! I don't even like him. Nobody at school likes him, either."

"Which is one of the reasons why I invited him to dinner." Julia's heart wrenched at the thought of Sam's recent despondency and aloofness. After watching the youngster gulp down the extra food from her lunch pail all week, she'd extended the dinner invitation to him. Offering him a chance to enjoy a decent meal was the least she could do. "Besides, it won't hurt us to be nice to him. Don't you think Sam needs some friends?"

After a long moment, Kate shrugged. "I guess you're right. Nobody at school likes Sam, and everyone makes fun of him for living in that old shack down by the river. He doesn't have a sister like you to make him a nice dinner for his birthday, either. So I guess I can be nice to him tonight, even if I don't really want to share my birthday with him." She nibbled on her lower lip. "You know something,

Julia? Sam probably needs a friend . . . just like Mr. Tyler."

Just like Mr. Tyler . . . The words echoed in Julia's ears long after Kate licked the mixing bowl clean and scampered outside to play. Kate had agreed to be cordial to Sam, even though she wasn't over-joyed at the thought of his presence at the dinner table. And for some reason Julia could not define, it seemed important to Kate that Tyler enjoy himself this evening.

Julia set a cast-iron skillet on the stove, ponder-ing the situation. If Kate could share her birthday with Sam, couldn't her older sister set aside her tumultuous emotions for a few hours and embrace the same attitude toward Tyler McRae?

Though he would never admit it, Tyler needed a sense of family in his life as much as Sam did. And it wasn't as if he were a permanent boarder. From all indications, he was almost recovered from his wounds. Common sense told her that he would not be staying at Hopewell House much longer. And if his presence meant so much to Kate on her birthday . . .

She pulled back her shoulders and lifted her chin. This evening she would set aside her misgivings about Tyler McRae for a few hours. She would be gracious and cordial to him, even if it killed her in the process.

For Kate's sake, of course.

At precisely six o'clock, Tyler stood in front of the beveled mirror and examined his reflection with a critical eye. His dark trousers were neatly pressed, his linen shirt spotlessly clean.

He leaned closer to the mirror, narrowing his eyes as he scrutinized the dark hairs sprouting over his upper lip. His jaw was smoothly shaven, without any nicks or cuts. Thank goodness his arm wasn't giving him any more pain. He'd managed to shave himself quite nicely. But he should have taken up Julia's offer to trim his mustache. It was much too long, curling over his mouth and—

"Judas Priest," he grumbled, grabbing a comb and ramming it through his hair. He'd been taking care of himself since he was ten years old. He didn't need a woman to help him. He straightened the collar of his shirt, sucked in a deep breath, and opened the door.

But he wasn't prepared for the scents and sounds that assaulted him. The clatter of dishes, the enticing aromas of fried chicken and some sort of fresh bread, the murmur of feminine voices, all swept over him, awakening memories he'd long forgotten.

Tyler's throat closed up. It had been years, an eternity, another world ago, since he'd been surrounded by those homey smells and sounds. He felt like he was being hurled back to another time . . . another place . . . another house full of love and laughter . . .

Shaking his head, he grimaced. "You damn fool."

He pulled back his shoulders and marched down the stairs. Sentimentality held no place in his life, after all. He'd traveled to Rome, Georgia, with one purpose in mind, and he couldn't afford to clutter up his thoughts by dredging up garbage from the past.

He was reminding himself to remain cool and distant during dinner when he saw Kate, standing at the foot of the stairs, waiting for him.

Tyler stopped cold, all his hard resolve shattering like fragile shards of glass. Blue ribbons dangled from Kate's hair, ribbons that matched the azure hue of the satin sash tied around her white dress. White stockings hugged her little legs, and a pair of dark shoes covered her tiny feet. All in all, she looked like a cherub, smiling up at him with those Cupid lips and vibrant green eyes.

"I'm so glad you're here, Mr. Tyler!"

Stunned by the genuine warmth of her greeting, Tyler felt his throat constrict as Kate threw her arms around his knees and hugged him. What had he done to win the heart of this child?

Taking him by the hand, she pulled him into the parlor. With high ceilings and elaborately carved woodwork, the room was large by most standards. Though the plaster was crumbling and the upholstered settee and chairs were threadbare, everything was neat and tidy. Not a trace of dust cluttered the furniture, and the wooden floors glistened with fresh polish.

And there was something else about the room, something Tyler couldn't ignore, no matter how hard he tried. Filling the spacious parlor was an aura of warmth and tranquility, a sense of welcoming so strong that Tyler had the urge to bolt out the door and jump on the next train out of town.

"Look, Elizabeth, this is Mr. Tyler! He's the man who got shot on the train!"

Seated on a rosewood chair by the fireplace was an attractive woman wearing a floral-print dress. Tyler surmised she was about thirty years old. Her dark hair was brushed back from her forehead and tied with a pink ribbon. Rising with an easy grace, she smiled as Kate led Tyler across the room.

"Good evening, Mr. McRae. Kate has told me a lot about you. I'm Elizabeth Fielding." She extended her hand to him. "I was sorry to hear about your problems on the train. I take it you're feeling much better now?"

He nodded stiffly. "Almost back to normal." Engulfed by the genuine sincerity in the woman's greeting and the homespun glow surrounding him, Tyler winced. After leaving Hopewell House, would anything about his life ever be normal again?

Kate wedged between them. "Elizabeth is going to marry my brother," she explained to Tyler. "He's not here tonight, but I know he would be here for my birthday if he could, 'cuz Lucas loves parties. But we're not exactly sure where he is right now and—"

"We know where Lucas is," a familiar voice interjected, coming up behind Tyler. "He's working with the railroad somewhere in Tennessee, restoring tracks that the Yanks destroyed during the War."

Hearing Julia's voice, Tyler straightened the collar of his shirt and inhaled a deep breath. Turning, he stared at her, studying the delicate lace on the collar of her sapphire green dress, perusing the tiny tucks of material draped over the full swell of her breasts, until his mouth went dry as cotton.

"I'm glad you could join us, Mr. McRae." A delicate blush blossomed on her cheeks. "It means a lot to Kate that you're here. She's talked of nothing else all week, and I know—"

"Miss Julia, Miss Julia!" A young boy with a thatch of red hair and a freckled face bolted through the doorway. Gasping with excitement, he darted toward Julia. "Miss Dorinda said the hogs haven't been fed. Can I feed them before dinner?"

Tyler thought the boy deserved to be thrashed for running through the house like a wild boar and interrupting an adult conversation. But Julia seemed unconcerned about the youngster's thoughtless behavior. On the contrary, she appeared delighted to see him. Running a hand through his tousled red hair, she flashed a smile of encouragement in his direction. "What a wonderful idea, Sam! The hogs and I will be eternally grateful for your help. Just be sure to wash up at the pump before you come back into the house."

Sam grinned. "I promise, Miss Julia." Whirling around, he sped across the room and disappeared into the foyer.

"What was that?" Tyler asked. "A whirlwind?"

Julia laughed. "No, that was Sam Springer. One of my students."

Tyler paled. "Are all your students coming to dinner?" Good God, he would never survive an entire evening trapped in a house full of children.

"No, just Sam." The laughter faded from her eyes and voice. "I have reason to suspect he's not getting enough to eat at home."

Tyler grimaced, knowing all too well what hunger felt like to a growing young boy. "He didn't seem like he's famished. The boy's got a bundle of energy in him."

"Maybe being here has lifted his spirits. He's acting more like his old self than he has in weeks." A shadow of darkness crossed Julia's face. "But he could use a hot meal, I'm certain. He's been quiet and withdrawn at school lately."

"Well, he's come to the right place for some good food," Tyler admitted, his mouth watering at the fragrant aromas wafting through the house.

A hint of a smile played on Julia's lips. "We'll be eating in a few minutes," she assured him.

"Come on, Mr. Tyler!" Kate tugged at his hand. "Let's go see what we're having for dinner."

They stepped into the dining room just as Odelphia set a platter of fried chicken on the table. "Look, Kate! Julia fixed all your favorites. We have sweet potato biscuits and—— "

"And green beans!" Dorinda waddled behind her sister, carrying a vegetable bowl. Turning to Tyler, she added, "It wouldn't be Kate's birthday if we didn't have green beans. Why, you've never seen a child eat green beans the way she does!"

"So I hear." Tyler looked down at Kate and winked. She grinned up at him, and what he saw written in that cherubic expression nearly knocked him to his knees.

Trust. She'd entrusted him with her secret—a silly one, no doubt, but of enormous importance to her—and he'd unwittingly honored that confidence. Judging by the adoration in her eyes, he ranked somewhere between God and the Virgin Mary. A ranking he neither wanted nor deserved.

Uneasy with the unmerited approval, he jerked his gaze away from those trusting little eyes just as Sam scrambled into the room and the group assembled for the meal. The matronly Hopewell sisters flanked each end of the oval table, and Kate positioned herself to sit next to Tyler. Elizabeth sat to Tyler's left.

Sam took the vacant chair next to Julia. "I fed the hogs real good, Miss Julia. You should've seen 'em! They were real hungry. And I washed up at the pump, too, just like you said."

"Wonderful, Sam!" Julia beamed down at him. "Now are you ready to eat?"

He nodded with such vigor that Tyler expected to hear his teeth chatter. He was still musing over the young boy's reaction when something small and warm slipped into his hand. He looked down, surprised to find Kate's little fingers entwined with his own.

"We always hold hands when we say the blessing," she informed him.

Elizabeth grasped Tyler's left hand just as Julia

began to pray. "Heavenly Father, we thank Thee for . . ."

But Tyler didn't hear another word. The innocence and sweetness of Kate, with her head bowed and eyes closed, cut through him like the sharp edge of a razor. An ache swelled in his chest as the long-forgotten memory of another little girl's innocence flashed through his mind. Rebecca, his sister. The sister he'd lost . . .

" . . . and for all these things, we thank You, Lord."

Following a chorus of amens, Tyler forced himself to remember that he was here to eat dinner and nothing more. He tried to ignore the conversation drifting so easily around the table, the laughter and smiles flowing as freely as water gushing from a swollen stream. Tried to overlook the serenity stemming from close companionships that he'd always assumed never existed.

Amid the clatter of china and silver, he concentrated on loading up his plate. Sam watched his every move, spooning out the same generous portions of each dish for himself. And, like Tyler, the young boy said little throughout the meal, focusing on the food instead of the casual bantering around the table.

Tyler ate until he thought he would explode. But as soon as he'd emptied the plate, his hostesses insisted on filling it up again.

"More mashed potatoes, Mr. McRae?" Odelphia shoved a bowl into his hand.

"How about another chicken breast?" Not waiting for an answer, Dorinda set a plump portion in front of him.

"Have another helping of green beans, Mr. McRae." Julia spooned out a generous serving.

Tyler offered no protests. If they wanted to treat him like royalty, let them. Tomorrow he would be gone. His stay at Hopewell House would be nothing more than a distant memory.

He stabbed a fork into some beans, unable to shake a growing sense of emptiness at the thought of resuming his old way of life. It suddenly occurred to him that he'd heard more laughter, seen more smiles, received more attention, since coming to Hopewell House than he'd ever heard or seen or received in his life.

He lifted his eyes, gazing around the table in stunned disbelief as a new revelation assaulted him. Was this what families were all about?

Good God, he was going daft. He was twenty-nine years old, not an innocent kid. He knew better than to think this sort of camaraderie and warmth, this glimpse of heaven, home and family, could last forever.

And it didn't. Within the span of the next few minutes, Sam spilled a glass of milk on the table, drenching himself and the linen tablecloth. Odelphia snapped at Dorinda for not helping clean up the mess. Kate fidgeted restlessly in her chair, pleading to open her presents.

And Julia smiled through it all.

She was calm, steady, patient, like an anchor keeping a ship at bay during a turbulent storm. She was the center, the heart, of this family, her love and concern for each one of them shimmering from the depths of her eyes and the curve of her mouth. Frowns disappeared beneath the soothing lilt of her voice. Discontentment became satisfaction with the tender touch of her hand. And the sudden burst of tension at the table vanished with her quiet suggestion to move into the parlor and continue their celebration.

As soon as the little group retreated into the next room, Kate sat down on the floor to open her presents. She took genuine delight in the simple hair ribbons from Elizabeth, doted on the rag doll from Julia, and squealed with pleasure when she received a new brush and comb set from her aunts.

But it was Sam who snared most of Tyler's attention. The lad sat quietly, watching Kate with a look of longing in his expression, obviously wishing someone cared enough to celebrate his birthday, too.

Try as he might, Tyler couldn't prevent a rush of old emotions from surfacing, their jagged edges piercing deep into his soul. All too well he could identify with the emptiness haunting Sam's barren eyes, the gnawing sense of knowing no one gave a damn about him.

After Kate opened the last gift, Dorinda dabbed at the moisture swelling in her eyes with a lace-trimmed hanky. "Oh, I wish our dear sister Capitola could be here to celebrate Kate's birthday with us."

"Mother would be delighted to know that Kate is growing up to be such a beautiful young lady." Julia's voice was choked and strained.

"She'd be proud of both of her daughters," Odelphia added.

Elizabeth, sitting next to Tyler on the settee, leaned over and whispered in his ear. "Capitola was Julia's mother. She died seven years ago today . . . giving birth to Kate."

Something tight and restricting gripped Tyler's chest. He shifted uneasily, giving a silent curse for exposing himself to this torture. He didn't belong here, didn't want to be here.

He wasn't cut out for the trappings of family life and all that went with it. He didn't want to celebrate birthdays, clasp hands around the dinner table, or give thanks for his meal to a merciless God. He simply wanted to view Julia Hopewell and her family with the same practiced detachment he'd held for everyone else who'd crossed his path since he was ten years old.

Because it hurt too much. Scared the living hell out of him to think he was capable of caring about anyone.

Dammit, he couldn't take any more of this sweet agony. He bolted to his feet, intending to make a hasty exit, just as an outburst of grunts and squeals erupted from the yard.

Julia shot up from her chair, raced to the parlor window that overlooked the rear lawn, and pulled back the drapes. Peering through the glass panes, she gasped in horror. "Oh, dear Lord in heaven, help us."

Whirling around, she picked up her skirts. Then she broke into a run, heading in the direction of the disturbance in the yard.

Chapter 7

The rest of the little group clambered to their feet and rushed outside. They stumbled to a halt beside Julia, who was standing on the back porch, gazing across the yard in stunned silence.

Tyler followed her gaze, surprised by what he saw. The hog pen was empty. The gate to the fenced enclosure was swinging to and fro, its hinges creaking to the rhythmic motions of the evening breezes. Five hogs were roaming through the yard, obviously enjoying their newfound freedom.

Two of the pigs were trampling through Odelphia's flower garden, crushing the colorful spring blossoms beneath their cloven hooves and pulverizing the blooms beyond recognition. A large black hog with white spots was poking its snout beneath the barn door. The two largest animals were invading Julia's garden, rooting through the freshly planted vegetables and wiggling their tails in delight.

"Oh, no." Julia's voice cracked with emotion. "Not my garden."

"And look what they've done to my flowers!" Odelphia shook a clenched fist into the air.

"Those fool pigs must think they're in hog heaven," Dorinda muttered in disgust. "Julia, do you think we can catch them with—"

But Julia was already halfway across the yard, skirts flying around her legs. Tyler, Kate, and Sam were close behind her.

"What are we going to do, Julia?" Kate asked.

"We'll have to rope them up as fast as we can, then get them back into the pen before they can do any more damage."

Sam raced past Julia, heading toward the barn. "We'll be just like cowboys on a cattle drive!"

"Roping cattle would probably be easier," Julia mumbled.

The hog near the barn door, the black one with white spots, looked up with bright, intelligent eyes as they approached. "Shame on you, Zachariah," Julia scolded, slapping her hand on the hog's coarse hide before hurling open the barn doors.

While the children tried to entice Zachariah back to the pen by calling, "Soo-ey! Soo-ey!" Tyler followed Julia into the barn.

"Sometimes hogs will cooperate if you threaten to hang them." She jerked on several lengths of rope hanging from a peg on the wall, making no attempt to hide her disgust.

Tyler casually leaned against the side of a stall and grinned. Did she realize how attractive she was? Anger complemented her, he thought. Those sparks of rage flashing from her eyes and those touches of crimson on her cheeks were quite appealing. "Sounds like you're speaking from experience."

"They get loose once or twice a year." She whirled around, her skirts rustling around her legs, and headed for the door. "It adds some excitement to my boring life, don't you think?"

"I don't know what to think just yet," Tyler admitted. "I've never chased hogs before."

"It's an experience you'll never forget, I can assure you." She tossed one of the pieces of rope to him.

"Tying up three-hundred-pound hogs isn't easy. Just pray we can get them back into the pen before they destroy everything in sight."

Outside the barn, Julia frowned in dismay. Zachariah was still not cooperating with the children. Each time Kate and Sam urged the animal in one direction, the black and white hog trotted away in the opposite one. Considering the animal's immense size, he was surprisingly swift and agile. To make matters worse, Kate's white stockings and dark shoes, as well as the legs of Sam's threadbare pants, were already covered with splotches of mud.

"Zachariah won't pay any attention to us!" Sam reported to Julia.

"He won't follow us anywhere!" Kate complained.

"Just keep trying," Julia encouraged the children. Then she turned to Tyler, fashioning a large loop in the end of the rope as she spoke. "If you can get Samson and Delilah out of the flower bed, I'll try to lure Naomi and Bathsheba out of the garden."

Between watching the serious expression on Julia's face and learning that each of the hogs possessed an absurd name, Tyler bit his cheek to keep from laughing out loud. Good Lord, she talked about those blasted hogs as though they were human! He wouldn't be surprised if she shed a few tears every time one of the massive creatures left for the slaughterhouse.

Five minutes later, standing between two obstinate hogs in the middle of the flower bed, Tyler discovered the situation was not as humorous as he'd thought. Each time he tried to slip the rope over the large head of one of the pigs, the animal buried its snout into the ground, refusing to budge.

Odelphia joined Tyler in the pitiful remains of her flower garden. After looking around at the uprooted stalks and crushed petals, she shook a bony finger at the hogs. "You're going to be the first ones to go to slaughter this year, you . . . you . . . you obstinate creatures!"

Dorinda waddled behind her, carrying a plate of sweet potato biscuits. "You know, hogs love sweet potatoes. Do you think these sweet potato biscuits would be appealing to them?"

As if to answer her question, Samson and Delilah raised their pink snouts into the air, sniffing at the plate in Dorinda's hand. Tyler leaped at the chance to slap the rope over the head of the larger hog— which he assumed to be Samson—while Odelphia plucked a biscuit from the plate. "Here, piggy!" She dangled the food in front of Delilah, a hefty white pig with black markings. "Follow me and you can have a biscuit!"

The biscuits worked like a charm. Samson and Delilah trotted back to the pen with relative ease as Odelphia and Dorinda dangled the food under their noses.

But the rest of the hogs were still on the loose, Tyler noticed. Sam and Kate were zipping across the yard, unable to keep pace with Zachariah's canter. Tyler couldn't tell which was louder—the children's shouts or the hogs' squeals.

Tyler swiped two sweet potato biscuits from the plate and jammed them into his pocket just before Odelphia and Dorinda turned their attention to helping the children lure Zachariah back into the hog pen. Then he paused for a moment, watching the struggle between Julia and her hogs. She tugged and pulled at the two sows who were invading the garden, pleading with them to return to their pen. But Bathsheba and

Naomi were much more interested in gobbling down the crop of strawberries than listening to their mistress.

Didn't she realize what she was up against? He was amazed at the woman's resilience and determination. Though the sows seemed oblivious to Julia's efforts, the line of her jaw was full of resolve, the look on her face full of determination. How many women would dare to wrestle with a hog who outweighed her by several hundred pounds?

"What are you staring at?" Exasperated, Julia straightened and glared at him. "If you'd quit standing there gawking at me, we might have a chance to get a rope around these sorry creatures."

"Maybe this will help." Tyler pulled a biscuit from his pocket, then pointed to the white sow in front of Julia. "What's her name?"

"Bathsheba." Julia gestured toward the other enormous white sow, rooting in the ground a few feet away. "And that's Naomi over there."

Bathsheba paid no attention to Tyler until she caught a whiff of the biscuit's scent. Then she jerked her head up from the ground and lunged at the food. Julia leaped up and snapped the rope over the sow's neck just as the biscuit disappeared into the animal's mouth.

A smile brightened Julia's face, then vanished when Bathsheba plunged her nose back into the ground. "Oh, good heavens," Julia muttered.

At that moment, Naomi grunted. Bathsheba's head jerked up. Then she bolted forward, heading toward her comrade in crime. Julia stumbled, her shoes slipping in the moist Georgia soil, and lost her grip on the rope.

Free from restraints, Bathsheba rammed straight into Tyler, knocking him to his knees. The impact of the jolt caused him to lose his balance, and he fell against Julia. Julia screamed just as they landed in the mud with a splat, arms and legs and bodies tangled together.

She struggled beneath him. "Get off me!" she demanded, tugging at the heavy weight of her skirts, now laden with mud. Tyler managed to pull himself off her, settling back on his haunches just as she sat up and glared at him. "What do you think you were doing, Tyler Mc—"

She stopped abruptly, her eyes widening in disbelief. Then she threw her head back and laughed.

"What's so funny?" Tyler wiped a clump of mud from his cheek.

Julia laughed harder. "You should see yourself!"

He reached out and wiped the mud off the end of her pert nose. "You're not exactly dressed for church, either, lady."

"But you...but I...but we..." Laughter choked off her words. "We're...sh...sh... shameful!" Tears filled her eyes as a new wave of laughter bubbled up from her throat. She doubled over, holding her sides.

Try as he might, Tyler couldn't help himself from laughing along with her.

And it felt wonderful.

Good God, he needed to laugh. He'd forgotten what a remarkable release it could be, wiping away tensions within the span of a second. He couldn't even remember the last time he'd let out a hearty chuckle or a genuine gust of laughter. But then, when was the last time he'd chased hogs and wallowed in the mud with the most enchanting woman in all of Georgia?

Maybe it was this woman sitting beside him in a muddy garden plot who was causing all that joy to swell up inside him and emerge from his throat as laughter. Maybe it was because he truly liked this mud-covered waif. Damn if he could think of a single thing he disliked about her. From the dirty roots of her hair to the muddy soles of her shoes, she was enchanting.

Something warm and muddy grazed his arm, and he looked down to find Julia's hand tenderly caressing the soiled sleeve of his linen shirt. Her laughter faded into silence, and the smile on her lips turned into a frown of concern. "Oh, Tyler, I'd almost forgotten . . . about your arm."

"My arm is fine," he lied, ignoring the gnawing pain in the muscles surrounding his wound. He wasn't going to let a little thing like the ache from a gunshot wound spoil the magic between them. Moments like these were too rare, too precious, to lose.

He pulled himself up reluctantly to a standing position, brushing off the bits of mud clinging to his clothes. Then he held out his hand to Julia and tried to ignore the strange stirrings in his chest as she stood up beside him.

But he couldn't overlook the uneasiness swamping him, no matter how hard he tried. Those uncomfortable feelings signaled a silent warning, alerting him about the dangers of enjoying himself too much, of letting down his guard. Nothing good ever lasted in his life, after all. Hadn't he learned his lesson? Better to put a stop to this nonsense now than to pay the consequences later.

With Julia at his side, he stalked toward the hog pen, where Sam and Kate were cheering on the silver-haired sisters. Using the remainder of the sweet potato biscuits, Odelphia and Dorinda were prodding the pair of mischievous sows back into the pen.

Once all of the animals were safely behind the fence, Odelphia examined the latch on the gate and frowned. "No wonder the hogs got loose. The latch won't hold." To prove her point, she demonstrated the ease with which the locking device slipped out of position.

The latch, a simple wooden slat that slipped behind a protruding piece of wood on the gate, hung loosely from the fence post. Secured by a nail that was on the verge of coming loose from the rotting wood, the latch rotated freely beneath Odelphia's fingers. Unless someone made the effort to securely fasten the latch, it could be knocked out of place with little effort.

Sam, who had been quietly observing the demonstration, suddenly stepped forward. "Maybe it's all my fault, Miss Julia. Maybe I didn't . . . I didn't . . ." He swallowed convulsively. "Maybe I didn't latch the gate after I slopped the hogs. I guess I . . . I just forgot."

"You forgot?" Tyler roared, unable to contain his anger. "What do you mean, you forgot?"

"I didn't do it on purpose! I was just in a hurry to get back to the house in time for—"

Tyler stomped toward the young boy and glowered at him. "Look at all the damage you caused by your carelessness! Don't you know that you're the reason for—"

"It's all right, Sam," Julia interrupted, stepping forward and placing her hand on Sam's shoulder. "We know it was an accident."

"Like hell it was an accident." Tyler scowled, unleashing his fury on Julia. "After half your garden and flower bed has been destroyed, you stand there and say it's all right?"

"The hogs trampled the garden and the flowers, not Sam. Besides, we all know the latch is loose. Any of us could have walked away from the pen and not realized that the gate wasn't locked securely. It happened to me last year, as a matter of fact."

"That's not the point." Tyler clenched his jaw. "The point is that someone's carelessness caused considerable damage, and that person should be pun—"

"It's all right, Sam." Ignoring Tyler's protests, Julia patted the young boy's shoulder. "Why don't you go back into the house and get cleaned up? Then we'll have some dessert to celebrate Kate's birthday."

"I guess I could use some cleaning up." Sam looked down at the mud on his clothes and frowned.

"Sounds like a good idea to me." Kate wrinkled her nose as she fingered the soiled sash on her dress. "I'd much rather be eating cake than chasing dirty old hogs."

Smiling, Dorinda held out her hand to Kate. "I know exactly what you mean, dear."

"Come on, children." Odelphia turned, heading back to the house. "Let's get moving."

Sam narrowed his eyes and cast a defiant glare at Tyler before spinning around and marching back to the house with Kate and the women. Stiffening at the sight of the belligerence in the young boy's expression, Tyler turned to Julia.

"How could you be so lenient on that boy? You, of all people, should be furious with him! It's your garden that's been ripped apart on account of him."

"Sam meant no harm, Tyler." She draped one arm over the fence railing and sighed. "I didn't caution him about the latch, and he had no way of knowing that it doesn't always shut properly."

"Which is no excuse for his reckless behavior," he snapped. "That little scoundrel deserves to be horsewhipped for his carelessness. All this destruction demands some form of reprimand."

"He probably should have been more cautious," Julia conceded. "But he's only ten years old, and I'm certain it will never happen again. I'm sure he's learned his lesson."

Tyler snorted his disgust. "If it were up to me, he'd never get another chance for anything like this to happen again."

"But it's not up to you, now, is it?" She lifted her chin. Sparks of anger danced in her eyes.

"Maybe not, but his age shouldn't be an excuse for his behavior. The boy should learn some responsibility. Why, when I was his age, I was—"

He stopped, catching himself just in time. When he was Sam's age, his world was a living hell. He hadn't told another soul of his secret agonies, hadn't mentioned it for almost two decades. Why in the hell was he starting to talk about it now?

He cleared his throat. "When I was Sam's age, I was responsible for my own actions," he finished curtly.

For a long moment, Julia said nothing. Standing quietly, she tilted her head to one side and studied him. But the look in her eyes spoke volumes. The compassion and understanding shimmering from their green depths drove a stake through Tyler's heart.

"I think he's already been punished enough," she finally said with a quiet firmness. "He feels badly, I'm sure, and he's aware of the damage and trouble he's caused."

"Kids like him, I can live without." Frustrated, Tyler raked a muddy hand through his hair. "Don't understand 'em, that's for sure. Never will."

"Children are simply little adults." A smile as soft as a spring breeze caressed her lips. "They're

the heart of most families I know. Besides, some
of my students are more mature in their thinking
than a few adults I could name. And most of the
time, youngsters are a lot more fun than grown-ups.
They're not held back by their fears, like some
adults are."

"But Sam has caused you a lot of heartache, Julia!
If he'd done anything like that to me, I wouldn't
be able to forgive him so easily." Unaccustomed
to acknowledging his faults, he dropped his gaze,
studying the toes of his muddy boots as he dragged
them across the ground. "In spite of my charm and
personality, forgiveness is not one of my redeeming
qualities. I don't see how you can forgive him so . . .
so . . . easily."

"What good would it do for me not to forgive him?
What would it accomplish? Forgiveness achieves
much more than holding grudges—for everyone
involved." She slowly lifted her hand and allowed
her fingers to glide along the line of his jaw,
caressing him as softly as the stroke of a feather.
"I've even found it in my heart to forgive you, you
know."

His head jerked up. Her touch felt like a flame
scorching his skin, but her words burned into his
very core. "For what?"

"For the way you kissed me the other day." Her
gaze focused on his mouth. "I've had time to think
about it, and now I understand why you kissed me
like a savage beast. You woke up in a strange place.
You'd been shot. You were angry, hurting. You
simply weren't in your right mind, I suppose."

Tyler's breath caught in his throat. He stepped
forward, unable to resist running a grimy finger
over her cheek with a quiet reverence, as if she
were as fragile as fine crystal. He was enamored by
this woman who loved so freely, forgave so easily.

"I don't think I've been in my right mind ever since I've been here." His voice was husky and low. "I think I'm going insane. And I think I'm going to turn into a savage beast again if I don't kiss you." He swallowed convulsively. "Would you be able to find it in your heart to forgive me again . . . if I kissed you one more time?"

"If you kissed me again," she said, nervously running her tongue over her lips, "I don't think there would be anything for me to forgive."

Tyler's gaze flicked down to the bare skin of her throat, then darted up to her lips. Could she see how much he wanted her? And if he kissed her, would he be able to tear himself away from those alluring, bow-shaped lips?

His hands trembled as he placed them on her narrow shoulders. God, she was innocent, vulnerable, much too good for a scoundrel like him. But how could he resist her? He pulled her to him and bent his head to kiss her.

The instant before their lips met, Kate's voice sang through the air. "Hurry, Julia! We want to eat some birthday cake!"

Julia broke away from Tyler as though she'd been slapped across the face. "Coming, Kate!"

Then she nervously brushed back the tangles of hair from her forehead, wiped her hands on her dress, and tried to force a bright smile on her lips. "I'd best be getting back to the house," she announced awkwardly, avoiding Tyler's eyes as she picked up her skirts and fled.

Chapter 8

Julia rushed across the yard, her cheeks burning from her audacious behavior. Good heavens, what had she done?

She'd practically thrown herself at the man, practically invited him to kiss her. Which was something no respectable woman would permit herself to do . . . especially the daughter of a God-fearing minister. Was she losing her mind? What had possessed her to behave like a woman without any standards, any morals to her name? And why would she toss aside all her principles of integrity and honor for the sake of a kiss?

Shame coursed through her as she stumbled toward the house. She knew she had not lived up to the biblical teachings of her minister father. Yet another part of her, some tiny part, felt a twinge of regret for missing the chance to feel the touch of Tyler's lips on hers.

Heaven help her, she *liked* Tyler McRae. And she'd wanted him to kiss her more than anything she'd ever wanted in her life.

She couldn't explain how her feelings of disdain for the man had turned into something entirely different over the course of the last few hours. But she had felt something changing, deep inside of her, the instant she'd slipped into the parlor and found him standing there, talking with Elizabeth and Kate.

From the dark waves of his hair to the leather tips of his boots, he was the most engaging sight she'd ever seen. In spite of her efforts not to gawk at him, her gaze had kept drifting in his direction throughout dinner. And she had discovered much more about the stranger in their midst than she'd expected to learn. Most of the time his expression mirrored the pugnacity in Sam's face, telling Julia that he was painfully, awkwardly, aware he did not belong in the center of this family affair.

Oh, he'd tried not to watch them, tried to ignore the laughter surrounding him, tried to overlook the merriment encompassing the little group. But he had unknowingly betrayed himself, showing just how much he'd wanted to belong. Julia caught fleeting glimpses of his inner turmoil—the twist in those intriguing lips, those sudden flinches in the strong line of his jaw, the way his eyes reflected the longing in Sam's expression, the longing for someone to care.

Seeing Tyler's uneasiness, Julia had wanted to plant a smile on his lips by teasing him, soothe his hurts by comforting him, tousle his hair as if he were no older than Sam.

And that was her downfall. Outside, alone with him, she'd let down her guard and teased him about kissing her. When the lighthearted bantering suddenly turned into breathless sparks of wonder between them . . . she'd fled from the allure of those beckoning lips like a deer running from the threatening presence of a gunslinging hunter.

Forcing herself to set aside all thoughts about Tyler McRae, Julia went into the house. Both she and Kate washed the grime from their hair and bodies, then donned clean dresses before returning to the dining room for dessert.

Kate immediately noticed Tyler's absence from the table. "I guess Mr. Tyler thought he was too dirty to eat with us." She slipped down from her chair and placed a hefty slice of cake on an empty plate. "I think I'll go outside and take a piece of cake to him."

Sam scowled, and Julia knew the reason why. After Tyler's dealings with the boy, Sam probably wanted nothing more to do with the Hopewell House boarder.

"Finish up with your cake before you have to leave, Sam," she urged as Kate scampered outside. "I don't want you roaming the streets after dark, and I certainly don't want your mother to worry about you."

Sam shrugged, avoiding her eyes as he crammed the cake into his mouth. "She won't be worried."

Which was exactly Julia's fear. No one was taking proper care of the boy, she thought later, sending Sam on his way home. He'd scarcely looked at her, scarcely spoken to her, after Tyler's outburst. Julia could only pray the evening had not been more harmful than helpful to the young boy's spirits.

For Kate, however, the evening had been far from disappointing. As Julia tucked the young girl into bed for the night, Kate merrily reported that Mr. Tyler had thanked her for bringing the cake to him. Then she threw her chubby arms around Julia's neck and kissed her on the cheek. "Oh, Julia, this has been a wonderful birthday! Mr. Tyler came to my party . . . I got some beautiful presents . . . we got to chase hogs . . . and we didn't even have to mop water off the floor this afternoon!"

What a day, Julia thought later, returning the last of the clean dishes to the china cabinet. She had just shut the cabinet's bow-front door when she heard the riveting clinks of a hammer striking against nails. Following the direction of the noise, she stepped onto the back porch.

It was a beautiful evening. Beyond the grove of trees at the edge of the Hopewell property, the last rays of sunshine were fading rapidly. Cicadas and crickets chirped at the first signs of twilight. Fireflies danced in the dusky light, while fragrant spring breezes rustled through the evening air. Julia tilted back her head, gazing into the sky, enchanted by the moonbeams smiling down on her.

The hammer clanked again, and Julia dropped her gaze. Beneath the brightness of the full Georgia moon, she could see the silhouette of a man in the distance. Her heart fluttered as she watched the contours of his muscular form, listened to the sounds of his hammer pounding into the loose latch on the gate.

Intending to thank him for making the repairs, she stepped into the yard. As she neared him, she decided that he must have washed up at the pump after their tumble in the garden. Though his hair was tousled in disarray, it glistened with beads of water. Bits of grime still lingered on his trousers and boots, but the clumps of mud had disappeared from his face and shirt.

He looked up, surprised, as she approached.

"You didn't have to do this, you know," Julia said quietly. "But I'm grateful you've taken care of repairing the latch for me. I'm not very handy with a hammer and nails."

Seeming somewhat flustered by the unexpected praise, he edged back and motioned for her to step up to the gate. "Try it out before you thank me."

She didn't need to test it. She already knew, just by looking, that Tyler had fixed it. But to appease him, she gave the latch a shake. When it didn't budge, she looked over at him and grinned. "It's as good as new! We shouldn't have to chase any more hogs out of the garden for a while."

Her hair, slightly damp and smelling of lilacs, flowed freely over her shoulders, unrestricted by hairpins or ribbons. Tyler sucked in a shuddering breath, unable to tear his gaze away from her. Could she sense how much he longed to thread his fingers through her hair? Know how badly he was aching to devour those smiling, pink lips of hers with his own?

With forced effort, he dragged his gaze away from her and focused his eyes on a sagging fence rail. "The latch should hold, but I'm not sure about the rest of the pen. There are several boards that should be replaced . . . or else Hezekiah and Jezebel will be on the loose again."

"Hezekiah and Jezebel?" Julia's laughter glittered like spun gold beneath the moonlight. "I don't have any hogs by those names."

He reveled in the delight sparkling from her eyes, the beauty of her delicate features. "What you call your hogs isn't much better, lady."

"My hogs have proper biblical names—Bathsheba, Naomi, Zachariah, Delilah, and Samson," she told him, tipping her head at a mischievous angle, exposing the graceful line of her neck as the wind whipped her hair over her shoulder.

"Pardon me." Tyler moistened his lips, yearning to run his mouth over that creamy neckline of hers. "Since your hogs have such common names, I can't imagine why I failed to remember them."

"'Twas my father's idea," she admitted, a wistful little smile touching her lips. "Papa was partial to the Old Testament."

"He might have chosen the names, but something tells me you were the one who insisted the hogs needed names in the first place."

"Oh?" Julia studied the toes of her slippers. "Why would you think that?"

Couldn't she see for herself? A woman who loved so candidly, so fervently, wouldn't hesitate to give names to hogs or any other living creature. Yet, with her innocence, the goodness spilling from her heart and encircling everyone around her . . . how could she know? "You're the type who doesn't ignore anything that breathes," he finally said.

She lifted one shoulder in an airy shrug. "It's easier to get the hogs' attention if you call them by name. Hogs are very intelligent creatures." She paused, turning slightly, gazing into the distance. "Besides, Papa liked calling them by name, too."

"And he doesn't anymore?"

For a long moment, Julia didn't respond. When she finally turned to answer him, bright tears were shimmering in her eyes. "Papa died this spring . . . only two months ago."

Tyler wanted to dig a hole in the ground and crawl into it. He wanted to run as fast and as far as his legs could take him, if just to escape the sight of the pain glistening from her eyes. "I never stopped to think . . . I didn't realize . . . I would have never . . ."

"Of course you didn't know." She forced a brave smile, even though her bottom lip was trembling. "Papa got caught out in a raging storm, and his cold and coughs developed into pneumonia. There was nothing . . . nothing Doc Kramer or I or anyone could do."

An ache swelled in Tyler's chest. Her loss was great, her love for her father deep and unending. It was apparent by the lines of sorrow etched around her lips, the slight tremble in her chin, the moisture brimming in her eyes. Yes, she regretted the old man's passing. The depth and extent of her love for him could not be denied.

During the War, Tyler had witnessed countless numbers of deaths. He'd heard the groans of anguish on the battlefield, shuddered at the sight of mangled limbs, watched in horror as dying soldiers struggled in pain. But he'd learned to wear a mask of indifference, depending on it to shield and protect him from the tragedies of war as much as his Confederate-issued Pulaski rifle.

But he'd never seen a wife grieving for her husband, never watched a mother's tears for the loss of a son. He simply hadn't allowed himself to get involved, to expose himself to that kind of pain. Even now, he didn't want to be witness to this daughter's grief for her father.

Unable to bear it, Tyler clenched the fence railing, his fingers ripping the wood into splinters beneath the force of his grasp. Sweet Jesus, why was life so cruel? Julia was too good, too virtuous, to deserve this insufferable pain. Only bastards like himself merited such agony.

"The end was very swift," she continued softly. "Papa suffered greatly for a few days. And then . . . and then he was gone. God was very merciful, I think. He took Papa quickly, before the pain became unbearable."

Merciful? Tyler bit his tongue to keep from arguing with her. God wasn't merciful. How could she claim her God was being gracious if He'd snatched her earthly father away from her?

Her voice grew softer, taking on a watery sound. "Poor Papa. We buried him in the cemetery behind the Methodist church. He was the gentlest, kindest, most trusting person who ever lived . . . and I . . . I . . . I m-m-miss . . . him . . . s-s-so . . ." She turned her face away from him, but not before he saw the tears streaming down her cheeks.

Tyler, who had never comforted anyone in his life, was at a total loss. He didn't know what he should say or do. Part of him wanted to be her refuge, to let his arms become the haven of comfort that he'd never had for his own grief and pain.

But if he pulled her into his arms, what would happen then? Could he resist kissing away the tears on her cheeks? Did he have the willpower to walk away without running his fingers through that glorious, wind-tossed mane of chestnut hair? And would he be able to leave without letting her know how much he wanted her?

She buried her face in her hands, muffling a sob. Watching her narrow shoulders heave with sorrow, Tyler swallowed convulsively. Sweet Mother of Jesus, what could he do? He was only an empty shell of a man.

But standing there by herself with errant moonbeams dancing off her hair, she looked so damned alone, so helpless, so vulnerable . . .

Something inside Tyler crumbled. "Damn it to hell!" he muttered, reaching out and spinning her around. He crushed her face against the wide expanse of his chest, clamping his arms around her trembling shoulders. Sniffling, she snuggled a tearstained cheek against him.

His fingers were shaking as he stroked her hair. "What's all this, Miss Julia?"

"I'm—I'm sorry," she choked out. "I—I haven't—haven't cried since the day of Papa's funeral. I hardly ever cry. But it's just that . . . Papa isn't here . . . and I—I . . ."

Rocking her in his arms as if she were no more than a child, he rested his chin on the soft crown of her head. "Cry all you want, sweet Julia. Nobody around here is going to stop you. You're the chief princess of Hopewell House, aren't you?"

That brought a soggy giggle. "I guess you could say that. But sometimes . . . sometimes I don't feel like I'm doing such a great job. There's so much to do around this place——so much that needs to be done—that I don't know where to start."

Her tears had subsided now, and he knew he should pull away. But he continued to rock her against him ever so slightly, swaying his torso against hers, unable to bear the thought of letting go. Nothing had ever felt so right in his life as holding this woman in his arms. "A couple of shutters are missing on the house, I noticed. And the porch steps are rotting, as well."

"How good of you to point out all of those flaws." Her halfhearted chuckle faded into a sigh. "At least the latch on the hog pen is fixed, thanks to you. I'm hoping to save enough money for a new roof by the end of the summer. But that all depends on how quickly I can get the rest of the house ready for boarders."

"So what's stopping you?"

She leaned back in the cradle of his arms, arching her neck, looking up at him. A bit of embarrassment tinged her sculpted cheeks as she slowly broke away from his hold. "Lack of time . . . labor . . . and money."

"I don't think you have to worry about the success of Hopewell House," he said, trying his best to offer a bit of encouragement. "Once word gets out about the meals you serve in this place, you'll have a full house every night."

"I hope so." Her voice dropped to a whisper. "A few moments before Papa died, I promised him that I would take care of the family. It was his final request, and I would never be able to forgive myself if I didn't live up to my promise. Taking in boarders seems like the only way to keep all of us together, the only way to keep Hopewell House alive."

Tyler had no doubts about her sincerity and determination to live up to her father's expectations. But he couldn't stop from wondering why Julia was so full of determination to be her family's sole salvation.

Was an overwhelming sense of responsibility simply part of her nature? Was it sheer determination that drove her to keep a deathbed promise? Or had someone taken her love, love she offered so freely, and used it to shatter her? Led her to the point that she'd wrapped herself up in her family and shut herself off from the possibilities of ever loving anyone else?

Tyler's jaw suddenly clenched with stubborn resolve. None of this was his damn business. And if he quit asking questions and stopped listening to answers, maybe he could forget all about this woman and her family and go back to his life the way it was before he'd come here . . . all alone.

He curled his fists into tight balls. For a gut-wrenching instant Tyler wished he'd never seen her, never touched the silky softness of her hair. He wished he'd never smelled that lilac scent of hers, never tasted the sweetness of her bow-shaped lips.

Distracted by his thoughts, he didn't realize that he'd slammed his hand into the rotten fence rail, shattering it into pieces, until he heard Julia's soft gasp of surprise.

"What in heaven's name . . . ?"

Behind the fence, the hogs grunted and squealed. Tyler glared at the animals, then swung his gaze toward Julia. "Don't worry about your damn hog pen. You've got a few extra boards stored in the barn, and I'll use them to fix the railing before I turn in for the night. I'm sure as hell not running after hogs twice in one day."

She lifted her chin. "Think you're so handy with a hammer and nails that you can repair that railing?"

"Damn right I am. I can fix anything around this place that needs fixing."

"Anything?" Her eyes held a glimmer of challenge.

"You name it."

She crossed her arms over her chest. "Can you replace porch steps?"

"Piece of cake."

"Fix broken shutters?"

"In an hour or two."

"Patch up a leaky roof?"

"Better than most."

"Repair crumbling plaster?"

"Of course."

"Remove wallpaper? Paint?"

"Nothing to it."

Her rapid-fire questions stopped as she curled her lips into a smile. "Then you can make yourself handy around here, Tyler McRae. I'll consider your room and board paid in full if you'll stay long enough to fix some things that need repairing. That way, I'll be able to accept new boarders much sooner than I'd planned."

Never one to back down from a challenge, Tyler stretched out his hand before giving any thought to the consequences. "You've got a deal, lady."

Julia placed her hand in his. It was a simple gesture, but the slight brush of their fingers jolted Tyler to the core. His heart seemed to stop as their eyes met and locked, their handshake tightened and froze in midair. Holy Moses, she was looking up at him as if she expected something wonderful to happen.

To his surprise, she lifted her free hand to his face. Lightly running her fingers over his mustache, she whispered, "And for good measure, I'll even throw in a few mustache trimmings as part of the deal. For free."

"I should have let you trim it the other morning," he admitted, his voice ragged and choked.

With the brush of her fingertips across his upper lip, a shudder of longing coursed through him. Sweet Jesus, didn't she know what she was doing?

Of course she didn't. She was too innocent to understand that the simple touch of her hand was driving him insane. Too inexperienced in the ways of a man and a woman to realize that she was igniting a fire within him, a fire that was in danger of soaring out of control.

Yet there was a certain look about her that said she wanted to understand. Her gaze, locked on his mouth, shimmered with a naive curiosity. And her lips were slightly parted, almost as if she were waiting for him to kiss her.

Tyler inhaled an unsteady breath, unable to endure another second of torture. He would kiss her, for certain, but it would only be a simple little kiss. Nothing more. Promising himself that he would stop if she resisted, he bent his head and brushed his lips against hers.

But the instant their lips met, Tyler forgot all reason. Her mouth was moist and warm, inviting and tempting. And the sweet taste of her was more addictive than anything he'd ever known. Sweet Jesus, he wanted more . . . much more . . .

Not wanting to frighten her, he moved his lips over hers, back and forth, slowly, seductively. "You taste so good, sweet Julia," he whispered into her mouth. "So damn good, I can't stop . . ."

He continued to brush his lips against hers, deepening the pressure of the kiss and slipping his tongue inside the lush sweetness of her mouth. She shivered, whimpering softly, as the tips of their tongues entwined. His loins burned as her tongue circled around his, shyly, hesitantly, then with more boldness.

He glided his palms to the sweep of her back, pressing her against him, hoping to pull her deeper into the kiss. As she slid her arms over his shoulders, he felt shudders rippling through her. Was she feeling the same dizzying need that was soaring through him?

Judas Priest, he wanted her. Wanted every part of her with a passion he'd never known. And he knew one kiss would never be enough. One kiss could never quench the fire raging through him, the desire scorching every part of his body. "God, you can't imagine what you're doing to me . . . Julia," he rasped, still kissing her.

Hearing the sound of her name, whispered with such unbearably sweet tenderness, Julia sagged against him. She was drowning in his body, totally absorbed by the way his mouth was moving against hers, the feel of his hands roving across her back, the sounds of his labored breathing rumbling from his throat. Her breasts, crushed against his chest, ached with a fierce yearning. Enveloped in the powerful strength of his arms, consumed by the blistering inferno of desire sweeping through her, Julia moaned beneath the increasing pressure of his lips.

His tongue plunged deeper inside her, surging and swirling, forcing her to open her mouth wider. His hands swept down her back and clamped over her buttocks, crushing her against him. With his arousal pressed hard against her thigh, waves of heat spread through her lower body.

He tore his lips away from her mouth, planting hot, hungry kisses down her neck and throat. "You feel it, too, don't you, Julia? You can't tell me you don't . . ."

Whatever denials Julia might have voiced were swept away by the waves of unfamiliar sensations washing through her. Her whole body was tingling, aching, burning with a fever hotter than she'd ever known possible. She was lost in the feel of his wet lips burning a fiery trail across her bare skin, the scorching touch of his hands clamped over her hips, the scalding pulse of his masculinity pressing against her.

Somewhere in the recesses of her mind, she became aware that this kiss was more mind-boggling than the first one. It wasn't the same type of kiss that had stunned her beyond words when Tyler had arrived at Hopewell House. No, this was a soul-jarring kiss that was even more dangerous and tempting and . . .

"Heaven help me," she whispered, her voice shaky and weak. Dear Lord, what was she doing? She edged away from him, ashamed of herself. "I should have never . . . we shouldn't have . . ."

"Maybe you're right, Julia." The unsteadiness in his voice revealed that he was shaken as deeply as she. He sucked in a deep breath, as if he were trying to quell the frantic thundering in his heart. "I didn't mean to get so carried away."

"I didn't, either." She nervously tugged at her dress, straightening it, not daring to meet his eyes.

Placing an outstretched finger beneath her chin, he forced her to meet his gaze. "But just because I went further than I'd intended . . . doesn't mean

I didn't enjoy every damn second. Christ, I don't think I'll ever be able to get enough of you—"

"Please stop," she pleaded, gazing up at him with eyes full of uncertainty and doubt. "Please don't make this any harder than it already is. And please don't make me feel more ashamed of myself than I already am."

He cringed, pulling his hand away from her face. "I know all of this is new to you, Julia. But dammit, you shouldn't feel ashamed! We just got carried away—"

"And I shouldn't have allowed things to get out of hand."

"Fine." Frustrated, he dragged a hand through his hair. "From now on, I'll keep my damn hands off you," he snapped. But even as he ground out the words, Tyler knew nothing short of a miracle could prevent him from touching her again.

"That might be wise, considering you've agreed to stay here for a while longer." She paused, dropping her gaze again, shuffling her feet across the grass. "You know, I—I never—never stopped to think that it may not be convenient for you to stay here. Your arm has nearly healed, and I'm sure you must have other things to consider in your life. You probably need to be on your way . . . to tend to the business that brought you here in the first place."

"If I didn't want to stay at Hopewell House for a while longer, I wouldn't have agreed to your deal, lady," he lied smoothly.

"Good." She forced a smile. "I'm glad to know you're a man of your word."

But as Julia turned and walked away, Tyler felt the blood drain from his face. Good God, he'd almost forgotten about Jeremiah Carey. That son of a bitch was the cause of all his troubles, the reason why he'd been shot and dragged to Hopewell House in the first place.

But how could he think about pursuing a thief with Julia's beautiful green eyes looking up at him, shining with hope and promises for the future? How could he walk away from a woman who was grieving for her father, an enchantress who left him breathless and joyous and confused like no other female ever had? And how could he deny his promise to repair her home, knowing she treasured the place more than anything else in the world?

He couldn't.

Cursing under his breath, he stalked toward the barn to find the lumber to repair the fence.

His pursuit of Jeremiah Carey would simply have to wait.

Within moments after awakening the next morning, Tyler sensed something was different.

The ever-present tension clutching at his chest, the infernal well of emptiness lurking inside him, were notably absent. In their stead, a remarkable sense of expectation was flowing through him, almost like springs of hope bubbling up from a mountain stream.

He couldn't pinpoint the exact cause for his lighthearted spirit, didn't want to delve too deeply into the motives for the sudden change inside him, for fear it would disappear. All he knew for certain was that he was embracing the new day with more joy than he'd ever known.

He hastily dressed, chuckling as he heard snips of conversation between Odelphia and Dorinda in the next room.

"Gracious, Odie! You don't mean to wear that hat with your black mourning dress, do you?"

"Of course I do, Dorie. If you'd put your vanity aside long enough to get some spectacles, you'd be able to see this hat looks perfectly fine with my gown."

Tyler took the stairs two at a time. At the landing, he paused, listening as an unfamiliar sound greeted his ears. Good God, he was *whistling*!

Grinning, he resumed his brisk pace. But his long strides slowed to a halt in the dining room when he saw Julia.

She was wearing a black dress trimmed with a dainty lace collar. A mourning gown, no doubt, in respect of her father's passing. In spite of the drab hue, the dress complemented her. She looked so elegant, so beautiful, so feminine, that Tyler wanted nothing more than to reach out, pull her into his arms, and . . .

She looked up at him and smiled. "I'm glad you could join us for breakfast."

"I am, too." And it was true, even though his voice sounded like he was choking on a piece of horsemeat.

"Mr. Tyler!" Kate shrieked, running toward him with arms spread wide, grinning as though she hadn't seen him in years.

"Good morning, Kate." For the life of him, he couldn't help but smile.

After flinging her arms around his legs, Kate looked up at him with wide, expectant eyes. "Are you going to church with us this morning?"

Church. He should have known this family would not ignore the Lord's Day. But he hadn't graced the doors of a church in years, and he didn't intend to start now. "Maybe some other time, Kate."

Odelphia swept into the room, carrying a platter of crisp bacon and scrambled eggs. Dorinda followed with two more platters filled with grits and stacks of flapjacks.

After the platters had been passed around the table, Odelphia peered over the top of her spectacles at Tyler, who was sitting directly across from her. "I hope you're getting enough to eat this morning, Mr. McRae. We normally eat a light breakfast on Sunday."

"On the Lord's Day, we eat our main meal around two o'clock, after we get home from church," Dorinda added.

Tyler gazed down, staring at the mounds of food on his plate. Good heavens, if this was a light meal, what constituted a heavy one?

The next few minutes passed quickly. By the time Tyler finished breakfast, he was positive he wouldn't be able to eat for at least another week. Rising, he pushed back his chair and groaned just as a rap sounded at the front door.

"That must be Elizabeth," Julia remarked. "She always comes by here on Sunday mornings to go to church with us."

"I'll let her in," Kate offered, scrambling out of her chair.

Odelphia, Dorinda, and Julia were clearing off the table when Kate escorted Elizabeth into the room. She was an attractive woman, Tyler assessed, noticing her dark hair, dark eyes, and trim figure. Like the rest of the women at Hopewell House, Elizabeth was dressed for church, wearing a wide-brimmed hat and a pink gown that appeared to be her Sunday best.

No, he could not deny that Elizabeth was a beauty. And he knew a beautiful woman when he saw one. They'd always been his weakness. He prided himself on flirting with them, catching their attention, and luring them into his bed with his charm.

But today Tyler felt none of those old urgings. He had no inclination to explore any kind of relationship with this friend of the family's. Because there was only one woman he wanted to pursue. *Julia Hopewell.*

"We'll be leaving for church in a few minutes, Elizabeth." Julia picked up a stack of dishes from the table. "I just hope we won't be late. I'm running a little behind schedule this morning."

Elizabeth's brown eyes twinkled with amusement. "I'm sure you'll manage. You've never been late for church a day in your life, Julia Carey."

"But there's always the first time." Grinning, Julia turned, heading for the kitchen with the dirty breakfast dishes.

As Julia left the room, Tyler sucked in a shuddering breath. A tiny pulse of fear pounded through his veins. Had he heard Elizabeth correctly? Surely she had been teasing . . .

"Is something wrong, Mr. McRae?" Elizabeth asked politely.

He shook his head, not wanting to admit anything, not even to himself. "I just assumed . . . I just assumed Julia's last name was Hopewell, like her aunts."

Elizabeth smiled graciously. "That's understandable. But Hopewell was her mother's maiden name. Julia's mother—Capitola, the dear lady we discussed last night—was a Hopewell until she married Julia's father."

"And Julia's father was . . . ?"

"Jeremiah Carey. The Reverend Jeremiah Carey of the Methodist church."

The air rushed from his lungs, as if someone had leveled a blow to his chest.

Judas Priest, what had he done?

Chapter 9

Stepping back into the dining room to retrieve the last load of dirty china and silver from the table, Julia smiled as Elizabeth mentioned her father's name.

"Papa served the Methodist church for nearly thirty years," Julia added to the conversation, making no attempt to hide the pride in her voice. "He worked a circuit route through North Georgia. And he also held tent revivals every spring in Tennessee."

Hearing a sharp intake of breath from Tyler's direction, she glanced up in confusion. His jaw was clenched, his eyes narrowed. Was she seeing struggle and torment in his expression . . . or merely surprise?

His smile seemed forced, strained. "A special breed of man, I'm certain."

"Everyone loved Reverend Carey." Elizabeth gave a wistful sigh. "He served his flock as if they were members of his own family. He was a very giving person."

"A man loyal to his calling, no doubt," Tyler returned in a clipped tone. With a curt nod, he abruptly stalked to the door. "Enjoy yourselves at church, ladies."

Turning to Julia, Elizabeth frowned as Tyler exited the room. "Did I say something wrong?"

Shrugging, Julia swept off the crumbs from the linen tablecloth. "I don't think so, Elizabeth. Tyler McRae isn't exactly the type of man who holds a fondness for righteous living. We've never discussed the subject of Papa's work, and I believe he was merely surprised to discover he has been staying with a minister's family during his visit to Rome."

At least she hoped that was the reason for the rigid set of his jaw and for his hasty departure. She didn't want to consider any other possibilities for his sudden change of spirits. And she certainly didn't want to believe that he might be filled with regret for kissing a minister's daughter . . . or even worse, shocked to think that one had *wanted* him to kiss her.

Welcoming the diversion of the Sunday services, she hastily finished dressing for church. After donning a small-brimmed, black hat trimmed with coral ribbons, she tucked a well-worn Bible beneath her arm and planted a bright smile on her lips before beginning the four-block walk to church with her family and Elizabeth.

The First United Methodist Church of Rome, a white frame building with a simple steeple, was located on the top of a small rise overlooking the town. Normally Julia found a sense of peace each time she worshiped in the small sanctuary, surrounded by family and friends.

But on this Sunday morning, peace eluded Julia. She squirmed uncomfortably on the hard wooden pew, sitting between Kate and Elizabeth, trying to shove aside the unsettling thoughts that plagued her like a prickly thorn in her side. She couldn't concentrate on the minister's words, couldn't think of anything other than the events of the last twelve hours.

Last night she'd merely intended to convey her thanks to Tyler for repairing the hog pen when she'd stepped outside to join him. She'd never intended to grieve so openly for her father. And she'd never expected a man like Tyler McRae to console her, comfort her, in ways that no one else ever had.

Under the bewitching light of the full Georgia moon, she'd found strength in the cradle of his arms, an unexpected sense of comfort from the words he'd whispered into her hair, a surprising amount of understanding in the tenderness of his touch.

At the time, asking him to make some repairs in exchange for his room and board seemed like the logical thing to do. He couldn't pay her, she knew. He'd been robbed of every cent to his name, hadn't he? And she needed someone to make repairs to the house so she could open some more rooms for additional boarders. Bartering seemed like the perfect solution.

She'd been surprised, but pleased, by his quick acceptance of the idea. Over breakfast, she had been even more delighted to discover that he actually seemed to be enjoying himself. The guarded look in his eyes had vanished, replaced with an openness, an eagerness, that Julia had never seen before. He'd laughed more freely, smiled more easily, than he'd laughed or smiled during his entire stay at Hopewell House.

Then, without warning, his laughter and good humor had disappeared. It seemed as though he'd stepped behind that invisible wall again, the barrier that kept his true emotions at bay, as soon as he'd learned Papa had been a minister.

But Julia sensed something other than the news about Papa had disturbed him. Was he remembering that soul-jarring kiss they'd shared in the moonlight? Had it affected him in the same earth-shattering way it had affected her? Or was he stunned because a minister's daughter had offered herself so freely to him?

Yes, she'd wanted him to kiss her. That much, she could not deny. But only because she'd been possessed with the crazy notion that one more kiss would miraculously sever the invisible cords that kept drawing her to the man. And if a second kiss did not affect her, it would certainly prove that her soaring emotions were nothing more than a figment of her imagination every time he was near.

But the instant she'd felt his lips brushing across hers, she knew she'd made a dreadful mistake. It was nothing like the rough, brutal kiss she'd received on his first night at Hopewell House. This had been a kiss filled with such deeply felt passion and longing that even now she trembled from the vivid memory of it. A kiss even more potent and dangerous, she realized, than the first one.

It revealed a different side of Tyler McRae, a side she longed to know, the part of him that could express compassion as fiercely as he tried to hide it . . . the part that had been needing someone for a long, long time.

It was just a taste, a sampling, of what was buried inside him, she knew. No woman would ever be loved more passionately, more fully, if Tyler McRae ever submitted to all those locked-up emotions.

If and when that happened, Julia wished she could be that woman. But, of course, that could never be. She'd pulled away from the sweet torture of his lips as soon as the revelation had occurred to her.

Yet if they were so wrong for each other, why did her heart leap with excitement every time he was near? Why did her pulse race, her knees tremble, at the mere thought of seeing him again?

And why was she thinking all these ungodly thoughts in the middle of the Sunday morning sermon?

The minister's voice bellowed through the sanctuary. "Let us pray."

Julia dutifully bowed her head and closed her eyes, acutely aware she needed all the help that heaven could offer.

"Damn it all to hell," Tyler roared, his voice echoing from the rafters in the empty barn.

His hands were raw with fresh blisters, his brow covered with sweat, his arms aching with pain. He'd chopped enough wood for three winters, cleaned out the neglected barn stalls, and now he was hurling hay over his shoulders with a pitchfork just for the hell of it.

He didn't know how long he'd been working himself into a frenzy, nor did he care. All he wanted was to purge himself of all the rage, the anger, the frustration, that was ricocheting inside him. Tyler figured if he worked himself long enough, hard enough, maybe he would drop dead from exhaustion and not have to think about it at all.

When he'd stalked out of the house, he'd gone straight to the barn, hoping to find some evidence of Jeremiah Carey's crime. But the two horses in the stalls were pitiful-looking creatures, nothing like the majestic breeds from his own livery. And the bits, bridles, and saddles bore no resemblance to the ones that had belonged to him.

Tyler slumped down into the hay, feeling as though he'd been beaten with a horsewhip. Sweet Jesus, how in the hell had it happened? Julia's father—*her father*, for cripes' sake—was the man he'd sworn vengeance against. The son of a bitch he'd sworn to make pay for his sins.

A hot surge of anger rushed through him. For cripes' sake, he should have seen it coming. When he'd learned that Julia's mother had been the sister of Odelphia and Dorinda, he should've realized that Julia's last name would be different from her aunts. But he'd been so caught up in trying to curtail his emotions last night that the thought had never crossed his mind.

Knowing he wasn't the only person who'd been fooled by the man who'd claimed to be a minister of God only made matters worse. Carey had even pulled the wool over the eyes of his own family. He'd led a double life, robbing the rich with one hand while pounding on the pulpit with the other.

At the moment, he despised the man almost as much as he hated his own father. He'd never forgiven his father for betraying him, for ripping their family apart. His feelings toward Jeremiah Carey were no different. Dead or alive, the scoundrel didn't deserve to be forgiven. If anything, he should've died a slow, agonizing death, not the swift, merciful one that Julia had described so tearfully.

But those bright tears on her face had affected him like nothing ever had. Tyler's throat tightened at the memory of the moisture swelling in those emerald green eyes, the heart-wrenching way she'd grieved for her loss, the awkward bits of comfort he'd so desperately tried to offer.

And her father had stolen a livery full of horses from him.

Leaping up from the hay, Tyler curled his fists into tight balls. He stomped through the barn, frustration mounting with each step.

Hell, what could he do about it? Worse yet, what was he going to do about *her*?

He frowned. Julia and her little band had given him more compassion, more tenderness, more caring, than he'd ever known in his entire life. They'd nursed him, fed him, watched over him. They'd made him laugh, made him feel wanted . . . and warm.

Running out on them was hardly the thing to do. And if he packed his bags, how could he justify his actions to Julia? Could he blame the woman for her father's sins? Was he man enough to admit that he couldn't paint her house, mend her fences, or fix her roof because he'd fallen under her spell?

Yet every instinct he possessed warned him to run as fast and as far as his legs could carry him. He wasn't any prize, especially for a woman like Julia Carey—a woman whose home and family were the joys of her life, a woman who would do anything to keep them safe from harm.

Julia deserved a man who was dependable, loving, and kind. A man who would adore her beauty, treasure her goodness, and love her family. And Tyler McRae was not that man. He didn't have an ounce of love left for anyone in his barren soul.

He'd stopped caring, stopped loving, stopped feeling, long ago. Nineteen years ago, to be precise. It was the day that his life had changed forever, that fateful day when he'd learned the bitter truth about his mother, when his father's wrath had ripped his family apart . . . when he'd seen Rebecca for the last time.

Tyler wearily leaned against the open door of the barn, gazing across the yard, feeling an odd ache growing in his chest. For some strange reason, he found himself wishing he could be the dependable, stoic man who loved kids and family, home and church, the type who was capable of forgiving

others as freely as he loved them . . . the man Julia
Carey needed . . . and deserved.

But he wasn't that kind of man. Didn't even
have the hope of ever becoming the man of Julia's
dreams. It was too late to rid himself of the ghosts
that had haunted him since childhood.

So leaving was the only thing he could do. No, he
wouldn't abandon her tonight, wouldn't go back on
his word to make a few repairs to her damn house.
But he'd fix up the place as fast as he could . . . and
then get the hell out of town.

At that moment a door slammed at the back of
the house. Tyler looked up just as a slight figure
stepped into the yard, basket in hand. Her black
mourning dress, the one she'd worn to church, had
been replaced with an apple green calico. Dappled
sunlight cast an ethereal glow over her upturned
face, highlighting the streaks of red in her chestnut
hair until they sparkled like gold.

Just the sight of her melted all of Tyler's cold
resolve. His mouth grew dry with longing.

He swallowed convulsively. Jesus Christ, would
it be such a sin to taste a bit more of her sweetness?
Couldn't he stay just long enough to ease that nagging sense of emptiness in the scarred remains of
his soul? Why couldn't he store away a few memories of this little slice of heaven, tuck them away for
all those cold, bleak winters ahead without her?

Tyler's fists clenched, his eyes narrowed. He had
the rest of his life to be eaten alive with hate and
bitterness, to wrestle with ghosts from the past, to
be alone . . . so damn alone. Would it be so awful to
stay here for a few more days? He only wanted to
be wreathed in the goodness of this woman and her
family for a little while longer. He wasn't asking
for anything more.

"Mr. Tyler, Mr. Tyler!"

Startled, Tyler looked up. Kate was running toward him across the yard, chubby arms waving wildly, laughter bubbling up from her throat, thick braids trailing behind her in the wind.

A lump swelled in his throat. Blast, he couldn't figure out why she doted on him so. He didn't deserve any little girl's adoration. Not after the way he'd cut out on Rebecca, leaving her stranded, alone, forlorn . . .

Kate tugged on his trousers. "It's almost time to eat, Mr. Tyler. Will you sit by me at the table?"

Tyler wanted to refuse, wanted to tell her that he shouldn't eat any more meals with the family of the man who'd wiped out his livery. But one glance at the precious child wiped away all his resolve. She was looking up at him with such eagerness, such innocence, that he couldn't bear to disappoint her.

He crossed his arms over his chest, twisted his mouth into a frown, and pretended to consider the matter. "All depends, I suppose. Are we having green beans?"

She giggled with delight. "Not today, thank goodness."

Winking, he reached out and tweaked her braids. "Then you lead the way, Miss Katy-did. As soon as I wash up, I'll be right behind you."

"You don't want another piece of my strawberry pie, Mr. McRae?" Dorinda's expression was a mixture of disappointment and disbelief. "I made it especially for you."

"And it was the most delicious strawberry pie I've ever tasted, Miss Dorinda. But I can't possibly eat another bite at the moment." Rising, Tyler flashed a charming smile. "Of course, if you could save me a piece for later . . ."

"Of course." Dorinda's eyelashes fluttered. "We'll have it waiting for you, right here on the table."

"Now, if you ladies will excuse me, I'll be heading back out to the barn."

Tyler was almost to the door when Kate scrambled down from her chair. "Wait for me, Mr. Tyler!"

Dorinda sighed wistfully as the young girl clambered after Tyler. "Mercy me, that man is a charmer. I never thought I would like having boarders in our house, but I have to admit I think I am going to hate seeing him leave."

"Actually, he'll be staying on for a while longer," Julia announced quietly, shoving aside her dinner plate. "He's agreed to make some repairs to the house for us in exchange for his room and board."

"I wondered why he's been working out in the barn all day." Dorinda cut a second slice of pie for herself and licked the sugary syrup from her fingers. "So how did all this come about?"

"It was my suggestion," Julia admitted. "The idea occurred to me after he repaired the latch to the hog pen last night. I figured if he couldn't pay us for staying here—since all of his money was stolen on the train—he might agree to provide the labor for our repair work in exchange for room and board. And he was very receptive to the idea."

A frown creased Odelphia's brow as she dabbed the corners of her mouth with a linen napkin. "But even if Mr. McRae provides the labor, repairs cost money, Julia. How are we going to pay for the new materials and supplies?"

"I'm hoping we can put off buying a lot of supplies until the money starts coming in from boarders. Our biggest problem is the leak in the ceiling, but maybe Tyler can patch the roof until we can afford to get a new one. We also have a few scraps of lumber in the barn that he can use for other repairs."

"And if we need anything else, maybe that nice Horace Bates will give us credit at his store," Dorinda suggested brightly.

"You know how I feel about buying anything on credit, Aunt Dorinda." Julia sighed. "Besides, I don't want to feel obligated to Horace Bates—or anyone else, for that matter—for anything."

At the end of the day, however, Julia had the strange feeling that she was becoming indebted to one particular person, whether or not she wanted to be. She'd only asked Tyler to make repairs to the house, but he was doing more, much more, than she'd ever expected of him.

When she'd returned home from church, she had been surprised to see all the freshly chopped firewood in the woodpile beside the barn. And when Kate had dragged Tyler into the house for Sunday dinner, she'd reported that she'd never seen the barn so clean.

After dinner, Julia had quietly observed Tyler from the corner of her eye as she repaired the damage to the garden. Though she'd tried not to gape at him, she couldn't prevent her eyes from drifting in his direction while she replanted some of the green sprouts that had been uprooted by the hogs.

He'd worked tirelessly by the grove of trees at the edge of the property, clearing an area that was choked with weeds and overgrown foliage. He had been careful not to strain his left arm, Julia noticed. She only prayed that his wound had fully healed. Yet she didn't have the heart to tell him that only necessary chores could be done on the Lord's Day. Working like a Trojan on Sundays had always been strictly forbidden by her family.

Besides, she had been too mesmerized by the sight of his lean, muscular form to utter a coherent sentence. Spellbound, Julia had watched in fascination as he'd shrugged off his shirt and flexed the powerful muscles in his shoulders, swinging a sickle back and forth across the branches and limbs. Watching his stalwart poses, observing the strength of his actions, numbed her thoughts to the point that she couldn't think of anything other than her longing to run her fingers through the dark nests of hair covering his chest.

Just looking at him made her fingers tighten around the fragile stem of a tomato plant. When the plant snapped beneath the pressure of her fingers, she shook her head in dismay. "Stop this nonsense right now," she scolded herself. It was the Lord's Day, and she had no business thinking such ungodly thoughts.

Though Tyler made a brief appearance at supper, it was well after dark by the time he returned to the house for the night. Kate had already been tucked into bed, and Odelphia and Dorinda had retreated to their rooms. Julia was alone in the parlor, mending one of Kate's dresses, when she heard the sound of his boots shuffling through the halls.

A few moments later, Julia set aside her mending and secured the house for the evening. Then she quietly slipped up the stairs to the third floor. But as soon as she opened the door to her room, she stopped cold.

Tyler was sprawled out on the bed. His head was propped up on a pillow, his hands locked behind his neck. The lantern on the table beside the bed cast a golden glow over him, highlighting the angular planes and grooves of his face. He was bare-chested, barefooted, and obviously at ease with himself.

Julia's breath caught in her throat. "Wh-Wh-What are you doing here?"

He flashed a decadent grin. "I'm just settling in for the night."

"I fail to see the humor in this situation, Mr. McRae. And if you don't leave this instant, I shall scream to the top of my lungs."

"Oh, that should work wonders. I'm certain your aunts would be delighted to discover that you're entertaining a gentleman in the privacy of your room."

Infuriated, Julia could feel the heat rising to her cheeks. What could she do? He'd backed her into a corner, and he knew it. Explaining his presence to her family was the last thing she wanted.

"No?" His voice was soft, taunting. "I didn't think so."

"Please leave." Sighing with exasperation, Julia wearily massaged the nape of her neck. "It's been a long day. Fighting with you does not appeal to me in the least. And I don't think you need me to remind you that you're in the wrong room."

"Ah, but that's where you're wrong. I'm in the right room, at last." Sitting up, he swung his legs over the edge of the mattress. Julia suddenly noticed that his traveling bag was sitting at the foot of the bed. "I should've been sleeping up here all along. Not you. It's high time I got the hell out of your room, lady. No sense in my robbing you of your bed any longer, now that I'm planning to stick around for a few more days."

"Fine. Have it your way," Julia snapped. Of course, he was right, and she knew it. But she didn't like the idea of being pushed back into her own room in the middle of the night. And she didn't know how to respond to the unexpected pleasure of finding him in her bed, didn't enjoy the uninvited emotions soaring through her at the thought of being alone with him in such intimate quarters.

"If you don't want to leave, I would be happy for you to stay here with me."

She glared at him. "I can just imagine how happy that would make you," she ground out.

She stormed across the room and jerked up some gowns draped across the back of a chair. She had just tossed the clothing over her shoulder when Tyler came up behind her. Reaching around her, he plucked up a remaining garment from the chair.

Looking down at the chemise dangling from his fingers, Julia cringed with embarrassment. She snatched the garment from his grasp, intending to flee before he could see the hot flush in her cheeks. But she'd taken only one step across the room when he gently caught her arm.

He whirled her around to face him. Julia looked up at him, determined to meet his gaze with a seething glare. But the touch of his hand and the blue of his eyes melted all of her resolve. "Please don't," she whispered. Her voice was shaky, pleading.

"Do I frighten you, Julia?"

"Of course not." It was her own violent reactions to this man that terrified her. "It's just that . . . "

"Have you never had a suitor before?" His voice was barely above a whisper.

"Yes." She swallowed convulsively, offering nothing more.

The line of his jaw hardened. "And is he still calling on you?"

"No." She inhaled a deep breath, then spilled out the words quickly. "He died in the War."

Something akin to sympathy flashed in his eyes. "Then it has been a very long time since another man has kissed you, I suppose." He paused. "Did you respond to his kisses in the same way that you responded to me last night?"

"Don't ask me that, Tyler," she pleaded. "I can't compare you and Brent. He was very different from you."

"In the way we kiss . . . or in the way we make you feel?"

Both, she started to say, but caught herself just in time. Brent's kisses had been chaste, simple pecks that had brought only a few flutters to her heart. Nothing like this man's passionate, soul-jarring kisses that bored straight through to her soul.

When she didn't answer, he reached out and tucked an errant tendril of chestnut hair behind her ear. "You can't deny that you wanted me to kiss you last night, Julia. You wanted it as much as I did. I could tell."

Her eyes widened incredulously. "But how . . . how did you know?"

"Everything about you said you wanted to be kissed. I could tell by the way you moistened your lips with your tongue . . . and by the way your mouth parted ever so slightly . . ." He traced the outline of her mouth with a callused finger, studying the bow-shaped contours with a gaze so intense that her breath caught in her throat. "Even your eyes were sending messages to me, sweet Julia. You were looking up at me like you *wanted* me to kiss you . . . the same way you're looking at me now."

She squeezed her eyes shut, not wanting him to see any more emotions written there. "I didn't . . . didn't realize I was so . . . transparent," she choked out.

His hand skittered across the fragile chords of her throat, sending a tingling sensation through her. "Wanting to be kissed isn't a sin, you know."

Her eyes shot open. "But the way you kissed me wasn't exactly chaste, Tyler!"

"God wouldn't have invented kissing if He didn't intend for us to enjoy it." Amusement sparkled from his eyes until his voice dropped to a husky timbre. "And God knows, I've never found more pleasure in any woman's kisses. So I suggest we take advantage of every opportunity we have to enjoy more of each other . . ."

Julia's heart thundered in her chest as he edged closer and bent his head. He was going to kiss her, she knew, and she wasn't certain she could deal with all the searing emotions that were certain to accompany it.

She stepped back, shaken to the core. Resisting the temptation of feeling his hot, hungry mouth on hers was the hardest thing she'd ever had to do. "We can't, Tyler. Not now. I'm not ready for any more . . ."

She heard his sharp intake of breath, saw every muscle in his long, powerful frame go whipcord-taut. "Then I'll try to wait. I'll try not to force myself on you until you're ready. But I can't make any guarantees that I'll be patient." His jaw clenched tightly. "Hell, I might have to lock myself in this damn room to keep my hands off you."

A few more encounters like this one, and he might not have to wait for long, she feared. Abating her sinful nature was not easy around a man the likes of Tyler McRae. Inhaling a shaky breath, she turned to leave. "Good night, Tyler," she whispered. "I'll see you in the morning."

Chapter 10

Shortly before noon on Monday, Julia gazed across the sea of restless students in the schoolhouse and frowned at the waves of discontent rippling through the one-room building.

Instead of focusing on their lessons, most of the children were seated at their desks, staring aimlessly through the window. Many of the younger students, including Kate, were squirming uncomfortably in their seats. In the back of the room, a gale of laughter suddenly erupted from one group of pupils, a group that was supposed to be working on a joint geography project.

Looking outside, Julia could see the reasons for their restlessness. The weather was beautiful, bright and sunny. Just the hint of a spring breeze rustled through the trees surrounding the schoolhouse.

The day was much too inviting to stay inside, and Julia could hardly find fault with the children for their lack of concentration. Even their teacher was finding it difficult to resist the temptation of forsaking the responsibilities of the day and stepping outside to enjoy the pleasant spring weather.

"Time for lunch, class," Julia announced, closing the textbook on her desk. "And when we resume our studies this afternoon, we won't be coming back into the schoolhouse. It's too beautiful to be

cooped up inside, so we'll be holding classes outdoors for the rest of the day."

As Julia suspected, the students responded with
whoops of delight. Setting aside their lessons, they
bolted up from their desks, grabbed their lunch
pails, and clambered outside.

Except for Sam. Unlike his classmates, the red-
haired youth did not dash out the door with a
smile on his face and a lunch pail in his hand.
He lingered behind the others, shoulders slumped,
mouth drawn, hands empty. As he trudged toward
the open door, his shoes shuffled over the planked
floor with a heavy weight, almost as if chains were
strapped around his ankles.

As she watched him, an ache swelled in Julia's
heart. She'd hoped and prayed that providing Sam
with a hot meal and a sense of family would lift
his spirits. But his brief visit to Hopewell House
had changed nothing, she realized. She'd been foolish to think she could wipe away his troubles by
changing his environment for a few hours. Sam's
worries were obviously much more serious than
she'd ever dreamed.

All morning she had been tempted to pull him
aside, wrap her arms around his frail shoulders,
and assure him that someone cared about his forlorn little soul. But she knew Sam would not submit to such an open display of affection without
putting up a fight. He was too proud, maybe even
too ashamed, to admit that he needed an affirma-
tion of love in his life, needed to know someone
cared.

Even his classmates were snubbing him, and Julia
knew the reason why. He was still wearing the same
clothes that he'd worn to dinner on Saturday evening, the same threadbare shirt and trousers that
had been streaked with mud during the wild hog

chase in the garden. To make matters worse, his hair, hands, and face were as filthy as his clothes. The stench was revolting, and Julia could understand why the children did not want to be near him.

Thank goodness she'd been able to open the shutters and doors and let the spring breezes filter through the building. Otherwise, the entire class would have been pinching their noses every time they caught a whiff of the foul odors wafting from Sam's direction.

With a troubled sigh, Julia picked up her lunch pail and went outside. Sitting on the schoolhouse steps, she placed a linen napkin in her lap. Then she pulled out a biscuit and a slice of cheese from the assortment of food stuffed into the tin pail. Though she'd packed four more biscuits, an apple, additional cheese, and a slice of cake, she had no intention of keeping the food for herself. Sam needed nourishment much more than she did. Julia suspected he had not eaten a meal since Kate's birthday dinner.

In the kitchen that morning, Tyler had peered over her shoulder and frowned at the exorbitant amount of food that she had set aside for lunch. "Good heavens, woman! Are you planning to feed the entire school?"

She'd tried to smile, even though her heart had twisted into a knot at the expectation of Sam snatching up the food like a starving animal. "I usually take more than I need, just in case one of the children forgets to bring his lunch."

His eyes narrowed suspiciously. "And does that happen often?"

"Almost every day. Some students are more forgetful than others."

"Some students . . . like Sam?"

"Sam is one of the children who doesn't always remember to bring food from home," she admitted. "He seems terribly hungry at times, and taking a little extra food with me seems like the least I can do."

Some sort of indiscernible emotion flashed across Tyler's face. "That kid will never learn to take care of himself if everyone keeps pampering him like a damn baby," he mumbled irritably before wheeling out of the room.

Caught up in the rush to leave for school, Julia did not have the chance to say anything more to Tyler. But now his misgivings about Sam haunted her thoughts. Why was the young boy such a tender subject with him? And why couldn't Tyler be more compassionate and caring? Didn't he realize that Sam was starving for much more than food?

Finishing the last bite of cheese from her lunch, Julia sauntered across the school yard. Following her established routine, she casually paused beside the old oak tree and set her lunch pail beside the trunk. Then she returned to the entrance of the schoolhouse, sat down on the steps, and waited.

A few moments later, Sam slipped up to the tree. Julia breathed a sigh of relief as he snatched up the food. At least I know he's getting one meal today, she thought.

But her breath caught in her throat when she noticed that Daniel Young was creeping up behind Sam. The red-haired youngster, concentrating on eating, was too distracted by the food to sense that anyone was sneaking up on him.

"Whatsa matter with you, Springer?" Daniel taunted. "That's Miss Julia's lunch, not yours! I saw her leave it here a few minutes ago."

Startled, Sam whirled around, his eyes wide with guilt and alarm. "This food ain't Miss Julia's, it's mine!" He rammed another biscuit into his mouth, then clutched the lunch pail to his chest with a fierce protectiveness. "I'm eatin' it, ain't I?"

Daniel snickered, obviously unconvinced. "Why can't you bring your own lunch instead of stealing Miss Julia's? Don't you like your ma's cooking? Or is she just too busy to fool with the likes of you?"

The lunch pail hit the ground with a clatter as Sam leaped up and grabbed Daniel's collar. The uneaten biscuits flew out of the tin container, sailing across the school yard. "Don't you talk about my ma!" he shouted. "If you say another word about my ma or her cooking, I'll smash my fist into your nose."

"Won't do no good to hit me," Daniel jeered. "It ain't just me that's talkin' about your ma. Why, everybody in town knows she ain't worth a hill of beans. Folks all over are sayin' they ain't seen your ma for weeks! My pa says she probably took off with that no-good man of hers, tryin' to get him to marry her. But my ma says ain't nobody gonna marry a sorry creature like your moth—"

"I ain't gonna listen to this!" Sam yelled. "Shut your mouth!"

"Make me, Springer," Daniel dared. "It's the truth, and you know it!"

Sam hurled back his arm just as Julia leaped down from the steps and shot across the yard. "Sam, Daniel, stop this foolishness right now!" she called.

But the boys paid her no heed. Sam crashed a closed fist into Daniel's jaw. Yelping, Daniel reached out, grabbed a chunk of Sam's hair, and yanked with all his might. Refusing to submit to the pain, Sam bent over and rammed his head straight into Daniel's stomach. At the same time, he grabbed the boy's knees and knocked him off his feet. Both boys crashed to the ground.

Within seconds, the rest of the students had formed a circle around the boys. Julia barged through the crowd of children, praying she could break up the brawl before either of the boys could get seriously injured.

"Get him, Daniel!" one of the older boys cheered.

"You can whip Sam with one hand tied behind your back!" another urged.

"Enough of this!" Julia shouted, shoving aside the students to get to the center of the fight.

By the time Julia broke through the crowd, the brawl was in full momentum. The boys were rolling on top of each other in the dirt, fists flying and legs kicking. Horrified, she reached down and struggled to pull the youngsters apart. "Stop it this instant, both of you!"

The lads stilled, though a thick cloud of tension hovered through the air. Sam reluctantly pulled himself off Daniel, brushing off the dirt from the sleeve of his shirt. "He's the one who started it, Miss Julia. Not me."

Daniel leaped up, wiping blood from his nose. "He's a no-account liar! He shoved me first!"

Julia placed a steadying hand on each boy's shoulder. "I want both of you to stand right here—without laying a hand on each other—and be quiet for just a moment." Turning to the circle of students, she announced, "As for the rest of you, there's nothing else to watch now. I want all of you—except for Daniel and Sam—to return to your proper seats in the schoolhouse. We'll be starting class in five minutes."

Moans of dismay filtered through the air. Kate stuck out her lower lip, crossed her arms over her chest, and glared at Daniel and Sam. "See what you boys did? Now none of us gets to stay outdoors this afternoon!"

Julia lifted one eyebrow and looked at Kate stern-ly. "No complaining, Kate. Just do as you're told." She motioned for the remainder of the children to go inside the building. "And that goes for the rest of you, too."

Amid sighs of protest, the children reluctantly followed Julia's instructions. Once the school yard had emptied, Julia turned to confront the troubled youths.

Sam's left eye was bloodshot and swollen; bruises were already beginning to form on his face. But the stubborn set of his jaw and the seething fury in his eyes told Julia that his anger was far from subsided.

Daniel did not look much better. Blood oozed from his nose and dribbled over a swollen lip; the sleeve of his shirt dangled by a single thread. And, like Sam, Daniel was still brimming with tension, itching to fight.

"Fighting with your fists doesn't accomplish any-thing, boys." Julia pulled a handkerchief from her pocket and dabbed at the blood running out of Daniel's nose. Then she tenderly tilted back Sam's head and examined his eye. He winced, pulling away from her, but she held him firmly until she was satisfied there was no sign of permanent damage from the nasty bruises. Stepping back, she inspected the unruly pair from head to toe with one sweeping, comprehensive glance. "Are either of you hurting anywhere else?"

Sam stiffened. "That sissy couldn't have hurt me if he'd tried."

Daniel crossed his arms over his chest defiantly. "No mama's boy is gonna whip me."

Sighing, Julia shook her head. Obviously nei-ther youngster would admit to any pain, even if he'd been mangled in combat. "Don't you think

it's time to settle your differences with words—
and not your fists?"

"It's all Sam's fault, Miss Julia!" Daniel burst out,
pointing an accusing finger at the red-haired boy.
"He's the one who started it."

"Am not." Sam's face was as red as his hair.
"You're the one to blame, Daniel!"

Julia wedged between the youths before one of
them could level another blow. "Both of you are
at fault, boys. I heard and saw the entire incident.
Daniel, I suggest you keep your opinions to yourself about Sam's mother. And, Sam, I suggest that
you keep your fists out of Daniel's face."

She paused, hoping to hear some word of apology from them. When neither boy broke the stony
silence, she heaved a weary sigh. "Both of you
will stay for one hour after school today and
clean the chalkboards as your punishment. If I
hear you exchange another word or dirty look
during the remainder of the afternoon, you will
have to remain after school every day for two
weeks. And I expect much better behavior from
both of you from now on."

Heads hanging low, the boys trudged back to the
schoolhouse, carefully keeping their distance from
each other. Julia walked a few feet behind them,
disheartened by the turn of events.

Vowing to unravel the mysteries behind Sam's
troubled state by the end of the day, Julia stepped
back into the schoolhouse. She wasn't exactly certain what she would do, but she knew she couldn't
sit back and watch Sam's problems continue to
escalate.

The rest of the afternoon dragged by slowly.
The children, restless and buzzing with excitement
about the fight during lunch, were hard to control.
And the atmosphere bristled with unspoken tension

between Daniel and Sam, even though they did not dare look at each other under Julia's watchful eye.

After dismissing school for the day, Julia sent Kate home with her auburn-haired friend, little Maggie O'Neill. Then she settled down at her desk, grading the work of her older students, while Sam and Daniel washed the chalkboards.

At the end of the hour, Julia looked up from her work. The chalkboards were sparkling, even though the boys were still glaring at each other. "You've done a good job this afternoon, boys, but I hope you realize that you could have avoided staying after school. Next time try to solve your differences more peacefully."

Daniel studied the toes of his shoes. "Yes, ma'am."

Sam remained silent, his mouth set in a hard line.

Still troubled over the dissonance, Julia gathered up her belongings to leave. The boys would be walking home in the same direction, and there was too much discord between them for Julia to feel comfortable with sending them off together. "Run on home, Daniel. I'll see you in the morning."

"Yes, Miss Julia."

As Daniel shot out the door, Julia turned to Sam, hoping a few moments of privacy would prompt the boy to open up to her. "Do you have anything you want to tell me about what happened today, Sam?"

His gaze was hollow, his eyes vacant. "You said you saw the whole thing, Miss Julia."

"Yes, but I'd like to hear your side of the story."

"It all started when Daniel saw me eating those stupid biscuits you'd left under the tree." He scowled. "I ain't never gonna do that again, not even if I'm—"

He stiffened, obviously realizing he was saying more than he should. Julia's heart rolled over. She kneeled down to meet his troubled gaze. "Sam, everybody gets hungry, especially growing boys like you. And you've got to eat enough to keep up your strength."

"I'm strong enough," he insisted. "But I ain't ever gonna let Daniel see me eatin' nothing of yours again."

Julia sighed. "Then maybe I should talk with your mother and remind her to pack something for your lunch every morning."

He went rigid. "Ain't my ma's fault that I ain't been bringing my lunch. It's . . . it's my fault. I just can't remember to bring it." Gulping, he paused. His brave facade suddenly crumbled as he glanced up at her, eyes wide with worry. "You ain't really gonna talk to my ma, are you, Miss Julia?"

She blinked back the moisture brimming in her eyes. Reaching out, she tousled the boy's thatch of red hair. She longed to press him to her breast and soothe all those hidden hurts and fears, to wipe away all the fright in his voice and eyes. "I just don't want you to be hungry, Sam. And I don't want you fighting with Daniel anymore, either."

His chin jutted with defiance. "I wouldn't have hit him if he hadn't been saying such mean things about my ma."

"Why do you think Daniel would say all those things about your mother?"

He swallowed convulsively, as if he were trying to get rid of a lump in his throat. "Not too many folks got anything nice to say about Ma." Turning, he shrugged. "I gotta get home, Miss Julia."

Inhaling a deep, steadying breath, she turned and set out in the opposite direction. She was still mulling over Sam's plight by the time she reached

Hopewell House. Distracted by her thoughts, she
sauntered over the walkway leading up to the
front door. It wasn't until she reached the steps
that she realized something was different about
the house. Looking down at her feet, she stopped
in her tracks.

Freshly cut planks of lumber had replaced the
old porch steps. The new boards were sturdy and
straight, a sharp contrast to the original, warped
risers. Kneeling, Julia ran her fingers over the raw
wood, silently admiring the workmanship when a
familiar voice broke into her thoughts.

"Think it'll pass your inspection?"

She looked up at Tyler, praying her face would
not betray the emotions reeling through her. Just
gazing at the man sent her pulse soaring through
her veins.

Never had he looked more handsome. Something
about the way the dappled sunlight splayed over
his long, lean form jolted her to the core. He was
standing on the porch, leaning against a white Doric
column, hammer in hand. The tousled waves of his
hair looked as though they had been brushed by the
wind. And a hint of a smile played on his lips, as if
he were pleased to catch her admiring his handi-
work.

"If you're fishing for a compliment, you don't
have to bait me," she insisted as lightly as she could.
"The new steps look wonderful. I don't know of
anyone who could have done a better job."

"Then you're easier to fool than I'd thought, lady."
Tyler motioned for Julia to step aside, then pulled
up one of the planks from the steps.

Julia stepped back in surprise. "You're not finished?"

"A few of the boards need to be planed. Then
I'll hammer the steps into place and paint them."

With quick, efficient movements, he set a wooden plane over the board and glided the tool over the raw wood, slicing off the uneven edges.

"You really know what you're doing," she commented thoughtfully. "Are you a carpenter by trade?"

"Hardly." He continued working. "But I learned a lot about woodworking from a master craftsman when I was growing up."

"From . . . your father?" she guessed.

"No, Pa wasn't much of a carpenter." His hands stilled. "Actually, my father wasn't around long enough to teach me anything. The last time I saw him, I was about Sam's age. He was sitting in a jailhouse cell in Tennessee, locked up for murder." Lines of anguish marred his face. "And Ma . . . well, by then, she'd already disappeared."

"Oh, Tyler." Julia's heart wrenched as she imagined the sorrow and confusion he'd endured as a child. "I'm so sorry—"

His head snapped up. "Don't feel sorry for me, Julia. There are lots of kids in this world who don't have the good fortune of being raised by two loving parents. And I was more fortunate than most. At least I had a place to live after the sheriff locked up my pa. A man by the name of John Osborne took me in a few days after my pa went to jail."

"The same man who taught you to work with your hands?"

Nodding, Tyler ran his fingers over the wooden plane, and gazed down at the tool for a long moment. His eyes clouded with distant memories. Setting the tool over the rough wood, he resumed his work. "John owned an inn and tavern in Chattanooga. His boy—and his wife—died with the fever a few years before I came to live with him."

"I'm sure you filled an empty void in his life."

"No, I was just a pair of hands to help him around the place." Tyler's eyes grew cold and hard. "It was strictly a business arrangement, Julia. He needed some help with the inn and tavern; I needed a place to live. Old John made sure I always had something to eat, a roof over my head, shoes on my feet. He even saw to my schooling. He couldn't read—or write, for that matter—but he insisted I needed an education to get by in this world."

His hands tightened over the plane. "But he attached a price to his generosity. The man was a slave driver who worked me from dawn until well after dark, even when I was as young as Sam. And anything less than perfection sent him into fits of outrage. Yes, he taught me how to repair everything from broken wagon wheels to rotting porch steps, but if I made one mistake, I knew I could expect a thrashing. He was an unforgiving sort, without a kind word for anyone—especially me."

"The loss of his wife and son must have made him a very bitter man," Julia mused.

"And I think he resented me, too. Looking back, I think he believed his own son should have been the one working beside him—and not me." He paused. "Yet, in spite of all his flaws, he showed me how to survive in this world. When the damn Yanks practically destroyed everything I owned during the War, I had to draw on every skill he'd ever taught me. Plank by plank, nail by nail, I had to rebuild my life . . ."

He shoved the plane across the rough lumber with quick, angry strokes, as if he were taking out his frustrations on the raw wood. She watched him in silence for a few moments, agonizing for the lack of love in his life as a young boy, wishing he would tell her more. But he remained silent, intent on his work.

She didn't realize that a frustrated sigh had escaped from her throat until Tyler glanced up at her sharply. "Problems at school today?"

Julia nodded wearily. "I'm afraid so. Sam got into a fight during lunch. One of the boys was bad-mouthing his mother . . . and Sam just couldn't handle it."

The grating stopped. Tyler's fingers tightened over the wooden plane. "Did he . . . get hurt?"

"He's got a whale of a shiner, but I think his pride was hurt more than anything else. The other boy fared worse, it seemed. Daniel ended up with a bloody nose and a ripped shirt."

Tyler placed the smooth-shaven plank in position on the steps and scowled. "I hope to God their fathers have the sense to tan their little hides when they get home."

"Unfortunately, I don't think Sam has ever met his father. And I suspect there may be more to Daniel's accusations about Mrs. Springer than Sam would dare to admit. Daniel claims Sam's mother isn't even living at home anymore. If it's true, that means Sam is living by himself." She drew in a shuddering breath. "I can't bear the thought of that child trying to survive by himself. And I'm not going to let him go hungry for one more day." Pursing her lips together, she turned to leave. "When Aunt Odelphia and Aunt Dorinda return from their walk, please tell them that I'll be home in time for dinner."

"Damn it all to hell," Tyler growled.

Julia had taken only two steps across the yard when Tyler took off after her. "What in the hell do you think you're doing?" he demanded, grabbing her arm and whirling her around to face him.

She boldly met his gaze. "I'm going to pay a visit to Mrs. Springer and get to the bottom of this mystery about Sam. I'm going to find out why he hasn't been getting enough to eat, why he doesn't take a bath, why he's been so sad and worried."

"Hellfire, Julia, you can't just barge into someone's house and make demands like that! It's none of your damn business how your students are treated at home."

"Why not? I'm Sam's teacher, and his performance at school is suffering. If that isn't my business, I don't know what is." She jerked away from his hold. "Now, if you'll excuse me, I have to hitch up the buggy."

"If you think you're going to traipse into some lady's house by yourself and demand an explanation for the way she's been treating her son, you got another think comin', woman," Tyler mumbled, stomping along beside her.

"Do you have a better suggestion?" she snapped back.

"Yeah, I do." He hurled open the barn door. "If you want to save this kid's soul and take your chances of getting blasted out the door by his mother, it's fine with me. But you're not going to stick your pretty little neck out all by yourself."

She blinked in confusion. "I'm not?"

"No, goddammit, because I'm going with you." He snapped the reins over the horse. "And let's get the hell out of here before I change my mind."

She's not your responsibility, Tyler told himself repeatedly as the buggy rattled down the road. Clenching the reins, he stared straight ahead and tried to ignore the touch of Julia's shoulder jostling against his each time they hit a rut in the road.

No, he wasn't responsible for Julia Carey. And he could not care less about the blasted kid who was the cause of all her worries. He should've let her embark on her little mission of mercy all alone. She didn't need to be poking her nose into something that was none of her concern. And he didn't need to be helping her cause.

Yet the thought of Julia walking into a potentially explosive situation—alone—made his gut churn. She was too innocent, too naive, to realize that Sam's mother might not welcome her with open arms. And too preoccupied with her concerns about the boy's troubles to consider her own safety. For God's sake, the woman could greet Julia at the door with a loaded shotgun!

The shriek of a steam whistle pierced the air, jolting Tyler from his thoughts. "What in the hell was that?"

"Nobel's Foundry." Julia pointed to a large building up ahead of them. "People around here set their clocks by that whistle. During the War, the foundry was the busiest place in town, making cannons for the Confederacy. Lots of folks depend on the foundry for their livelihood, but thankfully, they're busy making things other than Confederate arms now."

Following Julia's directions, Tyler veered the buggy through the town's bustling commercial district. He'd heard Sherman had burned most of the business and industrial sections of Rome, but it appeared the town had quickly rebuilt itself. The level of activity along the busy waterfront surprised him, even though he was well aware that Rome had been the center of commerce for North Georgia before the War.

Located in the heart of the Cotton Belt at the junction of three rivers, the city was the farthest inland point in the state that could be reached by riverboat. The Coosa River, formed by the union of the Etowah and Oostanaula rivers at Rome, had flowed heavily with traffic when cotton had been king of the South.

Though Tyler had visited the town's telegraph office, he hadn't seen much of the city during his stay in Rome. Now, taking in the sights, he was impressed by the town's adjustments to life after the War. Broad Street, bordering the Oostanaula River, was teeming with merchants and customers. Numerous vessels lined the wharfs along the riverfront, and crews were busy loading cargo from the docks.

What he didn't like were the men's crude stares and lewd glances directed at Julia as they rode past the docks. Suddenly filled with a surge of possessiveness, he tightened his grip on the reins.

The sweet lilt of Julia's voice soothed his raging thoughts. "Sam lives just around this corner." She pointed to a row of shacks beside the river.

Tyler's throat constricted as they pulled up to the ramshackle building. The place looked as though it had been pieced together with materials that had been discarded by previous owners. It appeared more like an abandoned fishing shack than a dwelling. "Are you sure this is the place?"

She nodded weakly. "I knew it would be bad, Tyler. But I never dreamed it would be like this . . ."

"It's not too late to leave."

She lifted her chin with determination, and Tyler knew she was focusing her thoughts on Sam. "We've come this far. It's pointless to go back now."

The stench of dead fish and rotting food assaulted them as they approached the building. "Most animals have better homes than this," Tyler muttered, silently cursing the injustices of life. No human should have to live in such a wretched place.

Julia drew in a deep breath and rapped on the door, which was warped and rotting. "Mrs. Springer, it's Julia Carey, Sam's teacher."

Silence was the only response. Tyler stepped closer to the door as Julia knocked for the second time. "Mrs. Springer?" she repeated.

She was getting ready to knock again when a whimper penetrated the stillness. Julia's hand froze in midair. "Did you hear that?" she whispered.

Nodding, Tyler shoved the door open. After motioning for Julia to remain by the entrance, he steeled himself and stepped inside. Slivers of sunlight from the open door allowed him to survey the dark interior.

It was a dungeon of filth and grime, a revolting pit of emptiness and despair, void of furnishings or any sign of life. Nausea jolted Tyler's stomach at the stench permeating the tiny, windowless room. He closed his eyes, grimacing, just as a tiny, frightened voice pierced through him.

"Wh-Wh-Who's th-th-there?"

Hearing Sam's frightened cry, Julia burst into the shack. "Sam, where are you?"

Something rustled in the corner, and Sam's white face peered out from the edge of a tattered quilt. "M-Miss-s-s J-Julia . . . is it . . . is it . . . really you?" His eyes were wide with fright, his voice choked and strained.

Julia flew to the boy's side. Kneeling, she pulled Sam into her arms and crushed him to her chest. "Yes, Sam. It's really me. And Mr. McRae came with me to check on you. Everything is going to be fine."

"B-B-But m-m-my ma . . ."

"Is your mother here?"

"No." The child flinched. "No—nobody's here except m-m-me."

"And your mother? Do you know where she is?" Julia's voice was as soft and warm as a spring breeze.

"I-I-I . . . haven't seen her . . . in t-two w-w-weeks." Finally releasing the turmoils and fears rolling inside of him, Sam burst into tears and buried his face in Julia's chest.

"There, there, now," she crooned, rocking him like a baby. "We'll find your mother, Sam. Do you have any idea where she might be?"

He lifted up his tear-streaked face, sniffling. "I th-think sh-she l-l-left t-t-town . . ." His voice breaking, he buried his face in her chest once again.

Watching it all, Tyler felt like someone had driven an axe through his chest. For a fleeting instant he actually thought he was going to vomit.

Tyler covered his eyes with his forearm, and the nausea subsided as quickly as it had arrived. But the hollow, sickening feeling remained, piercing deep into his soul. Tyler wanted to run, wanted to hide, wanted to forget he'd ever set foot in this godforsaken place.

He squeezed his eyes shut, trying to block out the long-forgotten memories that suddenly became all too vivid. It seemed as though he were reliving his own life all over again. For Christ's sake, he had been exactly Sam's age when . . .

"And you've been here . . . by yourself . . . the whole time?" Julia was asking.

"I-I-I didn't want to t-t-tell you, M-M-Miss Ju-Julia. Didn't want anybody to know. I know she'll come back. She will. She didn't mean to leave me here by myself. I know it's all a mistake . . ."

The denial was all too familiar to Tyler, ripping deep into the well of emptiness inside him. Putting on a brave front for all the world to see wasn't easy, he knew. Especially when you were dying inside.

One day the boy would learn, Tyler acknowledged to himself. One day soon, Sam would wake up and realize that his mother was never coming back, that his world would never be the same again. He'd find out that families and love brought nothing but pain and heartache.

Tyler shuddered, unable to contain the emotions roaring through him. "Dammit, boy! Why in the hell didn't you let somebody know that your ma ran out on you?" His voice sounded harsh, even to his own ears. "Why didn't you tell Miss Julia?"

"B-Because every day I th-thought Ma would be c-c-coming b-back," Sam stuttered. "B-B-But sh-she didn't come back, and I-I-I didn't know what to do."

"Well, we know what we can do about your situation now, Sam." Rising, Julia pulled the young boy to his feet. "You're going home with Mr. McRae and me. We're taking you back with us to Hopewell House right now."

Chapter 11

All the way home, Julia was acutely aware of the stiffness in Tyler's shoulders, the hard set of his jaw, the tight grip of his hands on the reins. Though he spoke not a word, his stony silence revealed much more than words could convey. Every movement, every expression, every action, shouted of anger.

She suspected Tyler's rage stemmed from his concern for Sam's welfare. Although he would never admit to caring for the boy, it was obvious that Sam's living conditions had appalled him.

Still, Julia was puzzled by Tyler's gruffness with the child. He'd been extremely harsh with Sam for not telling anyone about his mother's disappearance, and his brusque treatment of the frightened child irritated Julia. Couldn't Tyler see that the boy was obviously terrified? Didn't he know that Sam was trying to protect his mother, clinging to his last bit of pride?

She looked over at Tyler, who was staring straight ahead to the road. Then her gaze dropped to the little boy wedged between them on the buggy seat. And what she saw made her ache inside.

The differences between the two males were obvious. One was a boy, the other a man. Nearly twenty years separated them in age. Sam's freckled face and red hair bore no resemblance to Tyler's olive complexion and dark features.

But the two were more alike than either would dare admit. Both of them despised that supple, precarious side of themselves, and they fought to conceal their emotions beneath a tough outer shell. Even now their expressions were almost identical, full of anger, bitterness, and rage.

Julia heaved a troubled sigh. Was there more to Tyler's anger than merely seeing Sam's deplorable living conditions?

The buggy rolled to a stop in front of Hopewell House, jarring Julia from her thoughts. Tyler and Sam bolted down from the seat, glaring at each other. Julia wished there could be a bit of trust between the surly pair. But in her heart, she knew that was only wishful thinking. They were too much alike, sharing an animosity that wedged insurmountable obstacles between them. She could only hope the troubled man and frightened boy could find peace within themselves during their stays at Hopewell House.

"I ain't gonna take my clothes off in front of you!"

Standing beside the copper tub that Julia had just filled with hot water, Sam crossed his arms over his chest and jutted out his chin with a defiant toss of his head.

"Believe me, Sam, I'm not thrilled about this, either." Julia picked up a towel and handed it to him. "After you take off your clothes, wrap this towel around your waist and get into the tub. I'll wash your hair, and you can take care of the rest."

"And if I don't?"

"Then you won't be eating dinner with us." Withholding food from a starving child was the last thing Julia wanted to do, but she would not allow the boy to sit down at the dinner table covered with dirt and grime from head to toe.

His eyes, red and bloodshot, were full of suspicion and doubt. "If I don't do what you say, you'll kick me out of here, won't you?"

"No, Sam, I won't make you leave Hopewell House," Julia answered quietly. "Starting tonight, this is your home for as long as you want to stay or need a place to live. But living here means you have to obey our rules, like sitting down at the table with clean hands and washing up before you eat. All of us have rules to go by so we can live together, sweetheart. If you can't abide by the rules, you'll have to be punished for your actions. But I promise I will never send you away from here just because you don't follow my instructions."

He gulped. "You won't?"

She tousled his hair affectionately. "I promise, Sam. This is your home now, just like it's mine. And I promise to take care of you as long as you're here. You'll always have a warm bed and plenty of food. You won't have to worry about those things anymore by yourself."

Some of the tension disappeared from Sam's shoulders, but a trace of skepticism remained. Julia hoped she had eased some of his insecurities. Adjusting to life at Hopewell House might take some time for Sam, she knew, but she was prepared to deal with the consequences of opening her home to the young boy. And she would do everything within her power to keep Sam from having to fend for himself again.

Out of respect for Sam's modesty, she turned her back while the boy disrobed and stepped into the tub. Though he fussed and fumed as Julia scrubbed the dirt from his hair, he was careful not to squirm and lose his grip on the towel that was strategically draped over his lap.

After rinsing the dirty water from his hair with a fresh bucket of warm water, Julia handed a bar of lye soap to Sam and placed another towel on a chair beside the tub. "When you're finished, wrap up in the dry towel. I'll be back in a few minutes."

Sam was standing awkwardly by the tub, clutching the towel around his thin waist, when she returned to the room a few moments later. He looked up, his eyes widening in surprise, as Julia held up a pair of clean trousers and a muslin shirt.

"Those aren't my clothes, Miss Julia."

"They're yours now. They may not be new, but they're clean and serviceable. And I think they'll just fit you, too."

"But where . . ." Sam frowned in confusion. "Where did you get them, Miss Julia? You don't have any other boys my age living here."

"Oh, let's just say I have connections with the right people." Julia smiled, grateful to Odelphia and Dorinda for their thoughtfulness. As soon as the ladies had learned about Sam's plight, the dear souls had scurried to the church, rummaged through the baskets of used clothing maintained by the ladies' auxiliary for the poor and needy, and returned with two sets of clothing for a boy of Sam's size.

At the dinner table, the senior Hopewell sisters doted over Sam's freshly scrubbed face and hair. But the boy was too busy eating to respond to their compliments with anything other than brief nods. Tyler, like Sam, had little to say during the

meal, and quickly excused himself as soon as he
had eaten.

It was nearly dark by the time Julia had the
chance to step out on the verandah for a breath of
fresh air. Odelphia and Dorinda sat contentedly in
a pair of wicker rockers, chatting about the events
of the evening, as Julia sat down beside them.

"I hope you don't mind that I brought Sam home
with me today," she began slowly.

After listening to Julia's descriptions of Sam's horrid living conditions, Odelphia shuddered. "Heavens, Julia, you had no choice but to take the boy
away from that miserable place."

"His mother ought to be ashamed for the way
she's neglected that poor child." Dorinda munched
on an oatmeal cookie.

"I'm glad you found some clean clothes for him."
Julia shuddered at the memory of the pungent odor
that reeked from the boy's threadbare trousers and
shirt. "I intend to burn his old clothes tomorrow."

"He looked like a different person after you got
him cleaned up tonight," Dorinda remarked.

"You should see him, now that he's asleep. He
looks like an innocent little angel with his flaming
red hair and freckled face," Julia mused softly.

"Poor little fella probably hasn't had a good
night's sleep in weeks." Odelphia shook her head
in dismay. "As far as I'm concerned, he can stay
here with us as long as he needs to."

The two sisters soon retired for the night, leaving
Julia alone with her thoughts. She was still sitting
on the verandah, musing over the events of the
day, when Tyler stepped out on the porch.

At the sight of him, Julia's breath caught in her
throat. Would the man never cease to make her
heart race each time she looked at him? His
long, lean frame, silhouetted by the moonlight,

was imposing and powerful. His chiseled features seemed rugged and intriguing. The dark waves of his hair, spilling over the collar of his shirt, sparkled like ebony.

He propped one shoulder against a white Doric column. "Sam asleep?"

Julia nodded. "He was tired, I'm afraid. He fell asleep almost as soon as his head hit the pillow."

"And is he sleeping . . . in your bed?"

She glanced up at him sharply. "And what if he is? Do you really care where Sam sleeps?"

He pulled away from the porch column, his face tightening. "Look, Julia, I don't give a damn about that kid. He means nothing to me. But you didn't have to give him your bed, for God's sake! You didn't even have to bring him home with you. You could have made some other arrangements for him."

"Like what?" Rising, Julia swept across the porch and boldly stepped up to Tyler. "Should I have dropped him off at the docks and hoped some nice riverboat captain would give him a job?"

"Of course not," he snarled. "But there must be other alternatives for kids like him. Doesn't this town have a poorhouse . . . or an orphanage? Isn't there some childless couple who would have been willing to take him in?"

She caught her lower lip between her teeth, wondering why Tyler did not approve of bringing Sam to Hopewell House. "It won't hurt me to sleep in Kate's room for a while. I don't want Sam to be shuffled around like . . . like a piece of unwanted baggage any longer. He's been through enough trauma for a child his age. As far as I'm concerned, he can stay here for as long as he wants."

"You're asking for problems that you don't need," Tyler warned. "Can't you see that kid is nothing but trouble? Have you already forgotten he was responsible for almost destroying your garden the other night?"

"That was an accident, and I don't blame Sam." Julia's anger intensified with each passing second. "I've already told you how I felt about that situation."

"Well, you can't take in every stray person off the streets and expect to support yourself. You've got to use your rooms for paying boarders, Julia! And have you thought about the possible complications of taking in a kid like Sam? He's not your child. You have no legal claim to him. His mother might get furious with you for taking him out of his home!"

"What home? That horrid shanty wasn't a home for Sam, Tyler. It was a place to hide from the rest of the world. And it's obvious his own mother doesn't want him."

"Lots of kids aren't wanted by their parents, and they manage to survive, believe me. Besides, Sam has done all right by himself until now. He's smart, strong. He's not going to get himself into a situation he can't handle."

"But he hasn't done all right by himself, and he hasn't been able to handle his situation. You saw him, Tyler! When we got to his house, he was filthy, starving, terrified . . . and exhausted."

"But you didn't have to take him into your own home. You could have done something else with him. What makes you think you're the one who has to be his savior?"

"I'm not trying to save the world, Tyler. Just one little boy. I'm simply making sure that Sam has a decent place to sleep, some clean clothes, and enough food to eat," Julia countered quietly. "The same as I did for you."

Tyler paled, looking as stunned as if she'd smacked him across the face. Then a flash of regret flicked across his chiseled features. "I don't deserve you, lady." He tenderly grazed his knuckles across her cheek. "But I wish the hell I did."

Then, as if knowing he'd already said too much, he wheeled and stalked into the night.

"Look, Julia!" Skipping ahead of Sam and her sister during their walk home from school the next afternoon, Kate pointed in the direction of the house. "Mr. Tyler is climbing on our roof!"

Surprised, Julia paused as she gazed up at the familiar figure perched on the top of her three-story home. "He didn't mention anything to me about taking a look at the roof today," she mused aloud.

"I'd be scared to death if I were him, standing up there so high." Kate's eyes widened with awe. "Why, he's so far up in the sky, I bet he can reach up and touch the clouds!"

"Don't be silly, Kate," Sam scoffed, scrambling up beside the girl. "You can't touch clouds! And besides, climbin' up on a roof ain't so hard. I could climb up there, too, if I had a mind to."

"I think it's safer to keep your feet on solid ground, Sam," Julia cautioned. "And I'm certain Mr. Tyler is being very, very careful so he won't slip and fall."

"I'd be careful, too," the boy insisted. "If I got on the roof, I wouldn't jump up and down or turn somersaults or anything."

"Still, I don't believe we'll have any reasons for you to climb on top of the house anytime soon." Trying to divert Sam's train of thought, she hastily changed the subject. "You know, I believe Aunt Dorinda might have some nice treats waiting for you in the kitchen. She was planning to bake cookies today."

"Cookies?" Sam licked his lips. "What kind of cookies?"

"Oatmeal with raisins, probably," Kate answered. "That's her favorite. But she also likes molasses cookies and sugar cookies and—"

That was all Sam needed to hear. "Let's go!" he shouted, streaking across the yard.

As the children darted toward the kitchen entrance, Julia sauntered across the front lawn, looking up at Tyler, admiring his supple movements as he worked his way across the steep slope of the roof.

She knew she shouldn't be staring, but she couldn't seem to stop herself. Tyler's work shirt and trousers, drenched with perspiration from the unseasonably warm weather, were clinging to him like a second skin, emphasizing the long, muscular lines of his arms and legs. She was still gawking at him, mesmerized by the cords of muscles flexing beneath his damp clothing, as he descended the ladder.

When he reached the ground, he looked over at her and frowned. "Damn," he muttered. "You're home."

"How nice of you to notice," she shot back, wincing from the sting of his caustic greeting.

"Hell, Julia, I didn't mean . . ." He raked a hand through his hair in frustration. "It's just that I didn't expect you back from school so early. I was hoping I'd be finished with patching the roof by the time you got home."

"You've patched the roof . . . in one afternoon?"

"Not all of it. The job is taking longer than I'd expected. But I suspect I'll be finished in a few more hours." He paused, wiping the sweat from his brow with the back of his hand. "You usually get home later than this, don't you?"

"Yes, but I dismissed school early today. It was as hot as an oven in the schoolhouse this afternoon. The children were restless and uncomfortable, and we weren't getting a lot accomplished." She narrowed her eyes, gazing at him curiously. "I didn't think you'd ever noticed what time I got home from school."

"Oh, I've noticed." A slow, seductive grin sprouted at the corners of his mouth. "There's not too much I don't notice about you," he added meaningfully, his gaze roaming over the length of her mauve gown with blatant approval.

A flame of color scorched her cheeks. "I didn't realize you were planning to patch the roof today," she managed to say, struggling to hold on to her composure beneath the searing heat of his gaze. "But I . . . I genuinely appreciate all you've done."

"Just earnin' my keep, lady." Leaning against the ladder, he rested his arm over one of the wooden rungs. "And I'm just getting started. In the morning I'll take care of stripping off the old wallpaper from the rooms on the top floor. After that, I'll—"

"I don't expect you to do all the work by yourself, Tyler," Julia interrupted. "I'll be available every afternoon after school. And by the end of the week, I'll be free to work on the house every day. Friday is the last day of classes for the spring term."

He stilled. "You mean . . . you intend to work on the house with me?"

"Of course!" She cocked her head to one side. "Does that give you a problem?"

"It's just that I've never worked with a woman before." Reaching out, he skimmed his fingers across the dainty lace trim on the collar of her gown. "But I'll admit the idea appeals to me . . . especially if that woman is you."

The seductive tone of his voice nearly sapped the breath from her lungs. "The idea might not sound so appealing after you've worked with me for a while," she choked out with as much brightness as she could muster. "My students say I'm terribly demanding. A few have even accused me of being a perfectionist."

He seemed amused. "A real slave driver of sorts?"

"Sometimes." A smile blossomed on her lips. "But I'm certain you'll have the opportunity to form your own opinions in the next day or two."

"I've already formed my own opinions about you, Julia." He stepped forward, edging closer to her, brushing his fingers across the fragile chords of her throat. "I already know that your skin is softer than any I've ever touched." His fingers skittered across her mouth, tracing over the bow-shaped curves with a touch as soft as a whisper. "And your lips are sweeter than any I've ever tasted . . ."

"Then I guess . . . I suppose . . ." Gulping for air, she faltered for words. "Then you . . . and I . . . well, we shouldn't have any problem working together, should we?"

Subdued amusement sparkled from his lips and eyes. "I think not," he said, chuckling as she whirled around and raced into the house.

When Julia returned home from school the next afternoon, she pulled out a worn, dove gray gown from the back of her wardrobe. "No sense in ruining a good dress with plaster and paint," she mumbled.

After shrugging out of the high-necked green gown that she'd worn to school, she slipped the threadbare garment over her head and shoved her arms into the long sleeves. Straightening the folds of the full skirt, she peered into the mirror and groaned.

The hem of the dress dangled above her ankles, and the bodice was so tight, she could barely breathe. Struggling to button up the gown, Julia feared she would split the seams if she inhaled a deep breath.

But what other choice did she have? She possessed only a few gowns, and she didn't want to risk the chance of ruining one of the few good pieces in her wardrobe. The dove gray dress might not be appropriate for wearing in public, but it was quite fitting for an afternoon of plastering and painting. "Besides, Tyler won't notice what I'm wearing," she told herself as she headed up to the third floor. "He'll be too busy working to pay any attention to me."

Reaching the hall on the top floor, she caught a glimpse of Tyler, who was standing on a ladder in one of the bedrooms. She paused at the door, amazed by the transformation that had taken place. During the course of the day, Tyler had removed the crumbling wallpaper and patched up the cracks in the walls. Now, perched on top of a ladder, he was plastering the ceiling. A trowel laden with a thick mixture of wet plaster was poised in his hand.

She swept into the room, still admiring the improvements, as he dabbed the plaster into place directly over his head. "I can't believe how much progress you've made today! Maybe you don't need me around here, after all." Laughing, she whirled around, smiling up at him.

He stopped working, gazing down at her with an alarming intensity. Beneath his scathing appraisal, Julia's smile vanished. Just as a hot flush rose to her cheeks, she saw the fresh batch of plaster break away from the ceiling.

"Watch out, Tyler!" she cried.

But the warning came too late. The wet plaster landed on the top of Tyler's head with a splat, seeping into his dark hair and drizzling down the side of his face. "Damn it all to hell!" he roared, leaping down from the ladder and shaking his head furiously.

As the white, gooey mess trickled through the dark waves of his hair and streamed over his cheek, Julia almost choked on her laughter. Trying to bite back a smile, she grabbed a rag and held it up to his face. "Well, maybe you do need me around here," she mused, giggling like a schoolgirl as she wiped off the pasty substance from his cheek.

"And maybe not." He glared at her. "All of this is your fault, you know."

"My fault?" Her smile vanished.

"Yes, dammit! You distracted me. You and that damn gown of yours." He jerked the rag away from her grasp and plunged it through his hair with quick, angry strokes. "It's so damn tight that a man would have to be blind not to notice how it clings to your—"

"My gown is perfectly serviceable," she countered hotly. "Yes, it's a bit snug-fitting, but it's one of my oldest dresses! Did you expect me to wear something new while I'm painting walls and sanding floors?"

"Judas Priest," Tyler muttered in disgust, groaning as he yanked out a clump of plaster from his hair.

Julia stiffened her spine. "It appears we're not going to be able to work together with much success. Perhaps I should concentrate on working on another room while you're finishing up this one."

"Like hell you will," he growled. "As I recall, we agreed to work on these rooms together."

"Then perhaps you'll be able to carry on a decent conversation with me—without using foul language—as soon as you've washed up at the pump."

"And perhaps I'll be able to think straight once you put on another dress!"

"You don't have to yell at me," Julia returned in a wounded tone. "Your message is loud and clear."

After a long moment of silence, Tyler heaved a frustrated sigh. "I don't think you understand, Julia. Your gown isn't the only thing about you that I find distracting. Everything about you is distracting to me." His eyes darkened as he gazed down at her. "I'm distracted by the scent of lilacs that drifts around you like a fragrant spring breeze . . . the sound of your footsteps in the hallway . . . the way your eyes light up when you smile . . ."

Julia's heart pounded in her chest. Even with plaster clinging to his hair, the man could make her pulse race faster than if she'd sprinted across the state of Georgia. Dear heavens, why couldn't she control her emotions when she was around him? And why was she still longing for him to crush her into his arms and—

"Yoo-hoo!" Dorinda called from the stairs. "Ready for some cold lemonade?"

Hearing Dorinda's singsong invitation, Tyler suddenly laughed. "Distractions are quite common at Hopewell House, it seems."

"Comes with the territory, I'm afraid." She grinned. "What else can I say?"

"Julia, Tyler! Your lemonade is getting warm!" Dorinda sang out again.

Tyler threw up his hands in defeat. "Tell Dorinda that I'll be down for some cold lemonade as soon as

I wash up," he said, his mouth twitching with the hint of a smile as he ushered Julia to the door.

Julia took the precaution of wearing a loose-fitting, bibbed apron over her dove gray gown when she joined Tyler on the top floor of the house the next afternoon. Yet, in spite of her efforts to conceal the tight lines of her dress, unspoken tensions bristled through the air.

Though they exchanged pleasantries and shared brief bits of conversation as they worked, Julia became acutely aware that Tyler's eyes were constantly evading hers. He refused to allow his gaze to linger on her for more than a brief second when they were discussing the progress of their renovations. Was she still distracting him from his work?

It was very possible, she thought. At odd moments, he'd been stealing glimpses of her, she knew. Even now, as she brushed the first coat of pale yellow paint over the walls, she could feel his gaze roving over her, could sense the heated passion smoldering from his eyes.

Not until Saturday did Julia realize that she was guilty of stealing glimpses of Tyler, too. Several times, she caught herself gawking at the powerful stretch of his shoulders as he reached up to paint the ceiling. More than once she found herself mesmerized by the endearing way he caught his lower lip between his teeth when he was concentrating on a difficult task. And on a few occasions, she found herself savoring the stolen moments when she could observe him, unnoticed.

It was late in the afternoon when Tyler paused to rinse out his paintbrush. Observing the long length of his fingers running through the bristles, Julia forgot about the brush in her own hand until Tyler looked over at her and chuckled.

"I never realized how becoming yellow is to you," he remarked, biting back a smile.

Julia looked down at her dove gray dress, confused. "But I'm not wearing yellow . . ."

"Oh, but you are. Take a look in the mirror."

Peering at her reflection in the beveled mirror above the fireplace, Julia froze. Splotches of yellow paint covered her cheeks, and her nose was the exact color of a banana. "Oh, for goodness sake!" she muttered, cringing with embarrassment.

Chuckling, Tyler stepped down from the ladder and joined her beside the mirror.

"This isn't funny!" Julia moaned, furiously scrubbing her nose with a rag. Hearing another chuckle from Tyler, she glared at him. "And besides, you're the one to blame for this mess!"

"Me?" His eyes widened incredulously. "What in the hell have I done?"

"All kinds of things," she snapped, rubbing the rag against her cheeks. "Like flexing your muscles. Biting your lower lip. And looking at me when you thought I wasn't watching! Good heavens, with all that going on around me, how could I concentrate on painting?"

"So I was . . . distracting?" He flashed a wry smile.

"No." She stilled. "Yes."

"Yes?"

"Yes!" she spat out.

His grin broadened, emitting a devilish charm.

Horrified by her own admissions, Julia turned back to the mirror. She resumed scrubbing her face, grateful the heated flush in her cheeks was hidden beneath the yellow smears.

Four days later, Odelphia stood in the middle of the parlor with a bewildered expression on her face. "Now, where did I put those handbills we made up?" Squinting, she gazed around the room.

"Just where you left them." Dorinda waddled up to her sister and shoved a stack of papers into her hand. "Honestly, Odie, you'd lose your head if it wasn't attached to your neck. Did you ever find your spectacles this morning?"

"No, and I've looked everywhere."

"I imagine it's hard to look for your spectacles when you can't see to find them," Julia interrupted, coming up behind the ladies.

"Well, we can't go to the train station and put up these notices about Rome's newest boardinghouse until Odie finds her spectacles," Dorinda grumbled.

Julia quietly pulled out her aunt's spectacles from the pocket of her apron. "Perhaps this might help."

Odelphia smiled as she perched the wire-framed glasses on the end of her nose. "Now, where on earth did you find these, Julia?"

Julia grinned. "Would you believe the fireplace mantel in your room?"

"Oh, my." Odelphia's wrinkled face reddened with embarrassment. "Well, I guess I need to be more careful . . ."

"Especially if we're going to have all these strangers staying in our house," Dorinda noted with a frown.

"Now, Dorie, you know it won't be as bad as you make it sound," Odelphia cautioned. "You admitted it would be nice to have a lot of folks in the house again. And having Tyler and Sam here has been rather pleasant, hasn't it?"

"Well, I suppose so . . ." Dorinda conceded as she fell into step beside her sister.

As the two ladies headed for the train station, Julia could hardly contain her excitement. Hopewell

House was officially opening for boarders this afternoon! Finally, it looked as though all her hopes and dreams for the house would be coming true. Two of the rooms on the top floor would be ready for guests within a few hours.

And most of the credit belonged to a man named Tyler McRae, Julia conceded. His skillfulness with his hands far exceeded all of her expectations. There seemed to be nothing the man could not do. He could saw and hammer and plaster and paint as if he were born to it. As she worked side by side with him, her admiration for his talents and skills had increased with each passing day.

And her wayward thoughts had intensified, as well, she reminded herself with a grimace. She constantly wondered what it would be like to run her fingers through his hair, feel the hungry taste of his lips on hers again . . .

Forcing herself to set aside the disturbing thoughts, Julia climbed the stairs to the third floor. "Enough of this foolishness," she scolded herself.

In the yellow bedroom, Julia positioned a ladder by the window, hiked up her skirts, and stepped up on the rungs. Then she stretched her arms up over her head and placed a wooden rod holding a pair of faded drapes over the window frame. Though she longed for some new curtains to brighten up the room, the faded ones would have to do for now.

Stepping down from the ladder, she folded her arms over her chest and surveyed the room with a critical eye. Amazing what a bucket of paint could do, she thought. The soft yellow color was cheery and bright, chirping up the room with a welcoming hue.

At that moment, Tyler came up behind her. "Looks pretty damn good, wouldn't you say?"

She whirled around to face him. "No, I wouldn't exactly express my feelings like that." A shy smile played on her lips. "But I would say it looks wonderful, almost like a different place."

"If you think this room seems different, take a look over here," he invited, heading toward the second room.

Julia followed his lead, surprised to find that Tyler had already started applying the final coat of paint to the walls. The powder blue hue gave a light, airy feeling to the area, and Julia could not have been happier with the results. If possible, this room was even more inviting than the first one.

"I'm glad you suggested this color." She picked up a brush and dipped the bristles into the tin bucket. Only one wall remained to be painted with a second coat, and she was anxious to help. "You've accomplished a lot this morning. In fact, you've accomplished more around here in the last week than I ever dreamed possible."

He shrugged. "I've always liked doing this kind of work. But I appreciate it more now, after spending a couple of years with the First Tennessee. I'd much rather be fixing up houses than shooting at Yanks."

Julia's paintbrush slowed to a halt. Part of her was relieved he hadn't been with the Union, fighting against the very ground she loved. But another part of her was filled with curiosity about Tyler's experiences on the battlefield. "You must have seen a lot of action," she commented as casually as she could manage.

Nodding, he grimaced. "More than I care to remember. Shiloh, Kennesaw Mountain, Nashville, Chattanooga, Chickamauga—"

"Chickamauga?" Julia set down the paintbrush.

"Unfortunately."

She drew in a shaky breath. "My brother—and my fiancé—were at Chickamauga, too. Both of them served with the Fifteenth, Georgia, Benning's Brigade. That battle changed everything about my life." She swallowed convulsively. "Lucas—my half brother—has never been the same since fighting at Chickamauga. He's never wanted to settle down or come back home for more than a day or two at a time. And Brent—my fiancé—died on the Chickamauga battlefield."

"This Brent . . . did you love him?"

"Very much. Of course, the last time I saw him was in sixty-one, right at the start of the War. But I loved him as much as any sixteen-year-old could love a man," she admitted quietly. "I'm sure we would have had many good years together, with a house full of children, a life centered around our family. But all of that simply wasn't meant to be."

"It isn't too late for you to have a family of your own, Julia."

"I would like nothing more," she admitted, her voice quivering. "But apparently, marriage isn't for some people . . . like me."

"Why not?" He reached out and grazed his knuckles along her cheek, his expression filled with so much tenderness that her breath caught in her throat. "You sound as though you're repulsive."

Julia frowned. "Oh, I don't think I'm ugly. I'm just not beautiful . . . or elegant . . . like most women."

"Then you haven't looked into a mirror lately, Julia Carey." He whirled her around and positioned her in front of the beveled mirror hanging above the fireplace mantel. Standing behind her, he whispered into her hair. "Can't you see what I see? A woman who is not only beautiful, but desirable? A woman filled with so much beauty and goodness that she radiates with it?"

Could he really see all of that? "It's not just physical things," she tried to explain, her cheeks blossoming with color. He was standing so close that she was certain he could hear the rapid beat of her heart. "It's the fact that I already have responsibilities, obligations to take care of my family. And that doesn't make me the most eligible female in town for marriage. Most women's dowries aren't comprised of two elderly women, a small child, an abandoned boy, and a boardinghouse."

His steady gaze locked with hers in the mirror. "But most women aren't you, Julia. Finding a woman like you is like discovering a lost treasure . . ."

Julia shivered as his fingers moved through her hair and invaded the chignon at her nape. "Your hair is so soft," he murmured, removing one of the pins from the loose coil.

Within seconds, the remaining pins were scattered across the floor, and Julia's hair was streaming down around her shoulders like a tumbling waterfall. "Sweet Jesus, I can't help myself," Tyler whispered thickly, curling his fingers around the long, chestnut strands. "I've been dying to yank out those damn pins from your hair for days. I've been dreaming about—"

The sounds of splintering glass and Kate's screams cut off the rest of Tyler's thought. "Julia, come quick! Sam's been hurt!"

Horrified, Julia whirled around and raced from the room. Tyler followed at her heels, bounding down the stairs and running into the parlor.

Kate, standing by the fireplace, was sobbing hysterically. "Sam's hurt, Julia! He's bleeding!" She pointed at the boy, who was sprawled across the worn floral rug. Shards of glass surrounded him. In his hand were the remains of a broken crystal vase with jagged edges. Streaks of crimson dribbled down his arm.

Julia gingerly tiptoed over the broken pieces of glass and kneeled beside Sam. "Let me see your hand, Sam. It looks as though you've gotten a nasty cut."

The boy jerked away from her touch. "I'm not hurt," he insisted hotly.

"But you've cut yourself!"

He pulled himself upright and shrugged. "Doesn't matter."

"Maybe not, but we need to stop the bleeding. And we need to get the little pieces of glass out of your hand."

"I don't need you to help me," he insisted.

"Then you need to tell me how this happened," Julia returned quietly.

"He was chasing me!" Kate piped in. "He was chasing me through the parlor and— "

"I'm talking with Sam right now, Kate," Julia interrupted. "We'll hear your side of the story in a few moments."

Pouting, Kate shrank back. Julia returned her attention to Sam. "Now, would you care to tell me what happened?"

Defiance and belligerence filled his face. "Kate dared me to catch her. So I chased her. And I knocked over your stupid vase."

"That's not true!" Kate pointed an accusing finger at the boy. "You yanked on one of my hair ribbons. I started running, but you came after me and—"

Sam leaped up, crunching glass beneath him. "You're just trying to get me into trouble, Kate! You don't want me here, and you'll do anything to get rid of me!" His breathing was hard and ragged. "I don't belong here, anyhow. So I guess I might as well leave now, before I get kicked out of this place."

"No one wants you to leave, Sam." Julia grasped Sam's shoulders. "All of us— including Kate—want you to stay here. But as a member of this household, you've got to follow certain rules. We'll be getting boarders soon, and you and Kate can't be running through the house and disturbing our guests. From now on, you and Kate will have to refrain from running inside the house."

"From now on?" Sam blinked in confusion. "You mean . . . you mean you're not going to send me away?"

Julia's throat tightened. She hadn't realized how terrified, how insecure, he still was until this very moment. "Sam, everyone makes mistakes at times. But families don't turn their backs on someone just because he makes a mistake. I'm not going to send you away for running through the house and breaking a vase. But you will have to take responsibility for your actions. You'll have to clean up all this broken glass. And after dinner, I will expect you to help Aunt Odelphia and Aunt Dorinda with the dishes." She glanced over at her sister. "And that goes for you, too, Kate, since you're partly to blame for this."

"Come on, Sam," Kate grumbled, her head hanging low. "I'll show you where to find the broom."

As the two children left the room, Julia looked up at Tyler, who had been standing in the doorway, quietly observing the exchange. He was scowling. "You think I went too easy on Sam, don't you?"

"I would've blistered his hide if he'd broken something belonging to me," he admitted.

"You don't like Sam, do you?"

"I've told you, Julia. Kids and I don't get along."

"But you seem to get along fine with Kate."

"That's different. She's . . . she's just a little girl."

"And Sam's just a little boy," Julia reminded him quietly.

"A little boy who's too rambunctious for his own good."

"Who possibly reminds you of someone you used to know? Maybe someone . . . like yourself?"

"Nonsense. Sam and I have nothing in common," he lied smoothly. But even as he said the words, Tyler grimaced. He could see himself in Sam far more than he was willing to admit, even to himself. "He needs to be disciplined with a stern hand."

"In time, disciplining the boy with a whack across the seat of his pants might be appropriate on occasion. But right now, I think he needs to be disciplined with love."

"Love?" Tyler scowled. "What makes you think love will do any good?"

"Because love is the most powerful force I know. Love can fill the void, wipe away the emptiness, in a broken heart. It can be the mother who will never abandon you, the father who will never abuse you. Love can step in for the mother who never held you, the father who was never around to encourage you."

Something tight and restricting gripped Tyler's chest, crushing down on him like a heavy weight. He'd never known love like she was describing, never expected to find it.

But at that moment, he knew it existed.

Julia Carey was all the proof he needed. He could see it shimmering from the depths of her eyes, hear it in every word, every breath, that escaped from her lips. And he wanted nothing more than to crush her into his arms and fill his empty, hollow soul with all the love she could offer. Hell, he'd give his left arm for just one night of love by this ethereal angel.

Trying to ignore the gnawing ache in the depths of his heart, he planted a rakish grin on his lips. "But your definition doesn't include the kind of love that exists between a man and a woman, Julia."

"Why, everything I said about love can apply to two adults who are—"

He pulled her into his arms and clamped his mouth over hers, cutting off the rest of her thought. Claiming possession of her like a primitive savage, he ground his lips against hers, plunging his tongue inside of her mouth with a desperate urgency. Feeling her melt beneath the pressure of his hot, hungry kisses, he squeezed his eyes shut. Sweet Jesus, how much longer could he resist taking all of her? He was burning to explore all those secret, forbidden places hidden beneath her constricting garments.

Common sense suddenly invaded his tumultuous thoughts. *Stop, McRae*, he warned himself. *Much more of this, and you'll scare her off . . .*

He reluctantly ended the kiss. "That's physical love," he insisted, his voice husky and low. "It's hot, scorching, openmouthed kisses that leave you reeling for days. It's endless nights of passion and—"

She placed a trembling finger over his lips, silencing him. "I don't need to hear any more, Tyler." She tried to smile. "I've already learned more than I need to know."

At that moment Sam's voice rang through the house. "Miss Julia, my hand is bleeding again!"

"Pardon me." There was a reluctance, a shyness,

about her as she pulled back her hand. "Duty calls, I fear."

As she quietly slipped away to tend to Sam's cut, Tyler closed his eyes and sighed. "Damn it all to hell," he muttered, savoring the scent of lilacs still lingering around him.

Chapter 12

Julia carefully inspected the cuts on Sam's hand, plucked out one small shard of glass imbedded in his palm, then cleansed and bandaged the wound. Sam scowled and winced during the entire procedure, but recovered with remarkable speed. By the time he had cleaned up the remains of the broken vase from the parlor floor, he was acting as though he'd completely forgotten about the fresh bandage wrapped around his hand.

"Come on, Kate," he invited, motioning for the girl to join him. "Let's go back outside so I won't break anything else in the house."

Kate reluctantly trailed after the boy. "Just as long as you don't pull out my hair ribbons anymore," she warned.

"Don't worry," Sam assured her. "I'm never gonna touch your hair ribbons again! Those things get me in too much trouble."

Kate giggled, breaking the tension and prompting a grin from Sam. As the children scampered outside, Julia picked up her skirts and headed up the stairs. Tyler's familiar whistle drifted from the third floor.

She paused. A sudden longing swamped her, a yearning so intense that an ache filled her chest. She closed her eyes, trying to block out the searing memories of their reflections in the mirror, the way his hands had plunged through her hair, the strange tremblings of desire that had coursed through her as he'd branded her lips with his own.

Every instinct she possessed warned her that a relationship with Tyler McRae was not meant to be. But she wished—oh, how she wished—things could be different.

Tyler and Julia worked together for the rest of the day, preparing the two freshly painted rooms for boarders. After retrieving two bedroom suites from the attic, they arranged the furniture in each of the two rooms.

As Tyler positioned a cherry dresser between the two windows in the yellow bedroom, one of the drawers rattled open. Inside the drawer was a velvet-lined brass case containing a small tintype. The image revealed a man with a clean-shaven jaw and a stern expression on his face.

Tyler picked up the case from the drawer just as Julia came up behind him. Peering over his shoulder, she gazed fondly at the framed image. "That's Lucas, my half brother. It's a wonderful likeness of him, though he's usually smiling instead of frowning. As I recall, he wasn't too thrilled about posing for the photographer."

Tyler studied the image for a moment before handing over the case to Julia. "Your brother appears to be quite a bit older than you," he observed.

"Lucas is fifteen years my senior. His mother—Papa's first wife—died when Lucas was a child. But my own mother couldn't have loved him more than her own flesh and blood." She paused, gazing down at the tintype. "And I can see why. Lucas bears a striking resemblance to Papa. Even more so, in recent years. I fear the War aged my dear brother a great deal."

"The War took its toll on a good many men," Tyler agreed somberly.

After a final glance at the photograph, Julia closed the brass case over the tintype. She had just slipped the case into her pocket when Dorinda entered the room.

"Oh, my." Dorinda's voice was watery and nostalgic as she gingerly fingered the cherry dresser against the wall. "You've found Mama and Papa's bedroom suite."

"I believe Grandmother and Grandfather Hopewell would be pleased to know that we're putting their furniture to good use," Julia remarked quietly.

"This is very special furniture." Dorinda gazed at the elaborate wood carvings on the cherry bed. "I was born in this bed. And so was Odelphia and your dear mother, Capitola."

"No wonder it's so very special to you." Julia draped an arm around her aunt's round shoulders. "We'll always keep it in the family, Aunt Dorinda."

Dorinda gave a wistful sigh. "Odelphia and I have always hoped your children will be born in this bed, too."

"Maybe they will be." Julia smiled brightly. "In the meantime, I'm sure our boarders will enjoy the furniture during their visits to Hopewell House."

Her smile seemed forced, strained, Tyler thought. And he knew the reason why. Yet if any woman was born to be a mother, it was Julia Carey. She deserved a house full of children and a family to love more than any female he'd ever known.

"You'll never guess what happened!" Odelphia burst into the room, jarring Tyler from his thoughts.

"We already have our first boarders! A nice young couple with a little boy saw our notice at the train depot—and they're downstairs, wanting to rent a room!"

"My goodness!" Dorinda placed a chubby hand over her throat. "I never dreamed we'd get our first boarders so soon! We only left the handbills at the train station this morning!"

"Must be some passengers from the Atlanta train," Tyler commented. "It was due to pull into town about an hour ago."

"But what are we going to do with them?" Dorinda paled. "The rooms aren't ready! I don't have any pies made and—"

"Why don't you and Aunt Odelphia entertain our guests while Tyler and I finish up here?" Julia suggested. "There will be plenty of time to cook for our boarders while they're getting settled for the night."

"Julia's right," Odelphia insisted. "Come on, Dorie. Let's make our first boarders feel right at home."

As the ladies scurried to the parlor, Julia and Tyler set to work, putting the finishing touches on the room. Since the yellow room containing the cherry bedroom suite was large enough to accommodate additional furniture, they retrieved an iron bed from the cellar and set it up for the young son of the new boarders. Then Julia placed fresh linens on the mattresses while Tyler hung several pictures on the freshly painted walls.

All the while, Tyler felt a current of excitement flowing through him. Working side by side with Julia, transforming the dark, musty-smelling rooms into bright, cheery spaces, Tyler discovered he was enjoying himself as he never had. In fact, he'd never felt the same sense of pride with The McRae.

During the War, Union troops had seized the prosperous hotel to house the injured and dying. Almost overnight, The McRae was transformed from Chattanooga's most opulent hotel into a hospital for wounded soldiers. Thousands of injured Yanks and Rebs had been piled in boxcars and cattle cars and transported to Chattanooga for treatment, especially after the bloody battles of Murfreesboro and Chickamauga in 1863. Located near the train station, The McRae became the city's receiving center for the casualties of battle.

By the time all traces of fighting disappeared from the mountains overlooking Chattanooga, The McRae was in shambles. Tyler worked endlessly to restore the once majestic establishment to its former grandeur. When The McRae reopened in 1866, guests enjoyed elegant reception areas, walnut furnishings in every room, a spacious dining room, barbershops, billiard rooms, saloons, a telegraph office, and a livery stable. With its mansard roof, French doors, and observatory balconies that overlooked a shady lawn filled with flower gardens, The McRae quickly became the social center of Chattanooga.

As Tyler dressed for dinner, he suddenly realized that he had been so caught up in preparing Hopewell House for boarders that he hadn't even thought about his own business in days.

Good God, why should he care about this place? When Odelphia had announced the arrival of the first boarders, he'd felt like jumping for joy. But why did the success of Hopewell House matter so much to him? He had nothing at stake and nothing to gain or lose.

Not even the success of The McRae had produced such an emotional reaction from him. Yes, The McRae was his home, but he'd always viewed it from the cold harshness of profit-and-loss statements. Chattanooga's finest hotel was strictly a money-making proposition to Tyler McRae. Though it had succeeded beyond his wildest dreams, he'd never allowed himself to become emotionally attached to the business.

Yet the thought of welcoming the first boarders to Hopewell House sent a ripple of excitement running down his spine. Unable to comprehend the intensity of his emotions, Tyler was still contemplating his sudden sense of pride in Hopewell House when he stepped into the dining room for dinner.

The new arrivals at Hopewell House, Aaron and Violet Sprayberry, were already seated at the table with their young son when Tyler joined the group for the evening meal. Aaron was a stocky man with a thick neck and receding hairline. Edward, the young boy, had inherited his mother's light hair and pale complexion.

The first thing Tyler noticed about the couple was the differences in their personalities. Violet was timid and withdrawn, while her husband was gregarious and outgoing. Aaron's booming voice and hearty laugh contrasted sharply with his wife's shy smile and soft-spoken ways.

But the couple seemed to be in complete agreement about their accommodations at Hopewell House. As the group retreated into the parlor after dinner, Violet gazed around the house and gave a wistful sigh. "Oh, Aaron, isn't this the most charming house you've ever seen? It's big and roomy—yet warm and cozy at the same time."

"It's quite inviting," Aaron agreed, smiling at his wife as they sat down on an upholstered settee. "But I'm certain our own home will be just as charming."

"Do you plan to settle here in Rome?" Julia asked

conversationally, sitting down in a rosewood chair across from the young couple.

Nodding, Aaron scooped his sleepy-eyed young son into his lap. The boy rested his head on his father's broad chest and closed his eyes. "We plan to spend the next few days looking for a house to rent."

"Aaron has a new job with Nobel's Foundry," Violet added, her face beaming with pride as she gazed at her husband.

"How wonderful!" Dorinda exclaimed.

"We think so, too. We're pleased to be moving here." Aaron drew his son close to his chest and affectionately tousled the boy's thatch of blond hair. "Of course, we plan to build our own house eventually. But until we can purchase some acreage and draw up the plans for our home, we'll need to rent a small house with at least two bedrooms."

"Preferably three," Violet added, almost shyly. She patted her tummy, which was bulging slightly beneath the waistline of her gown. "We'll be needing a nursery around Thanksgiving."

Aaron glanced over at his wife, looking as though he wanted to pull her into his arms and never let her go. Violet leaned forward slightly, as if she were longing to be kissed by her husband. Tyler thought they were acting more like newlyweds than a married couple who were expecting their second child.

Love radiated between the young couple like a shining star, beaming with hope and bright promises for the future. Sitting on the settee with their young son cradled between them, they looked like the perfect portrait of happiness.

A strange, uneasy feeling gnawed in Tyler's gut as he observed the young, starry-eyed couple. Aaron

and Violet Sprayberry might be opposite in their
personalities and looks, he surmised, but their
common bond of love outweighed any differences
between them. It was obvious they shared the kind
of love that would last a lifetime.

"I'm sure Thanksgiving will be special to you
this year," Julia commented quietly. "With a new
baby in the house, you'll have lots to be thank-
ful for."

Her voice was watery and choked. Tyler looked
over at Julia, and what he saw in her expression
made his heart wrench with pain.

Envy.

Julia wanted what the Sprayberrys had. In spite
of her adamant insistence that her mission in life
was to provide for her family, she wanted a husband and a family of her own. It was written in
the slight tremble in her chin, the delicate twist
of her lips, the longing that shimmered from her
overly bright eyes. Her gaze drank in the sight of
the young family and lingered on the slight swell
of Violet's belly, revealing her secret yearnings in
a way that nothing else could.

At that instant, Tyler wished he could be the
one to give Julia her heart's desire, the man who
could fulfill all her hopes and dreams. He wanted
to plant his seed in her, fill her with child, create a
family with her. He wanted to surround her with
love, make all of her dreams come true, fill her life
with the joy she so richly deserved. He wanted
Julia to share his life, his home, his future.

It bewildered him, the strength of his desire for
her. He'd had dozens of women, women far more
sophisticated, women who knew how to satisfy a
man. Yet he didn't want any of those other women.
He wanted Julia.

He raked a hand through his hair in frustration.

Maybe he'd lost part of his brain when he'd been shot on the train. Maybe he should get Doc Kramer to examine his head.

All he knew for certain was that he wanted Julia in his bed, in his arms, in his life. But it went much further than that. On some deep, primitive emotional level, he wanted Julia to want him. He wanted her to need him. He wanted her to believe in him. He wanted her to look at him in the same adoring way that Violet Sprayberry gazed at her husband.

By the time he turned his attention back to the conversation, Violet was asking Julia about Hopewell House. "So have you lived here all of your life?" Violet asked.

"No, not always." Julia forced a smile. "My father was a Methodist minister with a circuit route, and we moved frequently until my sister, Kate, was born. That's when we moved here to live with Aunt Odelphia and Aunt Dorinda."

"Since you're from Atlanta, you might have heard of Julia's father." Odelphia sat primly on an upholstered chair by the fireplace. "He conducted revivals in lots of towns throughout Georgia and Tennessee."

"His name was Reverend Jeremiah Carey," Dorinda noted, her voice and face reflecting her fondness for her late brother-in-law.

"Why, I believe I have heard of the Reverend Jeremiah Carey." Aaron glanced at his wife. "Wasn't that the name of the minister who conducted the tent revival in Marietta last year?"

"It certainly was." Violet directed a shy smile in Julia's direction. "Your father was a wonderful preacher, Julia."

But Tyler didn't hear another word. *The Reverend Jeremiah Carey.*

He rose abruptly from his chair and excused himself from the room.

Damn them all, he thought angrily, stalking up the stairs. Damn the Reverend Carey for getting him into this mess. Damn the Sprayberrys for acting like two love-smitten fools.

And damn Julia for making him aware of the void in his life, the emptiness in his soul that only she could fill.

After escorting the Sprayberrys to their room, tucking Kate and Sam into bed, and cleaning up the kitchen for the evening, Julia was certain she would fall asleep as soon as she slipped into bed. But she tossed and turned for what seemed to be an eternity, tormented by strange stirrings in her heart that would not go away no matter how hard she tried to ignore them. Witnessing the devotion and adoration between Aaron and Violet Sprayberry had rekindled a host of wonderful fantasies that she hadn't dared to dream in a long time.

Restless, she rose from the bed and slipped a robe over her white cotton gown. Careful not to awaken Kate from her slumber, she tiptoed out of the room and went outside.

Standing on the verandah, she inhaled a deep breath. With the sweet fragrance of magnolia blossoms filling her senses, she leaned back against a white Doric column and gazed up into the evening sky. Stars twinkled brightly in the dark Georgia skies, and a half-moon smiled down over the rolling countryside. Just as she felt some of the tension dissipating from her muscles, a familiar voice split through the air.

"What in the hell are you doing out here?" Tyler demanded irritably, stepping out of the shadows.

Startled, Julia straightened, clutching the neckline of her robe to her throat. "I needed a breath of fresh air. It's a bit muggy inside the house, and—"

"Don't lie to me, Julia." The sharp edge in his voice diminished as he gazed down at her, concerned and troubled. "You know damn good and well that you're out here because you couldn't sleep."

"And what about you?" Lines of fatigue were marring his handsome features, she noticed, and shadows were circling his eyes. "Why aren't you in bed at this hour of the night?"

"Because I'm a damn sleepwalker," he snapped. "I always take a stroll at two in the morning."

She winced. "Well, you don't have to get so testy about it."

"Sleepless nights always make me testy," he grumbled, plunging a hand through the dark waves of his hair in frustration. "But I guess I shouldn't be too surprised that you're still awake, considering what happened in the parlor this evening."

She stiffened her spine. "My evening was quite pleasant, thank you. The Sprayberrys are a charming couple, and I enjoyed getting to know them."

"Of course you did. And getting to know them has gotten you so riled up that you can't even sleep." He shrugged. "But then, that's what jealousy can do to a person."

"I am not jealous!" She crossed her arms over her chest and lifted her chin, glaring at him in defiance. "Yes, I admire the Sprayberrys' devotion to each other—and to their child. And yes, I think it's wonderful that they're madly in love with each other—and aren't ashamed to show it. But I am not jealous of them!"

"Well, you sure as hell could have fooled me." He stalked to the edge of the verandah and sat down on the steps. Stretching out his long legs in front of him, he leaned back and leisurely raked his gaze over the length of her. "If you ask me, I think you've been so damn busy tending to everybody else's needs around here that you haven't allowed yourself to think about what *you* want out of life. And seeing the Sprayberrys reminded you about all those things you've been wanting . . . for a very long time."

Julia hugged her arms around her torso more tightly, acutely aware of her inappropriate dress. Yet the accuracy of his observations was just as disturbing to her as the scorching heat of his gaze.

Heaving a sigh of frustration, she leaned back against the white column and closed her eyes. "Well, maybe I was a bit envious of the Sprayberrys," she conceded with reluctance. "It would be wonderful to have a relationship like theirs. I've always dreamed of spending the rest of my life with one special man, raising a family together . . ." As her lashes fluttered open, her eyes swam with confusion and doubts. "Is that so much to wish for?"

Tyler's throat constricted. "Not for someone . . . like you."

She crossed the verandah and sat down beside him, arranging the folds of her gown over her legs and hugging her knees to her chest. "You know, my aunts are always insisting I should find some nice, rich man who will take care of us for the rest of our lives—someone who would take on the responsibilities of my family and this wonderful old house, too."

"Not a bad idea, I suppose," Tyler mumbled, vividly aware he wasn't the man they were searching for. Yes, he was rich, but . . . nice? He winced, silently cursing himself for his inadequacies.

"Before the War, I always assumed I would spend the rest of my life with Brent," she continued. "But

I wasn't much more than a child myself at the time. I wasn't old enough to understand what it truly means to love a man the way he should be loved, with total, complete devotion."

She tilted her head back, gazing up into the heavens. "But now I know what I want. I want what the Sprayberrys have . . . a sense of closeness and sharing, of family and devotion . . . a feeling of oneness . . . for all time." Her voice caught in her throat as she turned to him. "Do you know what I'm talking about, Tyler? Have you ever wanted that kind of relationship?"

"Me?" A harsh, bitter laugh rose from his chest. "Don't be ridiculous. I'm not a damn family man. I've never had time for a family. I've been on my own since I was a kid, struggling to make my way in the world."

"Even after your friend John . . . took you in?"

He shifted uncomfortably beneath the intensity of her gaze. "John died the year I turned seventeen. He willed the inn and tavern to me, and I was determined to make a success out of the place. I spent most of the next five years working like a Trojan, building up the business into a full-fledged hotel and restaurant. By the time the War broke out, I'd succeeded beyond my wildest dreams. And then . . ."

His laughter was coarse, hurting. "The Yanks destroyed everything I'd worked for. After I joined up with the First Tennessee, the Union seized my hotel and turned it into a hospital. When they pulled out of town, they left the place in shambles. And since the end of the War, I've been focusing all my attention on rebuilding what the Yanks destroyed. There hasn't been any room in my life . . . for a family."

Julia placed a trembling hand on his shoulder.

"Recovering from the War hasn't been easy for you, it appears."

"I've been more fortunate than most, I suspect. At least I've had the friendship of one good man along the way . . . a man who has become my family, of sorts." He paused. "I owe Forrest Utley a great deal, Julia. We served together in the First Tennessee. He took a bullet in his leg—a bullet that was intended for me. And I'll be indebted to him until my dying day."

"I'm indebted to him, too," she whispered, her voice strained and choked. "I'm very, very grateful to your friend for saving your life. Otherwise, I might not have had the chance . . . to get to know you." Her lashes fluttered closed with that revelation, and she nestled closer to him, nuzzling her cheek against his chest as if it were the most natural thing in the world to do.

Tyler sucked in a shuddering breath and draped his arms around her, stunned by the force of the unfamiliar emotions swarming through him. He couldn't put a name to the feelings he was experiencing. But nothing had ever felt so right in his life as holding this woman in his arms.

He tightened his hold around her. She was soft and warm and inviting. His fingers skimmed across her shoulders, drifted downward, and grazed across the soft swell of her breast. He cupped his hand over the tender mound, and her nipple hardened beneath his fingers. He groaned, feeling his groin tighten with desire. Merely touching her, he was burning to rip her nightclothes into shreds and explore every luscious inch of her bare flesh with his hands and mouth and eyes.

Yet Tyler hesitated, overwhelmed by the emotions rushing through him. Sitting there, rocking her in the cradle of his arms, he felt as though he were drowning in an exhilarating sense of rightness. He'd never known anything like it, never wanted the moment to end. It almost seemed conceivable that he could be the right man for Julia Carey, in spite of all his shortcomings.

She shifted her weight against him. "I should be getting to bed," she whispered.

Unable to restrain himself, he brushed his lips across her mouth and pulled her more tightly against him. "Are you certain you want to leave?"

"No." She edged back, slowly. "But I must . . . before . . . it's too late."

As she slithered out of his arms, Tyler struggled to hold on to all those wondrous, magical emotions that had made everything seem so right. But as soon as she disappeared from sight, the extraordinary feelings slipped away from his grasp.

Seconds later, sitting alone in the darkness, Tyler felt that god-awful sense of emptiness returning, clawing away at his soul like a savage beast that refused to be tamed.

Chapter 13

"**D**o you need a hammer, Mr. Tyler?"

"Not yet, Kate."

"How about the saw?"

"In a few minutes."

"Will you be needing the saw after you measure that piece of lumber?"

"Possibly."

Kate edged closer to Tyler's elbow, watching intently as he measured a length of Georgia pine. "What are you making, anyway?"

"A pair of new shutters for the house."

"But haven't you fixed all of the old ones?"

"Yes, Kate. But now I'm making a new set to replace the shutters that are missing."

"Will it take long?"

Silently counting to ten, Tyler closed his eyes and sucked in a slow, steadying breath. All morning Kate had been nipping at his heels, trailing behind him like a devoted puppy following its master. Though repairing the worn shutters and making a new set had required countless trips between the barn and the house, Kate's short legs had kept pace with Tyler's long strides every step of the way. For over two hours, an endless stream of inquiries had been spouting from those little pink lips. And the flood of questions showed no signs of running dry.

At the start of the day, Tyler hadn't minded Kate's company. For a time, it had been refreshing to see the world again through the wide-eyed innocence of a child. And he'd never ceased to be amazed by the uninhibited way she doted on him. She'd freely displayed her affection for him all morning. Each time he sat down to rest, Kate snuggled up in his lap, throwing her chubby arms around his neck and planting wet kisses on his cheek.

And those eyes of hers. Those trusting little eyes looked up at him with the kind of adoration that should be reserved only for saints. It was the same type of adoring gaze that Rebecca had bestowed upon him when he was a kid on the farm. The kind of blinding trust and adoration he neither wanted nor deserved.

All of which posed a problem for Tyler. Common sense and a lifetime of heartache warned him that Kate's unblemished view of the world wasn't a true reflection of reality. And memories of his own childhood made him acutely aware of the dangers of being swayed by the charms of a precocious little girl. All too well he knew about the empty, hollow ache that would lodge in his chest when he went on his way and never saw her again.

To make matters worse, he'd awakened that morning with the same dreadful feeling that had haunted him throughout a restless night—the bittersweet knowledge that he wasn't the right man for Julia or her family. He couldn't give his love to Julia and her little clan. He had no love to give. He was incapable of loving anyone. All of his love had died on that horrendous day back at the farm.

"So will we be working out here in the barn all day?" Kate persisted.

Exasperated, Tyler squared his jaw. Until this moment, he'd answered each and every one of

Kate's questions with the patience of a saint. But after a sleepless night haunted by impossible dreams, he was in no mood to contend with any more questions.

"Don't you have anything better to do, Kate?" He glared down at her, well aware that his expression matched the harshness in his voice.

He expected her to flinch, dart away, or even snarl her disgust at him. But Kate's reaction was much more disturbing that he could have ever imagined. Pain and shock clouded her cherubic, angel face. Those trusting green eyes, full of unquestioning faith only seconds ago, now swam with tears.

"I was just trying to be your helper, Mr. Tyler," she choked out, her bottom lip quivering. "Sam made friends with Edward this morning, and they don't want to play with me 'cuz I'm a girl. But I thought you were different. I thought you liked having me for a fr-fr-frien-n-d . . ."

"Damn it all to hell," Tyler muttered, reaching down and sweeping her into his arms. Lifting her to his chest, he fastened his hold around the little girl. Sweet Jesus, why was he always such a son of a bitch?

He hugged her tightly, wishing he could erase those tears swimming in her pain-stricken eyes, put an end to those soft whimpers of disappointment gurgling up from her throat. "You're probably the best friend I've ever had, Miss Katy-did," he said hoarsely.

Sniffing, she edged back in his arms. Her teary-eyed gaze was wide and solemn. "I— I—am?"

He nodded. "Not many folks can put up with me for very long. I've got a hot temper. I don't have a lot of patience. And I can say some pretty mean things at times."

"You can be a grouch sometimes, too," she pointed out solemnly.

He felt a rush of heat creeping along his cheekbones, knowing he could not deny his faults. "That's why you've been a good friend. You've stuck by me even when I've been grumpy and mean, just like a true friend should. And you've been the best helper I've ever had, too."

"I like being your helper." She beamed up at him. "If you'd like, I can be your helper all the time."

"As much as I'd like to keep you all to myself, I don't think it would be fair to Miss Julia or your aunts. They need your help, too, you know." He kissed the end of her pert little nose. "What do you think about taking a break until after lunch, partner? We've been working a long time now."

Dry-eyed and smiling, Kate wiggled out of his arms. "Want to play in the sawdust shavings with me until it's time to eat?" she asked eagerly.

He tousled her baby-fine hair, captivated by the brightness of her enchanting smile, determined never to be responsible for making those delicate brows crinkle in displeasure again. Of course, there was nothing more that he could do or say to plant a smile on those pink little lips. He, a bona fide son of a bitch, had nothing else to give to her. But if he could find some thing, some object, some trinket, that would give her endless pleasure and make her lips blossom into a smile again . . .

Seized by a sudden spurt of inspiration, Tyler turned and headed to the door. "I just remembered something, Kate. I need to take care of some business in town." Which was true, in part. While he was in town, he intended to send another wire to The McRae and inform Forrest that he would be staying in Rome for a bit longer.

"You'll be back in time for lunch, won't you?" she called out.

Pausing, he turned and grinned. "You can count on it, Miss Katy-did. Mark my word."

Preparing breakfast for six adults and three hungry children consumed most of Julia's morning. Though weary from tossing and turning for most of the night, she'd awakened before dawn and hurried to the kitchen, wanting to prepare a special breakfast in honor of Hopewell House's first official boarders.

Much to her relief and delight, the Sprayberrys raved about the flaky biscuits that Julia had prepared for them. The freshly baked bread quickly disappeared from the serving platters, along with generous portions of fried eggs, ham, and grits.

Cleaning up the kitchen and dining room after breakfast consumed another hour of Julia's morning. After clearing the table and washing the soiled plates, utensils, and serving dishes, Julia joined Odelphia in the parlor to dust the furniture.

Odelphia was standing at the parlor window, peering over the top of her spectacles, as Julia came into the room. "Looks like Sam has made a new friend," she observed with a nod toward the front yard.

Stepping up behind her aunt, Julia smiled as she gazed through the window. Sam and Edward were playing contentedly beneath an elm tree near the house, building a fort from broken twigs and sticks. Though five years separated the boys in age, the pair had taken an immediate liking to each other during breakfast. "It's nice to see Sam having a good time," Julia mused softly.

"I'm sure he's been longing for the company of another boy since he's been here." Odelphia pushed up her spectacles to the bridge of her nose. "He and Kate play together fairly well, but sometimes I think they're merely tolerating each other."

"Little boys and girls don't always see eye to eye on everything," Julia agreed.

"They can be downright cruel to each other at times, too. The children at school gave Sam a hard time about his mother, didn't they?"

"I'm afraid so." Remembering the harsh words and angry blows exchanged between Sam and Daniel, Julia sighed as she picked up a dustrag from the table. "Unfortunately, most of the children at school judged Sam by his mother's behavior. Since Edward is too young to understand Sam's situation, it looks like he's accepting Sam just the way he is —which is exactly the kind of friend Sam needs at the moment."

Turning away from the window, Odelphia nodded in agreement. "I imagine Sam is glad that you offered to let Edward stay here this morning while the Sprayberrys are looking for a place to live."

"At first I wondered if I'd done the right thing." Julia twisted her mouth into a frown as she wiped a thin layer of dust from the surface of a mahogany table. "Ever since breakfast, the boys have been acting as though Kate didn't even exist. I was concerned that she might feel slighted by the boys, but it looks like there wasn't any need to worry. Every time I've peeked out the window to check on her, she's been right by Tyler's side, looking as though she were happy to have him all to herself this morning."

Suddenly aware that she hadn't heard the clank of Tyler's hammer or the grating sounds of a handsaw for several minutes, Julia quickly set aside the dustrag. Picking up her skirts, she headed to the door. "Excuse me for a moment, Aunt Odelphia, but I believe it's past time for me to check on Kate."

She found her sister sitting on the ground near the barn, playing sanguinely, sifting sawdust through her fingers. Lost in an imaginary world, Kate didn't notice Julia until she kneeled down beside her. "Having fun, Kate?"

Grinning, the child looked up and nodded. "Look, Julia! I'm building a sand castle!"

"Sounds like a big project." Julia smiled as the child pressed a clump of shavings between her palms. "Has Mr. Tyler been helping you build the castle?"

"Mr. Tyler doesn't know anything about my castle yet." Kate set aside the molded chunk of shavings and brushed her hands together. "It's going to be a surprise when he gets back from town. He said he had to take care of some business. But he promised he would be back in time for lunch."

"Then I'm sure he'll return soon." *Unless he's like Lucas or Papa*, she didn't bother to add. As much as Julia loved her rebellious brother and dear, departed father, neither of the Carey men had ever learned to live up to his word. Promises to return home by a certain date or time were usually broken, and family responsibilities often lagged behind other interests and concerns.

Tyler McRae probably wasn't any different from Papa or Lucas, Julia thought with a stab of irritation. Not that it made any difference to her, of course. The man was free to come and go as he pleased, wasn't he?

Silently vowing to erase all thoughts of Tyler McRae from her mind, Julia rose and brushed off the dust clinging to her skirt. "Want to see how the garden is faring?" she asked brightly.

"No, thanks," Kate returned. "I promised Mr. Tyler I would wait for him right here."

With Kate patiently waiting beside the barn for Tyler, Julia walked across the yard and surveyed the garden plot with a critical eye. Much to her relief, she discovered many of the tiny shoots had survived the hogs' stampede. Miraculously, most of the crops were healthy and thriving, their rich, green leaves sprouting up from the moist Georgia clay and reaching out to welcome the rays of spring sunshine.

Julia swelled with a surge of optimism. By the end of the summer, Hopewell House's table should be overflowing with vegetables from the garden. As long as she could manage to keep the weeds at bay, she noted, squatting to yank a healthy bunch of unruly weeds from the tilled soil.

She was still weeding the garden when Kate shrieked with delight. Julia looked up just as the youngster streaked across the yard to greet the familiar figure who was rounding the corner of the house.

As Kate hurled herself at Tyler, Julia hastily tossed aside the last batch of weeds from the garden. She had just straightened her spine and smoothed down her skirts when Kate called out to her.

"Look, Julia, look! Look what Mr. Tyler got me!" Running across the yard, Kate cradled a wiggly ball of fur in her arms. "Look, Julia! A puppy! My very own puppy! Isn't he the most beautiful puppy you've ever seen in your whole, entire life?"

Kate stumbled to a halt in front of Julia, desperately trying to hold on to the delightful creature who was squirming in her arms. The puppy's bushy tail thumped across her chest, narrowly missing her face, while a little pink tongue darted out of his mouth and licked her arm.

The animal appeared clean and healthy, even though a shaggy mop of hair covered his eyes. His thick coat of fur was the color of wheat, mixed with hues of cream. Julia pushed back the hair from his face and found a pair of shiny dark eyes looking up at her. When she playfully scratched the top of his head, the puppy sniffed at Julia's hand, rubbing his cold, damp nose against her palm as if expressing his thanks.

"He's adorable, Kate." Though not exactly beautiful, the frisky mutt was certainly the perfect companion for a lively little girl, Julia thought.

"I already love him," Kate declared, hugging the puppy so tightly that the animal yelped. "Every day I'm gonna feed him and love him and play with him and hug him and . . . " Grinning, she paused as Tyler stepped up to join them. "And I'm gonna name him Mack 'cuz he was a present from Mr. Tyler McRae!"

Julia laughed. "That sounds like a good name to me."

Kate whirled around, hurling one arm around Tyler's legs while clinging to the startled puppy with the other. "Oh, Mr. Tyler, thank you for my puppy! Mack is the most wonderful present anybody has ever given me in my whole, entire life!"

Tyler had the grace to flush. "Let's just say he's a belated birthday present." A troubled look suddenly clouded the vivid blue of his eyes, and Julia heard the catch in his voice. "You know, my sister had a puppy once, and she—"

He stopped abruptly, shaking his head and tensing his broad shoulders, as if catching himself. Kate edged back and looked up at him, eyes wide and curious. "And she what?" she prompted.

Julia held her breath as she waited for Tyler's answer. All along, he'd insisted that he didn't have a family. He'd even made the point that he didn't care for all the trappings of family life and the troubles that came along with it. But now Julia sensed that nothing could have been further from the truth.

"And she . . ." Tyler's voice caught in his throat. His Adam's apple bobbed convulsively, and anguish shaded his eyes. "And she really loved her puppy," he finished, practically spitting out the words.

Seeing the lines of agony marring his chiseled features, Julia felt her heart wrench in pain. Obviously, talking about his family was not easy for him.

"That's because puppies are easy to love." Totally unaware of Tyler's inner turmoil, Kate giggled as the puppy licked her hand. Then she focused a solemn gaze on Tyler. "You know something, Mr. Tyler? I really love *you*."

For a fleeting instant, every muscle in Tyler's body stiffened. Then he hunkered down beside the little girl, running callused fingertips over her plump cheek with a gentle reverence. "Save some of your lovin' for that new puppy of yours, Miss Katy-did," he whispered in a choked tone.

Even if her life had depended on it, Julia couldn't have uttered a sound past the lump that was suddenly clogging up her throat.

At that moment, Mack squirmed out of Kate's arms and leaped to the ground. Kate took off across the yard, squealing with delight as her little legs struggled to keep up with the frisky puppy's pace.

Seizing the opportunity to slip away without being noticed, Tyler wheeled and stalked toward the barn. As his boots clopped over the ground, he silently chastised himself for his blunder. *You damn fool. You should have known better. What in the hell were you trying to prove, McRae?*

Absorbed in his thoughts, he didn't realize Julia was following him until he felt the pressure of her hand on his arm. "Tyler, the puppy . . ." She paused. "Well, it was very thoughtful of you."

"It wasn't anything," he denied, resuming his brisk pace across the yard. "I thought if Kate had a playmate, she wouldn't spend so much damn time tagging after me."

"Still, a puppy was the perfect gift for Kate," she rushed on. "And you must realize, of course, that you've earned a permanent place in her heart. Children never forget a person who is thoughtful and caring enough to give them something as valuable as a puppy—"

Unable to endure another word, Tyler stopped cold. "Dammit, Julia, you're making too much out of this whole thing! It's just a damn puppy, for God's sake. A farmer in town was giving away a whole litter of the blasted creatures, and I was foolish enough to take one. I wasn't being kind or thoughtful or caring. I simply took a damn puppy off a man's hands. And in spite of your opinion, I sure as hell didn't do anything special."

"You didn't?" Julia cocked her head to one side, narrowed her eyes, and twisted her bow-shaped lips into a frown. "Odd, but I thought Kate acted as though you'd given her the world on a silver platter."

Feeling like she had leveled a hard blow to his chest, Tyler tensed. He couldn't deny what Julia was saying; he knew it was true. But he hadn't meant for things to turn out this way. He hadn't meant for things to go so far. "Well, she didn't have to be so damn appreciative," he bit out, glaring at her. "And that goes for you, too. I sure as hell don't need both of you fussing over me like I'm a damn saint."

With that, he turned and stormed into the barn.

It took only an instant for Julia to take off after him. Kate's vows of love—and Julia's own expressions of gratitude to him—weren't the real source of Tyler's troubles, she sensed. It was his uncertainty in dealing with all the affection . . .

"Tyler!" she called. "Wait a minute!"

"What now?" He scowled as she scrambled up beside him. "You're almost as bad as Kate, traipsing after me everywhere. Good God, I can't get a moment's peace around this damn place between the two of you!"

"What a shame." Julia shook her head in sympathy. "I imagine it must be terribly difficult for you, snaring the attention of two sisters." She reached out, playfully fingering the buttons down the front of his work shirt. "Of course, we can ignore you, if that's what you really want."

Tyler sucked in a deep breath as her fingers brushed across his chest. "Hell, Julia. I didn't mean—"

"And I'm sure both of us can restrain ourselves from displaying any more affection for you—verbal or otherwise," she rushed on. Smiling, she skimmed the tips of her fingers across his mustache. "After all, we wouldn't want to make nuisances out of ourselves."

The tightness in his shoulders disappeared. His lips twitched with the hint of a smile. "I don't think you have any cause to worry about becoming a nuisance," he conceded, sliding his hands around her waist.

"That's nice to hear." She twinkled up at him. "Now I only have one worry to contend with."

"What's that?"

Her smile stole his heart. "Resisting you," she whispered, planting a light kiss on his lips before she spun around and darted away.

Thirty minutes later, Tyler returned to Hopewell House for lunch. As he stepped into the dining room, a noisy, boisterous group was crowding around the table. The Sprayberrys, who had just returned from their morning of house-hunting, were giving a detailed account of their tours of the properties available for rent in town. Sam and Edward, in high spirits from their morning of play, were scooping man-sized portions of food onto their plates. Kate was chattering non-stop, describing her new puppy in vivid detail to Odelphia and Dorinda. And Julia was pulling up an extra chair to the table to accommodate Elizabeth, who had apparently just arrived for lunch.

By the end of the meal, it was apparent that the excitement of the morning had taken its toll on Kate. When Julia refused Kate's request to bring the puppy into the house, the child became uncharacteristically argumentative. "You're not being fair, Julia! You're being mean to Mack and me!"

Julia pursed her lips together. "I believe you'll have a much better time playing with Mack this afternoon if you lie down and rest for a little while before going back outside," she said with a quiet firmness.

"But I don't want to take a nap! I want to play with Mack!" Whining, Kate rubbed a balled fist across her eyes. "Besides, Mr. Tyler needs me and Mack to help him finish the shutters this afternoon and—"

"There's too much work to be done on the shutters to finish with them in one afternoon," Tyler broke in. "We'll have plenty of time to work together on them later. I promise."

"Mack probably needs to take a nap, too," Odelphia pointed out. "He's just a little puppy, and I'd wager he needs to rest for a while so he can play with you the rest of the day."

"But I don't want to spend my whole day sleeping!" Kate whined.

Tyler plunged a hand into the pocket of his trousers, intending to retrieve his gold watch, check the time, and persuade Kate that the day was still young.

To his surprise, his pocket was empty.

Hadn't he shoved the watch into his pocket that morning when he'd dressed for the day? He rarely ventured outside without carrying the gold timepiece with him.

Elizabeth's voice broke into his thoughts. "I'll go upstairs with you, Kate," she volunteered, offering her hand to the young girl.

Kate contemplated the offer for a brief moment, then sighed. "Only if you'll sing some songs to me," she insisted wearily.

"We'll sing anything you'd like," Elizabeth agreed.

Giving a resigned shrug, Kate slipped her hand into Elizabeth's. After the pair left the room, Tyler rose from his chair and ventured up to the third floor.

Before retiring each night, he usually set the gold timepiece on the small table beside his bed. Certain he would find the watch just where he'd left it, he stepped into the room.

But his watch was not on the table.

He searched through his belongings, rummaged through his traveling bag, checked the pockets of the trousers that he'd worn the previous evening.

Nothing.

He paused, combing his memory. Weary from his restless night, he'd risen that morning in a groggy state and absently dressed for breakfast. Unable to recall his precise motions, he raked a hand through his hair in frustration. Could the watch have slipped out of his pocket during one of his many trips between the barn and the house?

Determined to retrace his steps until he located the watch, Tyler traipsed down the stairs. Irritated by his own negligence, he was cursing under his breath just as Elizabeth's melodious soprano voice floated into the hall and wrapped around him as softly as a warm summer breeze.

The lilting refrain captivated Tyler, stopping him in his tracks. He paused beside the door to Kate's room, mesmerized by the haunting melody and words.

> *"Alas, my love, you do me wrong*
> *To cast me off discourteously . . ."*

As Tyler listened to the soothing timbre of Elizabeth's voice, an uneasy feeling swept through him. He'd heard that song before, he was certain. But the memories had been buried so deeply, submerged so completely . . .

He closed his eyes, drifting back through time and space to the sounds of the familiar tune. Echoes of the past assaulted him. Memories, long forgotten, bubbled to the surface of his mind, beckoning to him with an appeal so powerful that he was unable to resist exploring them.

He was a boy again, snug in his bed, without a care in the world. He was content and happy, safe and secure. He could feel the comforting touch of a woman's hand on his forehead, brushing back some wayward strands of hair from his face. And he could hear the soothing tune and the familiar words that she was singing with such clarity that he could almost believe that he could reach out and touch her . . .

The singing stopped. Tyler's eyes shot open. Trembling, he leaned against the wall to steady himself. Sweet Jesus, his mother had lulled him to sleep dozens of times, humming that tune. He'd forgotten what a wonderful feeling it could be. Almost convinced himself that those wondrous feelings could never be possible again.

The door to Kate's room creaked open, jolting Tyler from his thoughts. He snapped to attention as Elizabeth stepped into the hall.

"Kate's finally asleep," she whispered. Shaking her head, she smiled. "But she put up quite a fight, I'm afraid."

Tyler sucked in a deep breath. "I heard you singing. That song . . ." He hedged, dying to know, not daring to ask.

"I'm sure you've heard it before," Elizabeth assured him. "Mothers have been singing that old English folk song to their children for years. As a matter of fact, my mother sang the song to me as a lullaby. Maybe yours did, too."

"Maybe so." With a curt nod and a stiff smile, Tyler bolted down the stairs. Then he marched through the foyer, stalked outside, and slammed the door behind him.

Exposing his soul to those sweet, torturous memories all over again was the last thing he needed.

What he needed at the moment was something to numb all those unwanted memories, something powerful and potent to deaden all those uninvited feelings swarming through him.

He quickened his pace across the yard.

What he needed could be bought in town for the price of a cheap bottle of whiskey.

Chapter 14

Julia was sitting in the parlor, mending one of Sam's shirts, when the thunderous crash of a door rattled the windowpanes. Startled by the sudden noise, she flinched, almost dropping the needle in her hand.

"Those boys," she grumbled, certain that Sam and Edward were responsible for the commotion. Deciding to investigate, she set aside her mending and dashed across the parlor.

Just as she reached the foyer, Elizabeth appeared at the top of the stairs. Her face was flushed, her brow lined with worry.

"What in heaven's name . . . ?" Julia began.

"It was Tyler, I'm afraid. We were talking about the song I'd been singing to Kate, and then a strange expression came over him. The next thing I knew, he was bounding down the stairs like he'd just seen a ghost." She paused on the last step. "Why would hearing an old lullaby upset him?"

"I'm not certain, Elizabeth." Julia opened the front door and stepped outside. "But maybe he'll talk to me about it."

Five minutes later, Julia located Tyler at the east end of the Hopewell property. He was standing beside the fence, every muscle in his body rigid with tension. His eyes were as turbulent as thunderclouds, and his hands were clenched over the railing so tightly that Julia feared the wood might snap beneath the pressure of his grip.

She approached him with caution. "Tyler . . . ?"

He whipped around. "What in the hell do you want?"

"I just wanted to make certain you were all right." She stepped closer. "I heard the door slamming as you left the house, and Elizabeth said you seemed troubled when you heard—"

"You and Elizabeth should be minding your own damn business," he spat out, turning his back to her. "You shouldn't be poking your noses into something that's none of your concern."

"Fine," she agreed crisply, wounded by his scathing rejection. "I'll leave you alone, if that's what you want."

She turned, intending to go back to the house. But she'd taken only one step across the yard when she realized that she wasn't the source of his anger. Something else—maybe some kind of demon from the past—was responsible for the bitterness and rage rolling through him. Turning back around, she stepped up behind him. "I don't want anything from you, Tyler," she insisted with quiet firmness. "I just want to know if there's anything I can do *for* you."

He snapped around to face her, intending to spit out another scathing reply. But a knot coiled in Tyler's throat when he saw her standing there beside him. In spite of his biting remarks and brusque manner, her face was alight with concern, her eyes shimmering with compassion. He wanted to bury himself in all that goodness radiating from her, assuage his pain by drowning himself in all she could offer him. Taking her, swift and hard, would make him forget, if only for a moment . . .

His hands whipped around her shoulders. He

jerked her up against him and clamped his mouth
down over hers. Somewhere in the recesses of his
mind, he sensed he was acting like a barbarian, but
he couldn't seem to stop himself. His hands groped
over her body with frenzied desperation, clutching
at her shoulders, the sweep of her back, then her
buttocks. Only the feel of her body, the taste of her
mouth, the touch of her skin, could calm his inner
torments.

A frightened whimper escaped from her throat
as his greedy mouth burned into hers. Hearing her
frantic cry beneath the pressure of his lips, Tyler
froze.

Good God, what was he doing? She didn't
deserve to be treated like this. Didn't deserve to
be mauled by a madman who couldn't control
himself . . .

He pushed her away. "Damn it all to hell," he
ground out, seething with fury as he whipped
around and stalked away.

Shaken beyond words, Julia sagged against the
fence as Tyler stormed across the yard. She ran her
fingers over her swollen lips, still burning from his
scalding kiss. Dear heavens, what was wrong with
him? What had ignited the anger that was soaring
through him like a raging fire?

Julia lingered beside the fence, struggling to
regain her composure before returning to the house.
As she waited, she saw Odelphia and Dorinda leaving for their daily stroll through town, accompanied
by Elizabeth, who was obviously walking back to
her own home in the company of the Hopewell
sisters.

The house seemed unusually quiet when Julia
returned to the parlor and picked up her mending basket. She settled down on the settee, trying
to concentrate on replacing a missing button on

Kate's white blouse, just as a rap sounded at the front door.

Julia scurried to the foyer, wondering who could be calling in the middle of the afternoon. When she swung open the door, a neatly groomed gentleman wearing a tan suit politely tipped a wide-brimmed hat and flashed a disarming smile. Judging by the expensive cut of his clothes, Julia surmised the stranger was a successful businessman.

"Good afternoon, ma'am. I'm Benjamin Whitley from Macon, Georgia. Would this lovely establishment happen to be Hopewell House?"

His charming manner brought a smile to Julia's lips. "Why, yes, this is Hopewell House."

"Wonderful! I've just arrived in Rome. I noticed your handbill at the train depot, and I was hoping you would be able to accommodate me during my visit here."

"At the moment, we happen to have one unoccupied room." Julia opened the door wider and stepped aside, gesturing for the man to enter. "Please come in, Mr. Whitley. I'm Julia Carey, and I operate Hopewell House with my aunts. Would you care to look at our accommodations?"

"I would be most grateful to you for opening your lovely home to me, Miss Carey." Benjamin stepped into the house in one long stride and graciously removed his hat with a sweep of his hand.

After viewing the room, he quickly agreed to rent it and paid in advance for one week's stay. When he returned to the main floor with Julia, a gleam of admiration sparkled from his eyes. "Hopewell House is quite charming, Miss Carey," he praised.

"Thank you, Mr. Whitley," Julia returned cordially. "When my aunts return from their afternoon stroll, I'll pass along your compliments."

"I'm looking forward to meeting them. And if they are as charming as their niece, I have no doubt that my stay at Hopewell House should be quite pleasurable."

Unaccustomed to such lavish compliments, Julia felt a rush of heat along her cheeks. "We'll be expecting you for dinner this evening, then, around six o'clock."

"Six o'clock is perfect. That will give me time to contact my business associates in town this afternoon and get settled here before dinner." Benjamin turned to leave, then paused. "After spending most of the day on the train, I've become terribly thirsty. Could I trouble you for a glass of water?"

"Getting a glass of water for you is no trouble at all," Julia insisted.

Rushing to the kitchen, Julia felt like leaping with joy. She fingered the bills in the pocket of her apron and breathed a prayer of thanksgiving. Another boarder! Maybe, just maybe, the income from more boarders like Benjamin Whitley and the Sprayberrys would pay for a new roof before the summer was over.

Her hands trembled with excitement as she picked up a glass pitcher from the table and headed outside to fill the container with fresh water from the pump. After placing the pitcher beneath the drooping spout, she walked around the pump and grasped the long handle between her hands.

Water usually gushed from the spout after a few vigorous pumps of the handle. But today the handle refused to budge.

Julia pressed down on the handle with all of her weight, then stepped back and wiped the perspiration from her forehead. "For heaven's sake," she muttered in disgust.

What was wrong with the pump? Since the spring rains had been heavy, there was no reason for the pump to run dry. And the handle had never gotten stuck before now. Surely she could figure out some way to get it operating again . . .

A smile suddenly blossomed on her lips. *Tyler*. Fixing the pump should be a simple task for him. She picked up her skirts, rushed across the yard, and swept into the barn. "Tyler!" she called.

Her voice echoed from the rafters. Julia stumbled to a halt as she peered around the empty barn. Where was Tyler?

Pivoting on her heel, she gazed across the yard. In the distance, Sam and Edward were playing with Kate's new puppy near the grove of trees at the edge of the property. The hogs were grunting and squealing, secure in their pen. A few chickens were rambling about, pecking at the ground and clucking at each other.

But Tyler was nowhere to be found.

A sinking feeling swept Julia. She wearily rested an elbow on the fence railing, suddenly aware she had not heard the clank of a hammer nor the buzz of a saw since Tyler had stormed away from her. "Just tend to your own business, and everything else will take care of itself," she reminded herself sternly. "You can't solve Tyler McRae's problems. But you can take care of getting a glass of water for your new boarder."

Pulling back her shoulders, she marched across the yard with renewed determination. After locating several bottles of cool water stored in the spring-house, she served a glass of water to Benjamin Whitley, just as she'd promised. Then she returned to the pump, rolled up the sleeves of her dress, and set to work, trying to put aside all thoughts of Tyler McRae.

*   *   *

Throughout the afternoon, Julia made every effort not to think about Tyler.

For a time, she succeeded. Repairing the pump required several hours of concentration, along with all of the diligence and determination she could muster.

But she was achingly aware of his absence at the dinner table. Though she tried to ignore the lump swelling in her throat each time she caught a glimpse of his empty chair, it almost seemed as though the most important part of her life were missing . . .

Yet she knew she was being foolish. Tyler McRae was not part of the family, after all. He was merely a boarder who was repairing the house in exchange for food and lodging.

Julia was tucking Kate into bed for the night when Tyler returned to the house. Slipping out of Kate's room, she stepped into the hall just as Tyler's voice bellowed from the third floor like the blast of a cannon.

"You'd better tell me why you were in my room, Sam!" he roared.

"I wasn't doin' nothin' wrong!" the boy hurled back.

At that moment, Sam raced down the steps, barreling past Julia as if the devil himself were nipping at his heels. Tyler stomped behind him, his face red with fury, stalking past Julia without so much as a glance in her direction.

The chase came to an abrupt halt at the foot of the stairs. Tyler caught up with Sam, grabbing his arm and spinning him around to face him. "You've got some explaining to do, boy. What in the hell were you doing in my room? And let me warn you—you'd better talk fast. Otherwise, I might be tempted to haul you over my knee and beat the living daylights out of you."

The boy flinched, but a spark of defiance flashed from his eyes. "I was just lookin' at your pocket watch!"

"My pocket watch, huh?" Bitterness tinged Tyler's harsh laugh. "Odd, but my pocket watch has been missing all day. You wouldn't happen to know anything about that, would you?"

Sam, who had been struggling to squirm away from Tyler's hold, suddenly stilled. "You knew . . . it was gone?" The boy's voice trembled, and the color drained from his face.

"You're damn right I knew it was missing! Good God, I'm not a damn fool." Tyler's grip tightened around the youngster's trembling shoulders, as if he were on the verge of shaking him until his teeth rattled. Then he abruptly released the boy with a rough shove. "Out with it, Sam. Face up to your faults like a man, not like some whimpering coward. You took the watch earlier today, and now you were trying to sneak it back into my room without getting caught, weren't you?"

Not daring to meet Tyler's gaze, Sam dropped his chin to his chest. "I didn't mean no harm," he mumbled. "Honest."

"You didn't mean any harm?" Tyler thundered, clenching his fists into tight balls.

Sam swallowed hard. "I just wanted to carry the watch in my pocket for a little while. I never had a pocket watch before. Miss Julia taught us how to tell time at school, and when I saw your watch—"

"You took it, you little thief," Tyler spit out, glaring at the boy. "For Christ's sake, you were stealing from me! Don't you have the sense to know you shouldn't take something that doesn't belong to you? Didn't you ever stop to think that you should have asked for my permission?"

"If I'd asked, you wouldn't have let me borrow it," Sam snapped back.

"You're damn right about that."

"Well, that's why I didn't ask." The lad's voice began to falter. "I knew . . . I knew you wouldn't let me touch it . . . and I thought I'd just borrow it for a little while . . . and then put it b-b-back-k . . ."

Julia, who had been quietly observing the confrontation from the stairs, stepped up behind the boy and placed a steadying hand on his trembling shoulders. "Sam, I believe you owe an apology to Mr. McRae. I'm certain you meant no harm, but it wasn't right to take his pocket watch without discussing the matter with him in advance."

Sam sniffled. "I'm s-s-sorry, M-M-Mr. M-McRae."

Tyler sneered. "And what good does that do? The damage has already been done."

As Tyler stormed out of the house, Sam's lower lip trembled. "Why does he have to be so mean all the time? I didn't hurt his old watch. And I was putting it back where I found it . . ."

Gulping back tears, he bolted around and shot up the stairs.

Horrified by the heated outburst, Julia remained frozen for a long moment, not knowing which way to turn. Finally she stepped up to the door and called out to Tyler. "I'll be back in a moment," she said. Turning in the direction of the stairs, Julia prayed she could find the right words to comfort both of them.

But soothing Sam was much more difficult than Julia anticipated. When she slipped into the room, the boy was sobbing into his pillow. She kneeled at the side of the bed, whispering words of assurance to him, wishing she could wipe away all his pain with a sweep of her hand. Brushing her fingers through his rumpled hair seemed to ease the rush of tears streaming down his face, and his choked sobs soon lessened.

It was late by the time Sam drifted off to sleep. Frustrated and troubled, Julia sauntered out to the verandah for a breath of fresh air. She inhaled a deep breath just as a whiskey-tainted voice slithered through the darkness.

"So, is the boy still awake?"

Startled, Julia turned in Tyler's direction. He was leaning against a white Doric column in a lazy stance, his hand curled around the neck of a brown bottle. His hair was mussed, his shoulders were drooping, and his face was void of expression.

"Sam is resting comfortably," she finally answered. "But he cried himself to sleep."

"Good for him."

The words were stinging, brutal. "For heaven's sake, Tyler! He said he was sorry for taking your watch."

"I'm not deaf," he growled. "I heard what the boy said."

"It was wrong for Sam to take the watch without asking for your permission, I'll admit," she rushed on. "But I'm certain he's learned a valuable lesson from his mistake. Next time he'll think twice before taking something that doesn't belong to him. I'm sure he wasn't really thinking about the consequences of his actions when he borrowed your watch this morning. It's just that he's never had a pocket watch of his own and—"

"Listen to yourself, Julia." His fingers tightened, curving around the bottle with such force that she feared the glass might shatter. "You're making excuses for a kid who is nothing but a thief! For Christ's sake, he'll never quit stealing if you keep justifying his actions!"

"But you have to admit there wasn't any harm done," she pointed out. "Your pocket watch is still working, isn't it?"

Grunting, he wedged the bottle beneath his arm, then plunged a hand into his pocket and yanked out the watch. Narrowing his eyes, he carefully examined the face of the timepiece. After checking the back of the gold case for scratches, he jammed the watch back into his pocket. "Looks like it hasn't been damaged," he admitted.

"Then why can't you let it go, Tyler?" Julia demanded. "Just look at yourself! Nothing has been lost, and you're still furious!"

His eyes blazed with anger. "You're damn right I'm furious, lady. How would you feel if one of your boarders took something of value from you?"

She frowned at the disturbing thought. "I suppose I wouldn't be pleased."

"And how would you feel if you caught someone in the act of trying to replace the stolen merchandise?"

Her frown deepened. "Well, I would probably confront him. Then I would listen to his explanation and discuss the matter of taking another person's belongings without permission. And then I would . . . forgive him."

"Forgive him?" Tyler echoed, staring at her in disbelief before raking a hand through his tousled hair in frustration. "Hell, of course you would. You'd find it in your heart to forgive your own damn family even if they'd abandoned you. But dammit, I'm not like that, Julia! I can't forgive that blasted kid . . . even if I wanted to."

"Why not?"

A shadow of darkness crossed his face. "Don't you see, sweet Julia? Can't you understand?" His voice, tinged with a mixture of embarrassment and shame, dropped to a husky whisper. "I don't know how to forgive anyone. I've never learned how."

Something tight and restricting gripped Julia's chest. Dear Lord, he was hurting, yearning for some peace within himself, longing to find a way to ease the anguish in his bruised and battered soul. Struggling with her own volatile emotions, she whispered in a shaky voice, "Mastering the ability to pardon others for their mistakes is something all of us have to learn, Tyler."

"You mean forgiveness doesn't come naturally to you?" His laughter was forced, strained.

"I don't think it's part of human nature to forgive easily." She paused, grappling for the right words. "But it's the right thing to do, I'm certain. After all, God tells us to forgive others . . . just as He forgives us."

"Well, God may be in the business of forgiving folks for their sins, but I'm not," he scoffed. The chiseled lines of his face tightened. "Some mistakes can't be forgiven, as far as I'm concerned. There is more ugliness and pain in this world than an angel like you could ever fathom, sweet Julia. And some people don't deserve to be forgiven by anyone . . . even God."

"People like who?"

His eyes darkened. "Like a father who commits cold-blooded murder in front of his own kids," he said in a low tone. "Like a parent who sells his children to the highest bidder."

A shudder raced through her at the horrid images painted by his words. In some ways, she wanted to press her fingers against those sensuous lips, to silence him. But she sensed an urgent need within him, a need to share a part of himself that no other soul had ever seen. She waited as he drew in a shaky breath and began.

"I was just about Sam's age when everything in
my life fell apart." His voice was low and ragged.
"At the time, I was living on a farm in Tennessee
with my folks and my little sister, Rebecca." He
paused, a bittersweet smile touching his lips at the
distant memories. "'Becca wore her hair in braids,
like Kate does. Kate reminds me a lot of her."

"And Rebecca . . . had a puppy?"

A hint of a smile played on his lips. "Rebecca and
her puppy were always tagging after me around
the farm, and Ma was always singing. I'd forgotten
how beautifully she sang . . . until today . . . until I
heard Elizabeth singing a song to Kate. It was one
of the songs that Ma used to sing to 'Becca . . .
and me."

He swallowed with difficulty. "But I discovered
our perfect little family wasn't so flawless, after all,
when my dad and his brother started arguing one
summer night. Turned out they were fighting over
Ma." He lifted the bottle to his lips and gulped
down the rest of its contents. "Seems Ma preferred
my uncle over Pa. She'd been sleeping with her
brother-in-law instead of her husband. When Pa
found out, he shot my uncle—his own brother—
in cold blood. Rebecca and I saw it all. Every grue-
some minute."

He hurled back his arm and tossed the bottle
across the lawn. "God, I wanted to die. Ma must
have figured that Pa would be aiming the gun at
her next, because she ran out in the middle of the
shooting. That was the last time I ever saw her."

"Oh, Tyler." Tears spilled down Julia's cheeks
for the pain he must have endured, for the heartache that still lingered. She reached out to squeeze
his arm and offer a bit of comfort, but he shifted
away from her.

"Pa might as well have shot 'Becca and me, too,

for all he cared about us. That bastard—" Shaking with fury, he rammed a balled fist into the Doric column. "He actually tried to sell 'Becca and me. *Sell* us, damn it. Can you imagine a father who could care so little about his children? We were just another piece of property to him, about as valuable as a couple of worthless Confederate greenbacks."

Julia bit her lip, shuddering at the image. "But surely he didn't mean . . ." Dear Lord in heaven, the thought was too horrible to fathom. "Surely you're mistaken, Tyler."

"No mistake." His eyes were cold and hard. "There are some folks in this world who are rotten to the core, sweet Julia. You're always too busy looking for the good in people to see the bad."

She didn't argue with him. She couldn't. It was impossible to utter a word past the lump swelling in her throat.

"To my dying day, I'll never forgive Pa for what he did. As soon as I caught wind of his plans to sell us to some strangers, I took off, running for my life . . . and I guess I haven't stopped since. God only knows what has happened to Rebecca. But I intend to find her, if it's the last thing I ever do . . ."

Grief lined his face, and his voice was raw with stark need. "When we found Sam in that wretched shack, I saw myself huddled in the back of that horrid place, terrified, frightened . . . so damn alone." He wrapped his hands around the Doric column so tightly, his knuckles turned white. "If I ever run into that no-account mother of his, I'll probably be hanged for wringing her neck with my bare hands. After the way she's neglected and mistreated that kid, she doesn't deserve to live."

Tyler wearily rested his forehead against the strength of the white Doric column. After a long moment of silence, Julia drew in a shaky breath. "Sophie Springer should be punished for abandoning her child," she agreed quietly. "But even if she doesn't get the punishment she deserves under the law, Sam will still have to find his own way to deal with the heartache that she has caused. Even though she may not deserve his forgiveness, Sam needs to forgive her—for his own sake."

His head snapped up. "Why in hell should he do that?"

"Because if he keeps carrying around all his bitterness and hurt and anger, it will grow and fester and . . . destroy him inside." She bit her lip. "Your father may not deserve your forgiveness either, Tyler, but you need to consider forgiving him for your own benefit. Not his."

The line of his jaw hardened. "It might do Sam some good to forgive his mother." Pain flitted across his face, mixed with a hopelessness so intense that an ache swelled in Julia's chest. "But it's too late for me to forgive anyone."

Then he turned and stalked away, disappearing into the darkness.

Chapter 15

Tyler awakened with a dull, throbbing ache in his head the next morning. "Damn it all to hell," he muttered, groaning as he struggled to open his eyes. Morning sunlight streamed through the windows, alerting him to the fact that he'd slept later than normal. Trying to ward off his sluggishness, he stumbled out of bed and dressed for the day.

But he was too late for breakfast. By the time he entered the dining room, the Sprayberrys were rising from their chairs, the children were scampering out the door, and the Hopewell sisters were clearing the table.

He wasn't surprised that he'd missed the meal, knowing he'd overslept. But Tyler was stunned by the sight of Julia standing beside a tall, fair-haired man. He stopped cold, staring at the couple in disbelief.

The man was gazing down at Julia as though he intended to devour her as the final course of the morning meal. Obviously flattered by the attention, Julia was smiling up at the stranger, lapping up his adoration like an innocent kitten sucking up sweet cream.

Tyler clenched his hands into tight balls. Other than yanking the rogue away from Julia by the roots of his neatly trimmed hair and tossing him out the door like a crate of rubbish, nothing would give him more pleasure than smashing his fists into the bastard's smooth-shaven face, knocking every tooth out of his head, and destroying that revolting smile.

He was still contemplating his next move when the man grasped Julia's hand and lifted it to his lips. As the stranger's mouth brushed across the tips of her dainty fingers, an indefinable emotion rocketed through Tyler.

Enough of this, he vowed. With long, confident strides, he crossed the room.

"When I considered boarding at Hopewell House, I had no idea the proprietor of this wonderful establishment would be one of the most beautiful women in all of Georgia," the man was saying as Tyler stepped up beside him.

"Actually, I'm not the sole proprietor," Julia corrected. "My aunts and I operate Hopewell House together."

"Miss Carey is too modest," Tyler broke in. "She's the one who oversees the daily operations of Hopewell House."

The man scrutinized Tyler with a quick, scathing glance, then turned his attention back to Julia. "You never mentioned that you have hired help, Miss Carey."

"Hired help?" Julia's thick brows narrowed. "I'm afraid you've misunderstood, Mr. Whitley. You haven't met Tyler McRae, but he—"

"Was hired with the understanding that he would take care of anything that needs fixing around the place," Tyler finished. "And I also pay particular attention to Miss Carey's welfare. If any man so much as looks at her the wrong way around here, he gets his nose flattened across his face." He poked an outstretched thumb into his own chest and flashed a triumphant smile. "And the hired help bestows the honors."

Benjamin dropped Julia's hand as though it had caught fire. Paling, he cautiously backed away from Tyler"s threatening scowl. "I'm afraid I must be leaving, Miss Carey. It's getting late, and I have an early appointment in town this morning." Without another glance in Julia's direction, he grabbed his wide-brimmed hat, sprinted across the room, and vanished from sight.

As Tyler chuckled with amusement, Julia whirled around to face him. Her fiery gaze crackled with anger. "I hope you have plenty of reasons for running off a good-paying boarder, Tyler."

He shrugged. "Everyone's money is the same color. You don't need his kind around here."

"His kind?" Julia scoffed. "I'll have you know that Benjamin Whitley was one of the most charming gentlemen to ever set foot in this house!"

"Charming? Scheming, deceitful, and conniving more aptly describes bastards like him."

Her eyes widened incredulously. "How can you make all those horrible claims about him? You don't even know the man!"

"But I know his type, Julia. He's the kind who will go to any lengths to seduce a woman who strikes his fancy. If his charming smile doesn't make her swoon at his feet, he'll try seductive looks, flattering words—"

"And you think I was about to become his next victim?"

"Well, you didn't seem to mind him ogling you," Tyler grumbled, stabs of irritation lancing through him. "I didn't see you trying to put a stop to all that sweet talk of his."

A heated flush colored her cheekbones. "Maybe not, but you didn't have the right to jump down his throat, either. You were inexcusably rude to him, Tyler, and I don't like the idea of you running off a customer! I'm trying to operate a business here, after all. And at the moment, I need all the boarders I can get."

"But you don't need any more boarders like Whitley." He grinned. "Unless, of course, you actually enjoy having a silver-tongued scoundrel slobber all over your hand. And as long as you don't mind looking like you're trying to get sand out of your eyes when you're batting your lashes at him. . . "

Julia tried to bite back a smile. "Are you accusing me of flirting with Mr. Whitley?"

"I'm just telling you what I saw. Seems to me you liked being sweet-talked."

"Sometimes it's nice to hear a man say nice things," she admitted in a shy tone. "Of course, you wouldn't understand, being a man and all."

"But maybe I do understand." Tyler's smile disappeared as he gazed down into her deep-set green eyes. "If it's flattery you want, I'll be happy to oblige. It wouldn't be difficult for me at all. In fact, I could spend hours and hours extolling all of your virtues. It might even take all night long. . . "

Her eyes widened, shimmering with wonder as their gazes met and locked. A heightened sense of awareness seemed to pass between them, transcending time and space. Though neither of them uttered a sound, the unspoken emotions sizzling through the air expressed far more than words could say.

"All night?" Julia finally echoed in a hushed whisper.

"Well, maybe not *all* night," Tyler conceded in a husky tone, stepping closer to her. "But as for the rest of the evening . . . well, I'm certain I could think of something else to occupy us for the remainder of the night. If we had trouble getting to sleep after a stimulating round of conversation, I'm sure I could think of some sort of physical activity that would leave us totally sated and exhausted."

"I'm sure you could, too. I imagine you would come up with some very interesting options for us." Julia grinned with complete understanding as she gathered up her hat and gloves from a corner table. "As much as I regret having to end this thought-provoking discussion, I should be running along now. I need to pick up a few supplies at Horace Bates's store."

She was slipping her fingers into her gloves when Odelphia and Dorinda entered the room. "I'm heading to town now," she informed her aunts. "If all goes well, I should be back in an hour or so."

"Be careful, dear," Odelphia called.

"Give that sweet Horace our best regards," Dorinda added.

As Julia swept out of the room, Odelphia motioned for Tyler to pull up a chair to the table. "Sit down, son," she urged in her brisk, efficient manner. "You need to start the day with a hot meal."

"Hardworking men can't afford to miss breakfast," Dorinda added. Shuffling to the table, she carried a plate brimming with hot sausages, pancakes, grits, and fried eggs. "When you didn't get here in time for breakfast, I made up a plate for you. I knew you'd be hungry since you weren't able to join us for dinner last night."

"Thanks, Miss Dorinda." Tyler took a seat as Dorinda set the plate in front of him. "Won't you ladies join me?"

"Why, I don't mind if I do." Dorinda plucked a sugar-coated pastry from a serving platter on the table, then lowered her plump frame into the chair beside Tyler's. "I only ate one of these wicked concoctions this morning, so I guess it wouldn't hurt to eat another one."

"How about you, Miss Odelphia?" Tyler asked.

"I'll join you for a cup of coffee," the elder Hopewell sister agreed, already pouring a cup for herself.

As Tyler stabbed a fork into a slice of sausage, Dorinda glanced over at him. "I couldn't help but overhear you talking about Mr. Whitley," she admitted. "Tell me, dear, do you really think he is as unscrupulous as you made him out to be?"

Taken by surprise, Tyler nearly choked. He hadn't realized anyone had overheard his conversation with Julia. He swallowed with difficulty, trying to dislodge the sausage stuck in his throat. "A true scoundrel lurks beneath all that finery, I fear," he finally croaked.

"Oh, dear." Dorinda daintily licked the sugar crumbs from the tip of her thumb and heaved a wistful sigh. "I was so hoping he might be the right young man for Julia."

"For some time now, Dorinda and I have been praying that Julia will meet a nice, wealthy young man," Odelphia explained, pouring a small amount of cream into her coffee. "Marriage for Julia would solve most of our problems—if the right man came along, that is."

"Of course, Julia will have none of it." Dorinda reached for a second pastry. "Ever since her fiancé died in the War, she thinks she's not supposed to marry anyone else, you know. Why, that precious girl believes she's supposed to spend the rest of her life taking care of us!"

"We don't want her to spend the rest of her life thinking about our needs over her own." Odelphia's voice was tinged with regret and sorrow. "No, Dorie and I don't want Julia to end up . . . like us."

"I'm not certain I understand." Tyler glanced from one sister to the other. "Do you mean you don't want Julia to remain . . . unmarried?"

"Precisely." Odelphia's lips formed a tight line. "Not that Dorie and I didn't have our chances to marry, mind you."

"Years ago, we were the most popular young ladies in all of Rome." Nostalgic memories clouded Dorinda's eyes. "Dozens of suitors came calling, vying for the chance to escort us on buggy rides and church picnics and long strolls down by the river . . . Oh, those were the days!"

"But all of that was a long time ago." Odelphia stiffened, as if trying to dismiss the subject.

"So if you had plenty of suitors . . . why did neither of you marry?" Tyler probed, genuinely puzzled.

A sorrowful expression crossed Dorinda's plump face. "Apparently, marriage wasn't meant for Odie and me. The love of my life was killed in a terrible accident down by the river docks a few weeks before our wedding day. And Odie's young man, well, he. . . " Her voice trailed off as she gazed sorrowfully at her sister.

"My young man, Alexander, neglected to tell me that he was already married." Odelphia twisted her thin lips into a frown. "Since he lived in a neighboring town, no one in Rome was aware of his philandering ways. On the very afternoon that we were planning our wedding, a gentleman stopped by the house to visit Papa. It just so happened that the gentleman lived in the same town as Alexander. Calling my young man by name, the gentleman politely inquired about his wife's health!"

"That was a horrible, horrible afternoon," Dorie commiserated with a woeful sigh. "A few months later, my own sweetheart met with his horrible demise. And by that time, most of the other eligible young men in town were already spoken for."

Tyler quietly finished off the food on his plate, mulling over the inequities of life. These gentle, silver-haired ladies seemed unlikely candidates for romantic heartaches. Yet their lives had not gone untouched by tragedy and pain, regret and remorse. For some odd reason, he found himself wanting to offer a bit of comfort to them. "It's unfortunate that life doesn't always work out according to plan," he finally commented.

"How true." Sighing, Dorinda propped an elbow on the table and rested her chin in her hand. "And sometimes history seems to repeat itself. Now that the War is over, there aren't very many eligible men left in town for Julia, either. Though she's a beautiful girl, time is passing her by, I fear. And she can't marry just anyone, you know. She has to find someone who deserves a sweet, loving woman who will be faithful and true to him. A man who will love her, treasure her, care for her. And, of course, he must provide for her comfortably for the rest of her life, too."

"I don't think we should give up all hope, Dorie." Odelphia set down her coffee cup. "Mr. Whitley may not have been the perfect candidate for a prospective husband, but I'm certain someone else will come along. And there's always Horace Bates, if Julia would just give that dear man a little encouragement. He's been smitten with her for years."

"He's quite well off financially, I'm certain. Bates's Mercantile and Dry Goods has become one of the busiest places in town since the end of the War. But Julia doesn't seem to have the least bit of interest in Horace." Dorinda turned to Tyler and patted his hand in a sympathetic gesture. "It's too bad all your money was stolen during that awful robbery on the train, dear. Otherwise, you and Julia might have been a lovely couple."

Appalled by her sister's brazen remarks, Odelphia gasped. "Dorinda Hopewell! I'm sure Mr. McRae does not need you to remind him that he's penniless!"

"And I'm sure I wasn't saying anything that he hasn't already thought of himself! Dorinda snatched the last pastry from the platter and smiled. "You know, maybe we shouldn't give up hope about finding a nice, wealthy husband for Julia. Who knows? With all these handsome young men coming into town on the train every day, the right man for Julia could be knocking at our door this very afternoon. Maybe he'll even take her into his arms, sweep her off her feet, and marry her on the spot!"

Though Odelphia laughed at her sister's romantic notions, Tyler found nothing amusing about the idea. The mere thought of seeing Julia in another man's arms made his blood churn. "I think I'll run down to Bates's Mercantile and help Julia with the supplies," he announced stiffly.

"I'm sure she would appreciate it," Odelphia said politely.

"Maybe she'll finally agree to allow Horace to come calling," Dorinda added wistfully. "With a little luck, Horace might even be the man who could sweep Julia off her feet!"

"There would only be one problem to that," Tyler mumbled to himself as he jammed a hat over his head and stalked out the door. "My dead body will be in the way."

Bates's Mercantile and Dry Goods, located at the corner of one of Rome's busiest intersections, was crowded with customers when Tyler walked into the frame building. After a few minutes of threading his way through the rows of well-stocked shelves, he found Julia standing by a long wooden counter, carefully counting out the proper amount of coins to pay for her purchases.

He couldn't help gawking at her like an awe-struck schoolboy. Dainty sprigs of lavender flowers trimmed the wide brim of her straw bonnet. Chestnut curls peeked out beneath the hat, framing her angelic face, and dangled down the sweep of her back like a tumbling waterfall. And her lavender day dress, though somewhat faded and worn, couldn't hide the shapeliness of her slender form. Tyler's mouth went dry with longing, just looking at her.

"I haven't seen too much of you around here lately, Miss Julia," remarked the scrawny-looking man who was standing behind the counter. He wiped his hands on the soiled apron tied around his thin torso before pocketing the change that Julia offered to him. "You haven't been having any problems, have you?"

"Every day has its own share of problems, Horace." Julia flashed a polite smile. "But so far, we haven't run across anything that we haven't been able to handle."

"Well, if money gets tight, you know I'd be more than happy to run a tab on your supplies. Course, I wouldn't do that for just anybody round these parts. But I'd make an exception for you, Miss Julia."

"I appreciate that, but you know how I feel about buying anything on credit." She paused, picking up her purchases from the counter and packing them into a large basket. "Besides, things are picking up, now that my aunts and I are accepting boarders."

"I hope you're not opening your door to just anyone." Horace leaned against the counter, narrowing his eyes. "Can't be too careful these days, Miss Julia. I have to admit, I've been concerned ever since Sheriff Mitchell told me that the young fella who got shot on the train has been boarding with you."

"That young fella has been quite a blessing, Horace. I don't know if we could have opened up Hopewell House without him. He's very skillful with his hands, and he's been making lots of repairs to the house since recovering from his injury."

Horace frowned. "Well, I would have been glad to help you, Miss Julia, if you'd only asked me."

"I'm sure you would have. But you have your hands full as it is, running your own business."

"That I do, Miss Julia. Course, I could use a little rest and relaxation every once in a while . . . and the company of a fine woman." He nervously slicked back his thinning hair with the palm of his hand. "You know, there's a picnic on the church grounds this Sunday after church. And I'd be mighty honored if I could escort you."

Before Julia could reply, Tyler stepped up to the counter and grasped the handle of the packed basket. "I'm afraid Miss Carey is too busy getting her business under way to take any time off on Sunday afternoons. Now that Hopewell House is open, the midday meal on Sunday requires a lot of preparation." Tyler flashed a charming smile in Julia's direction. "Isn't that right, Miss Carey?"

Julia's lips parted slightly, but her surprise at his unexpected presence vanished as quickly as it appeared. "Not necessarily, Mr. McRae. Other than breakfast, Odelphia and Dorinda are responsible for cooking most of the meals at Hopewell House." She turned back to Horace. "But I would hesitate to leave all the responsibilities for Sunday dinner to my aunts until they become more accustomed to serving a large group of guests."

A shadow of disappointment fell over Horace's thin face. Feeling a surge of triumph, Tyler picked up Julia's basket from the counter and escorted her to the door.

As he set the basket on the seat of the buggy, Julia placed a gloved hand on his arm. It was a simple gesture, yet Tyler felt like she'd branded him for life. "What was going on back there with Horace?" Confusion shimmered from her emerald eyes. "What were you trying to prove, Tyler?"

"I didn't say anything that wasn't true. You're much too busy on Sundays to be wasting your afternoon with a weasel like Horace Bates."

Julia pursed her lips together. "And why did you follow me here this morning?"

He shrugged. "I thought you might need some help."

"Then I'm sorry you've wasted your time." She removed her hand from his arm, picked up her skirts, and hoisted herself up into the buggy. "I've bought my own supplies and carried them home all by myself plenty of times. And in case you didn't notice, I even managed to hitch up the horses to the buggy all by myself, too. I'm not helpless, Tyler! I've been getting along without the help of a man for years."

"Well, maybe it's high time you had a man around to help you." He scowled. "And you're contradicting yourself, you know. I just heard you tell your doting admirer that you couldn't have opened Hopewell House without me!"

A becoming shade of crimson scorched her cheeks. "What I told Horace is true, Tyler. I don't know what I would have done without you making all those repairs to the house. And I truly appreciate all your help. But I'm perfectly capable of speaking for myself, for goodness sake! Twice this morning you've pushed a gentleman away from me. And I'm not accustomed to a man speaking and thinking for me."

"Well, maybe you need a man around to speak for you," he snapped, more harshly than he intended. "Can't you see what Horace is trying to do? He wants you to buy your supplies on credit so you'll be obligated to him. He wants to get a hold on you so he can have you all to himself!"

"He's been using the same old lines on me for years, Tyler. I know exactly what he's up to."

"Well, you don't seem to be too damned concerned about it," he muttered ungraciously.

"On the other hand, you seem quite disturbed," Julia pointed out. As she fingered the ribbons dangling from her bonnet, a smile sprouted on the corners of her lips. "Why, Tyler McRae, I do believe you're jealous!"

"Jealous?" he roared. He tugged on the brim of his hat, yanking it down over his eyes. "Lady, I don't have a jealous bone in my body."

Her eyes twinkled with amusement. "Whatever you say," she conceded with a demure nod. Then she grasped the reins between her gloved hands, called out to the horses, and drove away.

"Damn it all to hell," Tyler muttered as the buggy rolled over the dusty road and disappeared over the hill. Good God, could she be right?

No. He'd never been jealous of another man in his life. Never had a reason to be.

Until now.

Tyler shuffled his boots across the ground, heading back to Hopewell House, pondering Julia's parting words. Yes, his blood boiled at the thought of any man talking with her, laughing with her . . . touching her. Judas Priest, he'd acted like a jealous fool—not once, but twice in one morning! Never had he felt such possessiveness toward any human being.

And it was terrifying to think he could care so much about anyone.

Christ, how had it happened? Where was the cold, hardened man who'd been shot on the train? Had he become so soft, so vulnerable, so weak . . . that he'd actually begun to care?

"Damn it!' he roared, kicking a rock across the road with the toe of his boot.

He, of all people, should know about the dangers of caring too much. Every time he'd dropped his guard, he'd suffered the consequences. Getting trapped in the deceptive webs of love and caring, home and family, had never brought him anything but heartache and pain.

For a while, Julia had him dreaming of things he'd always assumed he could never have—a family, a place to call home, the warmth and love of a woman's touch. She had him looking inside himself, analyzing feelings he never knew he possessed, admitting to emotions he never knew he had.

But now Tyler sensed nothing was lurking inside his soul except a cold, bottomless well of emptiness. There was nothing inside him worth giving to anyone. He was no match for Julia or her little clan. He didn't know how to love anyone. Hell, he didn't even know how to forgive a little kid for swiping his pocket watch . . . or a dead man for robbing him blind.

But maybe it was better that way. Maybe it was better to be cold and unforgiving, heartless and unfeeling. If he learned how to forgive . . . or care . . . he'd only be setting himself up for disappointment . . . more hurt and pain.

No, nothing good could come from learning to forgive . . . or from loving a woman like Julia. Prolonging his stay at Hopewell House would only make matters worse. Eventually Julia would learn that he wasn't the man of her dreams. And it would break her heart when she discovered he was only an empty shell of a man with nothing to give to her . . . or anyone else.

Tyler trudged back to Hopewell House, knowing what he had to do, dreading the thought of it worse than death. Sweet Jesus, he'd give his right arm if he could change the circumstances that had brought him here . . . or if he could be the right man for Julia.

But he'd had his taste of heaven, home, and family. He'd gotten the house in shape for boarders, just as he'd promised. He'd even sampled the sweetness of Julia's lips, just as he'd dreamed. And though he wanted more—much more—he knew it was only wishful thinking.

Because it was time to leave. He had to leave Hopewell House before it was too late, before the pain became unbearable . . . before the price became too high to pay.

Chapter 16

The wide brim of Julia's straw bonnet cast a shadow over her face, shielding her eyes from the glare of the morning sun, as the buggy topped the hill and rolled down the well-traveled road. Soothed by the gentle sway of the carriage, the rhythmic clip-clop of the horses' hooves, and the sweet fragrance of magnolia blossoms drifting through the spring air, Julia loosened her tight grip on the reins.

She supposed she should have offered a ride to Tyler, but she needed a few moments of privacy to sort out her tumultuous feelings. The day had barely begun, and already it had been an eventful one.

From the start, she'd sensed it would not be an ordinary day. By the time breakfast was over, she was exhausted from contending with Benjamin Whitley's charming smile, gracious ways, and flattering words. His compliments were too thick and syrupy to be genuine, she discovered, and his sugar-coated phrases of adoration became almost sickeningly sweet.

But she'd never expected Tyler to practically threaten Benjamin's life! And just because she agreed with Tyler's assessment of the man with the silver tongue did not mean that she approved of his rude behavior to her newest boarder.

257

She might have dismissed Tyler's harsh treatment of Benjamin if it had not been for his second ill-mannered display of conduct at Bates's Mercantile. But how could she have disregarded the aggressive way he'd refused Horace's invitation on her behalf? And how could she have ignored the possessive tone in his voice, the protective touch of his hand as he'd guided her out of the store?

In the beginning, she had not immediately recognized the root cause of Tyler's behavior. Julia was inexperienced at recognizing the symptoms of a jealous heart. After all, there had been no reason for her beloved fiancé to envy any other man in her life. Before the War, the eligible men of Rome had not dared to intrude upon her relationship with Brent Harrington.

But this morning her feminine instincts had signaled a warning to her, and she'd heeded their call. As soon as she'd voiced her suspicions about Tyler's unseemly conduct, she had been certain her instincts were right. Though she'd only been teasing him about being jealous, his hot denial had condemned him with as much conviction as a written confession. And the tinge of disbelief in his expression said he hadn't stopped to think about the driving force behind his behavior until she'd pointed it out to him.

Yes, Tyler McRae was jealous, and his actions had embarrassed her and aggravated her beyond words. But in spite of her irritation with him, she could not deny that all the ruckus was a little bit flattering. And if Tyler couldn't bear the thought of another man kissing her hand or escorting her to a church picnic . . .

What did it all mean? Did he truly care for her? Had those well-tended walls around his heart crumbled last night when he'd shared the secrets of his past? Or were his actions merely the result of his hot temper and impatient ways?

The unanswered questions were still flooding through her mind when she guided the buggy to a stop at Hopewell House. Anxious to set aside the disturbing thoughts, she hastily tended to the horses and carried the basket of supplies into the kitchen.

Julia had just finished putting away her purchases when Violet Sprayberry's soft voice called out to her. "Oh, Julia, I'm so glad you're here! I've been looking all over the place for you."

Turning, Julia smiled as Violet stepped into the kitchen. She genuinely liked the shy, soft-spoken boarder, even though she had not had the chance to spend a lot of time with her. "Is there a problem?"

"Oh, no! I just wanted to ask a favor of you." Violet nervously fingered the lace edging around the collar of her dress. "Aaron and I found the most delightful spot near the river when we were looking at houses yesterday! It would be the perfect place for an afternoon outing. Would you mind if we take Sam and Kate with us on a picnic this afternoon? Edward would enjoy their company, I'm certain."

"How considerate of you! Of course the children may join you. And I'm sure they'll be delighted with the idea." As Julia untied the ribbons dangling beneath her chin and removed the wide-brimmed bonnet from her head, her smile widened. "You may have to take Mack along with you, too. I doubt Kate would be able to part with her new puppy for the whole afternoon."

"Aaron and I had already planned on that." Violet laughed. "We thought we would leave just as soon as we can pack up a nice lunch."

"I'm sure we can take care of filling up a basket with all the things you'll need for the afternoon," Julia assured her.

For the next half hour, Julia enjoyed Violet's company as they worked together in the kitchen, preparing a basket of food for the picnic. Violet's timid manner vanished while she chatted about the houses available for rent in Rome and the expected arrival of the new addition to her family in the fall. She also asked a number of questions about the area, which Julia patiently answered until a familiar figure passed by the kitchen window.

It was Tyler, arriving home on foot. Studying him through the glass panes, she immediately noticed something different about him. Normally he walked with bold, confident strides, shoulders thrown back, head held high. But at the moment, his pace was sluggish and hesitant, his stance desolate and forlorn. It almost seemed as though he dreaded entering the house.

Maybe he's just weary from walking back from town, Julia tried to tell herself, though she knew it wasn't true. Something was bothering him, pressing down on him like a heavy weight.

"Well, looks like everything is packed and ready to go," Violet announced, jarring Julia from her thoughts.

"I'll get the children ready for you," Julia offered, anxious to keep her hands busy and her mind occupied with thoughts other than those involving Tyler McRae.

After the Sprayberrys left with the children for the afternoon, an unusual quiet settled over Hopewell House. The place was too quiet, in fact, as far as Julia was concerned. When she joined Tyler and her aunts for lunch, she sensed an unspoken tension hovering around the dining room table. Tyler, who had little to say since returning from Bates's Mercantile, seemed distracted by wayward thoughts. Odelphia nibbled on her food and frowned as though she were battling a case of indigestion. And Dorinda yawned throughout the meal, struggling to keep her eyes open.

After Tyler mumbled something about going to his room and retreated up the stairs, Julia turned to her aunts. "Is something going on around here that I should know about?"

"Nothing out of the ordinary. I fear I'm just a tad drowsy, dear." Dorinda placed a hand over her mouth to stifle another yawn. "Must have been all those pastries I ate after breakfast this morning," she murmured.

"And watching you devour all those pastries made my stomach ache." Odelphia pushed aside her plate and sighed. "Reminiscing about the past this morning didn't help matters, either. Talking to Tyler brought back a lot of unhappy memories for me."

"What do you mean?" Julia asked.

"We told him about the reasons why neither of us has ever married." Though remorse tainted Odelphia's voice, she pulled up her thin frame from the chair with an air of renewed determination. "But there's no use in trying to change things that were never meant to be, now, is there? Come on, Dorie. Let's take our walk as soon as we clean up these dishes. Both of us need a breath of fresh air."

"I suppose it wouldn't hurt to take our afternoon stroll a bit earlier than usual today." Dorinda reluctantly pulled back from the table.

A few moments later, the Hopewell sisters were sauntering down the road, gloves in place, parasols in hand, and hats perched on top of their silver curls. As she watched them through the parlor window, Julia's heart swelled with love and admiration. Coping with shattered dreams and broken hearts could not have been easy for the women, but they'd dealt with their trials and pressed forward with their lives.

She was surprised that her aunts had confided in Tyler about their personal tragedies. Yet she couldn't imagine that Tyler would have been troubled by the stories of their long-lost loves. Something else was gnawing at him, she was certain. She only hoped he would be willing to discuss the matter with her.

Assuming Tyler would soon be going outside to continue his repairs to the house, Julia fully intended to take advantage of the rare, blissful moments of peace and quiet during the absence of her family and boarders throughout the afternoon. It seemed as though she never had enough time for all the things she needed to do, and she was determined to spend a few quiet hours in the parlor, catching up on her mending. Most of Sam's secondhand clothes needed altering for a proper fit.

She had just picked up a basket containing her needles and thread when she heard the slight shuffling of footsteps across the room. Looking up, Julia froze.

Tyler, standing at the door, looked almost like a stranger to her. Dear heavens, he'd shaved off his mustache! The clean-shaven skin beneath his nose revealed a thin upper lip so sensuous and beckoning that Julia's heart lurched with a stab of longing.

As she gawked at the sight of him, her lungs nearly stopped working. Since retreating to the privacy of his room, he'd changed from his cotton work clothes into a tailored suit. His broad shoulders filled the breadth of a black frock coat, which was open to reveal a brocaded satin vest hugging his trim torso. A gold watch chain was draped from the middle button to the pocket of his vest, and a black cravat was tied loosely around the collar of his white shirt. Black trousers covered the long length of his legs and disappeared into a pair of knee-high black boots.

All in all, he was dressed as though he intended to meet someone important. Julia was scrutinizing the changes in him with such intensity that she barely noticed he was carrying his traveling bag . . .

His traveling bag.

Her mouth went dry, her knees went weak. "You're . . . you're leaving?" she choked out, her voice barely above a whisper. "I . . . I had no idea . . ."

He stepped toward her, his face full of anguish and pain, his eyes full of sadness and heartache. "Julia, I—"

Thunderous raps crashing against the front door drowned out his words. "Open up! I know someone is in there!"

It was a woman's voice, one that Julia did not recognize. It was also an angry voice, brimming with rage . . .

Alarmed, Julia swept past Tyler and swung open the door. But her hand froze on the knob as she encountered the gaudiest-looking woman she had ever seen.

The woman's hair, wild and tangled, was the color of a carrot. Heavy layers of paint covered her pinched, drawn face, while a pair of cheap earrings dangled from her ears.

The woman scowled at Julia. "Where is he?" she demanded, the timbre of her voice as brassy and loud as her appearance. "I know you've got him in there somewhere."

"I'm afraid I can't help you." Julia lifted her chin, trying to retain an air of dignity in the wake of the woman's crude manner. "This is Hopewell House, a boarding establishment. I'm certain the person you're seeking could not be staying here."

"Well, I think you're wrong." Crossing her arms over her hefty bosom, the woman narrowed her eyes. "And I ain't leaving here until I get what I came for. I ain't takin' one step off this fancy porch until I get my boy."

A tiny pulse of fear throbbed through Julia's veins. "Your . . . b-b-boy?" she echoed in a terrified whisper.

"Yeah, the one with red hair and freckles. The one who goes by the name of Sam."

A sickening, dizzy feeling swamped through Julia. She staggered against the edge of the door, feeling light-headed and faint hearted. For a brief instant she actually thought she was going to faint.

This was Sam's mother? Julia had never expected Sophie Springer to be the kind of person who was full of love and concern for her son. But she'd never dreamed she would encounter someone as cold and unfeeling as this woman.

Trying to regain her composure, she drew in a shaky breath. At least Sam was gone for the afternoon, she thought wildly, hoping his absence would give her a chance to discourage Sophie from pursuing the boy. And she would endure a slow, painful death before relinquishing Sam to this atrocious woman. "Sam isn't here," she announced quietly.

"You're lying, lady, and you know it. The guys down at the docks told me that you and some fella come to my place and took the boy away with you." Sophie's eyes blazed with anger. "Who do you think you are, lady? You might live in some fancy house and your daddy might have been a God-fearing preacher, but you can't put on your self-righteous hat of Christianity, march onto somebody's property, and snatch a kid out of his own home!"

Waves of anger stormed through Julia. "And what gives you the right to abandon your own child? What kind of woman are you, leaving a helpless little boy all by himself for weeks at a time?"

"He's a tough kid. He knows how to fend for himself. I didn't raise my boy to be some whimpering fool who can't stand up on his own two feet." A bitter laugh escaped from her throat. "Most of the time, though, the damn boy ain't worth all the trouble he causes. His pa weren't no prize, and I'd wager Sam ain't been up to no good since he's been here."

"Sam is just a normal little boy . . . who needs lots of love and attention. And I'm certain he would be better off staying here with me," Julia stated quietly, even though her heart was pounding in her ears.

"That ain't for you to decide, now, is it? I ain't on trial here, and you ain't no judge in a court of law! And I'm ready to take my boy home."

"To the same place where we found him?" A knot coiled in the pit of her stomach at the horrid memory of Sam's miserable living conditions. "That wasn't a home, Mrs. Springer. That was a dump for discarded rubbish! My hogs live in better conditions!"

"Things are different now." Sophie's face grew red with fury. "I was down on my luck back then. But now I got me a man, a rich one who can take care of me." She held up a hand and wiggled her third finger, showing off a ring filled with tiny, dull stones.

"And what about Sam?" Julia trembled. "Is this man willing to assume responsibility for your son? Is he willing to feed him, clothe him, provide a roof over his head?"

"He'll do whatever I say. He loves me," Sophie announced flatly. "Now, I'm tired of arguing with you. I demand you turn over that damn kid to me right now, or I'll march down to Sheriff Mitchell's office and report you as a child snatcher!"

"I'll be right behind you, Mrs. Springer." Julia lifted her chin. "And I'll report you to the sheriff for abandoning your son."

"And what good would that do? Sam ain't got nobody but me. And I can't take care of him if I'm locked up behind bars."

"But I can take care of him," Julia responded evenly. "In fact, I want to take care of him."

She scowled. "If you ain't gonna turn my boy over to me, I'm gonna come in and get him." Sophie lunged at Julia. "Out of my way, lady."

Tyler, who had been quietly observing the confrontation from the foyer, could no longer restrain himself. After listening to Julia's scathing reprimand for his outspoken manner at Bates's Mercantile, he had been determined to stand back and let her wage her own private battles. But witnessing her courageous struggle to combat Sam's pitiful excuse of a mother, all his resolve vanished.

Tyler clamped a hand around Sophie's arm as she stormed into the house. "Didn't you hear what the nice lady said? The boy isn't here."

"Then I'll just wait until he gets back. I ain't nobody's fool. I know my boy has been stayin' here."

His grip tightened around the woman's arm. All too well he knew about women like Sophie Springer. Greedy and self-centered, indulgent and selfish, she was more concerned with taking care of her own needs than tending to a troublesome child. "But you don't really want the kid. He's just excess baggage to you, isn't he?"

Sophie raked her gaze over the expensive cut of Tyler's clothes. "Well, I might be willing to give him up. If the price is right, that is . . ."

Something snapped inside Tyler. Shoving the woman aside, he reached for his traveling bag. His hands shook with fury as he extracted a roll of bills from a hidden compartment, then hurled the money into Sophie's stunned face. "Damn it, woman! Get the hell out of here."

Greed and delight glistened from the woman's eyes as she snatched the money from Tyler's hand. After staring at the wad of crumpled bills for a long moment, she tucked the money into the low-cut bodice of her dress. Then she looked up at Tyler, patted her cleavage, and flashed a wicked smile. "The kid ain't worth this much, mister."

That was all Tyler needed to hear. Grabbing the woman by the shoulders, he spun her around. "Never let me see your face around here again, woman. If you come within a mile of that boy, I guarantee you'll regret it."

He shoved her onto the verandah, then slammed the door behind her with such force that the house shook from the impact. "Damn her!" he roared, smashing a balled fist into the closed door. "Damn her to hell!"

Consumed by a blinding fury, he ignored the pain searing through his hand. He stormed through the house and staggered through the rear entry, not knowing or caring where he was headed. All he knew for certain was that he had to get away, to escape from the horrors of reliving the nightmare that had haunted him for years.

Good God, Sophie Springer was just like Pa . . . willing to trade her own kid for the sake of a few measly dollars.

A few moments later, he found himself wandering near the edge of the Hopewell property. Feeling hot and tired, he shrugged off his frock coat and tossed it aside. Finding shade from the unusually warm spring afternoon beneath the canopied branches of a sprawling magnolia tree, he unhooked his watch chain, unbuttoned his vest, and dropped the brocaded garment to the ground. Then he loosened the cravat around his collar, propped his arm against the tree trunk, and dropped his forehead to his sleeve.

He closed his eyes, wanting to drown in the safe haven of darkness, longing to shut out the emotions reeling through him. He didn't move a muscle until he felt the gentle pressure of a woman's hand on his arm.

"Tyler, I want you to know how grateful I am . . . for what you just did."

Her voice fluttered through the air like an angel's, winging its way into the depths of his heart. He tried to ignore the strange emotions swelling up inside him. Without raising his head, he gave a bitter laugh. "Yeah, I'm a real hero, aren't I?"

"Don't be so hard on yourself, Tyler." Her fingers caressed the sleeve of his shirt with so much tenderness that it made him ache inside. "You just saved a little boy from a lot of pain and heartache. And I know it couldn't have been easy for you."

"Like father, like son, as they say." His eyes drifted closed again as he tried to block out that old, gnawing ache, the ache that refused to go away, no matter how hard he attempted to ignore it. "You know, I've always hated my old man for trying to sell off my sister and me. But I'm no better than he was. For God's sake, I just bought a blasted kid from his own damn mother!"

"But we both know you weren't buying a child! You were simply making sure that Sam has a roof over his head, food in his stomach, clothes on his back—all those things that his own mother wasn't providing for him."

"Don't try to make me into a saint, Julia. I didn't do anything for Sam's sake," he denied roughly. Pulling back from the tree, he straightened and brushed off bits of bark from his shirtsleeve. "I just didn't want that wretched woman to get her greedy hands on the boy. Judas Priest, she doesn't deserve to be his mother! You're the only one who deserves that title, Julia. You've probably given that blasted kid more love and attention since he's been here than his own mother has given him in a lifetime."

Not to mention all you've given to me, Tyler added silently, pausing to study the woman standing beside him. Sweet, sweet Julia had surrounded him with more love and concern than he'd ever known in his life. Like an angel sent from above, she'd made him feel warm and wanted and loved like no other woman ever had. Was it any wonder she made him ache, made him quiver, made him tremble inside?

"But you're the one who's given Sam the most precious gift of all . . . his freedom." Tears shimmered on her dark lashes. "Like it or not, Tyler, you're the one who has given the boy a real chance in life."

He dragged one hand through his thick waves of hair and tried to ignore her praise. He wasn't worthy of it, he knew. He'd rot in hell before he'd

admit to being the boy's salvation. "You wouldn't
think a mother—or a father—would stoop so low
as to trade a kid for a roll of greenbacks. Dammit,
I might have fought for the Confederacy, but even I
have the sense to know that people aren't supposed
to buy and sell other human beings in this country
any longer." Stretching out his arm, he grabbed
an overhead branch dangling from the magnolia
tree. The wood snapped beneath the pressure of
his fingers.

A white magnolia blossom sailed down from
the overhead branches, its sweet fragrance drifting
around them like a heavenly scent. Julia caught the
petals in an outstretched palm. "Papa used to say
money is the root of all evil. But then, money wasn't
a temptation for Papa. The poor man never had any
money to his name . . . not like some people, who
have more than they know what to do with."

Tyler cringed, biting his tongue, not wanting to
be the one to tarnish her love for the hypocritical son of a bitch who'd been her father. "Believe
me, money can cause more grief than it's worth at
times."

"I've never had a lot of money, so I wouldn't
know." She fingered the white petals in her hand.
"But it appears you do," she added in a soft, mean-
ingful tone. "Seeing you give all that money to
Sophie came as quite a surprise to me, I'll admit."

She was too saintly to accuse him of deceiving
her. Yet a thousand unspoken questions glimmered
from her overly bright eyes as she gazed up at him.
A knife seemed to tear into his gut. "I guess . . . I
guess you're wondering why . . . why I never told
you that the bastard who shot me on the train
didn't get everything I owned."

She rested her head against the tree, a troubled
look marring her delicate features. "I thought you

agreed to make repairs to the house in exchange for your room and board . . . because all your money had been stolen on the train."

He plucked the flower from her hand and tucked it behind her ear as gently as his trembling fingers would allow. "The son of a bitch who shot me only got the roll of bills I'd stuffed into the pocket of my jacket. I stashed away some more money in a hidden compartment of my traveling bag before leaving Chattanooga. I guess I should've told you, but I thought . . . I figured . . . I didn't know how to . . ."

Hell, he was babbling, rambling on like a mindless fool. He knew the money wasn't the root of her concern. Greed had no place in this woman's loving heart. No, she wasn't after his money, unlike some women he'd known. Julia Carey didn't care whether or not he had a cent to his name. But she was troubled because he hadn't been honest with her from the start. And he felt like a bastard for misleading her.

"Dammit, Julia, I didn't want you to know that I had any money! Truth of the matter is, I've got more money than I know how to spend. For all the damn good it does me." He crashed an open palm against the tree, venting his frustrations. "Having money—lots of it—attracts all kinds of people to you. Everyone claims to be your friend, but most only want you to lend money to them. And some are out to rob you blind. You learn to be cautious about who you take into your confidence."

"You even suspected me of trying to rob you," she recalled, "when you woke up in my room and found me rummaging through your traveling bag."

"You're damn right I did. For cripes' sake, I'd just been shot. I wasn't about to trust anyone. Not even you." He swallowed, hard. "Not at first, anyway."

"But what about later? You should have known that wealth doesn't impress me." A sudden flash of understanding brightened her troubled green eyes. "Unless you trusted someone else once, someone who hurt you very deeply . . . betrayed you, even . . ."

Would he ever get used to her perceptiveness? The way she could peer inside his soul and see all those secret, hidden places? Sometimes he felt like Julia Carey knew him better than he knew himself.

He wearily leaned one shoulder against the tree. "There was a woman, before the War. Her name was Sarah. When I joined up with the Confederate army, she promised to wait for me. But . . . she didn't keep her promise."

Julia sucked in a deep, shuddering breath.

"When the Union seized The McRae for a hospital, Sarah assumed I'd lost everything. So she decided to marry a carpetbagger from up North, someone who could give her all the things I couldn't." A harsh, hurting laugh escaped from his throat. "Odd, isn't it? She claimed she loved me when she thought I was rich. But she changed her tune when I was on the verge of losing everything."

"Did you . . . love her?"

"Hardly." Old feelings of bitterness swelled in his chest. "But I would like to see her again. I'd like for her to know that I've turned The McRae into the most profitable hotel in the South since the end of the War."

"I never realized . . ." Julia paused.

"When you assumed I'd been robbed of all my money, I didn't see any reason to tell you any differently. Besides, if I'd admitted to having money to pay you for my room and board . . . " He inhaled deeply. " . . . I wouldn't have had a reason to stay."

She stilled. "You didn't want . . . to leave?"

"No." He swallowed hard, trying to dispel the knot in his throat. How could she know that this place, this home, this family, were the closest thing to heaven he'd ever known? "Not then. Not even . . . now."

She traced the outline of his upper lip with trembling fingers. "I knew something was disturbing you when you got back from town this morning, right before lunch." Her fingers brushed across the smooth skin above his lip. "And when you got all dressed up—even shaving off your mustache—I thought you were planning to go somewhere special for the rest of the day. But then I saw your traveling bag, and I knew . . ." Her voice wavered.

"I thought it would be best for both of us if I went back to Chattanooga," he tried to explain.

"But . . . why?"

"God, can't you see?" He planted his hands on her shoulders. "Look at me, Julia! I'm so damn jealous that I managed to embarrass you twice in one morning!"

"It wasn't so terrible."

"Well, it was for me. I've never been jealous of another man in my life, for Christ's sake." He jerked away from her. "I'm not the right man for you, Julia. I'm no sweet-talker like Whitley. I'm not a family man like Aaron Sprayberry. I'm a damn loner. A coldhearted son of a bitch. Not the kind of man for a woman like you. Yes, I can buy you the world—but I can't give you what you *need*. I can't love you the way you deserve to be loved. I don't have any love inside me to give."

"I think you're wrong," Julia countered quietly. "I think you have lots of love in your heart. More than you realize. I think you—"

"Don't, Julia." He grimaced, closing his eyes for a moment, trying to block out the pain. "If I stay here much longer, we'll both regret it. I know you, damn it. I know you'd expect me to be someone I'm not. And I'd break your damn heart, lady."

"Maybe you already have." Her thick flashes fluttered. "The thought of you leaving . . . today or tomorrow or next week . . . is so painful, I don't know if I can bear it . . ." She choked back a sob and tried to blink back the moisture swelling in her eyes.

Something shattered inside Tyler when he saw the tears tumbling from her lashes and spilling down her cheeks. He was the one who'd caused those tears, and it pained him like nothing ever had. He draped his arms over her shoulders and pulled her close to him. "I can't stand the thought of leaving, either, Julia. If I leave, I'll never get to do this again . . ." He threaded trembling fingers through the thick, wavy tresses cascading down her back. "Or this . . ."

His mouth brushed through her hair, trailed over the soft curve of her cheek, then closed over her mouth. Her lips, soft and warm and pliant, parted shyly beneath the heated pressure of the kiss. His tongue snaked out, delving deep inside the lush sweetness of her mouth. She met the thrust with a soft swirl of her own, as if tentatively testing her own power. Coiling her arms around his neck, she pressed herself against him.

Feeling her breasts jutting against his chest, Tyler shuddered. He was starving for the taste of her, burning to touch every tantalizing curve and swell of her body with his tongue and his mouth and his hands.

"God help me, I can't get enough of you," he murmured, trailing wet, openmouthed kisses down the curve of her jaw and chin. His lips brushed across the high collar of her dress, secured around her neck by a row of buttons. Edging back ever so slightly, he slid the top button through the loop. After releasing a second button, he pressed his mouth to the soft skin at the base of her throat. A gasp escaped from her lips.

He undid a third button, then a fourth. When the fifth button fell away, he traced an imaginary line down from her neck to the top of the enticing crevice between her breasts. "Your skin is so soft, so smooth . . ." he choked out.

With the slow, seductive brush of his finger across her bare skin, a tingling sensation soared through Julia. She knew she should be pleading with him to stop or backing away from the touch of his hands. But she stood motionless, silent, captive to the strange new sensations she was experiencing.

"I've always known your skin was soft," he continued, his fingers working on the next button. "I knew from touching your face . . . your neck . . . your hands. But I've never touched you the way I really wanted to . . . never touched all the places I was burning to . . ."

The last button fell free. Tyler's eyes darkened as he gazed down at her, and Julia knew the reason why. Her thin chemise was almost transparent. She was certain he could see the outline of her nipples jutting out beneath the sheer fabric, and the darkness of the circles surrounding them.

Suddenly his fingers tugged at the dainty white ribbon securing the chemise across her breasts. Caught by surprise, Julia went rigid. "I can't allow . . . I shouldn't permit . . ." she sputtered, placing her hand over his, stopping him.

His eyes were desperate, pleading. "Please, Julia. Let me look at you. Just this once. It's all I've been able to think about, ever since that first night in your room . . ."

Her grip tightened over his hand. "But what if someone should—"

"No one will see us here. We're in the middle of a thick grove of trees, and we're sheltered from anyone's view beneath the branches of this magnolia." He gently removed her hand. "Please, Julia. I just want to see you . . ."

Without waiting for an answer, he tugged at the ribbon. As the chemise fell open, she closed her eyes, praying he would be pleased with what he saw—what no other man had ever seen.

He groaned at the sight of her naked breasts, full and ripe and swollen with desire. "You're beautiful," he rasped, skimming his fingers across the tips of her nipples.

She trembled. "You're not . . . disappointed?"

"Disappointed?" His eyes darted up to her face. "God, no, Julia. You're more glorious than I'd ever imagined."

He cupped his hand beneath one breast, gently squeezing the full mound as he brushed his thumb across the hardened peak. "So perfect," he whispered. "So high and full . . . and soft . . ."

Swooping down, he fitted his mouth over one rosy crest. As his tongue flicked across the hardened nipple, Julia arched her spine and tilted her head back, stunned by the sweet torture of his mouth on her breast. She plunged her hands into his hair, drawing him closer, deepening the pressure of his suckling.

"Oh, Tyler, I never realized . . ." She broke off, unable to express the feelings that shimmered just beyond reach.

"Let me show you more," he urged, cupping his mouth over her other breast.

Julia clung to him, swept away into a world of passion, blinded by the hot flames of desire burning through her. Just when she thought she was incapable of enduring another moment of his agonizingly sweet touch, he pulled away from her. She looked up in surprise as he shrugged off his cravat and shirt.

She admired the width of his muscular shoulders, the broad expanse of his chest, and the dark hairs curling over his torso. But it was the pink scar marring his upper arm that captured her attention. She reached out, tenderly brushing her fingers across the scarred flesh before pressing her lips against it. "So much pain," she whispered. "I wish I could take it all away."

Tyler shuddered, crushing her to him. The friction of his furred chest against her bare breasts was titillating to her. As they sank to the ground, the slow, simmering heat deep inside her belly erupted into blazes of passion.

He stretched out the full length of his hard, masculine frame against her, then plunged one hand beneath her skirts. He was impatiently tugging at her drawers and stockings when he heard Julia's soft whimper of protest. "Tyler . . . ?"

His hands stilled. Had he frightened her? Alarmed, he edged back, looking down into her face.

Her eyes were wide and questioning. "I've never . . . and all this is so new to me . . . and I'm not sure . . ."

"I'm not going to hurt you," he assured her. "Life has finally presented me with something rare and beautiful. And I couldn't bear the thought of inflicting any harm to the most precious gift I've ever received. God, I've never wanted a woman the way I want you. Everything about you sets me on fire, lady."

"But I want to—to make you happy," she whispered back. "I want to—please you. And I don't know how."

"You already know how to please me, Julia. Everything about you pleases me. Everything . . ."

He kissed her again and again. Still kissing her, he eased off her drawers and stockings. Then his hands traveled over her bare legs and worked their way up to the warm, moist juncture between her thighs. She gasped with pleasure as he touched her, kissed her, explored every part of her, in ways that no other man ever had.

Then, without warning, he suddenly stilled. "Julia?"

She was surprised to see the doubts flooding through his passion-filled gaze. Did he need to ask? Didn't he know she wanted him more than anything she'd ever wanted in her entire life? Heaven help her, she loved this perplexing, baffling man, and there was nothing on this earth that she would deny him. It seemed as though every minute of her life had been leading up to this one, as if she had been put on this earth for the sole purpose of loving Tyler McRae.

"Please, Tyler," she pleaded. "Please, now . . ."

Her boldness rocked him to the core. Yet he shouldn't have been surprised, he knew. He'd never known a woman who loved so fiercely, so openly, so completely. She was everything good and beautiful in a world filled with evil and ugliness, an earthly angel who had given him a taste of heaven on earth. Sweetness and goodness radiated from her like the soft, beckoning glow of a lantern, calling out to him, tempting him . . .

Desire, hot and raw, seared through him with such force that he gasped from the intensity of it. He wanted nothing more than to give in to his primal urges, to take her, swift and hard, to spill his seed deep inside her, to pour into her all the passion that was exploding inside of him. Yet another part of him wanted to go slowly, to savor every second of loving this heavenly creature.

"Love me, Tyler," she pleaded once again. "It's all I want . . ."

The urgency of her pleas left him gasping for breath. "I'll give you everything I have, sweet Julia. Everything . . ."

Tyler eased himself inside her, trying to be excruciatingly tender. In spite of his gentleness, she cried out, flinching as he broke through the delicate opening and plunged into the secret place inside her. "The painful part is over now," he promised. "So stay with me . . . stay with me . . ."

Flexing his hips, he moved with a slow, pulsating rhythm. Her cries of pain soon became passion-drenched whimpers. She wrapped her arms around him, sliding her hands down his back, digging her fingers into his skin. "I—I—think you're taking me —to heaven, Tyler."

"You are my heaven, Julia." He delved deeper and faster inside her, wanting to give her as much joy as she gave to him.

Suddenly pleasure flooded through her in pounding waves. She cried out, drowning in the overwhelming sensations. Tyler shuddered above her, clinging to her as if he never wanted to let go of the turbulent rush satiating both of them.

Then, one by one, his muscles began to relax. Sated with passion, he rested his head between the swell of her breasts, unwilling to remove himself from her. He felt an incredible sense of peace and wholeness that he'd never known. Was this what he'd been searching for all of his life?

He lifted his head, gazing up at her. "Julia, I've never known anything like this. I—— "

A frantic cry suddenly rang through the air. "Julia, come quick! Odie's been hurt!"

Dorinda's voice cut through Julia like the blade of a knife. "Dear Lord in heaven, something horrible has happened," she rasped.

Feeling Julia stiffening in alarm, Tyler straightened. "Judas Priest, what's going on?" he asked, rolling to one side.

She sat up, frantically groping for her undergarments. "I'm not certain," she admitted. "But I have to find out."

She dressed in silence, trying to summon up as much dignity as she could muster under the circumstances. Then she straightened her skirts, ran a shaky hand through her tangled hair, and ran toward the house.

Chapter 17

Propelled by sheer terror, Julia ripped through the grove of trees and raced toward the house. As she rounded the corner of the barn, she saw Dorinda pacing along the breezeway between the house and the kitchen, wringing her hands in dismay. "Julia, where are you?"

Julia's heart lurched with fear. "I'm right here, Dorie!" she called out. "I'm on my way!"

Gathering up her skirt and petticoats to her knees, she plunged across the yard. Stabs of guilt and shame lanced through her, intensifying as she picked up her pace. Was this God's punishment for her wanton behavior?

If something dreadful happened to dear Odelphia, she would never be able to forgive herself for not being at the woman's side. She didn't know how she could live with the guilt of not being available for her family . . . while she was consorting with a man in the most sinful of ways.

To make matters worse, Julia knew she must look like a fallen woman, too. Approaching the house, she was acutely aware of the tangled knots in her hair, the heated flush staining her cheeks, and the swollen curves of her lips. Dorinda, however, was too consumed with worry to notice her niece's rumpled appearance.

"Oh, Julia, it's terrible!" she cried. "Odie tripped

and stumbled down the stairs! I fear she's taken a terrible fall."

"Maybe it's not as bad as it seems." Though alarmed, Julia tried to remain composed for Dorinda's sake.

"But that's not all!" Dorinda shuddered. "The Sprayberrys came back early from their picnic with the children because Kate is terribly upset about something. And a young couple wants to board with us for several—"

"Stop, Sam!" Kate's cries pierced the air. "Stop it right now!"

Stunned by the terror in the child's voice, the women turned just as Sam darted around the corner of the house, hot on the heels of Kate's frisky new puppy. Kate trailed behind them, screaming hysterically. "Stop hurting him, Sam! Stop hurting Mack!"

"I ain't hurtin' your stupid dog!" Sam yelled. "I'm just playin' with him!"

At that instant, Sam caught up with Mack and yanked on the puppy's tail. As the animal yelped, the boy laughed with delight. "Atta boy, Mack!" Sam dropped to his knees, tucked the puppy under his arm, and rolled over in the grass with him.

Rushing toward Julia, Kate pointed an accusing finger at Sam. "Make him stop, Julia! He's hurting Mack! He's been pulling on his tail and making him yelp all afternoon! And he's just a little puppy . . ." Sobbing hysterically, the child hurled herself at Julia.

As Kate buried her tear-streaked face in the folds of her sister's dress, Dorinda tugged at Julia's arm. "We need to hurry, Julia. Odie is hurting!"

Torn between comforting Kate, settling the children's dispute, and rushing to Odelphia's aid, Julia felt as though her entire world were crumbling around her. The sight of Tyler rushing back to the house only made matters worse. She was too frazzled—and embarrassed—to even acknowledge his presence.

"Do something, Julia!" Kate pleaded. "Don't let Sam hurt Mack anymore!"

Deciding she would have plenty of time to fall apart later, Julia pursed her lips together with renewed determination and resolved to deal with one problem at a time. It was all she could do.

First she called out to the young boy who was still wrestling with Mack in the grass. "Mack needs to rest for a little while, Sam. He's too little to take so much rough play from a big boy like you. Besides, it's time for Kate to give him some food and water."

To Julia's surprise, Sam complied with her request without argument. And as soon as he turned the puppy loose, Kate's narrow shoulders stopped quaking. Julia wrapped her arms around her little sister. "I'll talk more to Sam later, sweetheart. Now, run along, and take care of your puppy."

Kate nodded, wiping the tears from her cheeks with the back of her hand. As the child scampered into the yard, Julia breathed a sigh of relief, then rushed into the house with Dorinda. Tyler followed behind them in silence.

But Julia's relief vanished when she found Odelphia sprawled out in a crumpled heap at the foot of the stairs, her wrinkled face contorted in pain. There was no doubt in Julia's mind that the dear soul had taken a rough tumble. Silver curls were scattered about her head in complete disarray, and her thick spectacles were dangling crookedly from the tip of her nose.

Julia kneeled down beside her. "Where are you hurting, Aunt Odelphia?"

Moaning, Odelphia pointed to her foot. "My right ankle, mostly. I'm afraid it might be broken."

"Let's take a look at it, then." Julia gently removed Odelphia's shoe and the white stockings that covered her thin legs. After examining the swollen, bruised skin around the woman's ankle, Julia prayed the fragile bone was not broken. "I think you've got a nasty sprain, Aunt Odelphia, but I'd like for Doc Kramer to take a look at it."

"What's all this, Miss Odelphia?"

At the sound of Tyler's voice, every nerve in Julia's body stood on end. Mindful of her shameful behavior, she could not bring herself to turn around and face him.

"I tripped down the stairs and twisted my ankle." Odelphia heaved a sigh of disgust. "I'm just a clumsy old biddy, I suppose."

"Age doesn't mean a thing," Tyler assured her. "Everyone, young and old, takes a tumble now and then."

"Regardless, she'll need to stay off her feet for a while." Dorinda sighed. "I fear she's taken quite a fall."

Still lacking the courage to face Tyler, Julia rose to her feet. "I'll get Sam to fetch Doc Kramer for us. In the meantime, let's get you settled in your room, Aunt Odelphia."

Julia stepped aside as Tyler hunkered down beside the injured woman. "Put your arms around my neck, sweetheart," he said with a teasing wink, "and I'll sweep you off your feet."

Taken aback by his humor, Odelphia managed to chuckle through her pain. Tyler scooped her into his arms and carried her up the steps as if she were no older than Kate. Dorinda waddled up the stairs behind them.

Assured that Dorinda would tend to Odelphia,

Julia rushed outside to locate Sam. Within a few seconds, she found the boy hanging from the branches of a tree near the verandah. "I need your help, Sam," she called out.

Though the boy scampered down the tree with the agility of a monkey, he approached Julia with caution. "I was just playin' with Mack, Miss Julia, and I didn't mean no——"

"We'll discuss Mack some other time," Julia broke in. "Right now I need you to run an errand for me."

After sending Sam into town to get Doc Kramer, Julia rushed back into the house and flew up the stairs. As she entered Odelphia's room, she was relieved to find her aunt resting comfortably in bed. Tyler was propping pillows beneath her injured ankle, while Dorinda was tucking another set of pillows behind her head.

Julia picked up a brush from the dresser. "Now, tell me, Aunt Odie. How did you get yourself into this predicament?"

As Julia brushed the tangles from her silver curls, Odelphia sighed. "I was coming down the stairs, carrying a load of soiled bed linens. Part of the bundle slipped out of my arms. Somehow my feet got tangled up in the sheets. The next thing I knew, I was skidding down the steps on my tailbone."

"I should have been the one responsible for changing the linens on Mr. Whitley's bed as soon as I rented out his room to that nice young couple." Sinking to the edge of the bed, Dorinda shook her head in dismay. "I shouldn't have left you with all the work while I was making up an extra apple pie for our new boarders."

The brush stilled in Julia's hand. "Our . . . new boarders?" she echoed in a tiny voice.

"Why, yes, dear." Dorinda beamed with pride.

"Odie and I met the nicest young couple down at the train depot this afternoon! They're just passing through town, and they needed a place to stay for the night."

"But we don't have an extra room available, Aunt Dorinda! Mr. Whitley has already paid in advance for an entire week. We only have two rooms available for boarders, and they're already occupied by the Sprayberrys and Mr. Whitley!"

"Oh, my." Dorinda paled. "But I thought . . . after Mr. Whitley left this morning . . . I figured he wouldn't . . . I didn't realize . . ."

Tyler suddenly stiffened. Sniffing, he wrinkled his nose. "Do I smell something burning?"

"Oh, no!" Dorinda cried, her eyes widening in horror. "My apple pies!"

Under any other circumstances, Julia might have been amused at the sight of her plump aunt springing up from the bed and rushing out of the room to rescue her pies from the oven. But at the moment, Julia felt more like crying than laughing. What else could go wrong in one afternoon?

At that moment, the tender touch of a callused hand threaded through her hair. Turning, Julia looked up at Tyler, meeting his steady gaze for the first time since scampering away from their secluded haven beneath the magnolia tree.

"If you'd like, I could stay on for a while longer," he offered, his voice husky and low. "I could help you get things under control here."

Her heart lurched. "I'd like that very much, Tyler."

"With Forrest looking after things at The McRae, there's no need for me to rush back to Chattanooga any time soon. And the boy . . . Sam . . . and I could share a room for a night or two. That would free up a room for the new boarders." A faint smile touched his lips as he tucked an errant curl behind her ear. "Sam and I may not get along very well, but surely we won't kill each other when we're sleeping."

Julia discerned a shadow of embarrassment lurking behind his tender smile, and an ache swelled in her chest. She'd never wanted him to leave, and she was moved beyond words that he'd decided to stay. And volunteering to share his living quarters with Sam could not have been easy for him. The relationship between the man and boy was far from amiable. Yet his simple sacrifice touched the depths of her heart in ways she never dreamed possible.

Standing in full view of Odelphia, Julia struggled not to reach out and coil her arms around his neck, to capture his mouth with her own, to show him how much she loved him. She settled for a hoarse whisper. "Thanks, Tyler," she murmured gratefully.

"No problem." He lifted one shoulder in a careless shrug. "When you're in the business of renting out rooms, you have to be flexible, you know."

"I'm learning, it seems." She mustered up a smile, remembering that he'd finally taken her into his confidence about his business. "And it appears I have an experienced teacher."

"You don't need a teacher, Julia." She could have sworn a flush of crimson was shading his high cheekbones before he turned to Odelphia. "You and your aunts are already turning Hopewell House into a success. Isn't that right, Miss Odelphia?"

Odelphia nodded, patting the silver curls around her forehead. "But Julia should get most of the credit. Taking in boarders was her idea, you know. She's the one who saw the need for another boardinghouse in town."

"A smart move," Tyler assessed thoughtfully, walking to the window. He pulled back the drapes and peered outside, as if appraising the town with one sweeping glance. "You know, Rome might need a genuine hotel in another year or so. I've been thinking about opening a hotel in Atlanta, but if Rome keeps attracting new businesses and families . . ."

As Tyler continued to ponder the possibilities of the town's growth, Julia quietly slipped out of the room. She was grateful to him for trying to keep Odelphia's mind off her pain. But she wished she knew of something that would make her forget her own troubles as easily. She retreated into the privacy of the parlor, hoping to spend a few moments alone to sort out her jumbled emotions.

She sank into a chair near the window, suddenly shaken beyond words. Dear heavens, what had she done? Waves of shame washed through her like a tidal wave. Not only had she neglected her family, but she'd committed an unpardonable sin. She'd fallen prey to the temptations of the flesh, going against her own moral standards and the biblical principles that had been part of her life for as long as she could remember.

It was bad enough that she'd given herself to a man without the benefit of marriage, but committing such a sinful act in the naked light of the spring afternoon only made matters worse. Julia was filled with regret for behaving so recklessly, so impulsively. What must Tyler think of her?

Though she had no way of knowing Tyler's opinion, she suspected he could not think any less of her than she thought of herself at the moment. Shame overpowered her with such intensity that she trembled from the force of it. She buried her face in her hands, muffling tremulous sighs of regret and frustration. She'd been a fool for giving herself to Tyler McRae with such reckless abandon, for wanting his love to last a lifetime.

God help her, she loved Tyler more than she'd ever dreamed possible, maybe even more than life itself. But deep inside her soul, she knew that loving him wasn't enough. It could never be enough.

Loving Tyler—the way he deserved to be loved—would consume every part of her, every thought, every breath, every moment of her life. Yet it was impossible to totally devote herself to him, to love him the way she wanted to. Her life was already crowded with too many other obligations and responsibilities, too many tearstained faces, too many shattered dreams.

How could she love Tyler and continue to care for her family? After the harrowing events of the afternoon, Julia didn't see how she could dedicate herself to both of them. During her stolen moments with Tyler beneath the magnolia tree, chaos had reigned supreme at Hopewell House. By the time she'd returned to her family's side, Julia knew her absence had been a grave mistake. In more ways than one.

Her aunts weren't getting any younger, and they needed her support as never before. Dorinda was becoming flustered more easily with each passing day, and now Odelphia would be confined to bed for several weeks with an injured ankle.

Then there was Kate. Julia had been more of a mother than a sister to the child since the day she was born. Who would take care of the precocious little lass if Julia were not around? Who would wipe away her tears, savor the sounds of her girlish laughter?

And now there was Sam's future to consider,

as well. She intended to fill the boy's life with all
the love and warmth that he'd never had and so
desperately needed.

All of which left very little of herself to give
to anything—or anyone—else. And how could she
honor her promise to Papa if she focused all of her
love and attention on Tyler McRae? Was there a
place in her life for the man who had stolen her
heart?

She thought not. An ache swelled in her heart,
an ache more powerful than any she'd ever known.
For the first time in her life, she could think of
nothing that could restore her hopes or revive her
spirits, nothing except . . . a miracle. Only a miracle could make her dreams of loving Tyler McRae
come true.

Tending to Odelphia's needs occupied much of
Julia's time during the next four days. She scurried
in and out of her aunt's room several times each
morning and afternoon. Though Odelphia had not
fractured any bones during her tumble down the
steps, Doc Kramer had advised complete bed rest
for the woman until the swelling and tenderness
around her ankle had subsided.

No longer able to rely on Odelphia to prepare
the evening meal, Julia assumed her aunt's duties
in the kitchen. Dorinda took over the daily ritual
of baking bread and biscuits, in addition to keeping a hearty supply of freshly baked pies and other sweets on hand. But the primary responsibility
of preparing three meals each day fell on Julia's
shoulders.

Which was no easy task, considering the steady
stream of boarders flowing in and out of Hopewell
House. As word spread about the establishment's
excellent fare and accommodations, the number of

new faces appearing at the door increased every day.

Benjamin Whitley left after only one night's stay—much to Tyler's relief—but a steamboat captain had immediately rented the vacated space. And within hours after the Sprayberrys had packed their bags and moved into their new home, their room had been occupied by another young family. To accommodate all of the houseguests, Sam was still doubling up with Tyler, and Julia was still sleeping in Kate's room.

Finished with most of the exterior repairs, Tyler plunged into working on the two remaining rooms on the third floor that had not yet been renovated. As Julia tended to boarders, cooked meals, waited on Odelphia, and settled squabbles between Kate and Sam, Tyler relegated himself to the top floor of the house, stripping and polishing floors, painting and plastering walls.

Yet, after four days without a moment of privacy with Julia, he was burning to steal away with her for a few precious hours. Late in the afternoon, he wandered into the kitchen, hoping to find her there.

She was standing in front of a chopping block, peeling potatoes. Tyler stopped at the door, awed by the power of the feelings she could evoke in him. His palms were sweating, and his heart was racing like mad.

Odd. Never in his wildest dreams could he have imagined that the sight of a woman peeling potatoes would be so appealing to him. For a long moment he watched her, admiring the gentle swell of her hips, the slight tilt of her head, the fragile curve of her jaw.

Then, without warning, she yelped in pain. Dropping the knife and half-peeled potato on the chopping block, she snatched a rag from the table and wiped off the blood oozing from her finger.

"Dear Lord in heaven, how much more can I take?" she cried, pressing the rag against her cut. "I've got a house full of people to feed, two kids who can't get along for more than five minutes without squabbling..." A sob choked off the rest of her unspoken thoughts.

Tyler's heart rolled over. It wasn't the first time he'd heard a woman lamenting over her problems. Most members of the fairer sex were masters at the art of complaining. Long ago he'd learned to shrug off their moans and groans without a second thought, labeling their protests as self-induced bitching.

But this wasn't just any woman. This was Julia. Kind, sweet, loving Julia. The woman who would sacrifice her own life if it meant making her loved ones happy. The woman who never uttered a cross word to anyone. In fact, Tyler couldn't recall hearing one word of complaint cross her lips.

Until now.

He stood at the door for another moment, studying her. Tiny lines of fatigue were etched into her angel face. The luster in her eyes was not as vivid as usual. And her shoulders were sagging...

Good God, it was no wonder her shoulders were sagging. The woman thought it was her responsibility to make everyone happy. She genuinely believed she had to maintain control of everyone's happiness and well-being at all times. If something went wrong, she shouldered the blame. And if Hopewell House wasn't functioning smoothly, she condemned no one but herself.

Her voice broke into his thoughts. "...and I've got an aunt who can't get out of bed, a roof that's

in pitiful shape, and I've given m-m-myself t-t-to a
m-m-man . . ."

A knot coiled in Tyler's gut. He'd taken her honor
and given her nothing in return. God, he wished
things could be different. She deserved a gold ring
on her finger, a white wedding gown, a man to love
and cherish her.

He silently damned himself. No, he couldn't love
her like she should be loved. Yet, in spite of his
shortcomings, he couldn't stop wanting her.

In the space of a heartbeat, he was standing beside
her, pushing back a wispy curl from her forehead.
"You look like hell, you know."

Something resembling a smile whispered across
her mouth until her bottom lip began to tremble.
"Thanks. I needed to hear that about as much as I
needed this cut in my finger."

He picked up her hand and gently brushed his
lips across the nick in her finger. "You don't have
to take care of everyone by yourself, you know."

"I really don't mind looking after everyone,
Tyler." She dropped her eyes and pulled away
from him, as if she'd been caught doing something naughty. "I'm just a little tired this afternoon."

"Tired?" He snorted. "Dammit, woman, don't be
so stubborn! You're not tired, you're exhausted!
You've been running around taking care of everyone around here . . . but yourself."

The curve of her back went rigid. "Unfortunately, I don't have a paid staff at my beck and call,
Tyler."

"Then just ask for some help when you need it.
Hellfire, I could help you with something . . ." He
surveyed the fresh vegetables she'd set out on the
table. "I could peel potatoes, snap beans, maybe
even slice up some apples."

Her eyes widened. "You, in the kitchen? Most men would say that's woman's work."

"Normally I'd agree. But when you're staking your livelihood on what comes out of the oven, it's a different matter. Believe me, I've whipped up a few dishes in the kitchen at The McRae on more than one occasion." Chuckling, he picked up the potato and knife. "On Sunday mornings. mostly, when the cook is too drunk to show up for work."

Before he could slice off the first bit of peeling, she snatched the knife from his hand. "I won't have you working in my kitchen, Tyler."

"And why the hell not? I eat enough of the stuff that comes out of here."

"Because I'm the one who should be taking care of my family. It's my responsibility to take care of them when they get hurt, to provide a place for them to live, to put food on the table—"

"That's not women's work, Julia. You're talking about a man's obligations to his family."

"Unfortunately, there have never been any men in my life who were willing to assume all of those responsibilities." A shadow of darkness crossed her face. "I dearly loved my father, but providing for his family was never one of his strongest assets. And Lucas . . ." She shrugged. "Well, Lucas is a different story entirely."

"What about this brother of yours?" He leaned against the table, genuinely curious about her elusive sibling. "Why in the hell can't you just ask him to come home and help you out for a while?"

"It's not easy to get in touch with Lucas, I'm afraid. He hasn't stayed in one place for more than a month or two since the end of the War. We couldn't even reach him in time to let him know about Papa's passing. Poor Lucas . . . didn't

get home in time for Papa's funeral." She heaved
a weary sigh. "At first he was always drifting from
place to place, picking up odd jobs while he was
searching for permanent work. Last year he finally
landed a good job with the railroad. But it's still
difficult to reach him because he's moving around
all the time, rebuilding the tracks that the Yanks
destroyed during the War."

"And he doesn't come home to visit very often,
I take it."

"I wish we could see him more than we do,"
Julia admitted, though Tyler noticed she wasn't
placing any blame on her beloved brother for not
taking the time to visit his family. "In his last let-
ter to Elizabeth, he mentioned something about
coming home around the middle of May. But we
haven't heard anything else from him."

She pursed her lips together and resumed her
work, picking up the knife and another potato. It
almost seemed as though she were trying to shove
aside her troubled thoughts by keeping her hands
occupied.

Frustrated, Tyler cursed under his breath. Why
in the hell was life so unfair? Julia's brother had the
love of a devoted sister and a beautiful fiancée, yet
he didn't seem to care enough about them to spend
a few days at home. Tyler wanted to wring Lucas
Carey's neck, even though he'd never even laid
eyes on him. "I hope your brother doesn't continue
to make a habit of disappointing the women who
love him," he admitted with genuine honesty.

Julia managed a weak smile. "Lucas doesn't
mean any harm, I'm certain. As Odelphia says,
he's sowing a few wild oats right now, and I'm
sure he'll settle down soon. Lucas is basically a
good person."

And I'm a damn angel with wings, Tyler thought

sarcastically. Slowly but surely, Julia's unwavering devotion to her undeserving brother was beginning to grate on his nerves. Couldn't she see the man for what he was? Even he could tell that Lucas Carey was an irresponsible, undependable rogue who had not a snippet of regard for his family's feelings. And he'd never even met the man. "Have you ever considered that Lucas is simply trying to avoid his family responsibilities? Maybe he doesn't come home because he's afraid of losing his independence. Or maybe he's fearful of getting tied down with family obligations."

"And what if you're right?" Julia set down the knife and glared at him. "Even if you are, Lucas wouldn't be the first man in the world to shy away from family life. As I recall, I've heard other men claim that families are nothing but trouble and bother."

Tyler felt a hot flush creeping along his neck. "I wish things could be different, Julia. God, how I wish . . ." He shook his head, knowing he couldn't change. "You know, you haven't been inclined to speak highly of families lately, either. Especially not in the last few minutes."

"I suppose you're right." Her voice wavered, and her eyes clouded with moisture.

She looked so tired, so vulnerable, so worried and burdened with troubles and doubts, that Tyler lost his last vestiges of control. "Damn it all to hell, woman," he muttered, catching her in his arms and crushing her against him.

Sniffing, she snuggled a damp cheek against his chest. "M-M-Maybe you were right, T-T-Tyler. M-M-Maybe families are m-m-more tr-trouble than they're w-w-worth."

He swallowed, hard. "That's what I'd always thought. Until . . ."

She leaned back and peered up at him, her tear-drenched eyes narrowing in confusion. "Until . . .?"

"Until you, sweet Julia," he whispered. "Until you."

Chapter 18

Tyler lingered at the table, dawdling over a cup of coffee, long after the rest of the household had finished with breakfast the next morning. He stared aimlessly into the murky brown liquid, wondering what in the hell he should do . . . about Julia.

The woman was working herself into an early grave. As she'd served breakfast to the hungry crowd, her smile had been bland, her step sluggish. Tyler suspected she hadn't rested well during the night. Lines of fatigue were etched into her delicate features, and shadows of sleeplessness circled her eyes.

But what could he do about it? He'd already warned her that she was overworked, exhausted. She was too stubborn, too independent, to ask for any assistance. And she would laugh in his face if he hired someone to help with the laundry or cooking . . .

Dorinda clattered through the adjoining foyer, jarring Tyler from his thoughts. Startled, he glanced up just as Julia came into view, trailing a few steps behind her aunt and cradling a pile of neatly folded bed linens in her arms.

"I used up the last of the sugar yesterday, dear," Dorinda was saying. "And I can't bake my pies this afternoon without sugar, you know."

"We're getting low on flour, too." Julia brushed her fingers across the freshly laundered sheets and heaved a weary sigh. "As soon as I change the bed linens, I'll run into town and pick up some sugar and flour at Horace's store. If I hurry, I can get back in time to fix lunch."

"There's no need to rush," Tyler called out, pushing back from the table and crossing the room.

Just as he reached the foyer, the front door swung open and all hell broke loose. Mack leaped down from Kate's arms and bolted into the house like a streak of lightning. Kate screamed. Sam vaulted through the door, scrambling to catch up with the puppy, but Mack skidded across the polished floor and slid straight into Dorinda's skirts.

Shrieking, Dorinda grasped the edge of the foyer table to keep from losing her balance. Mack yelped, shook the hem of Dorinda's skirts away from his face, then spun around and darted back outside.

Dorinda sagged against the table. "Oh, my," she whispered, clutching her throat in disbelief. "Oh, my."

Setting aside the bed linens, Julia clamped her hands around Kate's narrow shoulders. "How many times do I have to tell you that Mack isn't allowed in the house?"

The little girl's lower lip trembled. "But it was an accident, Julia! He jumped out of my arms and—"

"We're lucky that Aunt Dorinda didn't get hurt." Clearly troubled by the incident, Julia pursed her lips together.

"Run along outside and wait for me, Kate." Tyler retrieved his hat from a hook beside the door. "I'm going to pick up a few supplies for your sister at Bates's Mercantile, and you can go with me. Sam, too, if he wants."

Kate's face brightened considerably. "Can Mack go with us?"

"Of course. But you'll have to catch up with him first."

As Kate darted out the door in search of her beloved pet, Julia frowned. "I appreciate your offer, Tyler, but it really isn't necessary. I had already planned to go into town, and the children can go with—"

"No use arguing, woman. I've made up my mind." He shoved his hat over his thick waves of hair and pivoted around to leave.

He'd taken only one step when she called out to him. "Go on to the store, if you want. But you don't have to take Kate and Sam with you. They're my responsibility, after all, and I don't want you to—"

He spun around. "They're going with me, and that's final. And we're not going to rush back home, either." He couldn't resist reaching out and tucking a wispy curl behind her ear. "You need a few hours to yourself, Julia. Try to get some rest while we're gone."

For a fleeting instant Tyler thought she was on the verge of bursting into tears. As something akin to gratefulness flickered across her delicate features, Tyler felt a strange stirring in his chest. Good God, he never dreamed she would be so appreciative of such a simple gesture. How often did anyone bother to think about Julia's needs? Not often enough, it seemed.

She pulled some coins from her apron pocket and pressed the money into his hand. "This should be enough for ten pounds of sugar and flour. And maybe enough to buy a peppermint stick for each of the children."

He started to refuse, but ended up shoving the coins into his pocket without argument. He didn't

want her damn money, and she knew it. But any
refusal on his part would only wound her stubborn
pride. He supposed winning her permission to take
the children with him was victory enough for one
morning.

The walk into town was more pleasant than he'd
expected, considering he'd never volunteered to
take two kids and a dog with him anywhere.
Kate skipped along the dirt road, blond braids
flopping about her shoulders, while Sam tried to
keep pace with Tyler's long strides. Mack, trotting
beside the mismatched trio, wagged his tail as if he
were delighted to be included in the outing.

As the children admired the assortment of goods
on display at Bates's Mercantile, Tyler stepped up
to the counter. Horace greeted him with a frosty
glare. "You want something, McRae?"

"As a matter of fact, I'm here for Miss Julia. She
needs flour and sugar—ten pounds each." Tyler
pulled the money from his pocket and placed it on
the counter. "And I need two peppermint sticks,
too."

After snatching up the coins, Horace filled the
order without further comment. Though Tyler
wasn't surprised by the storekeeper's cool reception, he wondered about the extent of Horace's
fondness for Julia. He doubted he could be as
civilized if another man had shoved him out of
Julia's life.

Tyler stuffed the candy into his pocket, picked
up the bundles of supplies, and left the store. As
soon as they topped the first hill, he pulled out the
candy and presented it to the children. Though
Kate squealed with delight, Sam accepted the gift
with reluctance. "How come you bought this for
me?" he demanded, frowning up at Tyler.

He tried to ignore the suspicion tainting the

boy's voice. "I just thought you might like it," he answered with a shrug, though the question made him acutely aware of the lack of trust between them. Not that he cared, of course. The boy didn't deserve to be trusted, as far as Tyler was concerned.

Sharing a room had not eased the strain in their relationship. Though tempers had not flared, they had avoided each other as much as possible. And before retiring each night, Tyler tucked his pocket watch into the hidden compartment of his traveling bag, unwilling to leave the gold timepiece on the table beside the bed within reach of the boy's greedy fingers.

They walked along in silence for a few moments. Kate trailed behind them, playing tag with Mack. When Sam finished with the last bite of candy, he glanced over at Tyler. "How come you wanted me and Kate to go to the store with you?" he blurted out.

Tyler shrugged. "I thought Miss Julia needed a little peace and quiet."

"So *you* didn't really want us," Sam surmised hotly. "You just wanted to get us out of Miss Julia's hair for a while."

"Yeah, I guess you're right," Tyler shot back, irritated by the boy's attitude. He stomped over the dirt road, regretting that he'd offered to take the unappreciative lad anywhere. Consumed by his thoughts, he didn't notice the absence of Kate's laughter until Hopewell House came into view.

He paused and turned around, searching for her, trying to ignore the tiny pulse of fear throbbing through his veins when he saw nothing but an empty stretch of road behind him. "Come on, Kate!" he shouted. "We're almost home, and Julia will be waiting for us."

When the child didn't respond, a knot coiled in Tyler's gut. "Where's Kate?" he demanded roughly, glaring at Sam.

"She's not here?" Surprise flickered across the boy's freckled face. "She was right behind us a few minutes ago."

"She must be chasing after that damn puppy," Tyler grumbled. He set down the bundle of supplies beneath the shade of an oak tree. "Surely she and Mack haven't gone too far off the road. I'll go back over the hill to look for her."

As Tyler retraced his steps along the road, Sam darted off in the opposite direction. A few moments later, the boy rushed up to Tyler, breathless and distraught. "I can't find her nowhere, Mr. Tyler. And there ain't no sign of Mack, neither."

"Then where in the hell is she?" Tyler roared.

Sam flinched. "Maybe she's back at home. She might have taken a shortcut that we didn't know about."

"Maybe so," Tyler conceded, wearily kneading the nape of his neck in frustration. After retrieving the bundles of sugar and flour from the side of the road, he trudged back to the house.

As Sam searched the grounds for Kate, Tyler went inside the house. As he entered the kitchen, Julia rushed up to greet him. She looked rested, refreshed, and happy to see him. She smiled warmly as he set the parcels on the table.

"I can't thank you enough for all you've done," she gushed. "You were right, you know. I really needed a few hours to myself. I'm feeling much better now."

"I'm glad." He swallowed with difficulty. "So did Kate mention that I got her a peppermint stick?"

"Kate?" She frowned. "Kate isn't here. She is supposed to be . . . with you."

A sickening feeling swept through Tyler. "I was hoping . . . I figured . . ."

She stilled. "Where is she, Tyler?"

"To be honest, I'm not sure. On the way home, she was trailing behind Sam and me, chasing after Mack. Then, all of a sudden, I looked around . . . and she and Mack were gone."

"G—G—Gone?" Julia paled.

He felt something knot in his stomach, but met her anguished gaze as levelly as he could. "Sam and I looked everywhere for her—beneath every tree, behind every bush—along the road."

Ripping off her apron with trembling hands, Julia glared at him. "How could you have allowed something like this to happen? You were responsible for her, Tyler!" She slapped the apron onto the table. Fire blazed from her eyes and her voice. "I should have known something like this would happen."

Her words were like a lance cutting into his soul. "She's only been missing for a few minutes. She couldn't have gotten too far. I suspect she scampered off the road, chasing after Mack, and—"

"Mack!" Julia balked. "That puppy has caused problems ever since he's been here. I should have never allowed Kate to keep him, even if he was a birthday gift from you." Wringing her hands, she darterd to the window and looked outside. "Oh, dear Lord, where is she?"

"Sam suspects she might have taken a different route home. He's combing the grounds around the house right now, looking for her." Trying to offer some words of consolation, he added, "We'll find her, Julia. I'm certain of it."

"You'd better hope so." She whirled on him, all anger and anguish. "If anything happens to Kate,

I'll never be able to forgive myself for allowing her to go off with you. I should have remembered that she's my responsibility, not yours."

He reached out, wanting to wrap his arms around her narrow shoulders, longing to offer some sort of comfort in the midst of her pain. But she refused to be consoled. With an adamant shake of her head, she pushed him away. "We've already wasted enough time, Tyler. We've got to find Kate. I don't know what I would do if anything happened to her . . ."

Images of Kate, bubbling with laughter and smiles, danced through Julia's mind. It wasn't like the child to wander off by herself. What could have happened to her? Terrorized by the thought of never seeing her sister again, Julia plunged past Tyler as if her skirts had caught fire. She had to find her, and find her soon . . .

Just as she stepped onto the breezeway, Sam came rushing up to the house, gasping for breath. His face was as red as his hair, and his expression was full of dismay.

"Have you found any sign of Kate?" Julia could hear the frantic beat of her heart pounding in her ears. "Any sign at all?"

"Not yet, Miss Julia." Sam looked like he was trying to be very brave. "I've checked the spring-house and looked around the woods behind the barn."

"And what about the barn? Have you looked there?"

"No, but I—"

That was all Julia needed to hear. Tyler and Sam sprinted behind her as she raced across the yard, catching up with her when she hurled open the barn doors and lunged into the dimly lit building. "Kate, can you hear me?" she shouted.

Tyler bounded around her, peering into the first

stall, then the next. At the third stall, he stopped in his tracks.

Julia's heart lurched. "Tyler . . . ?"

A smile touched his lips. In Julia's eyes, never had there been a smile so wondrous, so welcome. He motioned for her to join him. "Look."

Holding her breath, she inched forward and looked around the edge of the wooden partition. What she saw brought tears of joy and relief to her eyes.

There had never been a sweeter sight. Kate was curled up in the hay, braids askew, one chubby arm coiled around her beloved puppy. The little girl's face bore an angelic expression, tainted with just the slightest hint of a smile. Her eyes were closed, as were Mack's. Wrapped in the protective arms of blissful slumber, both the child and her pet were oblivious to the panic and heartache they'd caused.

Julia sagged against Tyler. "Thank God," she whispered.

She was resting her head against the broad expanse of his chest when Sam rushed up and peered into the stall. "Well, I'll be damned."

"Samuel Springer!" Julia admonished, breaking away from Tyler with a start. "You know better than to use such foul language!"

Sam shot an accusing glare at Tyler. "Well, *he* says it all the time, and you never yell at him."

"Well, *he* doesn't have any more business cursing than you do, young man."

A soft whimper sounded from the stall. "Wh-Wh-What's all the yelling about?" a sleepy voice asked.

"Your sister is fussing at Sam and me for saying bad words," Tyler answered with a wry grin.

Kate propped up on her elbows. "Well, you

shouldn't be saying bad words, you know." Yawning, she rubbed her eyes with the back of her hand.

Sam looked up at Julia and frowned. "Well, aren't you going to yell at her for running away from us?"

"There will be enough time for that later." Relieved that Kate was safe and unharmed, Julia didn't have the heart to scold the child, no matter how much worry she'd caused. "At the moment, I think all of us need to wash up for lunch."

"Lunch, already?" Kate brushed Mack away from her lap and sprang up from the hay. "What's to eat? I'm starving."

Laughing, Julia held out her hand. "Anything you want, sweetheart. Anything at all."

Tyler leaned against the white Doric column, gazing across the front lawn. At the first sign of twilight, fireflies were dancing through the dusk-painted sky. Cicadas chirped in the distance, while the sweet fragrance of magnolia blossoms drifted through the evening air.

Yet, in spite of the serenity surrounding him, Tyler couldn't shake the troubling memories of the afternoon from his mind. Even now, he was still smarting from the way Julia had lashed out at him for losing Kate.

"Beautiful evening, isn't it?"

Julia's voice fluttered through the twilight as softly as the wings of an angel. His heartbeat quickened as she stepped up to join him, bathed in the soft golden glows of lantern light spilling from the windows of Hopewell House. "Not bad, as far as evenings go," he admitted in a curt tone.

"It's almost sinful not to take advantage of an evening as beautiful as this one." Her dark lashes dipped shyly, beguilingly. "You know, if a certain gentleman invited me to accompany him on an evening stroll, I would not be inclined to refuse him."

A rueful smile crossed his lips. "That's enough to make me wish I were a gentleman." But he, of course, was no gentleman. No gentleman would be burning to yank the constricting pins from her hair, longing to unravel the loose coil at her nape, aching to brush his fingers across every silken strand.

When he offered nothing more, she edged closer and looped her hand through the crook of his arm. "Please, Tyler. We need to talk."

Christ, how could he refuse? The touch of her fingers scorched through his shirt like a sizzling flame. For cripes' sake, didn't she know the effect she had on him?

Stars twinkled down on them as they trod through the grass. Tyler stole a glance at her. "Are we heading in any particular direction?" he asked.

"There's a creek just beyond the woods in the back. I haven't been there in a long time, but it's always been a beautiful place in the springtime."

"Then you lead the way."

They rounded the corner of the house, strolled past the barn, and crossed into the woods. After making their way through a small clearing, they followed a well-worn path to the banks of a gurgling stream.

Julia stopped at the edge of the water. A pensive look shadowed the brilliant green of her eyes. "I've been wanting to talk with you—privately—ever since we found Kate in the barn this morning." Her voice was strained, quiet. "I've been regretting all the things I said to you."

He winced, the memory still stinging. "Hell, I guess I would've been hollerin', too. If I had been in your place, I would've said things that could have burned your ears."

"But I usually don't lose my temper, or say things I don't really mean." She sank down on the moss-covered creekbank, looking so distressed that he feared she might cry. "You see, Tyler, I was terrified when I lashed out at you. I was afraid something horrible had happened to Kate."

"I guess I could've kept a closer eye on her." It was hard to admit, but he knew it was true. And he hated himself for being so careless, so reckless, for causing her so much heartache. He sat down beside her, feeling awkward, uncomfortable. "Hell, I could've—"

She pressed trembling fingers against his lips, stopping him. "You didn't do anything wrong, Tyler. Don't you see? Kate has never been anyone's responsibility but mine because I've never had the luxury of depending on a man for anything! And when I thought she was missing, I got mad at myself for thinking I could trust you with her . . . and angry at you for betraying my trust."

"It's no sin to get angry, Julia. Hell, I do it all the time." He tucked a stray wisp of hair behind her ear, noticing that a spring breeze had kissed a blush of color into her cheeks, wishing he had been the one to put it there.

"But I was wrong to think I couldn't trust you with my sister. You've never done anything to deserve that from me. In fact, you've acted more responsibly than any man I've ever known."

He couldn't have been any more stunned than if she'd slapped him across the face. "How in the hell have I done that?"

"In lots of ways. You stayed at Hopewell House and helped us out when you didn't have to. You defended Sam, giving him a whole new life. You didn't walk away when I needed you this morning, when I thought Kate was lost . . ." Her whole face was awash with dismay and heartache as she turned to him. "Oh, Tyler, can you ever forgive me for treating you so badly? For saying such awful things that I didn't mean?"

Her bottom lip was trembling. He traced the curve of her bow-shaped mouth with his thumb, knowing he could not deny her simple request. "I'd be a fool not to forgive you, sweet Julia, even though I'm the one who should be apologizing. Not you."

Of their own volition, his fingers brushed across her satin-soft cheek, skimmed across the tender skin of her throat. Letting his eyes drift shut, he lowered his head and kissed her. Her mouth was moist, her lips pliant and eager.

He was bewildered when she suddenly pulled away, even more astonished when he saw the joy sparkling from her eyes, the love glowing from her expression. "I don't know if you are aware of it, but something remarkable has just happened," she whispered, flattening her palms against his chest. "Right here . . . in your heart."

"I know." His throat tightened. "It's thumping so damn fast that I can't catch my breath."

She smiled. "That's because it's beating with a new spirit, Tyler. You've just accepted an apology from someone who has wronged you. And do you realize what that means? You've *forgiven* me."

Awestruck, he gaped at her, jolted to the core. Something crumbled inside him, something hard and brittle and callous, and a wondrous sense of serenity took its place.

"I've always suspected a very warm heart was lurking behind all those defensive walls of yours," she divulged, brushing her fingers along his chest with slow, seductive strokes. "But now I know for sure."

He couldn't have uttered a sound if his life had depended on it. Sweet Jesus, would he ever get used to the way she could reach out and touch all those hidden places inside him? Places no other soul had ever dared to wander or cared to explore?

"I've been catching glimpses of all those hidden feelings for quite a while," she continued, fingering the buttons on his shirt. "Like the time you gave a puppy to a little girl who adores you. And the day you protected a defenseless little boy from an uncaring mother, in spite of the pain of reliving your own heartache. And just this morning, when you were as worried and distraught about Kate's disappearance as I was."

The tenderness and compassion glimmering from her eyes enveloped him with more warmth and caring than he'd ever dreamed possible. "When we couldn't find Kate, I felt like the world was coming to an end," he conceded. "Then, when we found her in the barn, I knew exactly what you were feeling, Julia. All your pain, all your worry, all your joy and relief, were my feelings, too. I was sharing all of it right along with you."

"That's what loving is all about, Tyler." There were tremors in her voice, and he knew she was as deeply shaken as he. "It's sharing the joys and sorrows, the triumphs and fears. It's forgiving the mistakes, and caring in spite of someone's faults and flaws."

At that instant, Tyler felt a sense of healing flowing through the depths of his wounded soul. "Before I came here, I thought I had life all figured out." His voice was so choked with emotion that he could barely speak. "But I stumbled into a whole new world, one filled with more caring and love, more warmth and happiness, than I've ever known. I never thought I had any love inside of me to give to anyone, but now . . . God help me, Julia, I love you."

The happiness radiating from her face was so blissful, so joyous, that Tyler knew he'd never forget that moment, never in a thousand years. "I love you, Tyler, too. More than you'll ever know."

"Jesus, I never dreamed . . ." He shuddered from the power of the emotions coursing through him, trembled from the velvet touch of her cheek beneath his fingers. "Hell, you've got me thinking about things I'd never fathomed were possible, Julia. A real home. A family of our own. Maybe even a whole house full of little girls with deep-set green eyes, bow-shaped lips. And chestnut hair that sparkles with gold beneath the starlight on balmy spring evenings . . ."

Wanting to pour into her all the love that was exploding inside of him, he swept her into his arms. "My sweet Julia," he rasped, raining a shower of kisses along her neck and face before capturing her lips with his own.

His mouth devoured hers with hot, hungry kisses, as if he were starving and she were the magical source of his strength. A soft whimper escaped from her throat as their tongues entwined and splayed together. His hands plunged through her hair, ripping the pins from the loose chignon at her nape, letting the silken tresses fall free.

"Let me show you how much I love you," he whispered, his fingers skimming over the fragile sweep of her neck and down to her collar.

"Yes," she whispered back, her eyes aglow with passion as he unbuttoned the bodice of her dress. As the constricting garment parted, her breasts swelled beneath the heat of his gaze.

A firestorm raged through him, blazing with flames of passion beyond his control. Unable to restrain his desires, Tyler tore through the rest of her garments as fast as his trembling hands could manage. Then he shrugged out of his own clothing and pulled her into his arms. The contact of her soft flesh against his hot, hair-roughened skin sent tremors coursing through him.

They sank down onto the moss-covered bank, clinging to each other. She returned his caresses, hesitantly at first, then with more urgency. His lips explored the sweetness of her shoulders, the swell of her breasts, then suckled each rosy nipple. She moaned, writhing beneath him, curling her fingers through his hair, pressing his head against her breasts. Aching with the need to explore every part of her, he worked his fingers between the sweet cleft at the top of her thighs.

She was moist and pliant, ready for him. He throbbed with desire, burning to claim her as his own. As her legs parted invitingly, he sucked in a shuddering breath and pressed the length of his body over hers.

He propped one arm on each side of her, admiring the sweep of chestnut hair framing her face and fanning over the ground. He looked down at her, treasuring her, worshiping her, loving her. His angel-woman was teeming with passion, and her green eyes were shimmering up at him with so much love that he trembled from the intensity of it.

Burning to claim the love she was offering so freely, he thrust inside her. Once, twice, again and again, he thrust into that moist, warm part of her, praying he could fill her with all the love reeling through him. She splayed her fingers down the sweep of his back and cupped her hands over his hips, urging his hard, swollen shaft deeper inside her.

When tremors coursed through her, her passion-drenched lips cried out his name. He arched his head back and closed his eyes, plunging into her one last time. Shudder after shudder rocked through him, spreading light into the darkness of his soul, filling the emptiness in his heart with the promise of hope.

"I love you, sweet Julia."

Chapter 19

Julia scraped the last bit of corn bread batter from the mixing bowl, humming as she spooned the thick mixture into a matching pair of cast-iron skillets. Served with the leftover ham from last night's dinner, hot corn bread would taste delicious for lunch, she thought.

After placing the skillets into the oven, she picked up a knife and turned her attention to the smoked ham on the table. As she sliced off the remaining meat from the bone, a contented smile crossed her lips. Though life was still hectic at Hopewell House, her daily routine had become more manageable in recent days.

Odelphia was improving nicely, hobbling around the house on a set of crutches that Tyler had custom-made for her. With her steady recovery, she no longer required Julia's constant attention and care. Miraculously, Dorinda was assuming more household responsibilities, even though she continually fretted about ruining her lily white hands. And Kate was keeping Mack out of trouble by using a collar and leash that Tyler had fashioned from an old belt and a piece of rope.

Boarders were arriving daily, renting out rooms as soon as they were vacated. Ever since Tyler had finished with the renovations to the remaining rooms on the third floor, Hopewell House had been operating at full capacity. And best of all, opening up the additional rooms to boarders had provided Julia with enough money to pay for a new roof.

A new roof! Just this morning she'd made arrangements for the job with a pleasant boarder by the name of Noah Jenkins. A stocky man with thick shoulders and muscular arms, Noah looked as if he were no stranger to the manual labor required of a roofer. It almost seemed as though providence had guided him to her doorstep as soon as he'd arrived in town. When he'd revealed that he was seeking employment in the line of construction, Julia felt as if his arrival had been the answer to her prayers.

She'd hired him on the spot, advancing payment for the work so he could purchase the necessary materials. Noah had left with the promise to return in the morning with a wagon of supplies and a crew of workers. Though her coffers were now bare, Julia felt as though a heavy weight had been lifted from her shoulders. Tomorrow the roofing work would begin. All of the family's hard work to save their beloved home was beginning to pay off, and it was a wondrous feeling for Julia.

All in all, in the two weeks since she and Tyler had declared their love for each other, life had never been more glorious. Julia supposed she should feel guilty for her sinful behavior, but she hadn't been able to find a snippet of remorse in her heart for her wanton ways. Those heart-stopping moments alone with Tyler on the banks of the creek had been a wondrous celebration of their love, and she would treasure those moments of intimacy for the rest of her life.

But her worries had not vanished completely. Every day she tried to push aside her concerns about the future and enjoy the pleasures of each new moment, but she continued to struggle with the matter of making a permanent place in her life for Tyler alongside the family who needed her.

Still, she knew, without a doubt, she wanted a future with Tyler. "Maybe he'll ask me to marry him soon," she whispered just as she heard the clatters of a buggy rolling up to the house.

She peered out the kitchen window, delighted to see the Sprayberrys arriving for a visit. She quickly washed her hands, removed her apron, and scurried outside to greet the young couple and their son.

Tyler was shaking hands with Aaron as Julia crossed the yard, while Edward disappeared into the barn with Sam. "Aaron and Violet were just telling me that they're going to a dance in town tonight," Tyler announced when Julia stepped up beside them.

"How nice!" She flashed a warm smile at the couple, genuinely happy they were becoming part of the community so quickly. "I'm sure you'll have a wonderful time."

"Aaron and I always have a wonderful time together, wherever we go." Violet gazed up at her husband with a look of adoration before turning to Tyler and Julia. "But we don't know too many people in town yet, and we were hoping you—both of you—might join us."

"From what I hear, there's a dance in town every week," Aaron added. "And we thought it might be a good way to meet our neighbors."

Before Tyler could say a word, Julia spoke up. "I appreciate the invitation, I truly do. But I . . ." She lifted her chin, hoping she didn't appear as embarrassed as she felt. "But I wouldn't feel comfortable attending a dance, I'm afraid."

A shadow of disappointment shaded Violet's face. "Well, if you change your mind, we would love for you to join us."

As the foursome launched into a conversation about Aaron's new job and the Sprayberrys' move to their new home, Julia assumed the discussion about the dance was over. But Tyler brought up the subject as soon as the couple climbed into their buggy and drove away.

"Tell me, Julia." A puzzled frown creased his brow. "Why in the hell didn't you want to go dancing? Was it because . . . of me?"

"Of course not! I would go anywhere in the world with you. It's just that . . ." She dropped her gaze, pretending to study the scuffed toes of her slippers. What would he think of a woman who'd never learned to dance?

One callused finger tilted up her chin, forcing her to meet his concerned gaze. "There isn't any need to worry about your clothes. I saw a dressmaker's shop in town the other day, and we can—"

"It's not just the clothes, Tyler! A new dress wouldn't be of any use to me, even if I could afford to buy one. You see, I don't . . . I've never . . . I can't . . ."

As she floundered for words, he pulled her against him, nestling his chin in the soft crown of her hair. "Ah, I should have guessed. The preacher's daughter doesn't dance, does she?"

The tenderness in his touch, the understanding in his voice, allayed her fears about discussing the matter. "Papa never thought it was appropriate for a minister's daughter to be kicking up her heels in front of the entire town," she admitted.

Was it her imagination, or had his muscles tightened at the mention of her father? He edged back a few inches, studying her intently. "And how did the minister's daughter feel about that?"

Her thoughts drifted back to the days before the War. "At times she wondered how it would feel to be swept across the dance floor in the arms of a handsome suitor. And she envied her friends, with their beautiful new gowns . . ." She stopped, shaking her head. "But I knew it could never be that way for me."

"And now . . . ?"

"I've never given it much thought. Unfortunately, it's something that's never been part of my life." She forced a bright smile. "Besides, when do I have time for dancing?"

"Maybe you should make the ti—"

"H-H-Hel-l-p!" Sam's cries split the air as he shot around the corner of the barn. A bucket brimming with chicken feed dangled from his hand. Nipping at his heels was a fussy bantam rooster, strutting over the ground at a quick clip, flapping his black wings and bobbing his red crown.

When the rooster pecked at the cuff of the boy's trousers, Sam yelped like a wounded puppy. Lifting his leg to shake off the creature's hold, he lost his grip on the handle of the bucket. The tin container clattered to his feet, tipping over and spewing chicken feed across the ground. The cocky rooster jerked back his head in surprise and let out a noisy cackle.

Seizing the chance to escape, Sam dashed into the barn and slammed the door shut behind him. Crowing triumphantly, the rooster poked its beak into the spilled chicken feed. Within seconds, at least a dozen chickens were swarming around the rooster, clamoring to gobble up their share of the treasure.

Watching it all, Julia couldn't prevent a smile from curving along her lips. "Looks like Sam has just met his match," she observed, trying desperately not to laugh.

"Serves him right, I'd wager." Tyler scowled. "He was probably teasing the whole flock, and the rooster took off after him." He shook his head in disgust. "That blasted kid! When will he ever learn?"

Julia's smile disappeared. "Growing up isn't easy for any child, Tyler. Especially for a little boy like Sam. He's never had a father to look up to, a man to teach him all the things he needs to learn about life." She reached out, running her fingers down the front of his shirt. "We might see a lot of improvement in Sam's behavior if a man would be willing to take him under his wing. Of course, it would have to be a man who would be willing to spend some time with him . . ."

He paled. "Good God, Julia, surely you're not thinking . . ."

"Please, Tyler? Sam needs you in his life. He doesn't need cooking or sewing lessons, and that's all I can offer. What he needs is the influence of a man . . . a man like you."

"Damn it all to hell." He raked one hand through his hair and heaved a sigh of resignation. "Well, maybe it wouldn't kill me to take the kid fishing with me one morning."

Letting out a little cry of delight, Julia hurled her arms around his neck. "I knew I could count on you," she whispered.

"For cripes' sake, Julia! It's only one little fishing trip. I'm not promising anything more. Hell, I didn't even agree to have a good time!"

"I know." Julia beamed up at him. "But it's more than enough for now."

Late in the afternoon, Julia retreated into the kitchen to prepare the evening meal. She had just placed a kettle of water over the fire when Kate bounded into the room.

"Do you know when Aunt Dorinda is coming home?" Kate asked.

Julia blinked in surprise. "I didn't realize Aunt Dorinda was gone."

"She left a few hours ago. Aunt Odelphia saw her leaving with Mr. Tyler right after lunch. They were riding together in the buggy, heading toward town."

"Neither of them mentioned anything to me about going into town." Julia nibbled on her lower lip, wondering why they hadn't bothered to ask her to join them.

Kate shrugged. "Well, I'm sure they'll be home in time for dinner. Aunt Dorinda doesn't miss many meals."

And she was right. Just as the boarders were filing into the dining room, Tyler and Dorinda slipped into their regular places at the table. Although they remained silent about the reasons for their absence, the pair exchanged sly smiles across the table throughout the meal, as if they were sharing a deliciously naughty secret.

Which only provoked Julia's curiosity even more. Why would Aunt Dorinda go into town with Tyler for the afternoon? And why were both of them acting so secretive about everything?

Julia was still trying to solve the mystery after dinner. Mulling over the puzzling situation, she sauntered up the stairs. But as soon as she stepped into the room that she shared with her sister, she stumbled into another baffling surprise. Whose beautiful gown was draped across her bed?

She stepped closer, curious, unable to resist running her fingers over the soft fabric. Undoubtedly it was the most beautiful garment she'd ever seen. The skirt was wide and full, fashioned from three tiers of silk satin in a striking shade of cobalt blue. Flounces adorned the sleeves and trimmed the scoop neckline.

She caressed the gown as lovingly as if it were a priceless treasure, picking it up and pressing it against her breast in hushed reverence. "Oh, the joy of wearing a gown such as this . . ." she whispered.

"Oh, the joy of seeing you wear a gown such as this . . ." a familiar voice echoed behind her.

Wincing, Julia returned the garment to the bed, feeling as naughty as an errant child. Before she could turn around, a pair of strong hands slipped around her waist. "I was hoping you'd like it," Tyler whispered into her ear.

He felt her tremble as she spun around in his arms. "The gown . . . is mine?" Her face was awash with surprise and disbelief.

"All yours." How long had it been since she'd owned anything new? Too long, he thought, judging by her astonished expression. "When I saw it on display at the dressmaker's shop in town this afternoon, I thought it looked as if it had been made just for you."

"Then you and Dorinda . . ." Sudden understanding flashed across her face.

"I invited Dorinda along so she could advise the dressmaker on the sizing," he admitted. "And we waited at the shop while the gown was being altered."

"You did all of that . . . for me?"

He traced the outline of her lips with an outstretched finger. "A woman who is always thinking of everyone else's needs instead of her own deserves something new every once in a while." He draped the gown across her arms. "I'd like nothing better than to see you wearing it."

She brushed her fingers across the silky material. "But it almost seems shameful to wear a gown like this without a special reason . . ."

"Then we'll make this evening a special one."

Without giving her the chance to protest, he turned and left the room. A few moments later, he was standing at the foot of the stairs, wearing a brocaded vest and black frock coat over his white shirt and black trousers, waiting for Julia.

It suddenly occurred to him that he felt like a nervous schoolboy who was smitten with his teacher and trying his damnedest to make a good impression. His stomach was rolling, his heart racing, his mind as befuddled as if someone had smashed a rock over his head.

Matters only got worse when he heard the swish of a woman's skirts. Though he'd expected Julia would look ravishing, nothing could have prepared him for the sight of her. His heart stilled, his breathing stopped, as she swept down the stairs.

His eyes devoured her. The gown looked as though every stitch, every seam, every fold, had been molded and designed with Julia in mind. A scoop neckline revealed the enticing swell of her breasts and a provocative glimpse of cleavage, while the striking cobalt blue hue highlighted the creaminess of her complexion. The gown draped over her breasts with an elegant flow, cinching around the tiny span of her waist before flaring out into layers of silk satin around her hips. A hooped petticoat peeked out beneath the hem of the wide, full skirt.

A smile shimmered from the curve of her pink lips to the depths of her green eyes. Her face, framed by wisps of chestnut hair that had escaped from the loose bun at the nape of her neck, shone with a beauty so mind-boggling that Tyler could hardly breathe.

An ache of longing swelled within Tyler, an ache so powerful that he had to restrain himself from crushing her against him, burying himself in her.

She flushed beneath his blatant perusal as she swept down the stairs. "Does the gown meet your expectations?"

Speechless, he managed a brief nod before tucking her hand around the crook of his arm and leading her out to the verandah. The night was clear and enchanting, perfect for dancing under the stars.

He lifted her hand to his shoulder, then slipped an arm around her waist and twirled her around, humming the tune of a waltz under his breath.

Her laughter sparkled through the air. "What . . . ?"

"We're dancing, Miss Julia. Can't you tell?"

Her eyes twinkled up at him. "But I don't know how to dance."

"You could have fooled me." Her steps were graceful, light, following his lead with a natural, instinctive ease.

Beneath the light of the Georgia moon, they swayed across the verandah. Wrapped in Tyler's arms, Julia became mesmerized by the man who was responsible for the magical evening.

He was perfectly groomed, freshly shaved, smelling faintly of soap and cologne. The marks of a comb still lingered in his hair, and it was obvious to Julia that he had not dressed hastily. Dark trousers hugged lean hips and muscular thighs, while a pair of boots shone with the gleam of polished leather. The rugged appeal of his olive complexion became even more alluring against his white linen shirt, captivating Julia with such intensity that she could barely catch her breath.

Tyler continued to provide the music, slightly off tune, until Julia peered up at him and stole his heart with a smile. "No one has ever done anything like this for me," she confessed with a slight tremble in her lips. "Now I know what it's like to wear a beautiful gown and be swept across the dance floor by a handsome suitor."

"And how does it feel?"

"Like a dream come true." Love shimmered in her eyes as she gazed up at him. "I don't think any woman has ever loved a man as much as I love you, Tyler McRae. I swear I'll never stop loving you, for as long as I live."

Moved beyond words, Tyler closed his eyes, not wanting her to see the emotions written there. He'd been overwhelmed with the desire to snatch her away from the responsibilities of life for a little while, to give her a few hours of pleasure and laughter and joy. But he'd never expected anything in return, never dreamed she would vow her love to him for a lifetime.

His grip tightened around her waist as he whirled her across the verandah. Following his steps with a graceful ease, she tilted back her head and smiled. "I'm not doing too bad for a minister's daughter, am I?"

Tyler longed to agree, but the words snared in his throat. *A minister's daughter.* Judas Priest, he didn't deserve her. He wasn't good enough for a woman of her upbringing. For days he'd been trying to shove that nagging thought out of his mind, but now it was back, haunting him worse than ever.

She deserved far better than the son of a man who'd been hanged for murder. She merited someone far better than he ... someone who wouldn't dishonor her the way he had.

As he looked down into her face, all awash with love and happiness, he felt his soul ripping into shreds. "I wish I could give you everything you deserve," he said in a strained tone.

He crushed her against him, clinging to her with a need so desperate that a shudder coursed through him. Capturing her lips with his own, he sought refuge in the sweet taste of her before whirling her across the verandah again.

Still feeling giddy from the wondrous, magical evening of dancing with Tyler under the light of the Georgia moon, Julia practically floated into the kitchen to prepare breakfast the next morning. She couldn't remember a time when she'd felt so lighthearted and carefree. *Maybe I should go dancing with Tyler more often*, she thought with a wry smile. *And maybe he'll ask me to marry him soon ...*

Only one awkward moment had marred the perfection of the evening. Why was Tyler so uncomfortable every time she mentioned something about her father? Was it Papa's occupation that bothered him so? Tyler wasn't exactly the type of man who held a fondness for the ministries of the church, after all.

Setting aside the disturbing thought, Julia measured out the ingredients for making the day's supply of bread. She'd just finished kneading the dough when she realized that Noah and his workmen should be arriving at any moment to replace the roof.

Throughout the morning, she listened for the workmen's arrival, peering out the window each time a buggy or wagon rattled down the road. But by ten o'clock, a troubled frown was creasing her brow. Where was Noah? Had she misunderstood their agreement?

After lunch, she confessed her concerns to Tyler. "Picking up the supplies shouldn't have been any problem for Noah," she explained. "Since I paid him in advance for the work, he had the money to purchase the materials."

Tyler's eyes narrowed. "You paid him in advance?"

A tiny pulse of fear throbbed through Julia's veins, though she tried to ignore it. "Noah is an honest man, I'm certain. And I'm sure he has good reasons for not arriving on time this morning."

But the afternoon passed without any sign of Noah. When he failed to show up the next morning, Julia set out to find him. Late in the afternoon, she returned from town with a heavy heart, unable to locate a trace of the man.

Faced with an empty purse, a wounded spirit, and a leaky roof, Julia quietly admitted her foolish mistake to her family after dinner. Then she retreated into the privacy of her room for the evening. Grieving for the loss of her family's hardearned funds, she berated herself for lacking good judgment in such an important business matter.

A clatter of noise awakened her the next morning. Julia sat up in bed, rubbing the sleep from her eyes, as an incessant pounding rattled above her head. It sounded as if someone were ripping off the roof . . .

Noah was here! He hadn't failed her, after all. Julia shot out of bed, trembling with relief and joy. She hastily dressed, pinned up her hair, and scurried down the stairs.

The first light of dawn greeted her as she stepped outside. The sun was just breaking over the horizon, tinting the pale blue sky with soft streaks of mauve and gold. Two workers were unloading supplies from a wagon. Another man was perched on the roof, ripping off the rusted pieces of tin.

Though two days late, everything was just as Noah had promised, Julia thought. She was breathing a sigh of relief just as Tyler came out of the house. Two fishing poles were propped over his shoulder and a bucket of minnows dangled from his hand. "Looks like the whole world is getting an early start this morning," she commented brightly, pleased he was living up to his word about spending some time with Sam.

"How could anyone sleep with all the racket around here?" Grinning, he stepped into the yard to survey the work in progress.

She followed his lead, intending to scold Noah for his tardiness. But Noah was not among the men who were climbing over the roof. "Strange, but I don't see Noah Jenkins anywhere."

She glanced over at Tyler just as a swift flash of guilt crossed his face. Her heart lurched. "What do you know about Noah, Tyler?"

He heaved a weary sigh. "The talk around town is that Noah Jenkins is a master at the art of conning women out of their hard-earned money. He travels from place to place—"

"Preying on trusting women like me," she finished, flinching in disdain. She paused, watching the men rip off a rusted piece of tin from the roof. "But if Noah has already skipped town with my money, why are these men here?"

When Tyler offered no response, her eyes narrowed with suspicion. "This is your doing, isn't it?"

He refused to meet her steady gaze. "And what if it is? You're getting a new roof, just like you wanted."

"I don't want your charity, Tyler." Her voice was quiet, strained. "The gown was the most wonderful gift I've ever received from anyone, but a new roof is an entirely different matter. I made a foolish mistake by paying a stranger for his work in advance. And I should be the one to pay for my mistakes. Not you."

"But you've already paid for the work, Julia! And it will take months to recoup your losses. Use a little reason, will you? I'm just trying to make life a little easier for you and your family."

"I need your pity even less than your charity, Tyler." He could feel heated blazes of hostility crackling from her stormy gaze. "Is that why you've stayed long after your wounds have healed? Were you feeling sorry for a poor little minister's daughter who was struggling to make ends meet? I don't know why you even bothered to come here in the first place!"

"If you really want to know, I'll tell you why," Tyler snapped. Pride stinging and defensive instincts flaring, he lashed out at her. "I came here looking for your father, Julia. The Reverend Jeremiah Carey."

"Papa?" Her eyes widened incredulously. "But why . . . ?"

"Seems he snatched every horse and saddle from my livery stable in Chattanooga. And I came to Rome to make certain he paid for his crime under the justice of the law."

As soon as the words flew out of his mouth, regret sliced through him. He'd never meant to hurt her. But seeing all that anguish and disbelief marring her angel-face was enough to make him wish he were dead.

"P-P-Papa?" she repeated, stepping back, gasping in disbelief. "Why, that's impossible. Papa would have never robbed—"

"I'm not making flagrant accusations, Julia. I have more proof than you can ever imagine." God, he hated hurting her, wished he'd never told her. "You don't know how many times I've wished it weren't true. You don't know how many times I've wished everything could be different—"

He halted, cringing as tears spilled from her anguished eyes and streamed down her cheeks, hating himself as she picked up her skirts and fled.

Tyler shifted uneasily, wishing the serenity of his surroundings could soothe the turbulence raging inside him. Throughout the morning, he'd been sitting on the banks of the Coosa River, fishing with Sam. But not even the slow, lazy current of the river or the gentle sounds of the water lapping against the shore had been able to ease his troubled mind.

Next to him, four fish were flopping around in a bucket of water. A few feet away, Sam was gazing into the distance, fishing pole in hand. Apparently the boy was enjoying himself, though he'd said little since they'd left the house. Tyler figured he was still stunned by his invitation to spend the morning with him.

"Have you ever cried, Mr. Tyler?"

Startled by the abrupt question, Tyler flinched. "Men don't cry, Sam."

"You mean you've never cried? Not even once?"

His thoughts skittered back to his last few moments on the farm and the miserable days that had followed. He'd been scared out of his wits, terrified to the point that he'd puked out his guts on more than one occasion. But he'd never cried. "Not that I can recall. Why do you ask?"

Sam shrugged. "I was just thinkin' about that time you and Miss Julia came down to the place where I'd been stayin' with Ma. I was so scared, I couldn't do nothin' but cry like a little baby. But later, Miss Julia told me that cryin' wasn't nothin' for me to be ashamed of. She said that men who cry aren't afraid to show what they're feelin' inside."

An uneasy feeling rolled through Tyler. "That's Miss Julia's way of looking at things, Sam."

"Even Miss Julia cries," Sam rushed on, a sorrowful expression flashing across his freckled face. "Right before we left the house, I went by her room to tell her good-bye. But I heard her crying. She was real upset about something. I peeked around the door, and she was crying into her pillow . . ."

Tyler's throat constricted. The image of sweet Julia sobbing into her pillow was almost more than he could bear. Good God, he was the one who'd caused those tears to stream down that angel-woman's face. He was the bastard responsible for wrenching her heart.

A sickening feeling rolled through him. Why hadn't he kept his damn mouth shut? He'd lived with worse secrets, after all. He had no right to punish Julia for the sins of her father. Why should she suffer because he couldn't find a shred of forgiveness in his heart to pardon a hypocritical preacher for a theft?

He glanced over at Sam, jolted by another revelation. He'd never forgiven the boy for robbing him, either. And he wondered if he ever could. Just because he'd managed to forgive Julia for one little mistake didn't mean he could forgive anyone who'd wronged him. There was still too much anger lingering inside him, too many phantoms from the past plaguing his soul . . .

Tyler tried to shove aside the disturbing thoughts as he and Sam returned to Hopewell House, fishing poles and buckets in hand. Kate, playing with Mack on the verandah, leaped up to greet them as they approached. "Something wonderful has happened, Mr. Tyler!"

As Tyler set down his fishing gear, Kate grabbed him by the arm. "Hurry and come inside. You, too, Sam. Somebody special is here, and I want both of you to meet him."

Without further explanation, Kate rushed into the house. Tyler followed her lead into the parlor, where the atmosphere was bristling with excitement. At the center of attention was a man who looked vaguely familiar to Tyler. His light brown hair was peppered with streaks of gray, and he was wearing a grin that could only be described as devilish.

Lucas, Tyler realized, recognizing him from the tintype.

It almost seemed as if Lucas had cast a spell over his captive audience. Odelphia and Dorinda were clamoring around him like fussy mother hens, while Julia and Elizabeth were sitting on the edge of their seats, listening to his vivid descriptions.

"I wish you could've seen all those grand sights up North," he was saying. "The shops in New York City offer anything you could ever want. Why, the hotels are the fanciest places in the world, with big crystal chandeliers, and—"

At that instant, Kate bounded across the room. "This is the nice man I've been telling you about, Lucas. His name is Mr. Tyler. And this is Sam," she added as the red-haired boy darted up behind her.

After rumpling Sam's hair with an affectionate pat, Lucas rose from the settee to shake Tyler's outstretched hand. Though Tyler was aware of the difference in age between Julia and her half brother, he was still taken aback by the man's appearance. With the streaks of gray running through his hair, Lucas looked old enough to be Julia's father.

He'd aged a great deal since posing for the tintype, Tyler assessed. Yet hadn't Julia admitted as much? And hadn't she mentioned that her brother bore a striking resemblance to their minister father?

"With all your travels, maybe you've heard of Tyler's hotel in Chattanooga," Julia remarked. "It's called The McRae."

"The McRae?" Lucas shook his head. "Can't say that I've heard of it."

But Tyler sensed that he had. In the split second before Lucas had voiced his denial, something had flashed through his eyes. Had it been a glimmer of recognition . . . or fear?

Lucas swept Kate into his arms, spinning her around and whirling her through the air like a rag doll. "I declare, Miss Kate, you're growing up so fast that I can hardly believe my eyes!"

Kate was still shrieking with delight when Lucas set her down and pulled Elizabeth to her feet. He twirled his dark-haired fiancée around the parlor as if they were dancing to the majestic refrains of a symphony. "Ah, my beautiful Elizabeth," he murmured, his voice husky and low. "I've missed you more than you could ever know. And now that I'm home, I want to make up for all the time we've been apart."

Elizabeth flushed as she beamed up at him. "Oh, Lucas, I'm so glad you're home!"

Tyler couldn't explain the odd sense of protectiveness gnawing in his gut as Lucas whirled Elizabeth around the room. For some unexplainable reason, he felt like snatching her away from Lucas's hungry gaze and shielding her from any possible harm.

His uneasiness intensified throughout the day, in spite of the festive atmosphere. For the sake of Julia and her family, he supposed he should be happy about Lucas's return. But happiness was not the emotion soaring through Tyler. Anger was soaring through his veins. He wanted nothing more than to break Lucas Carey's neck for abandoning the family who adored him, for putting the weight of the world on his sister's narrow shoulders.

Tyler managed to restrain his emotions until dinner. But something snapped inside him as he listened to Lucas's bold plans for making further improvements to Hopewell House. Shoving aside his plate, Tyler glared at the man seated across the table from him. "And how do you intend to make all these changes, Lucas? Do you expect Julia to raise the funds and supervise the work all by herself—while you're off riding the rails and exploring the world? Of course, that's the way it is now, in case you haven't noticed."

"Tyler!" Julia shot up from her chair, trembling with fury. "How dare you!"

Her seething glare sliced through him like a razor, shattering something inside of him. It was the second time in the course of one day that she'd leaped to the defense of her family under his brutal assaults.

"Damn it all to hell," Tyler muttered.

He snapped up and stormed out of the room, too frustrated and angry to contend with Julia's unwavering loyalty to her family for another moment.

Give it up, McRae. You've tried. And you've failed.

Tyler shifted restlessly in the hard wooden pew, regretting his decision to attend church with Julia and her little clan. It had been an act of desperation, a final attempt in his struggle to become the right man for Julia Carey.

And it wasn't working.

He hated being here, despised himself for being such a hypocrite. Even more, he abhorred the anger and bitterness still lingering in his heart, knowing it was poisoning his chances for a lifetime of happiness with the woman at his side.

After the final amen, he left the church with Julia. Clutching a small bouquet of flowers to her breast, she sauntered toward the cemetery, located on the grounds behind the church. "I'd like to pay my respects to Papa," she explained in a quiet, hushed tone.

He fell into step beside her, not knowing why he couldn't pull himself away. He grimaced as she stopped to kneel beside her father's grave. Good God, why was he here? He couldn't pay his respects to any man who'd wronged him.

Trying not to bolt and run, Tyler steeled himself. As Julia placed the bouquet of flowers at the base of the tombstone, his gaze drifted across the words etched into the granite slab.

REVEREND JEREMIAH LUCAS CAREY
BELOVED SERVANT OF GOD
BORN FEBRUARY 3, 1809
DIED MARCH 15, 1868

Tyler froze, staring at the last line of the epitaph in disbelief. "Your father died in the middle of March?" he choked out.

She straightened, nodding. "On the fifteenth of the month."

He clutched her arm. "Are you certain?"

Her lashes fluttered in confusion. "Of course I'm certain, Tyler. I was at Papa's bedside when he died."

"Then that means . . ." So many thoughts were tumbling through his mind that his head started to spin.

Sweet Jesus, Jeremiah Carey couldn't have possibly robbed the livery. On the day his livery had been stripped of its contents, the man had been dead for more than a week. And if Jeremiah Carey hadn't been the thief, someone had been impersonating him, maybe someone who bore a striking resemblance to him . . .

"What's wrong, Tyler?"

He winced, not knowing if he should be elated or horrified. "We need to get back to the house right away," he said as evenly as he could. "There is something I need to discuss . . . with your brother."

Chapter 20

"**P**lease don't leave, Lucas! You've only been here for one day. Surely you can stay awhile longer . . ." Elizabeth's voice, laced with desperation, echoed through the rafters of the barn.

"Sweetheart, you know I'd stay if I could," Lucas returned smoothly, guiding a horse out of the stall. "But it just isn't possible right now."

Turning, he hoisted a saddle over the horse. As he adjusted the stirrups, Tyler stepped out of the shadows. "Leaving so soon, Lucas?"

His head snapped up. "Regretfully so," he answered in a brisk tone. "Unexpected business, you know."

"Too bad." Tyler brushed a hand across the horse's silky mane, immediately recognizing the animal as one that had been stolen from his livery. "Fine-looking horse you've got here. I wouldn't mind having a fine specimen like this for myself. Care to tell me where you found him?"

He avoided Tyler's probing gaze. "Bought him from a friend of mine," he mumbled, tightening the leather straps on the saddle. "Now, if you'll get out of my way—"

Elizabeth rushed forward, pleading with him. "Lucas, you can't leave like this! You haven't even said good-bye to your family!"

337

"I'm out of time, sweetheart. Give them my best, will you?"

"That won't be necessary." Tyler's voice was low and threatening. "You aren't going anywhere, Carey. This horse is stolen property, and you know it."

Lucas froze. The color drained from his face, shattering the last vestiges of his cool facade. "You can't prove a damn thing, McRae!"

But even as he spit out the words, his eyes were searching for a way to escape. When his gaze landed on the horse, he lunged forward.

"Please don't leave, Lucas!" Elizabeth reached out to stop him. "Not like this!"

"Get the hell out of my way, woman." He shoved her aside, slamming her into the side of the stall, before hoisting one boot into the stirrup.

"You son of a bitch!" Tyler roared, clamping an arm around Lucas's leg.

With one last, desperate attempt to escape, Lucas slammed the heel of his boot into Tyler's chest. The force of the impact knocked the breath from Tyler. He slumped to the ground, drowning in a sea of darkness.

Some time later, he felt the soothing touch of a soft hand on his forehead. His eyes fluttered open. Julia was bending over him, brushing her fingers across his brow with a featherlike caress. "Are you hurting, Tyler?"

More than you'll ever know, lady. Grimacing, he propped up on his elbows. His chest ached, but he could live with it. "I think your damn brother just knocked the wind out of me," he assessed grimly.

"I'm certain there must be some mistake, Tyler." Her eyes were pleading, clinging to his. "Lucas couldn't possibly be a horse thief!"

The ache in his chest intensified. He wished—God, how he wished—she loved him half as much.

He staggered to his feet. "Your brother isn't the angel you want him to be, Julia. He's a damn horse thief, for God's sake! Why do you refuse to see him for who he really is?"

Massaging her bruised arm, Elizabeth sighed. "I'm afraid Tyler is right, Julia. I don't think we know the real Lucas Carey at all. He was like a different person a few minutes ago . . . like someone I've never known."

"Surely Lucas has a good explanation for all of this." Julia shook her head in dismay, obviously refusing to believe the worst about her brother.

"Then maybe he can explain himself to Sheriff Mitchell," Tyler grumbled, stalking to the door.

He'd taken only two steps when Julia reached out and grasped his arm. "You're filing charges . . . against Lucas?"

"You're damn right I am, and there's not a blasted thing you can do about it." It sounded cruel and heartless, he knew. He lowered his voice to a husky whisper, trying to soften the blow. "You're not your brother's keeper, Julia. Lucas got himself into this mess, and he is the one who has to pay for his sins. Not you."

Unable to bear the anguished expression on her face, he turned and walked away.

It was well after midnight before Julia slipped into bed. But as she rested her head upon the pillow, she knew sleep would not come easily for her. Too many things had happened during the course of the day; too many dreams had been shattered.

She'd paced restlessly across the verandah for most of the afternoon, anxiously gazing toward the road, straining to catch a glimpse of Tyler as he returned from town. But the hours had dragged by without any sign of him. By nightfall the faint throb of apprehension in her heart had swelled into a despondency greater than any she'd ever known. And now she could no longer ignore the nagging suspicion that had been lurking in her thoughts throughout the afternoon.

Tyler was gone. And he wasn't coming back.

"You fool," she whispered into the darkness. "You should have known better . . ."

She paused, listening intently, hearing footsteps on the main floor. Who could be roaming through the house at this hour of the night? She slipped a robe over her gown and padded down the stairs, guided by the soft glow of a lantern.

When she reached the landing, she could hear the sound of boots shuffling through the foyer. Heart pounding in her chest, she halted just as her brother came into view. "Lucas! What are—"

"I won't be staying long, Julia." He sounded tired and troubled. "I came back to pick up a few things I'd left behind. And as soon as I gather up my belongings, I'll be leaving again."

Julia's heart sank as he evaded her puzzled gaze. Was this man the same affectionate brother she'd known and loved for years? She grasped his arm as he trudged past her. "Can we talk . . . before you go?"

He gave a weary nod. "I'll be back down as soon as I get my gear."

Confused and weary, Julia sank down on the steps. Surely none of this is happening, she thought. Surely she would wake up soon and discover that all of this had been a nightmare. She cupped her chin in her hands, sighing wearily. There were so many unanswered questions, so much she wanted to know.

But where could she start? What could she say to her wayward brother? She was still mulling over the situation when Lucas appeared, hat in hand. He placed a bundle of garments on the steps, then sat down beside her.

She drew in a steadying breath. "Tell me what's going on with you, Lucas. I need . . . to know."

"It's not what you think, Julia." His face was pinched and drawn. "It's not what you think at all."

"Then I would be very interested to hear what you have to say," Julia returned in a quiet voice, though not entirely certain she was prepared for what she might learn.

He fidgeted with the brim of his hat, twirling it around in his hand, not daring to meet her eyes. "After the War, I met up with some guys who'd served in Benning's Brigade with me. Like me, they hadn't been able to find steady work. And then we discovered it wasn't too hard to walk away from a poker table with enough winnings to tide us over from one job to the next." A harsh laugh escaped from his throat. "All of a sudden, everything got out of hand. We were losing more than we were winning. Everywhere we turned, someone was demanding money we didn't have. So we stayed on the run, traveling from one town to the next."

Julia's eyes narrowed in confusion. "But you were traveling from town to town with your railroad job . . . weren't you?"

He stole a glance at her, then turned away as a flush of remorse stained his cheeks. "Hell, Julia, I never had a job with the railroad. Never laid the first inch of track. I only told you and Elizabeth that I was working the rails so you'd think I had good reason for roaming from place to place all the time."

"Oh, Lucas." Moaning, she closed her eyes. Dear

heavens, she'd never dreamed her brother could be so deceptive.

"When we got to Chattanooga, my buddies and I were desperate." His fingers tightened over the tattered brim of his hat. "We figured the stock in McRae's livery was worth more than all our debts combined. So I got a job at The McRae, working in the livery."

"And you used . . . Papa's name?"

He nodded. "It was a crazy idea, I know. But at the time, it made sense to me. A lot of people were looking for Lucas Carey, and I didn't think it would be wise to use my own name. I figured I could always claim I was working at the livery to make ends meet between revivals if I ran into someone who had heard of Papa from his tent meetings. For the folks who'd met Papa, I figured I could just tell 'em the truth—that my pa and I shared the same name."

"How ingenious of you," Julia muttered. "To think you were impersonating Papa . . ." She shook her head in disbelief.

"No one ever suspected a thing," Lucas continued in a regretful tone. "I worked at the livery for several weeks, checking out the place, before we made our move. Then, one by one, my buddies came to the livery and rented out the equipment, piece by piece. Together we wiped out the place in a couple of days."

"So you set up a schedule for renting out the horses and buggies to your friends . . . knowing nothing would ever be returned?"

"I'm afraid so, Julia." He heaved a weary sigh. "We sold off the stock and equipment so we could pay off most of the crooks who were hounding us about our gambling debts."

So it was true. A sickening sensation rolled

through Julia. She clutched her arms around her stomach, feeling as though she might become ill at any moment. "But you must have kept some of the stock for yourself," she managed to say in a choked voice. "Elizabeth said Tyler recognized your horse in the barn this afternoon."

Turning, he glared at her. "For Christ's sake, I need that damn horse worse than McRae does!" With a rush of anger, he slapped his hat over his knee. "Hell, Julia, I would've never stolen a damn thing from the man if I thought it would've ruined him. But McRae's got more money than he knows what to do with. The cost of restocking his livery wouldn't even make a dent in his bank account."

"But Tyler's wealth doesn't justify what you did, Lucas! Surely you don't think you have a right to steal from someone just because he has more wealth or possessions than you!" Her voice was trembling, her insides quivering. "What has happened to you, Lucas? What kind of man have you become? Papa would be appalled . . ." A choked sob drowned out the rest of her thoughts.

"I'm not proud of myself, Julia," he admitted, covering his eyes with his hands and wearily shaking his head in despair. "And I'm tired, too. I'm so damn tired of running and lying, cheating and stealing . . ."

Julia's heart wrenched. She'd never seen Lucas this way, and she didn't know what to say or do.

He shifted uncomfortably. "McRae seems to like you, Julia. Do you think you can talk to him, maybe see if he'll forget this whole thing?"

For a long moment, Julia stared at her brother in shocked silence. Her eyes searched his face, trying to find a trace of regret written there. Instead, she saw nothing but weariness and desperation etched into his haggard features. He was tired, so very tired, and asking her to right all his wrongs for him . . .

"I can't help you, Lucas, even if I wanted to. Tyler isn't the type of person who could overlook something as serious as this. In fact, when he left here this afternoon, he was on his way to Sheriff Mitchell's office."

His eyes widened. "And you didn't stop him? Why in the hell didn't you tell me before now?" Without waiting for an answer, Lucas grabbed his gear and stormed down the steps.

As he bolted through the door and disappeared into the darkness, Julia's heart wrenched in pain. She buried her face in her hands, aching for the brother who had become a stranger to her, regretting that her blind devotion to him had driven Tyler away.

Searching her heart throughout the wee hours of the morning, Julia reviewed every word of her conversation with Lucas. In some respects, it had almost seemed as if he had been searching for a way to put a stop to his endless round of blunders. He seemed so very weary and so very desperate . . .

By the first light of dawn, Julia knew what she had to do. No longer could she pretend to be responsible for her brother's behavior. No longer could she assume responsibility for his happiness, nor defend his actions. Shortly after daybreak, she dried the tears from her swollen eyes and slipped into her lavender day dress. Knowing she must report Lucas's unexpected visit to the sheriff, she hitched up the horses and buggy with a heavy heart. Then she set off for town, not stopping until she arrived at Sheriff Mitchell's office.

The amiable sheriff looked up from his desk in surprise. "Miss Julia! What brings you here?"

"You don't know?" She paused, confusion sweeping through her. "Didn't Mr. McRae talk with you yesterday about a matter concerning my brother?"

Sheriff Mitchell shook his head. "'Fraid not, Miss Julia. When I saw McRae yesterday, he was boarding the train bound for Chattanooga. And we didn't have the chance to speak to each other."

A myriad of emotions swarmed through Julia. As the sheriff confirmed her suspicions about Tyler's departure, the heavy ache in her chest intensified. But waves of astonishment were also rolling through her. Why hadn't Tyler filed charges against Lucas, as he'd threatened?

It doesn't matter now, she told herself. *Tyler is gone. He isn't coming back. And Lucas can't go on running forever. It's time for you to stop making excuses for your brother's behavior . . .*

She drew in a deep, steadying breath and lifted her chin. "Sheriff Mitchell, I have some information to report to you. It concerns the theft of some horses. And it involves my brother, Lucas Carey . . ."

Everything was different. Yet nothing had changed.

Tyler shifted uneasily in the saddle as his gaze swept over the patch of land that he'd tried to forget for nineteen years. Though weeds were now choking the once fertile fields, and towering trees were standing in the place of young saplings, little else had changed, it seemed.

Memories suppressed for almost two decades took on new life as he guided the horse down the hill and over the winding trail. As his eyes devoured the old, familiar sights, a rush of nostalgia swept through him.

The old elm was still there, its sprawling branches sweeping over the trail like a sheltering canopy. At one time, he and 'Becca had spent hours beneath the shade of that tree, laughing and dreaming and playing together. His chest tightened at the thought.

But there was more. Amazingly, part of the fence was still standing. Wildflowers were still sprouting. And the view of the mountains hovering in the distance was just as breathtaking as before.

His grip tightened around the reins as he rounded a bend in the trail. As his eyes locked on the abandoned homestead, his breath lodged in his throat. Good God, why in the hell was he here? He wanted nothing more than to escape from the hurtful, agonizing memories attached to this place.

But it was his overwhelming desire to escape from the clutches of the past that had lured him here, he remembered. Since leaving Rome, he had become determined to confront the ghosts that continued to haunt him. Night and day, Julia's words had echoed through his mind. *Your father may not deserve your forgiveness . . . but you need to consider forgiving him for your own benefit. Not his.*

He dismounted. As if being led by some unexplainable force, he stepped up on the porch. Crossing over the rotting slats, he approached the warped, open door. Inhaling a deep breath, he edged his way into the cabin.

Though it loomed large in his memories, the place was small and confining. A few pieces of furniture were scattered about, some gnawed by animals, others rotting from neglect. There was an old table propped up against the stone fireplace, part of some shelving, and . . .

Ma's rocking chair. His fingers trembled, rubbing through the grime and the dust, tracing over the carving etched into the oak headrest. Overwhelmed by a rush of emotions, he slowly sank into the rocker. Closing his eyes, he could almost hear Ma's voice singing that old song . . .

> *"Alas, my love, you do me wrong*
> *To cast me off discourteously . . . "*

It was the same tune she'd been humming on that fateful night in 1849 . . .

He and Rebecca had been sitting on the front porch, playing with the puppy that 'Becca adored, waiting for Pa to come in from the fields for the evening. Uncle Willie, a frequent guest for dinner, had already arrived. He was inside the house, talking to Ma. The front door was slightly ajar, and Tyler could hear his mother humming that old, familiar song under her breath as she set the table for dinner.

"I think my puppy must be hungry, Tyler," Rebecca had observed. "He keeps gnawing on my finger!"

"I'll see if Ma has some scraps for him to eat," Tyler offered, scrambling to his feet.

He slipped inside the house just as Uncle Willie offered to open a jar of preserves for Ma. Sometimes the lids were hard to pry off the jars, and Ma often needed help to open them. Tyler waited, patiently, silently, knowing Ma would scold him for being impolite if he interrupted.

But it took only a few seconds for Tyler to realize that something wasn't quite right. Obviously his uncle and mother were not aware of his presence. Uncle Willie was standing behind Ma, his arms wrapped around hers, his hands clamped over the jar that she held in front of her . . . and Ma was closing her eyes, whimpering softly . . .

Tyler froze, stunned by what was happening.

Why was Uncle Willie kissing Ma's neck? And why was Ma acting as though she were enjoying it?

At that instant, Pa stepped up behind him. His boots clomped over the wood floor, announcing his arrival. Uncle Willie and Ma jerked away from each other, but not before Pa's eyes widened in disbelief. He ripped through the room with the force of a tornado, lunging at Uncle Willie. "Good God!" Pa's hands clamped around Willie's neck. "My own damn brother with my wife—behind my back!"

Willie's eyes took on an evil gleam. "You shoulda seen it comin', Vernon."

If Pa flinched, Tyler never saw it. Seething with rage, he shoved Willie into the table. Dishes clattered, crashing to the floor. "Get out of my house, brother," Pa warned. "Get off my land. And if I catch you here again . . . so help me God, you won't live to see another sunrise."

Now Tyler cringed as his memories grew more vivid. Uncle Willie picked up a butcher knife from the table. The sharp edges of the blade glistened as he hurled back his arm and lunged at Pa.

Reacting swiftly to the threat, Pa reached for his rifle and aimed it straight at his brother's heart.

Then there was the noise, the terrible noise. The thundering blast of gunpowder. Rebecca's screams. The thud of Uncle Willie's body crashing to the floor, followed by Ma's cries of despair.

And the faces. God, the faces. Pa, dumbfounded by what he'd just done. Ma, the shock and horror of it all. And Uncle Willie, a ghostly white . . .

Ma dropped to the floor and cradled Willie's head in her lap, rocking his lifeless body as if he was a babe. "How could you, Vernon?" she cried. "Your own brother . . . You killed your own brother . . . poor Willie . . ."

"Poor Willie!" Pa roared in disbelief. "For God's sake, Ruth, he betrayed me. You and Willie betrayed me . . ." Shaking with fury, he glared down at her. "Get the hell out of here, woman. Before I put you in the grave, along with your lover . . ."

Pa reached for his rifle again. The shame and guilt written on Ma's face suddenly vanished, replaced with stark terror. And then she was running, dashing out the door and into the fields, racing through the valley and over the hills, fleeing for her life . . .

Tyler remembered little about the next few days. He and Rebecca had been taken into the home of some kindhearted neighbors. On the morning of Pa's trial, he had been allowed to visit Pa at the jail.

Some strange men had been talking to Pa as Tyler approached the jail cell.

"If you don't hang for murder, McRae, you're gonna spend the rest of your life behind bars," the first man was saying.

"I'm telling you, it was self-defense! My own damn brother tried to stab me . . ." Pa's hands clutched the iron bars with desperation. "If they hang me, my kids will be the ones to suffer. Ruth is never coming back. And if I'm gone, who will take care of my kids?"

The second man narrowed his eyes. "You know, I've been looking for a boy to work for me around the farm."

"And my woman could use a girl to help her in the kitchen." The first man pulled out a roll of bills from his vest pocket. "Tell you what, McRae. I'll give you a fine sum for both of them."

Pa's eyes widened at the sight of the money. Terrified beyond words, Tyler bolted through the jail and fled into the streets, never once looking back.

Until now.

Until this moment, he'd never had the courage to relive all those horrible events in his life, second by second. Never realized how vulnerable and human and flawed his pa had been. And never known how a man could behave so irrationally when confronted with the threat of losing everything . . . especially a woman's love.

Now Tyler McRae was no longer a frightened little boy. He was a man who knew, firsthand, about the power of love and the frailty of the human spirit. He knew what jealousy and betrayal felt like, the damage they could cause.

Wrought with emotion, Tyler's eyes burned with tears. No, he would never be able to approve of the things Pa had done . . . but he could understand more clearly why he'd done them. Self-defense had caused Vernon McRae to aim his rifle at his own brother. Rage had prompted him to dismiss his wife from their home. And desperation had led him to the point of taking money for his children.

Tyler buried his face in his hands. His throat constricted, his chest tightened, his eyes burned. Hot tears spilled from his lashes and streamed down his face as his shoulders heaved with sorrow.

He had no idea how long he sat there, letting the tears fall free, washing away years of bitterness and despair, cleansing the memories of a ten-year-old boy with a man's understanding of the human heart. When he finally wiped away the last bit of moisture clinging to his lashes, Tyler felt a lifetime of anger draining away from him.

Yet he stared in disbelief at the tears on his fingertips. Judas Priest, he never cried.

He stilled, recalling the words of a freckle-faced

young boy. *Miss Julia told me cryin' wasn't nothin'
for me to be ashamed of. She said that men who cry
aren't afraid to show what they're feelin' inside . . .*

Tyler rose, feeling as if he had been freed from
the pits of hell.

Thunder rumbled through the Georgia skies as
the women of Hopewell House gathered in the
dining room to set the table for dinner.

Peering over the top of her spectacles and gazing
through the window, Odelphia studied the dark
clouds overhead. "Looks like rain is a-comin' our
way."

"We don't have to worry about the threat of rain
anymore, Odie." Smiling, Dorinda waddled around
the table, setting out the china plates. "With our new
roof, we won't have to be bothered with dumping
out buckets and mopping up water anymore."

"Mr. Tyler would be real glad to know we don't
have to put buckets in his room anymore." Kate
sighed as she folded a linen napkin between her
chubby fingers. "You know, I miss Mr. Tyler. He
was one of the best friends I've ever had."

"I miss him, too," Dorinda confessed, pausing
beside the table as a wistful expression crossed
her face. "He was the most charming man. Why,
I'll never forget the afternoon we went into town
together. I've never seen a man so concerned about
buying the perfect gown for a woman."

"It's a pity everything turned out the way it did."
Odelphia shook her head in dismay. "It breaks my
heart, just thinking about it all."

"Poor Lucas," Dorinda commiserated. "And poor
Tyler, too. After his confrontation with Lucas in
the barn, it's no wonder the man went back to
Chattanooga in such a hurry."

"It's a shame . . . for all of us," Odelphia agreed.

"And we were such fools. Why, the perfect man for Julia was right under our noses, and we didn't even recognize him!"

Quietly listening to the discussion, Julia felt a lump swell in her throat. After placing the last stem of crystal on the table, she slipped out of the room.

Five days had passed since that fateful afternoon in the barn, five of the most agonizing days of her life. Even though she had relinquished her feelings of responsibility for her brother, her dreams for a future with Tyler had been crushed beyond all hope. Her loyalty to Lucas had destroyed Tyler's love for her, she knew. And Tyler would never be able to forgive Lucas for all the horrible things he'd done.

"It doesn't matter now," Julia whispered to herself. "Tyler is gone. And he isn't coming back."

She opened the front door and stepped outside for a breath of fresh air. As she closed her eyes and inhaled a deep breath, the sound of a familiar voice drifted through the summer afternoon.

"Any rooms left for the night?"

Her eyes flew open. Heart pounding and pulse racing, she whirled around just as Tyler stepped onto the verandah. He dropped his traveling bag to the ground and edged forward, never once taking his eyes off her.

Her breath lodged in her throat. She longed to reach out and brush her fingers through the dark waves of his hair, hurl her arms over his neck and press herself against him, feel his mouth claiming hers.

But standing there, gazing at him in disbelief, she stilled. Something was different about him. His hair was tousled, his clothing wrinkled, as if he'd been traveling for a very long time. Yet there was a peace about him, a peace that transcended all the pain and hurt of the past, as if his long journey had finally ended. The ever-present anguish in his eyes had disappeared, replaced with glimmers of hope . . . and love.

"It seems like forever since you've been gone," she admitted in a choked voice. "I thought you weren't coming back."

He reached out and brushed his knuckles along the curve of her cheek with so much tenderness that Julia quivered inside. "I didn't want to leave you, not even for a moment. But I knew it was time for me to tend to some unsettled matters back on a farm in Tennessee."

A rush of joy surged through her. He didn't have to tell her that he'd made peace with his past. Everything about him said that all the years of heartache and anguish had been resolved.

"And now I'm here to settle another unresolved matter," he continued, his gaze raking over her delicate features as his fingers brushed through her hair.

"You mean . . . Lucas?" Her heartbeat quickened. "I wondered why you didn't file charges against him before you left town."

"I didn't come back to report your brother to the sheriff, Julia," he assured her. "I don't want to inflict any more pain on you. That's why I couldn't bring myself to file charges against him before I left town." He winced. "I've already hurt you enough by wrongfully accusing your father of a crime he didn't commit. As far as I'm concerned, the matter of Lucas is no longer an issue."

Only the heart of a man with a forgiving spirit could set aside his misgivings so easily, Julia knew. Her throat tightened with emotion. "The matter of Lucas has been settled permanently, Tyler. Sheriff Mitchell apprehended him on Monday afternoon."

His fingers stilled in her hair. "But if I didn't press charges against him, how did Sheriff Mitchell know . . . ?" His eyes narrowed. "You?"

"I forced myself to look beyond my love and devotion for Lucas," she admitted, her voice breaking. "And I discovered I can't be responsible for his happiness—or his behavior. Loving my family doesn't mean that their problems and needs have to consume every part of me."

"That couldn't have been easy for you to acknowledge, Julia."

"Knowing that my blind devotion to my family had driven you away was even harder to accept." She drew in a shaky breath. "Is it possible you could find it in your heart to . . . forgive me?"

"That might be possible." Love glowed in his eyes as he gazed down at her. "I can't fault you for loving your family, Julia. It's one of the things I love about you."

"Then . . . everything is settled between us?"

"Not quite. There's one more matter we need to discuss—a very important one." A hint of a smile played on his lips. "We need to talk about getting you a new gown."

"A new gown?" Her brow furrowed in confusion. "But you've already bought me the most beautiful gown in the world."

"You'll be needing a new one," he insisted, sliding his hands around the tiny expanse of her waist and pulling her close to him. "It will have to be white, with lots of delicate embroidery and fine lace. The kind of gown that's suitable for a bride to wear on her wedding day. *Our* wedding day." He paused. "Will you be my wife, sweet Julia?"

"Oh, yes, Tyler!" Tears of happiness sprang to her eyes as she slipped her arms over his shoulders. "Nothing could make me happier."

"Nothing?" His eyes were teasing and warm. "What about sharing our lives with two wonderful ladies, a freckle-faced boy, a little girl with a penchant for puppies . . . and five or six children of our own?"

"I couldn't ask for anything more," she whispered, feeling as if her heart might burst from the happiness swelling within it.

At that moment a stream of sunlight broke through the cloudy skies, shining down on them with bright promises for the future. Julia lifted her lips to his, basking in the joy of loving Tyler McRae.

Epilogue

A soft spring breeze whispered through the open windows of the third-floor nursery, soothing the whimpers of the tiny baby nestled in her mother's arms. Tyler stood beside his wife, beaming as he gazed down at their dark-haired daughter.

"Next to her mother, she's the most beautiful creature on earth," he insisted.

Julia smiled. "You've said that every day for the last seven months."

"Well, it's true! Both of you get more beautiful with each passing day." He slipped an arm around his wife's shoulders. "Sometimes, looking at the two of you, I feel like I'm in the middle of a wonderful dream. It's hard to believe that both of you . . . belong to me."

After placing the sleeping baby into her cradle, Julia returned to her husband's side. "Do you ever miss anything about your life back in Chattanooga?"

"How could I? Selling The McRae to Forrest has given me the freedom to finish up all the renovations to this house and spend some time working on the construction plans for our new hotel here in town." He wrapped his arms around her waist, smiling. "Besides, everything I've ever wanted is

356

right here with you." He chuckled. "With all of you."

She twinkled up at him. "I'd say you've adjusted to family life quite admirably, Tyler McRae. Almost as if you were born to it."

His smile faded, replaced with a pensive expression. "Only one thing could make my life more complete, Julia. Someday, I have to find . . . Rebecca."

"We'll find her, Tyler. I'm sure of it. Between all the letters we've written and all the people we've contacted, I'm certain we'll find her soon. And I know she'll be thrilled when she discovers that she has a namesake."

Their loving gazes shifted to their daughter, still sleeping peacefully in her cradle. Tyler brushed his hand through Julia's hair as she snuggled up against him.

"I'm glad we named our daughter Rebecca," he mused.

"I am, too," Julia agreed. "But we'll be needing to think of another name soon."

His hand stilled in her hair. "Another . . . name?"

She smiled. "For the newest addition to the McRae family. She—or he—will be arriving around Christmastime, I believe."

Elated, Tyler moved his hands down to her abdomen. Already he could feel the gentle swell of new life growing there, created by the union of their love. "Feels like a boy to me," he said, grinning at the prospect.

At that moment, Rebecca stirred, cooing softly in her sleep. Julia reached down into the cradle and lifted the baby to her breast.

And Tyler embraced them, love overflowing from his once barren heart.

Avon Romances—
the best in exceptional authors
and unforgettable novels!

MONTANA ANGEL   **Kathleen Harrington**
77059-8/ $4.50 US/ $5.50 Can

EMBRACE THE WILD DAWN   **Selina MacPherson**
77251-5/ $4.50 US/ $5.50 Can

MIDNIGHT RAIN   **Elizabeth Turner**
77371-6/ $4.50 US/ $5.50 Can

SWEET SPANISH BRIDE   **Donna Whitfield**
77626-X/ $4.50 US/ $5.50 Can

THE SAVAGE   **Nicole Jordan**
77280-9/ $4.50 US/ $5.50 Can

NIGHT SONG   **Beverly Jenkins**
77658-8/ $4.50 US/ $5.50 Can

MY LADY PIRATE   **Danelle Harmon**
77228-0/ $4.50 US/ $5.50 Can

THE HEART AND THE HEATHER   Nancy Richards-Akers
77519-0/ $4.50 US/ $5.50 Can

DEVIL'S ANGEL   **Marlene Suson**
77613-8/ $4.50 US/ $5.50 Can

WILD FLOWER   **Donna Stephens**
77577-8/ $4.50 US/ $5.50 Can

Buy these books at your local bookstore or use this coupon for ordering:

Mail to: Avon Books, Dept BP, Box 767, Rte 2, Dresden, TN 38225   C
Please send me the book(s) I have checked above.
☐ My check or money order— no cash or CODs please— for $_____ is enclosed
please add $1.50 to cover postage and handling for each book ordered— Canadian residents
add 7% GST).
☐ Charge my VISA/MC Acct#_____ Exp Date_____
Minimum credit card order is two books or $6.00 (please add postage and handling charge of
$1.50 per book — Canadian residents add 7% GST). For faster service, call
1-800-762-0779. Residents of Tennessee, please call 1-800-633-1607. Prices and numbers
are subject to change without notice. Please allow six to eight weeks for delivery.

Name_____
Address_____
City_____ State/Zip_____
Telephone No._____   ROM 0894